Ihsan Abdel Kouddous (1919–1990) is one of the most prolific and popular writers of Arabic fiction of the twentieth century. Born in Cairo, Egypt, Abdel Kouddous graduated from law school in 1942 but left his law practice to pursue a long and successful career in journalism. He was an editor at the daily *Al-Akhbar*, the weekly *Rose al-Yusuf*, and was editor-in-chief of *Al-Ahram*. The author of dozens of books, his controversial writings and political views landed him in jail more than once.

Jonathan Smolin is the Jane and Raphael Bernstein Professor in Asian Studies at Dartmouth College in the US. He is the translator of several works of Arabic fiction, including *Whitefly* by Abdelilah Hamdouchi and *A Rare Blue Bird Flies with Me* by Youssef Fadel.

I Do Not Sleep

Ihsan Abdel Kouddous

Translated by
Jonathan Smolin

First published in 2021 by
Hoopoe
113 Sharia Kasr el Aini, Cairo, Egypt
One Rockefeller Plaza, 10th Floor, New York, NY 10020
www.hoopoefiction.com

Hoopoe is an imprint of The American University in Cairo Press
www.aucpress.com

ISBN 978 1 649 03098 6

Library of Congress Cataloging-in-Publication Data

CIP data applied for

1 2 3 4 5   25 24 23 22 21

Designed by Adam el-Sehemy
Printed in the United Kingdom

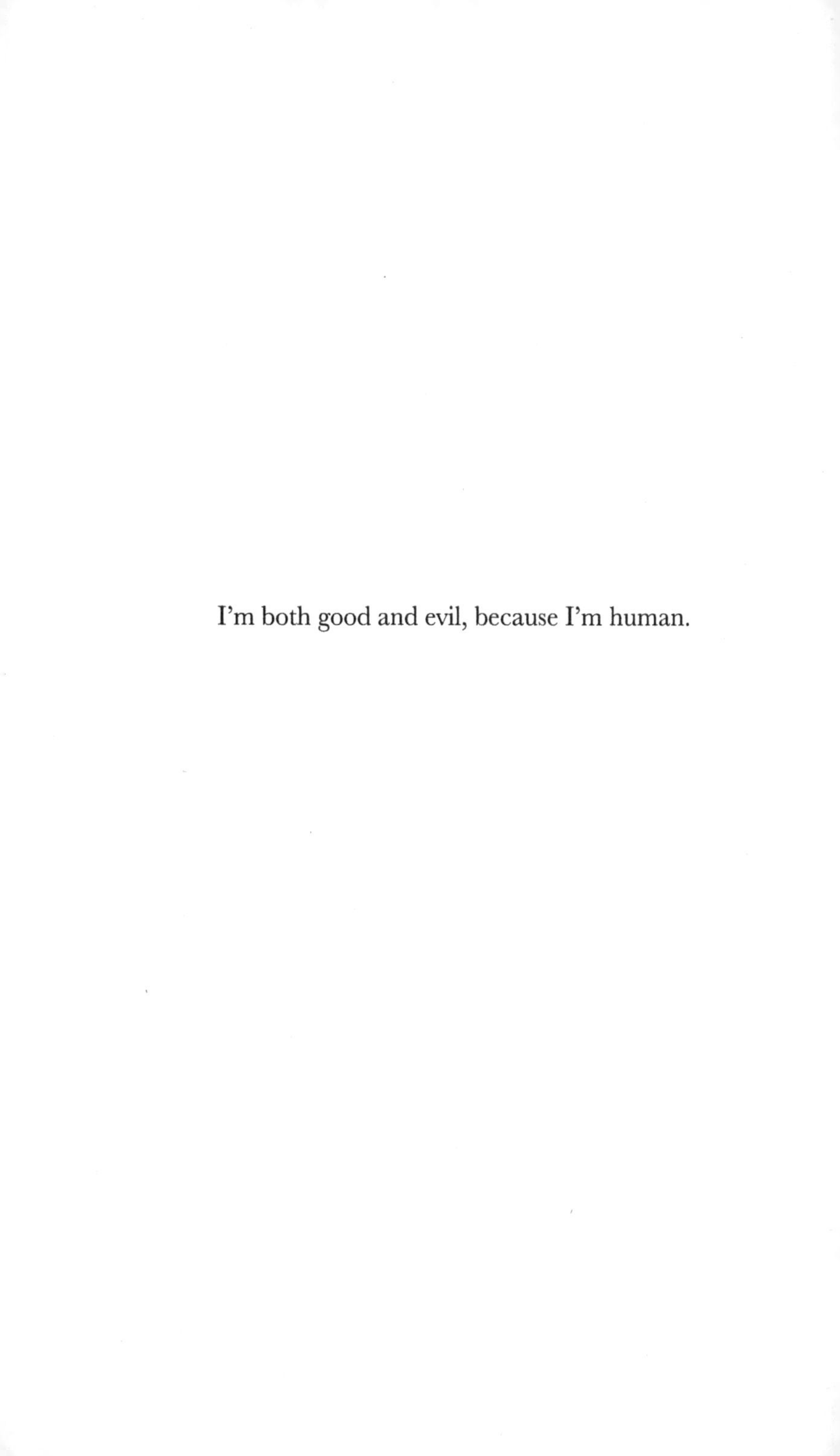

I’m both good and evil, because I’m human.

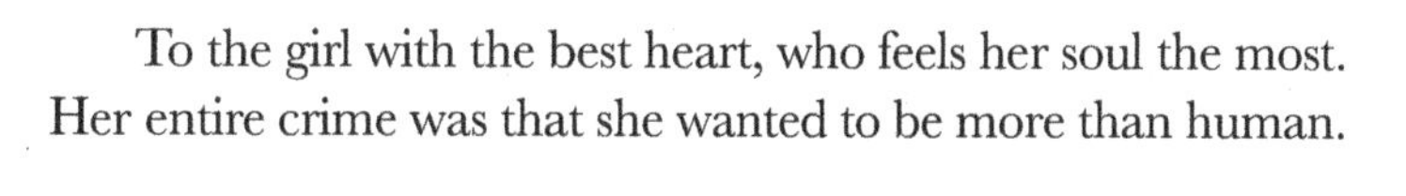

To the girl with the best heart, who feels her soul the most.
Her entire crime was that she wanted to be more than human.

To "N." She gave me her story, and then went far away after
she took a handful of my days and a piece of my heart.

Introduction

It is shocking that Ihsan Abdel Kouddous is still largely unknown outside of the Arab world. In the Middle East and North Africa, he was perhaps the most popular and prolific writer of the twentieth century. Known affectionately throughout the Arab world by just his first name, Ihsan began his literary career in the 1930s as a teenager writing humorous articles of youthful misadventure for Egypt's leading weekly political-cultural magazine, *Rose El Youssef*, which his mother founded and owned. By the mid-1940s, he was already a rising star as an incendiary journalist. He stirred up scandals to inflame public anger against the corruption of the old guard, laying the groundwork for the public embrace of the coming 1952 revolution. Ihsan would go on to become editor-in-chief of not only *Rose El Youssef*, but also important weeklies such as *Sabah al-Khayr* (Good Morning) and *Akhbar al-Yawm* (News of the Day). During the Sadat and Mubarak eras, he was in charge of *al-Ahram* (The Pyramids), Egypt's daily newspaper of record. From the early 1940s until his retirement in the 1980s, Ihsan was among the most prolific journalists in the Arab world, consistently publishing at least one weekly political or cultural article, frequently two or three.

Yet it was not Ihsan's journalism that made him a household name. Instead, it was his fiction. When he began writing *I Do Not Sleep* in 1955, Ihsan was already considered Egypt's most popular writer. By the time he died in 1990, he had published more than sixty books, including twenty novels and some six hundred short stories. Ihsan was known in particular for writing about sex, love, and romantic obsession, typically employing first-person narratives by young women as they discover their sexuality and seek love—or carnal desire—in the face of repressive and outmoded social traditions. Highlighting sexual desire—especially as seen through the eyes of young female protagonists—was shocking for many segments of Egyptian society in the 1950s and 60s. Just as Ihsan began gaining popularity for his taboo-breaking fiction in the late 1940s, the well-known critic and writer Abbas Mahmud al-Aqqad labeled him the "writer of the bed," dismissing Ihsan as someone who focused on sexual titillation instead of serious literary matters. This title stuck with Ihsan throughout his literary career. Although it certainly helped the sales of his books and magazines, it turned "respectable society" against him. Despite his popularity, Ihsan later recalled that during the 1950s and 60s, people would frequently not invite him to their houses or even admit to reading his work for fear of being associated with questionable morality. Young people—and women in particular—did not want to be caught by their parents or husbands reading his fiction, or even in possession of *Rose El Youssef* magazine, where most of his fiction was serialized. Of course, these parents or husbands might have had their own copies of Ihsan's work or magazines, which they read when their children or wives were not around.

Ihsan was not simply one of the most popular and prolific writers in the Arab world during the twentieth century. His work was disseminated more widely than any other writer's. All of his novels and short stories were first serialized in the pages of the highest circulation weeklies in Egypt before they were collected in book form and subsequently reprinted in dozens of editions. His fiction formed the basis of some of the most important and popular films in the history of Egyptian and Arab cinema, such as *I Do Not Sleep*, *There's a Man in My House*, and *My Father's Up a Tree*. Legends of the Arab silver screen such as Omar Sherif, Lubna Abdelaziz, Abdel Halim Hafez, and Faten Hamama bolstered their careers thanks to their performances in his films. In total, forty-nine Egyptian films were based on Ihsan's short stories and novels. Dozens of radio plays and television series were also adapted from his work, some lasting for hours and broadcast over months, and aired repeatedly by state radio. Ihsan's work is still being revitalized for new audiences, most recently with the 2017 Ramadan television serial adaptation of *Don't Extinguish the Sun*.

While Naguib Mahfouz won the Nobel Prize for literature in 1988, Ihsan Abdel Kouddous has been almost entirely ignored by critics and academics, both in Egypt and abroad. My forthcoming book on Ihsan will be the first in any language focusing on his fiction and his central role in the production and dissemination of Arabic popular culture in the twentieth century. Until this translation of *I Do Not Sleep*, not a single novel by Ihsan has been available in English. There are many reasons for this neglect. In addition to discomfort over the depiction of sexuality in his fiction, critics dismissed him because of his simple, direct style. Unlike Naguib Mahfouz, Ihsan employed simple vocabulary and sentence structure in a way that appealed to the widest possible readership—especially young people—but not to literary critics. Starting as early as 1943, he repeatedly called for the simplification of literary Arabic so that it could be used as a vehicle not only to build large audiences for the press but also to touch the emotions of ordinary Egyptians.

Throughout his career, both in his journalism and fiction, Ihsan strove to transform Arabic from the language of the elite to that of the masses, occasionally making fun of the complex vocabulary and syntax of writers like the "Dean of Arabic Literature," Taha Hussein, and the future Nobel laureate, Naguib Mahfouz. The pressures and demands of press serialization—not only selling magazines, but also keeping readers coming back week after week for the next installment—played a critical role in Ihsan's style. Nearly all of Ihsan's novels were serialized weekly for months, sometimes for over a year. He was highly attuned to the importance of sales since his magazines depended on circulation, not advertisement, for revenue. His clear, crisp, simple prose had been a key element in his success as a political journalist. Employing a similar style in his fiction gained him a massive audience but cost him the attention of critics, who insisted that his work was neither serious nor literary. Thus, while his books remain wildly popular in the Arab world, the lack of support by critics meant that publishing houses outside of the Middle East neglected his fiction. The publication of *I Do Not Sleep* in English is, thankfully, a first important step in rectifying this decades-long oversight.

We now know that when Ihsan began serializing *I Do Not Sleep* in October 1955, he had been deeply involved in the 1952 Egyptian Revolution and had a close personal relationship with Gamal Abdel Nasser in particular. During the 1940s and early 1950s, when Egypt was still a monarchy, Ihsan had used his platform at *Rose El Youssef* to call repeatedly for revolution, urging a strong, masculine leader to rise up, uproot the old system, and cleanse the political terrain of corruption. He met secretly with members of the Free Officers—including Nasser and Anwar Sadat—collaborating with them to uncover and publish scandals designed to spark outrage at the ruling elite. When the Free Officers finally launched their coup on 23 July 1952, they invited the ecstatic Ihsan to the barracks to participate in negotiations to form a new government. While Ihsan later claimed that he did not know about the coup beforehand, he was a particularly enthusiastic supporter of the Officers and the coup in the weeks and months that followed. No doubt, Ihsan initially believed that Nasser and the Free Officers were carrying out his own vision of the revolution, performing the cleansing operation that he had envisioned, eliminating the monarchy and the collaborating elite while laying the groundwork for democracy.

By early 1953, however, it became clear that the Officers were instead establishing a military dictatorship. Ihsan was horrified. He once again took to his platform in *Rose El Youssef*, this time dissenting against the Free Officers, and calling for the rapid implementation of democratic reforms. While these calls were muted at first because of political pressures, Ihsan took advantage of the lifting of censorship in March 1954 to express his anxieties about his own role in laying the groundwork for the coup and supporting the Free Officers in its aftermath. In a series of editorials during that fateful month, Ihsan called for the end of the revolution. He demanded that Nasser and the other Free Officers leave the army and form a political party that would participate in free and fair elections. In response, Nasser had Ihsan arrested and subjected him to a harrowing three-month imprisonment.

Ihsan left jail in summer 1954 chastened. He would never again contest Nasser so openly in his editorials. That did not mean that Ihsan abandoned writing as an act of dissent. Starting in fall 1954 and continuing for a decade, Ihsan began publishing fiction—either a short story or an installment of a novel—almost weekly. As I show in my forthcoming book on Ihsan, in many of these works he used the cover of metaphor and symbolism to explore his deep sense of guilt, anxiety, and regret for his personal role in laying the groundwork for the 1952 coup and inadvertently helping to install Nasser as a dictator. Starting after his release from jail, Ihsan repeatedly returned to the theme of a very particular type of family betrayal. In his novels and stories, a protagonist suffers psychological trauma after inadvertently bringing a traitor into the family home. Since the details of Ihsan's complex relationship with Nasser and the 1952 coup were little known, most readers never picked up on the significance of the repeated echoes of anxiety, guilt, and regret in his fiction.

I Do Not Sleep is Ihsan's first masterwork from this period, the first in a series of classics that he would write over the next decade. It was his first long novel, serialized in *Rose El Youssef* on a weekly basis for over five months. The novel captivated the public, leading to skyrocketing sales of the magazine. *I Do Not Sleep* seized the imagination of readers unlike any of Ihsan's work up to that point. Nearly every issue of *Rose El Youssef* during its serialization included at least one reader's letter about the novel. Some readers were shocked and appalled at the supposed immorality of the novel, writing to the magazine to accuse Ihsan of spreading heresy and atheism—or, even worse, existentialism. Others, believing that the narrator Nadia Lutfi was indeed a real person, had fallen in love with her. One man even wrote to Ihsan to put him in touch with Nadia so that he could propose marriage. The Emir of Kuwait at the time, Abdullah al-Salim al-Sabah, was so taken with the novel that he wrote to Ihsan: "*I Do Not Sleep* cannot be fiction. The author cannot have made up all these situations from his imagination. They have to be real, and they must have happened to the author himself!"

No doubt, the novel suggests many readings. It could be read as a metaphorical confession of regret and guilt about plotting to orchestrate the 1952 coup and the horror of subsequently embedding a traitor into the fabric of the nation. Or, with its enticing language and sexual sensationalism, it could be read as a celebration of the new freedoms of popular culture in Nasser's Egypt. It could also be read as one of the first explorations of the complexities and nuances of a female narrator in modern Arabic literature. Regardless, what matters is that readers outside of the Arab world can finally discover Ihsan, this giant of Arabic literature and popular culture, for themselves.

Jonathan Smolin
Norwich, Vermont

Part One

1

Dear Ihsan,

I'm Nadia Lutfi.

You don't know me, even if I did turn your head both times you saw me. Once on Sidi Bishr beach in Alexandria and another time at the Semiramis Hotel in Cairo. Each time, I didn't pay much attention to you, as I'd gotten used to turning men's heads.

I've been writing you this letter or notebook for three months. I never meant to write you such a long story . . . my story. All I meant was to ask you a single question.

Does God exist?

But I realized it was a ridiculous question. I really do feel the existence of God.

Terror fills me whenever I mention Him. I even spent years praying five times a day, wrapping a white veil around my head, wearing a white shirt that rose up to my neck, with long sleeves hanging down by my sides, whenever I stood praying like an angel being conducted to heaven, to the unknown, to God.

Yes, I'm convinced that God exists; so convinced that it made my pen tremble as I wrote those words, doubting His existence—tremble from fear. And here I am, repeating to myself, "*I take refuge in God the Magnificent, I take refuge in God the Magnificent.*"

Maybe I wanted to ask you: what is God?

Yes.

What is God?

Tell me.

God is truth, virtue, and goodness, since the Prophet couldn't have called us to worship deception, sin, and evil.

He's the Powerful One, since the people of the earth couldn't have united to worship a weak god with no power or strength.

So, why does the Powerful Truth leave us to practice weak deception?

Why does virtue abandon us to sin?

Why is evil victorious over goodness in us?

Tell me.

Why?

Tell me.

What is God, then?

I was told that God the Almighty created us; that He created our intellect and will so we could distinguish between good and evil. And that He left us in life to put our behavior to the test, like an exam. Whoever passes has paradise as the reward and whoever fails has hell.

I was told this. I tried to be convinced, but I wasn't.

There can't be a ministry of education in heaven that gives us sheets of questions and then takes the answers to give them to committees for grading.

And then suppose that I failed the test. Who'd be responsible?

My ignorant mind and weak will.

And who put this ignorant mind in my head and furnished me with this weak will?

Who created me like this?

God.

God is the one responsible for me failing the test of heaven. How can I be punished for a crime for which I'm not responsible? How can I be burned for a sin I didn't commit, simply because heaven oppressed me by giving me a limited mind and weak will?

No, a thousand times no. This can't be God. God doesn't need to give people a test, because He has known them ever since He created them. He's too merciful to leave them to a fight in which they're torn between good and evil. He's not like the Roman emperors who used to let lions loose on their subjects, to be entertained by the sight of the battle between wild animals and men, by the sight of blood spilled in the Colosseum. He's God, the Merciful, the Compassionate. He's love and peace. There has to be another explanation. There has to be another explanation for good and evil, for heaven and hell, for the scales of judgment in heaven.

Or have I become an infidel?

I feel my heart pound. I feel as if there's another woman inside me slapping her cheeks, screaming and wailing as if she's throwing me down to hell.

I repeat again: "*I take refuge in God the Magnificent, I take refuge in God the Magnificent!*"

God will no doubt forgive me, since He knows that He didn't push me to all this questioning and doubt and that I'm a victim of myself, which always defeated me and always pushed me to evil, to sin.

Yes, dear Ihsan, I'm evil. I'm hooked on evil.

Despite that, you can't see evil on me. My face is innocent like a child's, untouched by age even after I've stood on the earth and walked in crowds of people, my purity unpolluted by the crush of life. My eyes are the color of green fields wet with dew. None of what is inside me ever flashes in them. Even when I cry, they don't express my grief. Instead, tears flow over them like a strange hand coming forward to cleanse them. My small mouth is traced by two firm lips. I never need to put on lipstick since my lips are always the color of cherries, as you would describe them in one of your stories, Ihsan, so that as soon as you touch them, you'd think that blood would burst out. My hair is blond like eighteen-karat gold, a deep color without sparkle, like a valuable treasure left to rust. Sometimes I tie up my long hair and sometimes I let it hang down in two braids like arrows of tightly woven gold pointing to my chest and my heart.

Quite simply, I'm beautiful. One of the most beautiful girls in Cairo. I told you that I'm used to turning men's heads, including yours. But I'm not bragging or boasting about my beauty. Beauty hasn't saved me from evil. Rather, it might have been one of the things that pushed me to it. How I wish that God, who granted me my looks, would take it back from me, and in exchange would show me the path of goodness.

I've described myself so you know there isn't anything in my appearance to show you what my soul has to work with, and there is nothing in my face to warn you about me. On the contrary, there's only that which would attract you to me and reassure you about me. My appearance of innocence might deceive you into fearing for me as I encounter people and the world. But I only fear myself, and I only ask for protection against myself.

Don't think, however, that I've killed someone or stolen something, or that the evil I'm talking about represents a crime that the law prohibits or that could be brought before the courts. No. Never. But is evil only killing and stealing? Could the law prohibit every kind of crime?

Only the law of heaven punishes my crimes. They are only brought before the court of the conscience.

Let me tell you about one of my crimes.

I was twelve years old. I was coming home from school, running through the streets of Dokki with our black servant chasing after me, carrying my bag.

I noticed a young man standing on the side of the road, looking at me with his mouth wide open as if he were thunderstruck.

I still remember him today. He was about sixteen, tall and broad-shouldered; he looked like he'd be one of the top athletes at his school. His face was brown and strong, but the signs of his physical strength couldn't hide his goodness and naiveté. Indeed, they might have revealed that he wasn't so smart.

He would be standing on the side of the road when I walked home from school. He was always looking at me with his mouth wide open like he was thunderstruck. At that age, I recognized my beauty and I understood the young man's look. I started smiling whenever I caught him out of the side of my eye standing in his place. I began strutting a little while walking past him, intentionally averting my face to make him think I felt his presence.

I'd get back home and think about him, but then my thoughts started taking a wicked direction without me realizing it. I was like a child thinking about destroying her doll for a reason she didn't know, other than the desire to destroy. I wanted to see him destroyed, even though he hadn't done anything wrong.

Unconsciously, I was driven to execute the wicked plan.

I started smiling at him. I began slowing down as I walked by. Whenever I passed him, I purposely talked loudly with the servant so he would hear my voice and wake up from the thunderbolt that hit him whenever he saw me. He started smiling at me and walking a few steps behind me, until the servant would notice him, and then he'd run off.

When the plan was ready and the decisive hour approached, I left school and ran away from the servant, who was waiting for me at the door, heading home alone. When I passed the young man, I gave him a big smile—bigger than the one I usually gave him every day.

He noticed that the servant wasn't following me, so he came after me. He got so close that I could hear his breath.

"Bonsoir."

I heard his voice for the first time.

I didn't speak, but I shook my head so my braids rocked back and forth as if they were responding to his greeting.

He was quiet, as if collecting his courage.

"Can I talk to you?" he asked.

I didn't respond. Instead, I sped up the plan. In my chest was a wicked torrential feeling whose nature I didn't understand—a feeling of fear, pleasure, terror, and hesitation, like the feeling of the gambler as he's betting everything he's got.

"Could you stop for a minute?" he continued.

I didn't respond. I hurried along as the delightful wicked feeling in me intensified, together with the pounding of my heart.

We were getting close to my house. I was afraid he'd stop following me, so I turned to him and gave him another big smile, walking right next to him.

"Finally," I heard him say. "What's wrong? Why do you keep going like that? Slow down or I'll lose you!"

We'd reached the door of my house. Suddenly, I turned to him.

"That's enough!" I yelled in his face as angrily as I could. "It's impolite! What do you want from me? Why are you running after me?"

The young man once more looked thunderstruck.

Othman the doorman woke up at the sound of me screaming and ran over. He looked at the young man staring at me, and took in what was happening. He reached out and punched the young man hard in the chest.

"Get out of here!" he yelled.

The young man was upset that the doorman hit him—especially in front of me—so he punched the doorman back. Othman let out a scream like a howl, and all the neighborhood doormen and servants ran over. They all pounded on the young man, beating and slapping him until he fell to the ground. He got up and ran away as fast as he could.

I stood at the door, watching everything.

My plan had succeeded. I'd destroyed the doll.

But was I happy?

I'd been terrified when I saw the poor guy in the hands of the doormen and servants. I almost screamed at them and rushed over to save him. But something nailed me to the ground and silenced me. When I was able to move, I ran to my room, threw myself on the bed, and started crying. I cried for a long time, but the tears couldn't soothe me or wash away my crime.

I didn't sleep that night, and passed a number of sleepless nights. I remained so depressed that the blood almost stopped flowing in my veins. Every time I remembered what I'd done, I felt ashamed. A bitter, painful shame like a knife cutting my chest, until I was forced to do something—to scream, to fight with one of the servants, to break something in the house, to hit my dog—to hide my shame at myself.

Why?

Why did I commit this crime? What pushed me to it, and at such a young age?

Why didn't God stand beside me to divert me from evil?

Or was I a victim of Satan?

What is Satan?

Is he not a creation of God? Then what's God's wisdom in making a creature that pushes us to sin?

If Satan is an angel who's no longer obedient to God, why didn't God punish him and erase him from existence to deliver us from his wickedness? Why did He leave him among us and then hold us accountable—we humans—for the evil that Satan pushes us to do?

I take refuge in God since He has to have wisdom in that.

I often take refuge in God, but that hasn't diverted me from evil.

My crimes multiplied. As I got older, I got better at setting more complicated plans, executing them perfectly.

And immediately after each crime, I'd be overwhelmed by this terror occupying me. Terror at myself. I'd spend sleepless nights, tortured by my clenched heart, despicable soul, tormented thoughts, and the painful, bitter shame that cut through my chest.

A number of months passed before I forgot the crime I told you about. It was a small crime that didn't leave behind any lasting effects, except that my father insisted I go back and forth to school by car, despite the short distance from our house.

But I remember there was also a bigger crime.

I was fourteen. I had an older schoolmate named Kawthar.

Kawthar wasn't my friend, but I liked her. She was dark, beautiful, stylish, confident, and nice. She walked as if she were floating on air and talked as if she were singing a beautiful tune. Her smile was radiant and when she let her long black hair hang down her back she was like an angel protecting night from day.

All the girls loved her.

During summer break, I met Kawthar on Sidi Bishr beach in Alexandria. There wasn't anything between us but a passing "hello" that we'd exchange every morning while we were walking on the beach. Days passed, and I noticed that my cousin Medhat was following her wherever she went. He'd spend the day under the umbrella in front of her cabin, only getting up from under it when Kawthar left her cabin.

It was easy to see that love had sprung up between them. That kind of pure, innocent love that grows between a girl whose family kept a close watch over her and a young man with strong character and good intentions; a love that doesn't usually go beyond words exchanged stealthily behind the cabin, far from the family's eyes.

My cousin didn't tell me about his love, but he became more interested in me, inviting me to sit with him under his umbrella. He'd talk to me for a long time, finally ending with him chatting about my school and classmates. He knew Kawthar was my classmate. He wanted me to talk about her, but I ignored what he was after and I kept quiet. When you read my story, you'll know that I'm good at staying quiet.

Then Kawthar became interested in me. She started trying hard to befriend me. She insisted on inviting me to her cabin and giving me ice cream. But, without thinking about it, I blocked her attempts, ignoring the friendship she was offering me.

The wicked feeling started creeping into my chest.

I started feeling the ugly desire to destroy the doll . . . and there were two dolls in front of me to destroy!

I wonder what pushes children to destroy dolls.

I swear to you that I resisted this feeling and desire as hard as I could, with all my will and all my nerves. There wasn't any rational reason making me revolt against this pure, innocent love. I loved my cousin like a brother and I wished nothing but the best for him. I just about loved Kawthar, and I wanted the best for her too. I had no excuse to hate them or envy them or fear one could harm the other. So why did I think about destroying them? Why did I commit a crime against them?

I succeeded in controlling this evil feeling all summer. All I did was spend a lot of time with my cousin, sitting with him under his umbrella and having fun with him, especially when Kawthar was in her cabin. Up until that time, I hadn't launched into any set plan.

We returned to Cairo and went back to school, where I was surprised by all the girls talking about Kawthar's love for my cousin Medhat.

I pretended to ignore all this talk. I didn't join in and I didn't encourage anyone to talk about it with me. But it started fanning the flames of evil in my chest, and the craving to destroy started to overwhelm me. When I went to bed, I started not being able to sleep. I'd think and think, until I came up with a plan and started executing it. I began savoring the feeling, savoring the fear, terror, and hesitation, the pleasure of putting my intelligence to the test, the intoxicating anticipation, the excitement of the gambler as he bets everything he's got.

I was friends with one of the neighbor girls, who wasn't a classmate. I came to an understanding with her and then told her about the plan.

I called Medhat and when I heard his voice, I handed the phone to my friend, who spoke with feigned anxiety and fear, as if someone were keeping tabs on her. I kept my ear pressed against the phone next to hers so I could hear.

"Hello? Medhat? How are you?"

"How are you?" he asked. "Who's this?"

"You don't know my voice, Medhat?" she asked. "It's Kawthar."

"Kawthar!" Medhat cried in a trembling voice. "I didn't know how I could see you or talk to you since—"

"I can't talk now." My friend cut him off, mimicking Kawthar's voice. "Au revoir."

"But listen, Kawthar—"

"Later, later, Medhat." She hung up.

I was exhilarated—by the cleverness of my own plan!

Two days later, we talked to Medhat again, my friend speaking as if she were Kawthar, using the same scared voice, rushed as if someone were keeping tabs on her.

"Listen, Medhat, come by tomorrow in front of the school as we're leaving so I can see you. Au revoir."

The poor guy didn't get a chance to say a word.

The next day, I went to school pretending to be absent-minded, confused, and sad. I put my arm around one of my classmates.

"Can I tell you a secret?" I whispered, leaning toward her. "But swear you won't tell anyone."

My classmate's eyes sparkled in delight. None of the girls at school knew a single secret about me. My beauty—and I'm not exaggerating if I tell you that I was the most beautiful girl in the school—pushed the other girls to try to gain my friendship and learn my secrets, but I'd frustrate them and not tell them a thing. I relished the knowledge that I was a locked box to them.

"I swear!" my classmate declared. "I swear I won't tell anyone!"

"My cousin is driving by the school door to see me," I told her, pretending to hesitate shyly. "I want you to distract Principal Zeinab so I can talk to him quickly."

My classmate opened her mouth wide in shock.

"Your cousin Medhat?" she asked.

"Yes."

"Do you love him?"

"Please. *He's* the one who loves *me*."

"So why haven't you talked with your family about it?"

"I'll tell you later."

"Tell me, Nadia, so I know how to play along with you."

"He came to propose, but Daddy won't agree to it until he finishes university, when I'll be nineteen. He hasn't come back to the house since."

My classmate's eyes became so wide that she looked like an idiot.

"But, but . . ." she stammered, then fell silent.

"But what?" I asked, knowing what she wanted to say.

"Nothing!"

I don't need to tell you that my "secret" spread like wildfire among the students that same day, until it reached Kawthar.

I saw her from a distance, anxious and miserable, as if she'd aged a hundred years.

We walked out of school.

I played the role of the confused, nervous girl. I started looking around until I saw my cousin in his car. I then looked at my classmate as if asking her for help, pushing her to follow through on her promise. And, indeed, she started talking to Principal Zeinab while the students were getting in the school vans.

I walked toward my cousin's car and started talking to him anxiously and hurriedly, as if I were committing a crime. I asked him about my aunt, his brothers, and my uncle in a tone closer to sweet nothings. He responded curtly, looking around shyly and hesitantly for Kawthar. I kept moving my head in front of him so he couldn't see her.

I left my cousin and went over to get in the school van.

The students greeted me with winks and smiles, except for Kawthar, who was silent and introverted. Her face was pale, as if I'd sucked out all of her blood.

My classmate came over to me.

"What did he say?" she asked impatiently.

"He wants to meet me away from school," I whispered. "But I don't want to."

I smiled to myself. I felt a wicked intoxication—the intoxication of conceit about my own intelligence.

After that, I was able to make my cousin wait in front of the school gates twice. Each time, I played the same role, sucking more of Kawthar's blood.

I then moved on to the second part of the plan, as if the first hadn't been enough.

For days, we didn't call my cousin. Then my dear neighbor and I called him again.

"Where have you been, Kawthar?" I heard him say as if his heart were crushed under the weight of his desire. "You made me so worried that I looked through the phonebook for your number until I found it. But whenever I call, I hear a different voice and I hang up. Where have you been?"

"I can't, Medhat," my friend responded as I whispered the words to her. "I can't call because the telephone is in the office and my father sits there all day long."

"What then?" Medhat asked, as if looking for the path to salvation. "Will we just go on like this? For two weeks, I've chained myself next to the phone, waiting for you to call."

"Listen, Medhat," my friend said, pretending to be in a rush. "Send me a letter and I'll write back. There's no other way. Au revoir!"

"But wait, Kawthar!"

"I can't. My father's coming. Au revoir!"

Two days later, I went to the post office and got Medhat's letter. I opened it and read it. I felt my heart plunge like it was running away from me. It was a pure, tender, elegant letter full of passion, love, and torture restrained by pride, like a man's tears that didn't fall but remained shining in his eyes.

I didn't sleep.

I spent the night on a bed of hot coals. I tried to free myself, but I couldn't. I tried to renounce my crime, but it only clung to me more. My head was on fire and my soul was screaming, almost tearing up my body.

I was tortured that night. I was tortured so dreadfully.

The next morning, I decided to fix everything—to turn back from completing this horrible crime.

But as soon as I saw myself among my classmates, the wicked feeling came back, sweeping me away like the soldier who finds himself in the middle of the battlefield and the desire to kill overwhelms him, even if he kills his own cousin.

I remember laughing with my neighbor, making fun of the two lovers.

I remember the students' whispers about my presumed engagement to Medhat.

I remember my delight and conceit at my intelligence as I watched my plan succeed.

All of a sudden, I was pushed forward to act out the play I'd begun. I purposely sat in an isolated spot in the schoolyard and starting reading Medhat's letter. I gave a loud fake sigh.

One of my classmates came over and asked about the letter. I tried to hide it from her, but she begged me and swore secrecy until I showed her part of it, after folding under the part with the words "My love, Kawthar."

The story of the letter was broadcast among the students. Each of them came to look at it. I caught a glimpse of Kawthar from a distance. She was so pale she looked like there was no more blood left in her for me to suck.

I let myself get carried away by my intoxication.

I went back home and called my friend. We sat together writing a letter to Medhat, signing it as Kawthar. We were laughing at every word. We resorted to romance stories and magazines for expressions of love and passion, until we came up with a letter packed with thick, fabricated words of love.

I sent it to Medhat.

I got the response a few days later. And then I went into the schoolyard again, sighing loudly.

Finally, I was convinced that I'd destroyed the doll.

I destroyed the pure, innocent love that had grown up between my classmate and my cousin, a love that could have lasted forever.

At the same time, I grew bored of this game. I grew bored of calling my cousin, writing love letters to him, and playing the role of the lover.

Weeks passed and I didn't do anything, except that I felt the tightness and screaming of my soul every time I saw Kawthar.

She wasted away until her cheekbones stuck out. She was no longer chic or confident. Instead, she was nervous and coarse, fighting with her classmates for one reason or another, then keeping to herself, as if she were digesting her pain. She started getting sick and began missing school for days at a time.

I was always trying to convince myself that I didn't have a hand in what happened to her; that I only played one of those little jokes that schoolgirls play on each other.

But I wasn't convinced.

I started not sleeping.

Until my cousin came to me one day. He too was withered and miserable, like a diseased apple tree. He sat alone with me in a corner of the room.

"I'm going to ask something of you, Nadia," he whispered as if he didn't have the strength to hold his breath. "I've never asked this of anyone."

I widened my eyes innocently, feigning surprise as grief percolated through my heart.

"What is it?" I asked.

"Something very important," he said, still whispering. "My entire happiness rests on it. If not, I wouldn't have asked you for this."

" What is it?" I asked, still pretending to be surprised.

"You know Kawthar, your classmate?" he asked, his lips beginning to tremble.

"Yes," I responded.

"Give this to her," he said, taking a letter out of his pocket.

"I don't understand," I said nervously.

"Don't ask about anything." He cut me off. "I beg you, don't ask!"

He moved away like an emaciated ghost.

He left me aghast, my breath almost choking my chest.

What should I do with this letter?

I had no plan. I could only lie or tell the truth.

Why didn't I tell the truth?

Why didn't I confess my crime to my cousin and Kawthar and save their love and their future?

I couldn't.

I wasn't strong enough.

I spent the night tortured, sleepless.

The next day, I went to school with the letter in my pocket. I didn't have to pretend to be distraught and upset. I really felt that way, torn apart by confusion between my evil, cowardly self and my sober, sleepless conscience.

Sometimes my conscience got the upper hand and I almost went to Kawthar to confess and give her the letter, but it didn't take long for my evil self to vanquish it, and I retreated once again from confessing.

The day ended.

I went home to find my cousin waiting for me, anxiety traced on his face.

"Kawthar wouldn't take the letter," I told him before he asked, dodging his eyes. "She told me she's engaged."

It was as if I'd stabbed him with a knife.

His face went so pale it lost almost all its color. His lips trembled until I thought they were going to fall off his mouth. His eyes drifted until he looked like he couldn't see.

"Merci," he said in a weak, hoarse voice like a rattle, reaching out to take the letter. "I'm very sorry, Nadia."

And he left.

I swear to you that what befell Medhat and Kawthar befell me too. I couldn't eat anymore, or laugh or sleep or taste life. I lost weight and became emaciated. My face turned pale and my father started sending me to doctors.

I felt like my crime was seeping out of all the pores of my body. I felt like each breath was a hollow drumbeat in my funeral procession. I felt like my heartbeats were a tight fist clenching around my neck.

Yes, I was tortured horribly for many days.

I don't need to tell you what happened after that.

Kawthar was engaged the following summer. It was as if she'd committed suicide. Her fiancé was the least likely person possible to achieve her hopes and dreams.

As for Medhat, he allowed the passage of time to mend his heart with the threads of forgetting.

But this crime remained a black spot inside me. I'd see it every evening as I took off my clothes. I'd remember it every time I saw Medhat.

I wondered whether Medhat could have been Kawthar's husband. Was I the one who destroyed the nest of their dreams?

I wondered what pushes a child to climb a tree to destroy a bird's nest and then cry when the bird dies.

What pushes him to commit this crime?

And then what pushes him to regret?

Answer me.

But you can't unless you know me and my story. Maybe after you know my story, you'll know it's too late for me—that you won't be able to help me with your advice or reach out to save what's left of me.

But let me write to you to ease the weight on my chest. Maybe I'll be able to relax.

And maybe after that I'll be able to sleep.

2

Where do I begin my story?

I'm confused. Every day could be a beginning and every day an end. But there's one day in particular that I can't forget. A day when I felt like my life began moving violently; when I felt that events started driving me instead of me driving events, and that I was no longer master of the world but the world had become master of me.

I was sixteen, and I'd been making the rounds at a number of Arabic, English, and French schools until I got to Madame Orly School in Maadi as a boarder.

My father came to school one afternoon. I remember it was a Tuesday. He asked for permission from the school director to take me home.

He seemed nervous. His face was so flushed that I smelled his breath as he was kissing me to check that he hadn't been drinking. It was as if he were suffering from a crisis of shame or was hiding something in his chest that he didn't know how to reveal or shake off. I walked next to him silently until we were out of the school and got in the car. I sat next to him in the front seat. We were both quiet as he drove toward Cairo.

I tried to break the silence and encourage him to talk. I asked him about Nanny Halima.

"She's good," he responded curtly, with a stiff smile.

I asked him about Abdou, the butler.

"He's good," he responded with the same curtness and smile.

I asked a third question, this time about the farm.

"It's great," he responded in the same tone.

I then decided to keep quiet. I turned to the window and bided my time, watching the road until I heard him clear his throat like he was gathering his will to talk. He cleared his throat a second time.

"You know, Nadia," he said, "I'm not happy with you living at that boarding school."

I turned to him. He didn't look at me but his eyes were not on the road; they wandered as if he were searching for something inside himself.

"Why, Daddy?" I asked, coming to life and moving closer to him. "It's a good school."

"Even so," he said, his eyes still avoiding me. "No matter how good it is, I don't like that my daughter is being raised in boarding schools. You know, I put you there against my better judgment. But, when you became a teenager, you couldn't stay home alone with me and live in a house without a woman to take care of you."

He fell silent for a bit.

"Nanny Halima is great," I said. "She loves me like a mother and more."

"But she's a maid," he said, his eyes fixed in front of him. "She doesn't know how to make a woman of you."

He turned to me quickly, and then went back to looking in front of him.

"You don't know how I've spent my whole life worried about you," he continued in a tender voice as if his heart were beating on his lips. "There are many things in your life that I want to be sure about, but I can't because I don't know how to talk to you about them or how to ask you about them. Things only a woman can talk to you about. But when I put you in boarding school, I started worrying about you more. I'd stay up all night wondering if you were sleeping or not, if you ate dinner or not, if you were happy or not. I went crazy, always missing you. I'd gotten used to beginning each day saying good morning to you and ending each day kissing you goodnight. With you gone, I felt the entire world had become empty. I hated the house and I hated the farm. I started drinking more, drinking without eating. Every time I thought about taking you out of boarding school and bringing you back home, I'd get worried about you living with me, about you living in a bachelor's house, in a house without a woman."

I wasn't moved by the affection overflowing from my father's words. Instead, I felt that he was aiming at something he hadn't revealed; something that was making him uncomfortable.

"But I've never complained about anything, Daddy!" I said, the words going dry on my tongue. "I've never felt that I've been deprived of anything. When I miss you at school, I know everything you're doing is for the best."

My father stopped the car by the side of the road, under the shade of a thick tree. He turned fully to me and started playing with my braids, as usual. He tried to give me a big smile.

"It's in your best interest and mine that we live together from now on," he said, giving me a sad look as if pleading with me. "The day you get married, I'll make it a condition for your husband that he marries us both!"

He tried to laugh, but it fell flat, as if it had dropped into a shallow well.

I too tried to laugh, but I couldn't even fake it. My heart began to get tighter and everything inside me was trembling as if I were standing on the edge of an abyss, afraid of someone pushing me forward.

My father was silent, swallowing his laugh. "There was no way for you to live with me and for me to have peace of mind about you unless I got married," he said, putting his hand on my shoulder tenderly, trying to bring me closer to him.

My eyes widened as if I'd seen a ghost.

"You got married?" I asked, cutting him off.

"Yes, Nadia," he said, avoiding my gaze. "For fourteen years I've lived without a wife, for you. But now I had to get married, for you as well."

I was almost in tears.

"The only condition I had for the woman I picked was that she could take care of you and look after you in your youth, that she could help me make you happy. I'm sure you'll love her."

"What's important is that you love her," I said in an almost sarcastic tone.

"If you love her," he said sincerely, "I'll love her too."

"Congratulations."

"That's it?" he said, tugging my braid.

I got closer to kiss him.

"All I care about is your happiness, Daddy."

"Merci," he said, seeming to be in terrible anguish.

We were both silent as we drove back to Cairo.

I couldn't interpret my feelings that day. It felt that at that moment, a fight between my emotions and my mind broke out. My emotions convulsed, writhing as if they'd touched a red-hot rod. My mind mocked my emotions, accusing them of egotism and denial.

I had to come down on the side of my mind. My father was thirty-nine, still young. He had the right to get married. I'd even asked myself many times why he didn't get married. Whenever I saw a beautiful woman, I imagined her as his wife.

You don't know what there was between my father and me. You don't know that I wasn't simply his daughter. I had all the rights of his wife.

I have no memory of my parents being together. They divorced when I was only two years old. My mother married another man and left me to my father.

I don't know why they got divorced or why she left me to my father when I was so young.

Why did she forgo raising me? Why did she give up her right to me and take away my right to her?

I don't know. My mother and my father both kept the story of their divorce to themselves. Members of the family would exchange surreptitious glances whenever the topic came up around me. I grew up with the story of the divorce whispered about behind my back. I rarely thought about it. If I did think about it, I felt that I was lost in the middle of a thick cloud or that I was before a locked box tossed into the house and I didn't have the key.

All I knew was that my father married my mother for love and that it caused an outcry in the two families. Both families opposed their love and their marriage, so my father and mother had to elope, forcing their families to face a fait accompli. At the time, my father was twenty-three and my mother was seventeen.

But their tempestuous love couldn't protect their marriage, and after three years it dissolved in divorce. I was the only remaining trace of it.

I grew up holding my mother responsible for her failed marriage to my father. I don't know why. Maybe because I was more attached to my father than to her and I felt responsible for defending him and his actions, including divorcing my mother.

My father gave his entire life to me.

He oversaw every minute of my life. He supervised my meals and sat with me until I finished eating. He went with me to the bathroom and washed me himself. He bought my clothes and spent the night next to me in my bed if I was sick. He always read children's books to me, and he studied books about parenting and children's health so he knew how to raise me and take care of me—books he still had in his study.

He was never satisfied with any of my foreign nannies. None of them could understand how involved he was with me, and they'd quit to go somewhere else. All of that was at the cost of his youth. He gave his youth to me without enjoying it himself. He never missed lunch or came home late after I went to sleep. I didn't know if he had a woman in his life. All I knew was that he usually drank three glasses of whiskey every night. He drank them at home sitting and reading, or listening to the radio or records.

As I got older, I felt I had no one in life except my father and that he had no one but me.

I also began to sense my position in our home. I felt I was the woman of the house. It was a big house in Dokki, with two stories and a large garden, which the family owned. My father and I lived on the first floor, while my father's brother lived upstairs. He was a bachelor who never got married. Instead, he was known for his many adventures with women. His personality was totally different from my father's. He was a year younger and was an artist and a painter. He was a bohemian and madc fun of everything around him. He talked a lot and laughed a lot. He didn't worry about anything or take anything seriously.

The only thing he shared with my father was his love for me. He loved me, but the way he showed his love was different from my father. He didn't take responsibility for me. Instead, he pampered me and always drowned me in gifts and kisses. I loved him and I liked his happiness and playfulness, but I didn't cherish him the way I did my father. In his seriousness and dignity, my father was my highest ideal in men while my uncle was, in my view, a flighty young man. I loved him, but he wasn't suited as a father, either for me or any other young woman.

When I got older—eight or nine—I began to consider myself responsible for the big house and everyone in it.

This responsibility made me seem older than I was. I'd purposely act stern before the servants. Even when Nanny Halima, who became like my mother, came to me, I always put up a barrier between us. I always made her feel that I was the mistress and she was the servant. I didn't let her kiss me or sit next to me. Instead, she always sat on the ground at my feet, telling me stories or the neighbors' news. I didn't even let her call me by only my name.

"Nadia, my daughter," I remember she said to me one day.

"Please, Nanny," I said dryly, giving her a harsh look. "I'm not your daughter!"

I felt the shock almost rip out her heart.

"Miss Nadia, I only meant—" she replied as she lowered her head submissively, and then finished what she was saying.

I started savoring that responsibility and those powers that I had granted myself in the house and that my father encouraged me to assume. I began giving orders to the servants and taking pleasure as they rushed around to carry them out. I fabricated reasons to blame them for things, and sometimes to fire them. I'd savor my power as they stood in front of me submissively or left the house abjectly. They knew I was the absolute authority and that my word was irrefutable, no matter how much of the nonsense of children there was in it. They knew that angering me meant angering my father, and that my father cared little about anything other than whether someone made me upset.

I considered myself responsible for everything in my father's life. I was occupied with his food and I sat with him at the table—when I wasn't at school—making him try everything I put in front of him. I'd go into his room and work with the servants to organize it. I'd stand with him as he was putting on his clothes, giving him his shoes and socks, picking out his tie. I'd sit with him in the evening as he was having his three glasses of whiskey and I'd try as hard as I could to understand what he was saying about the farm, cotton, wheat, and the peasants.

My father was happy with my involvement in his life and the running of the house. He'd encourage me to do it and, as if he were getting me ready for life, he'd reveal to me little by little our family position and the details of our financial situation.

I went so far as to start to reprimand him. I'd scold him if he was late or if he told me that he'd sold some land. I'd chide him whenever he was annoyed at my uncle. He was happiest when he heard me holding him accountable. He'd give me an explanation like I was his wife or mother, and then go overboard spoiling me.

This life occupied my youth and childhood. I wasn't inclined toward playing with girls as much as I was to giving the servants orders and ensuring that they carried them out. I wasn't interested in talking with my girlfriends and hanging out with them as much as I was in talking with my father and spending time with him. I didn't even try to have close friends. I don't have close friends even today. The friendships I had were all with girls I met by chance or at school. I purposely picked people who were less well off than me. I'd get to know them for a bit and then cut them off and ignore them. Maybe I befriended them simply because I needed them to carry out a particular plan I'd hatched, or to entertain myself when I was bored. I then forgot them by eliminating my need for them. None could enter my life or become a confidante or occupy a part of my heart.

There was no one in my life except for my father. There was no one in my heart except him.

Even when I began to feel myself becoming a woman, when my mind started opening up about what happens between young men and young women, none of the neighbor boys or the ones who chased after me could excite my interest. I thought they were all "kids." I'd hear about the adventures of my classmates with those "kids" and I'd make fun of them. I'd come up with "tricks" to break them up with their boyfriends. I'd laugh until regret overwhelmed me at what I'd done, and then I'd cry.

Despite this, the neighborhood kids and those who chased after me sated my conceit. I couldn't imagine one of them passing me by without turning to me or showing me more attention than another girl.

I remember when I was thirteen, one of the neighbor boys started going after me. He was the handsomest boy in the neighborhood, the eldest son of the richest family. He was loud and spoiled, with a car in which he'd roam the streets of the neighborhood day and night. He'd bother everyone with the way he kept honking the horn to the rhythm of different songs. He was the dream of all the neighborhood girls. His name was Hasan.

Hasan wasn't yet sixteen.

He usually drove around my house a bunch of times each evening after I got home from school, honking to the tune of the song "Take the pacifier and be quiet, take it and go to sleep!" He'd wait for me until I went out in our car, either with the driver or my father, and then he'd follow us, honking the same tune. I couldn't go to the movies or head out shopping or to the beach without finding him behind me.

The girls of the neighborhood knew Hasan was chasing me and loved me.

Hasan thought I was his and that he was the only one who had the right to go after me. He'd fight with any guy who tried to do the same thing. There were a bunch of violent confrontations between guys in the neighborhood because of me and Hasan.

All that happened without him getting anything from me, not even a smile. I purposely gave him a sharp, loathing look whenever my eyes fell on him, a look he'd greet dejectedly. But he'd keep following me. I really thought of him as a kid, since he didn't stir up anything in me or capture any part of my heart. Whenever he followed me, I'd block him.

All he did was please my ego. And my ego remained so greedy that his passing by the house each evening, honking out his song, became like a satiating dish.

Hasan got tired of chasing me.

He got tired of begging the neighbor girls to convince me to meet him or talk to him on the phone or smile at him.

I refused the intervention of the neighbor girls, telling them that he was just a kid.

He heard that I was describing him as a kid. A week later, I saw him sporting a mustache—a thin, light mustache, like the shadow of his nose above his lips.

I laughed when I caught sight of his thin mustache. I continued to insist that he was a kid, and still despised him.

Suddenly, Hasan cut me off.

He didn't chase me anymore and I didn't hear "Take the pacifier and be quiet" anymore.

I began to feel annoyed. I started feeling like I'd been insulted, as if my dignity had been trampled before the neighborhood girls.

I asked around until I found out that he was chasing after another girl, Mervat.

Mervat was a good-natured, easygoing girl who laughed a lot and clowned around. I can't deny that she was beautiful. I had to leave Hasan to her and leave her to Hasan, since I didn't want him and all he stirred up in me was my conceit.

But this conceit was enough to drive evil plans into my head. I began not sleeping. I began to resist myself so that I didn't commit a crime against the good-natured, easygoing, innocent Mervat. But I couldn't.

One day, I went to Mervat's house when I knew she wouldn't be there. Her mother met me graciously, affectionately, and tenderly, since it was rare for me to visit one of the neighborhood families.

"Is Mervat in?" I asked innocently.

"No, my dear," she responded, taking me by the hand to sit me down next to her. "She went to visit her cousin."

"I came to congratulate her," I said, still feigning innocence.

"Thank you so much, but for what?" her mother asked with a confused look.

"For her engagement," I said naively. "Even if she still hasn't invited me."

"Her engagement?" her poor mother asked, stunned. "To whom?"

"To Hasan," I said, without losing my nerve.

I stopped when I saw the mother's sharp glance, as if she were terrified. I pretended to be nervous, confused, and shy, and started pressing my hands together.

"Uh . . . uh . . . Mervat didn't get engaged?" I stammered.

"No, my dear," her mother said, collecting herself, trying to lower her voice. "She hasn't gotten engaged." She looked me straight in the eye. "Where did you hear that from?" she asked. "Who told you that?"

"My friends," I said, looking away from her. "Excuse me," I said, standing up and trembling. "Daddy's waiting for me. I'm very sorry!"

The poor mother said a cold goodbye at the door.

The result of this simple plan was that strict family supervision was imposed on Mervat to intervene between her and Hasan. Mervat's mother went to Hasan's mother to complain about her son chasing after her daughter. Hasan's parents then took his car away from him as punishment.

The entire neighborhood knew that I was the one who had come up with this scheme. The neighborhood girls stopped talking to me. But the strange thing was that Hasan went back to chasing after me. He went back to cruising past my house every evening. He started walking by instead of driving by in his car. I went back to despising him, looking down on him, and feeding my ego.

But I was tortured. Not because the neighborhood knew I was behind this trick or because the girls stopped talking to me.

I was tortured by regret.

I regretted a crime I had committed against an innocent friend—a crime I didn't need to commit. I became so depressed and anxious that my blood almost froze in my veins. I suffered from being ashamed of myself: a bitter, painful shame.

I started creating crises in the house. I'd fight with the servants or break something or hit the dog to hide from this shame at myself.

Weeks passed, and I couldn't sleep.

There were a lot of other reasons that prevented me from sleeping.

There was a side of my life, a side of my personality that was torturing me, eating up my chest and nerves, drinking my soul, and leaving me hard and dry like a stone . . . a beautiful stone.

But my great love for my father—the love that was my entire life—couldn't fill the big emptiness that my loneliness with him left.

I loved him so much that I couldn't complain to him. I considered myself responsible for his happiness to the point that I didn't dare disturb him with my complaints. I wanted to convince him that I was happy and that I wasn't lacking anything, to the point that I hid all my pain and confusion from him.

There were a lot of things troubling me that I needed to dispel by sharing them with someone, things that happen to every child and every girl. I was confused about them and I needed someone to help me understand them. There were changes in my body that I didn't understand or have anyone to ask about.

I didn't dare talk to my father because I was afraid of what my complaints would do to him.

I didn't ask him about the things I was confused about because I was too embarrassed: he was a man, and I thought he wouldn't understand such women's issues.

When my father broke the news about getting married, he was right when he said that there were many aspects of my life he couldn't discuss with me because only a woman could talk about them with me.

Yes. This was true. There was much in my life that no one knew about except me.

I still remember the day when my periods started. I was eleven. One morning, I felt the change in my body and it carried on, day after day, accompanied by a pain that got worse, hour after hour.

I was confused.

I didn't know what to do.

No one told me what I should do. There wasn't anyone around I could ask. I didn't dare ask Nanny Halima, since the barrier I'd erected between us prevented me from revealing any secrets to her. And I thought that what was happening to me must remain a secret—the deepest secret—and I was too proud to reveal it to anyone.

Days passed in pain and confusion. I locked myself in my bedroom, crying and pressing down on my stomach. I'd then do what I thought I had to: I'd dry my tears, stand up straight, put a smile on my lips, and leave the room to see my father.

All my father noticed those days was the pallor of my face. I reassured him and told him I had a slight cold.

That was until Nanny Halima discovered my underwear. She came to me with an anxious look and a smile on her lips.

"I want to cry out in joy, Miss Nadia! You're growing up, and soon I'll see you as a bride in your husband's house!"

I met her words coldly, even though I was eager to get her advice and listen to her. I listened, surrendering my pride and my status as her mistress.

No doubt Nanny Halima told my father what was happening to me. In the following days, he kept asking about my health, scrutinizing my face more than usual, spoiling me excessively, and doing whatever I asked. But he never dared bring up the subject of what I was suffering.

That was how it went with all the problems I had.

One result of me repressing my complaints was that I got used to being silent.

This silence helped me hide what was in my head and heart. No one ever knew what was going on behind my innocent face and my green eyes. I was a locked secret. I used to savor that.

All of my family, classmates, and servants knew this about me and feared me. They feared my intelligence. They approached me very carefully.

But where was my mother in all of this? Home with her husband.

She was a spoiled wife who only knew the happy side of life. The only thing she paid attention to was picking out her clothes and going to parties. That didn't mean she was flighty, only that she was pampered. She would still be concerned for her reputation, her house, or the love of her husband.

There was always something thick, something enormous, separating me from her, and not only because she was living in a world totally different from mine. Maybe it was my feeling that she was responsible for the divorce. I sometimes even felt that I blamed my father for marrying her; that this marriage was the one mistake in his life, even if my existence was the result of it.

Or maybe it was because I didn't resemble her at all. I have a light complexion like my father, while she's dark. My eyes are the color of my father's and her eyes are black. I'm tall like my father and she is of medium height. I keep my feelings in, making me seem cold—like my father—while she would let her feelings out, playing on her femininity.

Maybe all of that was what separated me and her. Nonetheless, I loved her. It was a love with plenty of reserve and discontent.

I'd visit once a week. I'd spend the entire day with her, her husband, and my half-siblings—two boys and a girl—but I never tried to bring her into my private life. And she didn't insist on knowing anything that wasn't obvious. Maybe without meaning it. Maybe because I'd feel deeply embarrassed whenever my father or my life with him came up.

Nonetheless, I'd visit her, happy because she was happy. She would pour joy into each day. Every time I went to see her, she sat at the piano, played the song "Dance of the mistresses," and taught me to dance. I learned from her and I got good at it. My mother was so happy with my dancing that she made a red belly-dance costume for me. She put it on me and I'd dance in front of her, just the two of us. I kept dancing for her until I was fourteen, and then I stopped.

That was my mother.

She never had a real part in my life. She could never know her daughter.

That, in brief, was me as I was the day my father broke the news about his marriage.

And then we got home.

I got out of the car and went up the stairs as if going up to a new, unknown world.

I thought there was something cold in the way Abdou the butler greeted me, as if he'd deposed me from my throne—the throne of the "mistress of the house."

A young woman came out to welcome me.

I knew she was my father's wife.

3

SHE WAS DARK LIKE MY mother, and was twenty-seven years old.

There wasn't anything particularly striking about her looks. She possessed the kind of beauty that imposes itself gradually, like the beauty of trees or the sunset or the beauty of millions of women . . . a beauty that doesn't dazzle you or turn your head. You could easily miss it as you pass by.

Perhaps the most prominent thing about her was the calm that radiated from her, like the tranquilizing scent of perfume. Everything about her was calm: the expression in her eyes, her smile, her hair, her modest clothes, her walk, her low voice, and her relaxed, sedate way of talking.

This calmness pushed you to respect her, feel at ease with her, and trust her.

Despite that, when my father introduced me to her for the first time, I couldn't match her calmness. I couldn't get control of my smile. It almost fell from my lips. I couldn't get control of my hand as I reached out to greet her. It trembled in her hand. I searched for something to say, but only came up with nervous sounds, like radio static when you can't tune in to a station.

My father stood between us, between his wife and his daughter. He was nervous too, and contented himself with a simpleminded, meaningless smile.

She was the first to talk.

"Welcome, Nadia," she said, giving me a tender, good-natured look. "You're much more beautiful than your picture."

"Merci, Auntie," I stammered.

My father smiled when he heard the word "Auntie," as if he'd found a way out of his discomfort.

"You'll have to excuse me," he said, still trying to hide his uneasiness. "I have an errand to run. I won't be gone for more than half an hour."

And he left us alone.

We sat in the salon. Safi—the pet name for Safiya, my new stepmother—began doing her very best to engage me in a long chat. But I was reserved, as if something in my head were urging me not to talk with her.

I was thinking about my new life with her and about my new position vis-à-vis my father, the servants, and the house.

Which one of us was the mistress of the house?

She was, of course.

And me—what was my position, what was my share?

I couldn't define my new status in the house. I would begrudgingly have to relinquish one of the rights I'd earned. I knew I had to give it up, whether I wanted to or not.

When I got annoyed at this thought, I looked at her talking and asked myself: Couldn't my father have found someone more beautiful?

Would I have preferred it if my father had picked a wife more beautiful than this one?

Maybe. If he'd picked a beautiful, wanton, pampered, and fickle wife—and I knew those kinds of women were chasing after him—I could have found a hundred reasons to hate her and plot against her. But this calm, respectful, modest wife . . . how could I hate her? In other words, please forgive me if I plot against her or cast on her the evil spirit that lives inside me.

From the first moment, I felt that this woman was stronger than me—stronger than me in her nature and in her desire to make my father and me happy, her concern for our home showing her desire to stay in it forever.

We sat together for a while. We talked about many things—about school, the servants, the family.

She told me about herself.

And she asked about me.

My father was gone for a while, so I asked permission to go off to my room to change my clothes.

"I let myself go in your room while you were at school," she said, getting up with me. "Let me congratulate you on your taste! Everything in your room is beautiful and lovely, just like you."

I felt like she was exaggerating. My room wasn't that beautiful. The entire house wasn't beautiful before she arrived. It was crammed with expensive antiquated furniture lined up along the sides of the rooms, just as my mother had left it before she and my father got divorced fourteen years ago. Neither my father nor I had tried to move the furniture around or add anything new.

My room was the only one that had new furniture.

And I didn't have anything to do with it. Once I got older, my father called Pontremoli, the furniture sellers, and had them design the whole room for me. Pontremoli picked the "modern style" and organized it all. Even the drapes, the color of the walls, and the pictures. I wasn't involved at all.

It was expensive, but it wasn't beautiful . . . rather, its beauty was manufactured, not an expression of my personality or taste.

Auntie Safi hadn't tried to change anything in my room, but she'd turned the house completely on its head without adding anything new. She'd moved pieces of furniture from one place to another, rugs from one room to another, and reorganized the flowerpots and all the beautiful porcelain so that the house looked as if it had been refurnished, as if everything in it were bought just for her, on the occasion of her marriage.

She was indeed the mistress of the house.

I couldn't deny that.

Auntie Safi left me at the door of my room.

I locked myself inside and threw myself on my bed, crying.

I couldn't explain the reason for my crying, but I had never cried with such intensity. My tears had never gushed out like that before. I felt I would wear myself out through my tears, as if I'd lost my father forever.

I locked myself in my room for a long time. I began to feel like this room was all I had left in this big house.

When it was time for dinner, my father came and knocked on my door. I wiped my tears and fixed my hair and clothes before opening the door for him.

"Where have you been, Nadia?" he asked happily, looking ten years younger. "We're all waiting for you for dinner."

"I was just so tired," I said, trying to smile. "I slept for a little."

My father looked me in the eye, trying to figure out what I was really thinking.

"Okay, let's get going," he said, trying to dispel the doubts swirling in his head. "We're throwing a party for you!"

I put on new clothes. I braided my hair into a single braid rather than the usual two hanging down on my chest. I wanted to look older, like my father's wife.

I joined them in the parlor. My father was sitting with a glass of whiskey in front of him. His wife was sitting next to him wearing a black dress of shiny faille. It was a modest dress that covered her arms and neck, but it was chic and refined, like part of a bridal gown. She was drinking a glass of strawberry juice. My uncle Aziz—I mentioned before that he lived upstairs—was sitting opposite her, laughing as always, but drinking more than usual.

Auntie Safi met me with delight as if I were her daughter. My father smiled, proud of me and my beauty. Uncle Aziz hugged me and kissed my cheeks.

"That's it!" he said, laughing. "Now that Daddy's gotten married, you have to too!"

"If you'd like to marry me," I said, trying to laugh, "I'm ready to get married right now!"

"I'm sure your father wouldn't like that," he said, chuckling.

"Could he find someone better than you, Uncle?" I asked. I looked at my father. "Ever since I was young, I wanted to marry Daddy!" I said, unable to clear the bitterness from my voice.

"I don't think there's a man in the world who deserves Nadia," my father's wife said in a happy and innocent voice.

"Even Daddy?" I asked, challenging her.

"Is there a man in the world like your father?" she asked cleverly.

As soon as I sat down next to my uncle, Abdou the butler came over to bring me a glass of strawberry juice.

Who taught Abdou to bring me a drink I hadn't asked for?

Abdou had worked in the house for five years, but he'd never thought about bringing me something I hadn't asked for. He'd only bring coffee for guests, or whiskey if they were my father's close friends.

And what was the story with this strawberry juice?

I knew there were always bottles of Coke or soda water in the fridge, but there was never strawberry juice or anything like it.

What had happened?

She was the mistress of the house!

She was the one who put strawberry juice into the refrigerator. She was the one who taught Abdou to present it before dinner.

This was a new world that she built for me and my father to live in—a world I couldn't have offered him when I was mistress of the house.

We moved to the dinner table.

She sat at the head of the table with my father on her right, my uncle on her left, and me at the opposite end.

The butler brought out the plates. He went to her first, and then came to me.

This was the natural order that had to prevail in the house. She was first and I was second, but I was struck by it. I'd gotten used to being the first and only. I'd gotten used to sitting at the head of the table.

We talked as we ate dinner.

I spoke the least, and I was the last one they directed conversation to.

My uncle spoke to her, giving me only passing comments.

My father was talking more than he usually did. He wasn't as serious and reserved as usual. Instead, he bantered with my uncle, exchanging little jokes with him and looking at his wife between mouthfuls as if thanking her for this blessing.

She was clever at steering the rudder of conversation. She was directing it, trying to get everyone to participate, even me.

"I learned from your father that you like moussaka," she told me. "I told the cook to make it just for you."

I really did like moussaka, but on this day, I wasn't interested in eating moussaka or anything else.

After that, I would get accustomed to her making everything I liked. She was doing it to try to please me. But it was a mistake. These flatteries annoyed me and made me feel like I was a guest in my own house. I tried hard to break free from them. I hid from her what I liked and what I didn't. I sometimes purposely ate things I didn't like just to confuse her. But she kept trying to please me, trying to convince me that I was the most important person in the house.

If she hadn't tried so hard to please me, would I have forgiven her?

I don't think so. I figured out afterward that what annoyed me about her wasn't her trying to please me, but that she closed all the doors through which I could vent my hatred and loathing for her, from which I could let out the evil in my heart.

We finished dinner.

We went back to the parlor.

My uncle stayed for a little as he drank coffee. He then excused himself and left.

Auntie Safi sat next to my father sewing a piece of needlepoint as I began playing some records.

They were whispering to each other as if they were exchanging sweet nothings. Their whispering sometimes got so loud that I could hear it as I sat next to the turntable. Sometimes it went quiet so that I only heard a light flutter, as if their lips were the wings of angels hovering in the air.

All of a sudden, I noticed they had stopped whispering. Their silence went on for a while. I turned toward them and saw him give her a look. He was infatuated, as if he were kissing every part of her with his eyes. She looked down intently at the piece of cloth she was sewing, her cheeks blushing. They were looking at me in silence, then exchanging looks with each other as if there were a conversation happening between their eyes that my presence was ruining.

My blood boiled.

I felt that I was a burdensome uninvited guest, that I was a stranger in my own house.

For the first time, I felt like my father didn't want me next to him, like he wanted to get rid of me.

I felt as if something in my chest were crying and tearing itself apart, that a cold tremor was creeping through my veins, that my body was shriveling around my bones. I wanted to revolt, to destroy something, to pounce on my father and shake his shoulders, to wake him up to my existence, to make him remember me, to make him remember that I was everything in his life.

I pressed down on my nerves mercilessly. I decided to leave.

"Bonsoir," I said, feeling a weight on my tongue like a piece of clay. "I'm going to bed."

"Don't forget to lock the balcony door," my father said calmly and unenthusiastically, as if tossing me out.

"You're going to sleep already?" Auntie Safi asked, pretending to insist that I stay.

"I'm tired, Auntie," I said, unable to smile.

I leaned over my father, kissing him as usual. As if his love for me woke up when his lips touched my cheeks, he pulled me to his chest with great tenderness and gave me a bigger kiss than I was used to, a kiss with more affection and love.

I reached out to my father's wife and she pulled me to her and hugged me to her chest too.

"Good night, my dear," she said, pressing her cheek against mine.

There was a ring of sincerity, friendship, and love in her voice—as I remember it now—but my ears had become blocked from hearing anything except for my heart, as it pounded between my ribs like the church bell in a small village ringing out loudly to announce the attack of devils.

I went into my room and locked the door.

I didn't usually lock the door, but that night I locked it automatically, without meaning to, as if someone were calling out inside me, trying to protect me from an intruder coming in while I was sleeping, grabbing me from bed, and tossing me into the fire of hatred and loathing, the fire of feeling irrelevant.

I took off my clothes with nervous hands as if tearing them from my body. Throwing myself on the bed, I stared at the ceiling.

I didn't cry.

I didn't sleep.

My eyes stayed fixed on the ceiling. Images from my life passed through my mind, mixing with the noise filling my chest and burning in the fire that spread in my veins.

My room was next to my father's. The two rooms opened onto a single balcony overlooking the garden. I'd often see him from the balcony, and he'd come see me the same way. Often we both stood out there, he in his pajamas and I in my nightgown, talking for a while.

I heard my father and his wife walk to their room.

I heard my father let out a light-hearted laugh.

I heard her laugh mingle with his like a lump of sugar melting in a cup of hot tea.

I heard them shut the door behind them.

And then I didn't hear anything.

My imagination suddenly shuddered at the thought of what could be happening between them, between a man and his wife in the bedroom.

The imagination of a sixteen-year-old girl who hadn't known a man before and had only heard passing words from adolescent classmates about what happens in the bedroom.

My imagination started picturing incredible things.

I smiled, as if watching an exciting and entertaining movie, and then was disgusted, letting out cries of pain, when my adolescent mind came up with violent, harsh images.

I was revolted and filled with jealousy when a third kind of image jumped to my mind—a gentle image of kindness and love. My father, who gave his life to me, loved and was being tender with another woman.

My imagination persecuted me. It wasn't only dripping those images into my head, it was also dripping its poison into my body. I felt as if drops of cold water were falling on me in monotonous successive rhythms, like droplets of condensation slipping down a pane of glass or water dripping from a faucet that needed fixing.

It was the most intense physical feeling I had experienced in my life.

My imagination wore me out.

I was so exhausted and felt tortured.

I tried to kick my imagination out of my head and my body, but I was gripped by something like a state of anxiety. I hit the pillow with my hands. I lifted up the covers with my feet and turned on my side violently, as if I were writhing on coals.

I got up in bare feet to close the veranda door. But as soon as I got close to the door, I stopped.

I heard whispering coming from the neighboring room, a whispering that was more like moaning.

Words that I could almost make out, until they popped in the air like soap bubbles.

Distinct sentences torn apart with no meaning except what my imagination gave them.

Moans, agony, intoxication, rebuke as if delight, repulsion as if supplication.

My ears opened up. All of me became the ears of an adolescent girl. I took another step toward the balcony, like a thief, as all my confused emotions formed a gang to hijack my ears.

I stood there for a long time with my eyes wide open like an owl in the dark, my breath trembling as I tried to subdue it so it didn't drown out the sounds from the next room.

I heard everything.

Then I didn't hear anything.

Everything went silent.

I closed the balcony door and went to my bed in my bare feet like a sleepwalker.

But I couldn't sleep.

4

It was a morning like every morning that came after it.

A morning in which light dawned on the whole house except for my heart.

My father woke up like the rising sun, joyful and happy, almost kissing the furniture, walls, and servants with his smile. He went into the bathroom and sang in the shower so loudly that I could hear him from my bedroom, as if he were totally drunk. As soon as he saw me, he lifted me in his arms as if he were proud of a new strength pulsating in his body. He sprinkled loud kisses on my face, kisses crackling in the air as if they were the trills of joy the morning after a marriage ceremony.

My father's wife woke up as if her youth were renewed every day, as if the flower hidden under her brown cheeks would never wilt. She filled the entire house with activity from the first moment she opened her eyes on it. She wandered through the rooms to oversee the servants, then disappeared with my father until he got dressed. She sat with him at the breakfast table and said goodbye to him at the garden door, embracing him with her eyes like she was guarding him from envy. After my father left, she went upstairs, where Uncle Aziz lived, to oversee arranging his rooms.

I was the only one who woke up groggy, with puffy and withered eyes, absentminded, irritable. I stayed in bed for a long time, trying to collect myself and get control of my will so I could find a smile to hang on my lips when I encountered my father and his wife.

I was annoyed at this new happiness filling the house: the happiness of my father with his wife and her happiness with him. A happiness in which I played no part and for which I got no credit.

The fumes of evil began filling my chest and rising to my head. Fumes climbing from the crucible of a sorcerer preparing black poison.

Dozens of plans filled my head, all of them destroying this happy house, but I knew I'd destroy my father if I destroyed his house. I knew that if I tore his wife from him, I wouldn't be able to compensate him for her.

I loved my father. I loved him so much that I'd kill myself before I dared harm him. A violent battle rose up inside me between this love—my love for my father—and my hatred for his wife.

My love was victorious over my hatred. I throttled the black plans filling my head before I moved to carry them out. I alone was the victim. I was the one who was eaten alive by it and I was the one who didn't sleep, my eyelids coming down over my eyes only when I was completely exhausted.

Nonetheless, I could hide all of that behind my beautiful, innocent face, behind the smile on my lips. No one noticed how thin I got except for my father's wife. She suggested calling a doctor to give me a revitalizing shot.

My father's wife tried everything to make me a part of the happiness that she showered on the house.

She took me to Rita, the seamstress, and to Babaziane, the shoemaker. It was the first time I had clothes or shoes made for me. She spent hours with me flipping through fashion magazines. Then she'd spend hours with me in the kitchen without her making me feel like I was being given a lesson. Instead, it seemed as if we were playing a game, that we were children entertaining ourselves.

"Let's play a trick on Daddy," she said suddenly. "We'll make him lunch ourselves!"

Joyfully, she took me by the hand and we went into the kitchen, driving the cook away from the stove. She ordered the kitchen boy to peel the onions, Nanny Halima to crush the tomatoes, and the cook to prepare the chicken, and then she had me melt the butter over the fire.

I lost myself in this entertaining "trick." I looked at her as she was immersed in cooking, wisps of her black hair hanging down over her face.

I envied her. I envied her for her strong personality, the goodness of her heart, the sweet joy that she spread around her, and the love that surrounded her—the love of my father, of my uncle, of all the servants. Envy would oppress me sometimes and it would turn into hatred. I almost lost control, but I pretended that I was tired and ran out of the kitchen to hide in my room, locking the door behind me.

Despite that, I learned a lot of things in the kitchen from her. I learned how to take the cook to task, how to prepare the house budget, how to cook the moussaka I loved, and rice with curry, Circassian chicken, and baba ghanouj. Before Auntie Safi, I didn't know how to fry an egg and I got flustered if I tried to make a cup of coffee.

Every week, she put on a big dinner, inviting members of both families. I started noticing that she was very interested in my appearance and my clothes at those dinners, and that she'd purposely invite young men from the two families, and some of them invited their friends, who were young men too. I was sure she was doing all that to find a husband for me.

It would have been natural for me to be grateful for this kind, well-meaning effort that she was making on my behalf, but I wasn't. All I imagined was that she wanted to marry me off to get rid of me, to empty out the house for herself and my father.

I began to be stubborn.

I started resisting her efforts to marry me off.

I'd claim that I was sick just before the guests would arrive, and I'd lock myself in my room. If I went out and had dinner with them, I'd scowl in their faces and fill them with distaste for me. I wouldn't encourage a single one of them or open a door of hope for them. I'd sit among them with my eyes fixed on my father as if he were my only man. I didn't want anyone to take me from him or anyone to take him from me.

Maybe Auntie Safi noticed my scowling, and maybe she understood that I was only feigning illness, but she never tried to stop what I was doing or show me her displeasure.

I got used to her being more of a friend, not a mother or stepmother. A reserved friend with boundaries that she didn't cross. It wasn't her right to restrict my freedom or boss me around or criticize me.

But did I accept her friendship?

Never.

The happiness that she brought with her into the house almost reached me. I knew that I could have participated in it if my heart or mind had been different or if my psyche wasn't so shredded and complicated. But my heart and mind forbade me from accepting her friendship.

I blocked her from me as if a devil from my thoughts were standing between us.

I was fleeing from her love and kindness.

I was wishing evil on her. I was still setting the plans that would bring the whole house down on top of her, my father, and myself. I'd then resist those plans with all my will so that I didn't move forward to carry them out.

Until the day my will finally weakened.

The three of us were sitting in the parlor after we'd finished dinner. The telephone rang. I was closest to it, so I picked up the receiver. I heard the voice of one of my stepmother's friends.

I don't know what devil possessed me at that moment or filled me with evil, but I didn't respond to the friend who was talking. Instead, I started repeating, "Hello? Hello? Hello?" I repeated it a number of times, as if the person on the other end didn't want to respond to me. I hung up and turned to my father and his wife.

"There was no one there!" I said, appearing awkward and embarrassed.

I knew that the friend would call back.

And she did. Not a minute passed before the phone rang again.

I picked it up and brought it over to my father's wife.

"You answer, Auntie," I said, with the same naiveté mixed with embarrassment.

Auntie Safi took the receiver with total innocence and started talking to her friend.

I looked at my father, but I didn't see anything on his face indicating that he understood something was wrong or that he was even paying attention to what was happening.

He was smoking his cigarette and sipping his coffee as if he were the calmest and happiest husband in the world.

Auntie Safi finished talking on the phone.

My father didn't ask her anything. He didn't even ask the name of the friend she was talking to.

The conversation resumed among us.

"You know, Daddy," I said suddenly, "I decided that I'm not going to talk to my friend Aliya anymore."

"Why?" he asked calmly. "She's good-natured and cheerful."

"No she's not," I said innocently. "Imagine—I was at her house and she left me alone while she sat and talked with one of her boyfriends on the phone. She was talking with him while her mother was home with us!"

"Don't say that," my father said disapprovingly.

"She was talking with him like he was one of her girl-friends," I said, raising my voice and enunciating my words.

"The strange thing is that she didn't miss a beat. She didn't make a single mistake!"

He gave me a wide-eyed stare.

I searched his eyes for something to please the devil that had taken me over. I wanted him to understand that his wife was talking with a man, not one of her friends. But he didn't understand a thing.

"What does that have to do with us?" he asked, taking a drag on his cigarette.

"Believe it, Ahmed," his wife said, her eyes on the piece of cloth she was sewing. "Girls these days get away with all sorts of things!"

What she said came as a shock to me.

She hadn't noticed anything either. She hadn't caught on to the game I was playing.

My father changed the subject.

Everything became calm again, as if there were no attempted crime, as if the devil weren't there sitting with them, hiding behind a beautiful face with green eyes and blond hair.

I found myself silent.

I imagined this entire house demolished, and that I was the one who'd obliterated it with the seeds of doubt that I was trying to sow in my father's mind, just like mine workers when they dig holes to stuff sticks of dynamite into and then destroy the mountain.

I imagined my father under the debris of this house after I destroyed it. I imagined him as a corpse torn apart. I imagined myself trying to collect his limbs, to bring my father back to life, happiness, love, and tenderness. But I couldn't.

I imagined all that, and then I let out a cry hidden inside me that tore up my chest. I felt every drop of my blood howl like stray dogs running forward and barking as if I'd announced the revolution.

The revolution against the devil of evil.

The revolution against myself.

Maybe the trace of all those images appeared on my face. Maybe my cheeks turned red from my rushing blood, or maybe the pupils of my eyes widened or my hands trembled. I woke up from my sick fantasy at the sound of Auntie Safi speaking to me tenderly.

"What's wrong, Nadia my dear? I feel like something's wrong."

"No, nothing," I said, getting up from my chair. "I think I didn't eat enough."

"Okay," she said with a worried look. "Take a pepsin before you go to sleep."

"Yes, ma'am," I said in a barely audible voice.

I hurried to my room, almost tripping over my feet, and threw myself on the bed without taking off my clothes. My breath roiled, my eyes fixed on the ceiling. A long time passed as I was lost in the vortex of my black thoughts, until I heard myself whisper, "Oh Lord!"

And as if God came and wiped His hand over my eyes, I cried.

I kept crying until I heard my father and his wife head to their room. I heard his quiet laugh. I heard her laugh melt in his like a lump of sugar in a cup of hot tea.

Then I heard the door of the room close behind them. I got up from my bed barefoot, my tears still on my cheeks. I stood at the balcony door to listen to their whispers—the whispers of a man and his wife in their bedroom.

This had become my habit every evening.

Six months had passed since my father's marriage, and every evening of those six months, I snuck to the balcony door to listen to those whispers. I heard moans, agony, intoxication, delighted rebuke, and unrestrained supplication

It was as if I had an appointment with them every night. I would even start grumbling whenever they were late going to their room. I started almost urging them to go.

"Aren't you going to bed?" I'd ask them sometimes without thinking.

I'd say it innocently and honestly, not showing any of the deviant feeling pulsating in my veins. They'd often respond to my invitation. They'd exchange looks of love mixed with desire and bashfulness. Then they'd go to their room, but not before I beat them to mine.

Sometimes I'd stand on the balcony and listen in to catch some words. But then I couldn't hear anything except for the rhythmic breaths of two people drowning in calm, deep sleep. I'd be disappointed, as if my love had missed his appointment, as if I were going to sleep hungry and thirsty.

Was this deviant?

Something even more perverse happened. My imagination, stirred up by the whispering in my father's bedroom, evolved and began to overwhelm my pure, chaste body. I started imagining myself every evening in the arms of a man: my father. Yes, I was imagining myself in my father's arms, his arms around my body, his breath heating my face, hearing from him the same words that he whispered to his wife. I whispered in his ears the same words that she whispered to him, the words popping in the air like soap bubbles.

I was in agony, intoxicated, rebuking him in delight, repulsed yet pleading for more.

I was being tortured.

I knew how deviant my mind was.

Torture pushed me to look for an escape route from my imagination.

Thinking with a new logic, I knew that I couldn't give my father what his wife gave him.

But there had to be a man who could give me what my father was giving his wife.

This line of thought, began directing my life.

I started looking for a man.

A man who could give me what my father gave his wife, to whisper in my ears the same words he whispered to her.

I began looking at men in a new way. I began looking at them like I was shopping for clothes or buying a slave. With my eyes, I was taking the measurements of every one of them, examining the shape of their smile and the way they talked. I'd then compare each one to the image imprinted in my mind—the image of my father.

I examined a lot of men until I found him.

I found the man.

The first man in my life.

5

My father, his wife, and I were invited to dinner at the Mena House with some family friends.

I saw him there, having dinner with a family we knew. He was sitting next to the family's daughter, a girl around my age, blond like me, though she was less beautiful.

He wasn't young. He was, as I came to know later, thirty-six, three or four years younger than my father. Unlike my father, his skin was brown, the color of medium-rare steak. His hair was black and wavy, and he didn't pay much attention to brushing it. The most notable parts of his face were his eyes and lips. His small eyes emitted a razor-like intelligence. Because they were so sharp, they almost hid the goodness of his heart and could give someone who didn't know him the impression that he was dangerous. His lips were sensual. I couldn't look at them for long without thinking about kissing them!

I knew who he was. At any rate, I knew his name. I'd seen him before, on Sidi Bishr beach in Alexandria. He'd spend all day under an umbrella reading a book, lifting his eyes every page or two to glance at the flocks of girls, and then going back to his book. He'd then get up from under the umbrella and wander around to his friends' cabins. Every cabin welcomed him, since he was well known. He was from an important family, rich, seductive . . . and a bachelor.

We girls were walking in groups, each one almost blocking the promenade along the row of cabins. We knew the spot of every young man on the beach. We knew that it was so-and-so's cabin after two steps and someone else's cabin after another three steps. We'd cross the entire beach until we passed all the young men, every girl with us making sure to pass by the young man she'd chosen for herself.

We didn't look directly at anyone. But we knew young men—I mean the interesting young men—by the sound of their footsteps behind us. We knew that this was Ali's cabin, this was Mohamed's, and that Samir's. We felt the looks directed at us without needing to turn toward them. Each of us had a sixth sense we'd use to pick up their footsteps and looks without us letting on.

None of us young girls tried to pick up Mustafa's steps or looks. He was a distant hope for us, and none of us dared dream of him as our own.

Despite that, Mustafa once gave me a look. Just one, he didn't repeat it, as if he'd had his fill of me with that single look, or as if I didn't deserve more than one.

This look remained suspended in my imagination for a number of days. Then I forgot about it.

Until I saw him sitting having dinner at the Mena House with this family, next to that girl.

He talked to her for so long that I thought their conversation would never end. She kept laughing as if he were tickling her heart. Here and there, he let out shaky laughs with her as if he were a young child whose lungs weren't strong enough to bear much laughing.

He then got up to dance with her.

I noticed his arm around her back, rising until his palm fell on her shoulder. I noticed that he was pressing her to him until her chest disappeared in his, his nose plunged into the folds of her hair. He then moved her in slow, short, gentle steps as if he were swimming with her in the air.

My blood boiled.

I was furious.

I asked my father to get up to dance with me. I directed my father so we got near them. I looked at him. I looked at him with all of my eyes. I looked at him as if I were calling to him.

He lifted his head and gave me a single look from behind her back. Then he plunged his nose back into the folds of her hair.

Just one look.

As if he still could get his fill of me with a single look, or as if I still wasn't worth more than one.

I was even more irate.

I started staring at the girl. What did she have that I didn't? If she was beautiful, I was more so. If I was so young that I didn't deserve more than this look from him, she was around my age, maybe even younger.

I found myself making a decision.

I decided I'd take him from her.

I decided I'd take him for myself.

We got up to go. We passed by his table on our way out. I looked at him again. I stared right at him. But he didn't turn to look at me, or even notice me. Instead, he just kept on talking with her, while everyone was saying goodbye to me, some looking at me with glances of desire and some with sorrow.

I became more insistent on my decision.

I'll take him no matter the price.

I'll punish him for ignoring me.

I found myself pursing my lips as if collecting my resolve, as if finalizing the decision that I'd made with an official seal.

When I went to bed, I didn't sleep. But I didn't try to eavesdrop on the whispers of my father and his wife next door. It was the first night in six months that I didn't go out in bare feet to steal something that wasn't mine. I stayed in bed with my eyes wide open, searching my mind for the details of the plan by which I'd reach him. I kept going until I pictured myself with him. I saw him bow down at my feet. I saw myself point to him. He got closer to me, kissed my cheek and lips, and enveloped me in his arms, whispering in my ear the same words that my father whispered to his wife.

I looked at the phonebook. I started flipping through it impatiently until I found his name and number.

I hesitated a little before dialing.

I didn't know exactly what I'd say or how I'd start talking with him—my first real conversation with a man.

I closed my eyes, squeezing them shut as if collecting my strength. I then took the receiver and spun the dial. I heard the sound of the phone ringing like light knocks on my heart. A rough voice answered.

"Is Mustafa there?" I asked, making my voice as sweet as possible.

"He's sleeping," the rough voice replied curtly.

"Merci," I said quickly.

I dropped the receiver as if I were tossing something burning, like someone who'd been shocked with electricity.

I looked at the clock.

It was still eight in the morning.

I smiled. He had the right to sleep until eight, especially after his night out yesterday. I got up to wander around the house, doing nothing special. I didn't pay attention to the things I normally noticed every morning. I wasn't preoccupied by my father's happiness or his singing in the shower. The activity of my father's wife didn't annoy me. I didn't notice her at all. What filled my head and body was the new world whose door I was trying to knock on, a world whose throne Mustafa was sitting on . . . and I was sitting next to him on the same throne.

It was nine o'clock when I spun the dial again, as if I were turning years of my life.

The same rough voice responded.

"Is Mustafa awake?" I asked.

"He's in the shower," the voice responded curtly. "Who do I tell him is calling?"

"Don't worry about it," I said, disappointment dripping from my words. "I'll call back."

I hung up.

At ten o'clock, I picked up the receiver and called again.

"He's gone out," the same rough voice responded curtly.

I slammed the receiver down so hard that I almost smashed it. I felt I'd been insulted and my dignity ripped to shreds.

How could he not wait for me? How could he go out before I talked with him?

But he doesn't know me. He doesn't know that I want to talk to him.

I was able to convince myself to calm down.

I spent the morning waiting for lunchtime, when I tried calling him again, thinking I'd find him at home then. But he wasn't there. I was confused, unable to do anything except stare at the telephone as if I were trying to talk to it. I couldn't eat lunch and I refused to leave the house. I holed myself up in my room with the phone on my bed, spinning the dial every hour or so.

Finally, at seven in the evening, I heard his voice.

He didn't even say hello.

"Yes?" he said in a lazy voice, as if the strings of his voice were all tenor.

"Mustafa?" I asked, getting control of my nerves so the trembling of my heart didn't come through in my voice.

"Yes."

"I'm someone . . ." I fell silent, as if waiting for him to take over the conversation. But he didn't say a word. He was quiet for a long time.

"Who?" he asked finally, in a voice even lazier.

"Someone," I said, making my voice more delicate. "You don't want to talk to someone?"

"No."

"But I'm sure you'd like to talk to me!" I said flirtatiously.

"Why?" he said, throwing the burden of conversation back onto me.

"You'll find out soon enough," I said provocatively.

"Fine," he said coldly. "Call me soon enough."

I stiffened at his coldness.

"No," I said sharply. "I'll talk to you now, whether you like it or not!"

"No," he said, still colder than ice. "I don't like it."

"But I want to talk to you now!" I said like a little girl stamping her foot on the ground, insisting on what she wants.

"Go ahead, talk," he said.

I was silent. I didn't know what to say.

He kept quiet for a bit. Then he asked, "Is someone forcing you?"

This opened a door for conversation.

"Like who?" I asked awkwardly.

"How would I know?"

"Of course, you know a lot of women, and any one of them could push me to you."

"Not a lot . . ."

"Yesterday, for example, who were you with?"

"Yesterday? I wasn't with anyone."

"Liar! Who you were dancing with yesterday at the Mena House?"

"Who do you mean?" he asked innocently.

"Nagla," I said, as if revealing his secret.

He let out a broken chuckle like that of a child whose lungs aren't strong enough to give a full laugh.

"My dear, shame on you. She's like my daughter!"

"You do all that with your daughter? You dance with her like that?"

"I swear to you, I always dance like that." he said, still laughing.

"And you're swearing to me too?" I joked.

"To everyone dear to me. All of them, I swear. But please tell me, who are you?"

"I'm someone who likes you."

"So, you saw me and you know who I am?" he asked, trying to persuade me to reveal myself.

"Yes."

"And it's not shameful for you to talk to someone you know but who doesn't know you? That's selfish."

"Why selfish? You're talking to me just like I'm talking to you."

"The difference is that you're talking to someone you know—someone you can picture before you as you're holding the phone. But I'm talking to a voice in thin air—a voice without a body. The whole time I'm talking with you, I'm asking myself who you are. Are you beautiful or not? Who made you call me? This is crazy."

I was almost persuaded to tell him who I was, but I held back.

"Bear with me a little." .

"For who?" he said nervously. "For the air that's talking to me?"

"I'm not air. I'm someone who won't regret the day she met you."

"So you won't tell me who you are?"

"Later. After I'm reassured."

"About what?"

"That you deserve me."

"Empty words, my dear," he said sharply. "Someone's sitting in his house peacefully and a girl comes like a voice in thin air to test him, to see if he deserves her or not! Has anyone told you that I'm lacking women, my dear? Did I ask you to call me?"

"I want it like this," I cut him off coldly.

"Yes, ma'am," he said mockingly. "I'm at your command. But I just got home. Let me go change and wash up.

That way I can be sure that I'm chic and more presentable so I deserve you."

"I don't like chic men," I said, still cold.

"Okay, let me go and dishevel myself a bit."

"Fine. Au revoir," I said, laughing. "When do you want me to call back?"

"Whenever you want."

"So, when?"

"Half an hour."

"Bye."

"Bye."

I put the receiver down gently. I felt that I was flying into the new world I'd imagined. I was walking with my arm in Mustafa's toward the throne we'd sit on together. I didn't pay attention to the triviality of our conversation in which I appeared like a child who hadn't talked with a man before. The feeling of the adventure that I'd embarked on and that filled my entire being was enough for me to open the door for him.

Exactly half an hour later, I lifted the receiver and turned the dial. The rough voice that I hated responded.

"Who do I say is calling, miss?" he said with dry politesse.

"Tell him someone . . ."

"He's not here, miss."

I slammed the receiver down as all my dreams collapsed.

I was furious, my blood boiled. But instead of seeking to preserve my dignity and changing my plan, my fire was transformed into stubbornness.

This was the first time that I felt there was a man who didn't want me and was fleeing from me. But I tried to convince myself: he doesn't know me. He doesn't know how much he wants me.

I started calling back. I dialed his number dozens of times. Every hour, day and night. Sometimes I'd sneak out of my room at three in the morning and tiptoe over to the phone to call. But I didn't get through. The servant always answered, asked me my name, and when I told him "someone" or "he knows," he'd say he wasn't there.

I started giving myself fake names. I said I was Mervat or Suad or Fatima, but the servant would always make me wait for a moment.

"One minute while I see if he's here," he'd say.

Then he'd come back like a torturer to carry out the harsh judgment.

"I'm afraid he's just gone out."

I almost went crazy.

There was no other way to get in touch with him besides the phone. But he was driving me crazy. I started calling him more than fifty times a day.

And after five days, I finally got him.

He responded himself—maybe by mistake—and recognized my voice.

"You've totally worn me out, my dear," he said, as if pleading with me. "You've worn out my butler too. The whole house. Stop calling, please!"

"You've worn me out too, Mustafa," I said. "Why are you doing that?"

"For heaven's sake!" he said, as if pulling out his hair. "My dear, did I do something to you? You must be crazy!"

"I'm not crazy, Mustafa," I said, keeping calm. "If I were crazy, I would have told you who I was the first day."

I said his name informally as if I'd known him for a long time.

"Okay, listen, sane lady," he said as if giving me a lesson, "this story of the telephone stopped a long time ago. The world's changed. Now there are parties, clubs, and social circles for people to get to know each other. It doesn't make any sense that a girl who shows half her body on the beach hides her name on the phone. People don't have time for all this hypocrisy anymore. The whole thing doesn't take more than a few words: 'I'm so and so, hello! Where are you going today? Such and such place! Okay, I'll see you there. Great!'"

"So you wanted me to pounce on you at the Mena House?" I asked as if resisting my conviction. "I just say to you, 'Come and love me'?"

He laughed. "You love me?"

"I don't know," I said, fixing my mistake. "That's not what I meant, but—"

"Since it's gotten to that point, perhaps you could tell me who you are."

"No, not today," I said stubbornly. "I still don't know if you deserve me."

"I'll count to three, and if you don't tell me who you are, I'll hang up."

I was quiet for a bit.

"One."

"I won't say."

"Two."

"I still won't say."

"Three."

I kept quiet.

He was quiet for a second, and then hung up.

I was terrified. I immediately dialed the number again, like I was drowning, clutching a life jacket.

"Yes!" I heard him scream as if he'd gone crazy.

"I'm Nadia Lutfi," I said hurriedly. "My father is Ahmed Lutfi. I live in Dokki. I'm tall, beautiful, and blonde. You've seen me before and you liked me. Happy now?"

"And when will I see you?" he asked calmly, like he'd gotten an official report that he was sure would arrive.

"Not right now, Mustafa," I said, as if pleading with him. "Wait a little."

"I beg you, Nadia," he said confidently. "If we must meet each other, today is better than tomorrow."

It was the first time I'd heard him say my name. It felt like the first time I heard my name pronounced from a man's heart.

"Tomorrow," I said submissively. "Tomorrow at four thirty."

"Where?" he asked without showing any happiness.

I thought a little.

"In front of the Furousiya Club," I said.

"Make it five," he said.

"No, four thirty," I said stubbornly.

"Yes, ma'am," he said. I could picture a mocking smile of victory on his lips.

"Au revoir," I said, worn out from my defeat.

"Au revoir," he said, without trying to prolong the conversation.

He left me to my thoughts.

There weren't any thoughts, just a thick white cloud through which I could only see blurry images of me and Mustafa in a single frame.

Hours passed as I tried to interpret those images.

Had I made a mistake?

Was I embarking on a new crime?

I didn't know.

I no longer knew anything about what was going on around me except that I was confused, lost, with an unknown hand pushing me to an unknown fate. I felt that I wanted someone next to me. I wanted someone to guide me, to take my hand and show me the path of protection . . . someone to whom I could confess my confusion, my torture. I couldn't ask my father for advice, or his wife or my mother, who was oblivious to me. I didn't have a friend I could entrust my secret to.

I felt lonelier than ever.

I felt that I was alone with Mustafa. But I didn't know Mustafa or what he could do to me.

I was scared.

I was scared because I felt he was stronger than me, older than me, more experienced, because he was the first person who could destroy a plan I'd made.

My ploy was to let him chase after me, to stir him up so much that I'd divert him from his world. Then I'd decide what I wanted to do with him.

But he had upended the plan, and I had become the one chasing after him. I was the one diverted from my world. He was able to impose his will on me and drag me to meet him after only the second time I spoke to him on the phone. And I didn't know what he wanted to do to me after that.

I spent the night thinking about breaking my meeting with him.

But I didn't.

I felt like I wanted to flee from something that I knew was torturing me to something that I didn't know was torturing me.

I went to meet him with the white fog still filling my head and heart. All I did to get ready was tie my hair up and put on lipstick so I looked older than I was.

I didn't find him in front of the Furousiya Club.

I purposely went five minutes late but I didn't find him there.

I decided to leave. I walked away slowly, as if my feet were sticking to the ground.

Then I heard the sound of a car following me. Turning, I saw him in the driver's seat.

He stopped his car next to me and smiled.

I hated his smile. He was smiling as if he were victorious over me, or maybe I hated myself at that moment since I was the one defeated by him.

He didn't say anything.

Neither did I.

I went around the front of the car. He opened the door for me and I got in next to him.

"Please drive quickly," I said as he drove over Galaa Bridge. "Everyone knows me here!"

I lowered my head so none of the Dokki kids would see me.

"Watch out," he said, looking at me and smiling. "Everyone in the bus next to us can see you trying to hide."

That was the first thing I heard from him in our first meeting.

What he said made sense, so I sat up without discussion, as if he'd given me an order I couldn't refuse.

After that, he got me used to thinking that what he said always made sense. He had a smooth, clear logic that you could not help being convinced by. He turned to me as we drove out on Haram Street.

"I've seen you before," he said, looking at me with his dark, narrow eyes that hid the goodness of his heart. "But I didn't realize you were so young."

"I'm not young," I said defensively. "I'm eighteen." At the time, I was still sixteen.

"How old do you think I am?" he asked, smiling.

"Twenty-five," I said, hypocrisy dripping from my words.

"I wish," he said, laughing in self-pity. "I'm thirty-six. Double your age!"

"So what?" I said, trying to make him feel better. "Didn't our Lord say that man was double woman?"

He let out his high, broken laugh. "Our Lord said, 'To the man, a portion of two women,'" he said. "That means when I'm thirty-six, I have to go out with two girls, each of them eighteen!"

I laughed with him, and then my laugh trailed off. "So, for example, you'd like to bring Nagla along with me?" I asked bitterly.

"I told you that Nagla is like my daughter," he snapped. "Her father is my friend. Please believe me."

I pretended to believe him. But there was always something in my heart that left room for doubt. We reached al-Naziliya.

Throughout the drive, I kept to myself in the corner of the front seat, far from him, near the door, as if I were ready to jump out at any moment. I was looking out the window as I was talking with him, only turning to him now and then as if stealing a glimpse at him. I was afraid. No, not afraid . . . I was frightened of the adventure and I had little confidence in myself. I didn't know exactly what I'd do. Despite that, I felt I was being driven on a path paved with happiness—a happiness making me forget myself and the evil operating inside me.

He stopped the car on a calm street in al-Naziliya. Then he turned toward me and set his eyes on me.

I didn't find anything in his look to embarrass me or make me feel ashamed. There wasn't any desire or sin in his eyes. He didn't move his eyes to my chest or my thighs. He was only looking at my face. He was looking at it like an artist examining a painting or the face of a model to transfer it to his canvas.

I felt calm before his gaze. I even moved my head so he could see my face from different angles.

"I wish you'd let your hair down," he said without taking his eyes off me.

I smiled, then raised my hand to my head and pulled out the pins holding my hair so the two braids fell across my chest.

I didn't say a word, but I felt the blood rush to my cheeks, turning them red—as if I was going to extremes to please him, as if I was a slave girl showing her beauty to the sultan.

His eyes widened.

"My God!" he sighed.

He reached out and stroked my braids, exactly like my father did. I lowered my head, not saying a word.

"Do you see your cheek bones?" I heard him say. "It's what all the great artists spend their lives looking for and trying to paint."

This was a new kind of praise that I hadn't heard before. Maybe I didn't understand him, but I understood that he was praising my beauty.

"Merci," I said shyly.

"Tell me about yourself," he said, moving his eyes away from me.

I turned to him as if it were my turn to sate myself with his face. I thought he seemed young for his age. I thought we were about the same age.

"You tell me about yourself," I said. "All I know about you are things to be afraid of."

He laughed the laugh I loved.

"Look, my dear," he said, "I . . ."

He didn't finish, as a group of construction workers had come up to the car. They lingered and started tossing obnoxious comments at us, mixing them with laughs and whistles.

"Do you like that?" he asked with a mocking smile.

"What do these boors have to do with us?" I said.

"It's not their fault," he said, as if giving me a lesson. "If people walk by someone beautiful, it's their right to stand and look at her. If people see a man and a woman sitting in a car parked on the street, it's their right to stand and look at what they're doing. The street isn't yours or mine. It belongs to everyone. Everyone has the right to watch what happens here."

"Yes," I said as if convinced, though I wasn't at all.

"If we don't want someone to look at us," Mustafa continued, "we shouldn't be parked in the street."

I didn't respond.

He didn't continue. Instead, he turned on the ignition and drove away.

"Where do you want to go?" he asked as we got back on Haram Street.

"I think I have to go home. I'm very late," I lied.

And he believed me.

He drove toward my house slowly, exactly like my father. He was talking so slowly that I felt as if my heart were yearning after every word for another. We didn't talk about any one thing. As soon as we started talking about something, we found ourselves talking about something else. As if we wanted to jam the conversation of a whole life into a single hour.

He stopped on a side street in Dokki near my house.

"If I call you, will you pick up?" I asked, reaching out to him. "Or will it still be the butler?"

He took my hand gently. "Give it a try," he said, looking at me like he had the first time, with the look of an artist examining an amazing painting. He turned my hand in his, leaned over, and kissed my palm.

I felt his kiss flow through my veins, reaching every part of my body.

It was the first time a stranger's mouth had touched any part of me.

I pulled my hand from his as if I were pulling it out of a hot oven. I opened the car door and got out, forgetting to say goodbye. I walked to my house nervously, not daring to turn back. I thought his eyes were following me like the headlamps of a car shining a bright light on my back.

I walked a bit slower when I turned onto the side street leading to my house. A delicious, beautiful feeling started filling my chest. I felt like I was a different person, like I'd grown taller, like I'd become an experienced woman. I now had my own secret, like all the other women with secrets.

I met my father's wife in the parlor. I looked at her as if I were looking down on her. I felt we'd become equals. She had a man, and now so did I.

"How are you?" I asked, giving her a confident smile as if I'd lifted the formality between us.

"Bonsoir," she said, noticing the change that happened to me. "Why are you so happy? Is everything okay?"

"Everything's good," I said with a wide smile.

I didn't say anything else. I headed toward my room and stopped to open the door to my father's room.

"Bonsoir, Daddy!" I said happily, trilling in joy.

My father looked at me. He responded to my greeting with his eyes, a smile on his lips. He then went back to reading his book. The smile dropped from my lips at the thought of breaking the news to him that I now had another man.

That evening, I talked to Mustafa on the phone.

I talked with him the next morning, then every morning and every evening. There was nothing in my head, heart, or world except him. My father and his wife didn't interest me anymore. I didn't care anymore what he said or what she said, or where they went or when they came back. I was living each day to talk with Mustafa.

I knew exactly when he'd be home. He always answered the phone himself. Whenever we began talking about something, we always found ourselves talking about something else, but we didn't talk for long. We didn't talk for hours. Our conversations didn't last for more than ten minutes. Then I'd feel that I had to hurry to end it. I lived for those ten minutes in the morning and ten minutes in the evening.

Three days passed without him asking to meet me. I started craving him. My craving began to cross through clouds of doubt. Maybe he didn't like me. Maybe he thought I was too young. Maybe there was another girl.

"You know, Mustafa," I said on the fourth day, "Daddy and his wife went out alone yesterday. I could have seen you. I called but I didn't get you."

I was lying. I could have concocted a way to meet him, whether my father and his wife went out or not.

"When are they going out again?" he asked in his lazy voice.

"Tomorrow afternoon," I said impatiently.

"Okay, let's meet tomorrow," he said, much more patiently than I.

"Where?"

"I'll give you the address."

"Address of what?" I asked, alarmed.

"Of the apartment."

"No, Mustafa," I said as if chasing away a ghost. "Impossible. Never."

"Why?" he asked calmly. "If you want to meet me outside, we could only meet at a café, because a café is the only place where people can sit together outside."

"No. Impossible. We can meet at the aquarium garden."

"I'm too old for that, Nadia."

I was silent. He was reminding me that I was young. "If you like fish," he said, laughing, "I can buy a couple of pounds and bring them to the apartment for you."

I didn't laugh. "But Mustafa," I said finally, as if throwing myself into the sea.

"But what?"

"Promise you won't do anything that upsets me," I said, almost hearing the pounding of my heart.

"I promise."

The address he gave me wasn't where he lived.

6

I COULDN'T SLEEP, WAITING FOR the next day.

There was another person in my chest talking with me, never silent, never having mercy on me.

A deviant, insane person, who terrified me then enticed me, who sometimes made me a coward and sometimes made me reckless, who screamed in my ears, "How could you go to him, crazy girl?" Then this crazy person would shrug indifferently, give me a sarcastic smile, and say calmly, "Look around you. Don't you loathe this room and its sterile furniture? Don't you loathe this whole house? Don't you loathe your father's wife? Your father? Yourself? What would happen if you didn't go to him? You'll end another day in this room, in this house. Nothing in your whole life will ever change. You'll just keep hating your father's wife. The evil plans will just keep collecting in your head. Go. Go to him—break out of the horrible chains that have shackled your life."

I was almost convinced. I almost fell asleep, making up my mind to go, but the voice coming out of my chest, driving sleep away from my eyes, was now saying, "You believed it, crazy girl? You're going to go to see him? Didn't you ask yourself what he could do to you? You'll be alone in a room with him. In an apartment with only the two of you. Anything could happen. He could ruin your entire future and your whole life. Don't think that you're stronger than him. Don't trust your will. Don't be fooled. He's a man—a very strong man."

I opened my eyes as wide as possible and pressed my lips together firmly, deciding not to go.

But before long, the voice came back, calm and melodious, as if it were a bewitching flute.

"Yes, he's a man, a strong man, but he's *your* man. He's become your man as your stepmother has a man. He's become the secret you're graced with, as every girl has a secret she's been graced with. How can you sacrifice your man and your secret? Why are you afraid of him, and why don't you trust him? Go to him!"

This back and forth inside me continued until morning.

I got out of bed the next day as if I were a ghost. My eyes were heavy, my thoughts distracted. I walked slowly, as if I were afraid that if I moved I'd have a heart attack.

Our appointment was at five o'clock. But I found myself at eleven in the morning leaving home without telling anyone why I was going out. I took a taxi and went to the address he'd given me.

It was a big building on Qasr al-Nil Street. I walked in front of it and gave the door covert looks as if everyone on the street were watching me, as if they all knew I'd be coming back here at five o'clock to meet Mustafa in his apartment.

I passed by the building and walked to the end of Qasr al-Nil Street. I then returned on the same sidewalk and passed in front of the building's door again like a criminal carrying out surveillance on the location where she'll commit her crime.

This time, I read some of the signs hanging on the door: Doctor, Seamstress, Lawyer, Company.

I told myself that if someone saw me leaving or going into the building, I could say I was at the seamstress's. I memorized the name of the seamstress as if, with that, I'd solved a big problem.

I then went and bought some red lipstick, a little darker than the natural color of my lips. I bought pantyhose with a dark heel that I hadn't used before because I was too young for them. I also bought an ornate hairclip.

I did all that even though I was still not sure if I'd go to see him.

I was still hesitating.

The discussion between me and myself was still ongoing. I was carrying on this discussion in my head and my chest, pushed forward by an unknown force.

I lost my will.

I became another person, not the strong girl who keeps control of herself and all of her actions.

I went back home.

I couldn't eat a thing at lunch. Every part of me was trembling so much that I felt I had colic, as if I couldn't handle a bite of food in my throat.

I couldn't even drink the glass of tea I usually had after lunch.

I was aching as if there were a vortex in my head, as if there were a feverish tremor in my body.

I stood before the mirror. I didn't know how to tie my hair, put on lipstick, or pick out my clothes.

I was still pushed forward by an unknown force. The discussion was still going on inside me, but it had become distant, as if between two strangers who didn't know each other and whose voices I couldn't make out.

At five o'clock, I stood in front of the door of the building on Qasr al-Nil Street. I hesitated, and then took a long, deep breath.

I went in.

I stood inside the elevator, my sides cold and moist. My eyes alert, I looked at the mirror in the elevator. The sallow color of my face terrified me. I gave my cheeks some quick hard pinches with my trembling fingers to bring the color back.

The elevator stopped on the sixth floor.

I looked around for apartment number twenty-eight. The apartment numbers were all blurry, so I thought at first that they were all twenty-eight.

I reached out to ring the bell.

I pulled my hand back as if I'd decided to go back, but I couldn't. I couldn't go back.

I reached out again and pressed the bell. I thought I heard it ring inside the apartment like a trill of joy that angels let out in the glee of paradise.

I was terrified . . . terrified of paradise.

The door opened slowly and without a sound, as if opened by a magical force.

I saw him in front of me—Mustafa!

He was wearing a full suit and he had a calm, relaxed smile on his lips, like a doctor receiving one of his patients.

He didn't speak.

He didn't say bonsoir or hello or anything. He made way before me silently as the color of his eyes wrapped me in gentleness and tenderness. He closed the door gently behind me, without a sound. Taking my hand, he turned it over and kissed my palm.

I gave him a hesitant, trembling smile, my heart in my feet. I was still afraid. I lifted my eyes and began looking around the apartment as if expecting to find a devil or a dagger or a bottle of poison behind every chair.

He followed my gaze.

"Would you like a tour?" he asked in his lazy voice.

I didn't respond. I walked behind him through the apartment.

It had two rooms. One had a wide couch with a small table in front of it and a big fauteuil with open arms, practically imploring you to sit down. There was a desk that ran the length of the wall, half of it for books and the other half for records. Then a radio and a record player of dark almond wood. The couch and the fauteuil were covered with fabric that had wide stripes of dark green and red, with a thin yellow line between them. There were curtains, also dark green, hanging on the door of the balcony overlooking Qasr al-Nil Street. Under them was another curtain of light cotton in ochre or beige. There was nothing on the wall but an oil painting of a peasant by Inji Aflatoun, and on top of the radio was a strange sculpture by Gamal al-Sagini.

There was no door between this room and the other. Only an arched room divider with a red curtain. It was a room with a bar with black marbelite sides and bar stools covered in red leather. There were three small fauteuil chairs, also covered in red leather, a glass table with wonderful oil paintings on it, and a lot of funny caricatures hanging on the walls.

Then there was the bathroom, which was green.

There was a small stylish kitchen with a fridge and a stove.

There was no bedroom in the apartment. I don't know why I felt better when I didn't see a bedroom.

"You have great taste," I said, pulling my voice from the bottom of my throat as if my vocal cords had grown rusty from not speaking.

"You'll know soon enough that my taste is something else entirely, not that of this apartment," he said with the calm smile still on his lips.

We were standing at the entrance of the office, as I called it, and he gestured toward the room.

"Do you want to sit here?"

I sat down on the edge of the big chair as if I were sitting on my nerves. All my senses were focused on any movement by him. I thought he might pounce on me and kiss me by force or pull me to him roughly and take me in his arms. I gathered the sides of my dress around me, afraid he'd pull it off me.

But he didn't do anything of the sort. He turned around, picked up a pretty box of candies, and offered it to me.

I reached out to take a candy. Then I pulled back, afraid . . . afraid that there was a drug in it. Who knew!

That was how afraid I was of him.

That was how much I lost my confidence.

He didn't insist. He took a piece for himself and then put the box back. He sat on the wide couch and opened a big book that was on it—a volume of works by the painter Toulouse-Lautrec.

"I was looking for a picture that resembles you exactly," he said flipping through it. "I can't remember who made it or where I saw it."

"Do you know how to paint?" I asked, still clinging to my chair, waves of fear crashing in my chest.

"My dear," he said looking up from the book, his smile wider, "I love art, but I don't know how to paint. I love music, but I don't know how to play. I love flowers, but I don't know how to plant them. I love stories, but I don't know how to write. I love beauty, but unfortunately I don't know how to create it."

He was quiet for a bit as he lit his cigarette.

"Sometimes I feel that I could make sculptures," he said as if talking to himself. "My fingers move in the air as if there was clay in front of me and I can see myself making a statue. Then I go buy clay and try to make something from it, but I can't. Sometimes I think I can play the violin. My head fills with songs and tunes. Then I go buy a violin and try to play it, but I can't. I go crazy, and then I break it."

He was quiet as if he were in pain, grieving for himself.

"I call myself a critic," he said in a low voice. "I understand the arts, but I'm not an artist, not a creator."

I felt for him. I felt that he was complaining about something in himself that I didn't understand. He wasn't complaining to me per se, rather he was complaining to himself, complaining about fate.

I liked it. I liked that this was Mustafa. I'd thought he was too strong to complain about anything, too strong to feel deprived of something. I'd thought he was like my father. But now I saw him as more sensitive than my father; he was living in a world that wasn't the same as my father's, a world that he couldn't make out because it was muddled like the waves of the ocean, with no fixed beginning or end.

I began to feel better about him.

I began to regain my calmness and self-confidence.

"Well, as far as I can see, you have great taste," I said, consoling him.

"Let's talk about something else. Do you want to listen to some records?"

Without waiting for my answer, he got up, opened the turntable, and put some music on.

"How many girls have come into this apartment before me?" I asked as he had his back to me—a question that had been pestering me before I came here.

"A lot," he said simply, without turning to me.

I was furious. I was expecting him to lie as a way of flattering me, and expecting that I'd talk with him about his lie. I was expecting him to try to convince me that I was the first to enter his nest, or at any rate that I'd be the last. But he didn't lie and he didn't flatter me. As I came to know later, he was simply honest. He confessed truths, no matter how awful they were, and then justified them with a smooth, convincing logic.

"I'm just another in this 'a lot' of yours?"

He turned to me, still holding the records. "Ask me in two weeks. Then I'll know the difference between you and the others. Regardless, there's already an obvious difference."

"What?"

"You're the youngest," he said as the record started spinning, releasing its music.

"I'm not young!" I said, insulted.

"You're all of sixteen!"

"Eighteen, please!"

"You're still the youngest."

"I never liked young men."

"You like very old men?" he asked, smiling.

"You're the first," I said, looking at him quickly and then lowering my eyes again. "The first one I've known."

He bowed his head as if thinking about a big problem, as if someone had just hung a big responsibility on him.

"I'm afraid of you, Nadia," he said, tapping the table in front of him nervously.

"Of what?" I whispered.

"Of myself," he said sadly, matching the somber music coming from the turntable. "You don't know who I am or what I could do to your life."

"It's enough that you're afraid of me." I said, hesitating.

"And you? You're not afraid of me?"

"Not now," I said as the record ended and another one by Abdel-Wahab came down in its place on the turntable. "When I first came in, I was so terrified that I didn't want to take any of the chocolates you offered me. I was afraid you put something in them."

He let out a sweet, broken laugh. "You mean that I'd drugged them?"

"Yes," I said, smiling.

"And after I drug you," he said, still laughing, "I'd assail the dearest thing that you have, just like in cheap pocket novels and in the movies!" His smile tightened. "It's not only chocolate laced with hashish or opium that drugs girls," he said seriously. "Sometimes the girl is the one who poisons her own mind. She keeps convincing herself of something until she's drugged, and afterward she wakes up with regret."

"The day I start convincing myself, you'll catch me before I drug myself," I said, blocking all the paths where he could drive me away. "I trust you, Mustafa."

I looked him right in the eye.

Despite that, I didn't trust him, not that day or for many days. I was trying to get to know him, and when I did, my confusion about him only increased, as if I were in an ocean, and as I got deeper I became more and more afraid of drowning.

Everything about him seemed contradictory. His narrow eyes revealing a sharp, dangerous intelligence, his lips bearing goodness and simplicity. His light-brown skin and strong jawline suggesting harshness and violence. His long, thin fingers that were refined and weak. He was rich, but all his friends were poor young men. His opinions were so extreme that they were practically communist. He had a degree from Cambridge University, but he didn't have a job and wasn't looking for work. He began his nights out at the Semiramis and ended them at Fishawi's. He'd read a book about philosophy and then put it aside to grab the humor magazine *Ba'kuka*, chuckling at the jokes. Even the bunch of records that he put on the turntable clashed with each other. There was Beethoven, then "Oh, Mason!" by Shafiq Galal, Umm Kulthoum, followed by some harsh, rapid jazz.

How could you control this kind of person?

How could you trust him?

Despite that, he left me alone that first day, but his personality occupied my entire being.

I went back home without him touching me.

I went back home with the secret that I bore in my chest having grown so big that it almost lifted me off the ground and flew me away—the secret that I had been to a man, the secret of first love.

I felt this secret was bigger than me, stronger than my chest. I felt that I needed someone else to bear it with me, a person I could talk to about everything, with whom I could share my happiness and fear, my confusion and all my thoughts. A person I could beam in front of, show my pride that I'd grown up, that I now had a man, an adventure, a secret!

At that moment, I looked at Auntie Safi and wished she was my friend so I could tell her everything, but she was looking at me silently and coldly, as if searching for my secret on my face.

I was late. I got back at eight o'clock. I should have apologized, but I didn't have to since my father hadn't come back yet. Auntie Safi didn't ask me anything, but gave me silent, serious looks. Maybe she was waiting for me to talk, to say something. But when I didn't, she didn't say anything. That's what I came to expect from her—not asking me about anything or holding me accountable for anything or giving herself any rights over me.

I don't know why, but that day I felt the distance between us grew even greater, that the thick curtain separating us had become even thicker. I felt that her presence in the house annoyed me, that she was a fetter on my freedom and my actions, like she was a silent supervisor watching me whenever I came and went. I felt that she understood me well, and understood everything without saying a word.

I pretended to ignore her.

It was easy for me to ignore her as I thought about Mustafa. I thought about Mustafa day and night, with my heart, mind, and body: a confused heart hearing the knocks of love on its door, a lost mind that didn't know right from wrong, and a body tense like the strings of a new guitar that hadn't yet softened in the fingers of its owner.

I went to him again in his apartment on Qasr al-Nil Street, once more full of fear. I was thinking that if he'd spared me the first time, he'd seduce me when I went to him the second.

But he was even more reserved than the first time. He didn't try to touch me except for the kiss that he planted on my palm as he welcomed me and when he said goodbye.

After that, I went to him a lot.

I wasn't interested in or excited about anything anymore except going to see him. But he always remained reserved and cold.

I enjoyed listening to him talk about his life, books, opinions, and experiences. I was happy to hear his records, which he didn't stop playing. I liked the paintings he collected and that he would spend hours telling me about, revealing to me the secrets of their beauty. And I was happy talking about myself, about everything in my life: my childhood and youth, my father and his wife, my mother and Uncle Aziz, Nanny Halima, our butler Abdou, our driver Mohamed, and the cook. He was the first to learn any news about the house—what we bought, who visited us. He even knew what was in the fridge and in our kitchen.

He was the only man who could push me to talk about myself so naturally, and talking about myself would calm me and open me up to life. I still hid a lot of things from him, but what I told him, I'd never told another person.

I was happy.

Happy with this wide new world that Mustafa opened up before me. A world I didn't know and hadn't dreamed of.

But I wasn't satisfied. I was waiting for something to happen.

I was waiting for him to kiss me.

Yes, to kiss me!

Why not?

Every love story begins with a kiss. I saw kisses in every picture, every magazine, and every movie. I could almost hear them from the bedroom next to mine—the bedroom of my father and his wife.

So, where was my kiss?

When would my love story begin?

Maybe he didn't love me. Maybe he considered me like his daughter, as he once described my friend Nagla.

Or maybe there was another woman. A man like him couldn't live without a woman.

These thoughts tortured me and I started not sleeping.

As soon as I left his apartment, I began imagining that there was another woman going in after me. As soon as I got into bed, I imagined another woman getting into his.

I almost went crazy. Whenever I had the chance, I'd leave my house and go by his building, looking for his car parked out front to make sure he wasn't in his apartment with another woman. Whenever I went with my father and his wife to the movies, I'd find a way to make them go by Qasr al-Nil Street so I could look with crazed eyes for his car parked out front.

But it didn't prove anything.

I wasn't certain he was with another woman and I wasn't certain he wasn't.

I asked him, "Who are you with besides me, Mustafa?"

He looked at me as if he understood what I meant.

"These days, nobody," he said simply and honestly.

"Impossible," I said, agitated. "A man like you, a bachelor, all alone without anyone?"

"A man my age can spend his whole life without anyone," he said, smiling.

"Why? You're thirty-six. Daddy got married when he was thirty-nine."

"He had to find someone worth marrying."

"And you? You still haven't found anyone?"

He looked at me. "Not yet," he said, then averted his eyes as if chasing an idea from his head.

I felt a lump in my throat. I felt a cold breeze that Mustafa unleashed on my heart. I decided to stay silent.

We had this kind of conversation several times. Each time, it ended without him soothing the doubt, but rather torturing me: the suspicion that he had a relationship with another woman, an older woman who might be cheating on her husband or a divorcée, not a girl like me who wasn't yet seventeen.

I started prodding him.

I started prodding him toward me.

I clung to him whenever we sat to read a book. I put my hand in his and kept his hand in mine. I let my hair down so it fluttered on his face.

No doubt he felt all this provocation, and had to exert all his will to resist it. He'd find any excuse to jump up from next to me or pull his hand away from mine or move his face away from my hair.

I felt his resistance.

Whenever he resisted, I provoked him even more.

I'd get ready for this provocation before I went to him like I was setting out on a hunting trip. I put on the perfume that he loved and I wore clothes that showed off my charms—as much as I understood charms at that age.

I'd stand naked in front of my mirror. Looking at my body, bit by bit, as if picking out parts that Mustafa liked, as if looking at myself with his eyes, at my thighs, torso, waist, breasts, shoulders, and back, which a light shadow cut through, reaching from the top of my shoulders to my lower back. I knew all the secrets of my beauty. I counted the beauty marks that adorned my white skin: one on the top of my thigh and another on my side.

I was anxious whenever my eyes stopped on my chest. My chest was a little small for my height. I knew this, but I didn't care at all, until I imagined getting myself ready for Mustafa. Until I started standing naked in front of the mirror, imagining Mustafa standing next to me.

I started flipping through fashion magazines, looking for a bra that would fit my chest and make it look more pronounced under my clothes. I bought dozens of bras of all brands, all the American and Parisian designs. I hadn't thought that this minor flaw on my body could wear me out so much. My feelings got so intense that they gave me a complex that pushed me to examine the chests of all the women I met, comparing theirs to mine, and it pushed me to feel that the only reason anything happened to me was because of the small size of my chest. It got to the point that when I went to Mustafa, I started looking closely at his eyes, afraid that they'd fall on my chest.

But Mustafa never looked at my chest or my body. As usual, he only looked at my face, as he had since we first met.

Until one day . . .

Mustafa was standing next to the turntable putting on some records, murmuring the words to one of the songs.

I came and stood next to him, putting my hand on his shoulder. He'd taken off his jacket. I leaned over the turntable pretending to read the names of the records, and then I turned to him so that my lips were almost touching his.

"I like this record a lot!" I said, giving him a flirtatious look.

He didn't respond. Instead, he looked at me for a while. I saw something new and alluring in his eyes, as if he'd finally decided something that he'd been thinking about for a long time.

I felt him breathe faster than usual. I noticed a slight blush on his brown face.

"That's it," he said in a voice I hadn't heard before, as if talking from deep within. "Have you released me from my promise?"

"What promise?" I asked, my lips still near his, my voice almost a whisper.

"You don't remember that I promised you the first time that—"

"No," I said, cutting him off. "I don't remember."

He broke into a smile that disappeared quickly. I then felt his face come close to mine, his cheek rest on mine. His lips moved forward and touched mine.

Finally he kissed me!

I felt nothing but delight at this first kiss, the kiss I'd been waiting for all those weeks.

He put down the records in his hand and pulled me to his chest. He lifted up his hand and plunged his fingers into the folds of my hair while his other arm still held me tightly. I wished it were tighter. Leaning over, he kissed my neck dozens of times.

He raised his head and looked at me as I was still in his arms.

"I've resisted so much, Nadia!" he said in a trembling, breathless voice. "I . . ."

He didn't finish. He looked at his shirt and saw traces of my lipstick on it. With a big smile, he unbuttoned his shirt, pulled it out from under his pants, took it off, and tossed it on the floor.

I saw his bare chest.

I'd looked at men's bare chests many times at the beach. I'd even seen Mustafa's bare chest at the beach. But I never thought that a bare chest could arouse in me all the emotions that it did that day. I felt as if a burning heat were coming out of his chest. I felt as if a great strength were emanating from this bare chest, pulling me to it.

I was confused, as if I'd become weak, as if everything abandoned me, as if I were no longer able to stand on my feet, as if a fire had broken out in my veins, smoldered inside me, and then melted me.

I couldn't look at him or his bare chest anymore.

"I'm sorry," he said in a rough, broken voice.

I didn't respond.

He was quiet for a while. I felt his eyes looking over my face.

He then reached out, pulled me to him, and pressed my head to his chest. My lips pressed onto his skin, onto a part of his flesh.

7

Did I make a mistake?

When I was with him, I didn't feel the meaning of sin or the taste of it.

Everything happening between me and Mustafa flowed easily and simply, like the flow of life itself. I never felt that I was committing a crime. I never had one of those enormous terrifying feelings that happen in stories. I never felt afraid of him and I didn't sense the future. All I felt was that I was living, that I was living the happiest moments of my life.

A lot happened between Mustafa and me. The age difference between us disappeared, as if each of us were born the same day. The day he kissed me for the first time I became his and, with the passing of time, he became mine.

I gave him everything he wanted and I took everything he gave me. I didn't feel that I was losing something, or that he taking anything by force. Nature itself—the nature of being—was what was taking from me and giving to him and taking from him and giving to me: a systematic, predestined nature, every impulse of it with a time and motive. His kiss always came at the right time and his touch always in the right place.

There was nothing artificial between us. I never felt that he was preparing anything in advance. I never went to him knowing what would happen. Never. All I knew was that I'd meet him and enter his world, and then we would let nature dominate us. The wind might blow. It might rain. Night might follow us or daytime might stay with us for a long time.

For the most part, we met only on words that we exchanged.

He'd always find something to tell me.

I always loved what he said, and was convinced by it. All his ideas were new to me. I hadn't heard them before; I hadn't heard anything like them in my life. He was destroying all the traditions that I lived by. They fell around me silently, as if they'd never existed. Then he built a new world in my mind, a world with a shiny golden dome that was so dazzling you no longer saw anything to be afraid of.

The world with the golden dome that Mustafa was building with his opinions was a world composed entirely of love. Its heaven was love, its earth was love. It had no evil, no evildoers, no crime, no criminals. People, as Mustafa saw them, were all the same—simply people. The criminal and the virtuous were the same for him, since the virtuous man was pushed to virtue by his circumstances and the criminal was pushed to crime by his circumstances. The day that circumstances were the same for everyone, there wouldn't be virtuous people or criminals, and the meaning of virtue and criminality would change. There would be one concept on which all traditions would be based and which all people would follow, without a single person deviating from it, since the circumstances in which all individuals lived wouldn't push anyone to deviancy. We wouldn't call the man who gave money to another charitable, because giving between people living on an equal footing isn't charity. Similarly, the girl who ran off with a boy wouldn't be considered an eloper. She'd simply be a girl who went with a boy.

This was the world that Mustafa was constructing with his opinions.

I didn't understand Mustafa's opinions completely at the time, but I was convinced by them because he said them and because I was with him.

All I understood was that he always found an excuse for everything, an excuse with which he pardoned every crime.

I told him once the story of a wife I knew. She was cheating on her husband. I told him the story, angry at the wife and her adultery.

"She must not love him," he said simply.

"She cheats on him because she doesn't love him?" I asked, still angry.

"Why is he staying with her if she doesn't love him?"

"And why is she staying with him?"

"She's forced to," he said. "Society around her is forcing her to stay because divorce means scandal. It means ruining homes."

"So why's she lying to him?" I asked. "And making him think that she's faithful?"

"She's protecting herself," he said, as if giving a lecture. "Protecting her status in society. Society is the one that's wrong, not her. Society is the one forcing her to lie, deceive, be hypocritical, and cheat because she prefers to live in society and maintain her respect. Like the farmer who lies, deceives, and steals from the landowner. He's forced to because he doesn't have any other weapon to defend his rights."

"So every woman who doesn't love her husband can cheat on him?" I asked, resisting his argument.

"If she isn't betraying him with someone else she's betraying him with herself by giving him false emotions and a lifeless body. She's thinking about his salary more than him. She's thinking about when he'll die more than how long he'll live. She's thinking about when he'll leave the house more than when he'll come home."

"You're crazy, Mustafa," I said, confused. "Or am I stupid?"

"You're not stupid," he said, smiling. "And I'm not crazy. I just see what you don't. Soon enough, the world will be fixed. Society will advance. You won't find two married people who don't love each other. You won't find a woman cheating on her husband or a man cheating on his wife. People will advance and love will have a higher meaning than it has now."

"And when will that be, God willing?" I asked mockingly.

"In a thousand years," he stated, as if establishing a truth. "After people stop being victims and decide they've had enough and have to fix themselves."

"And what will we do for the next thousand years?"

"We'll continue to be confused. All you can do is have pity on people and forgive them. The woman who cheats on this husband of hers—if you were in her place, you'd cheat on him too. So have mercy on her and pity her and her husband, and the man she's cheating with too. All of them are victims—victims of a poor, confused society."

"You're right," I said, still thinking about it.

That was how we talked all the time. It always ended with me being persuaded of his point of view. Maybe those opinions of his were what was hiding my sin from me and hiding God from me.

But this conviction only lasted while I was with him. As soon as I left him and went back home, my confusion returned.

What confused me most was Mustafa himself. As soon as I was away from him, his image blurred before my eyes and a wave of doubt oppressing my mind overwhelmed me and my heart, wrapping around my nerves. I'd doubt my conviction about his opinions. I'd doubt his faithfulness and his love.

Does he love me?

Does he love me?

Does he love me?

A question that hammered in my chest like the ticks of a large, interminable clock counting the seconds. It only quieted down when I was with him. Immediately, I'd forget the questioning. I'd forget my doubt and confusion. I'd gather my whole being into a single feeling when I was with him.

Then I'd leave to go back to my confusion.

When I was alone, I couldn't trust that he loved me, or loved me like I loved him. His personality was too big in my mind to be satisfied with me. His persistently simple honesty made him seem complicated and mysterious—that he wasn't like everyone else. He wasn't living like them or talking like them, so he had to be smarter or more dangerous than everyone else. His opinions didn't calm me since he was a man who didn't believe that there was something called virtue and sin, things that were forbidden and others that were permitted. He didn't believe in traditions. Instead, he believed that circumstances were what drove people. So how could I trust the circumstances surrounding him and determining his behavior? How could I know that these circumstances wouldn't put another woman in his path?

My confusion would tip into jealousy.

I became jealous of him to the point of torture.

I kept going by his building to check for his car, to make sure that he wasn't at his apartment without me. Then I began suspecting that he was going there without his car, so I started tipping the doorman generously.

"Is Mustafa Bey upstairs?" I'd ask him whenever I came by.

"I swear he hasn't come today, miss," was his usual answer.

"Did he spend last night here?"

"Yesterday? No, miss," the doorman would reply awkwardly.

The doorman knew what I was after, so he appointed himself as a spy on Mustafa. He'd give me all his news, fleecing me for it. I hated myself on those days. I hated myself because I'd brought myself down to the level of revealing my secret to a doorman. But that was more merciful than the jealousy torturing me.

Spying on Mustafa didn't save me from my confusion. It didn't cool down my jealousy. Even Mustafa himself was too honest to hide anything from me.

The doorman told me once that Mustafa spent the night at the apartment with some friends. As soon as I met Mustafa, he started telling me the details of the evening, before I asked him anything or took him to task. As he was talking, I searched in his eyes for anything that would confirm my doubts. I only found the delight of the world, my world, with him.

The only solution was for me to be with him in his world in order to feel calm.

I kept going to him. I met him almost every day, but I always had to leave before six o'clock, before my father got home. Then that was no longer enough for me: I wanted to spend the night with him.

I began putting the plans in place.

I started by showing my mother more attention. I began talking with her on the phone every day. I discovered that talking with her and then recounting the conversation with my father annoyed his wife, which filled me with delight at her suffering, so I started talking more about my mother in front of my father and his wife. I turned my mother into a ghost living with us. I'd tell them where my mother went that day, what she bought, who visited her, and what she told her cook to make. Everything I heard from my mother, I'd tell them, rejoicing in my stepmother's misery.

My father didn't say anything about me getting closer to my mother. Maybe he attributed it to my loneliness at home after I stopped going to school. Maybe he attributed it to me getting older and needing my mother more.

One day, after my closeness with my mother had become well known in the house, I pressed my finger down on the line while I was talking to her on the phone. The conversation was cut off, but I kept talking.

"But do I have to ask Daddy's permission?" I asked as if the call was still going on between us.

I turned to my father.

"Mother's inviting me to the movies tonight. Can I go?"

My father nodded.

"Daddy says yes," I said into the receiver.

I was quiet for a bit.

"No. Don't come by here," I said. "I'll go to your house at eight. We'll have dinner and then go to the movies."

I put the receiver down in the cradle.

After a bit, I called my mother again.

"Something cut us off," I told her innocently.

At eight o'clock, our car took me to the building where my mother lived in Zamalek. I got in the elevator and went up to the top floor. After our car left, I went back down again. I then took a taxi and went to Mustafa's.

I told him everything.

I told him the details of my plan to meet him and stay with him until midnight. He looked at me in surprise. Maybe mingled with his surprise was admiration for my intelligence. Maybe there was some fear too at my audacity. But he didn't criticize me or warn me away from my plan.

He needed to be with me too. He was happy I would stay with him until midnight, but gave a slightly confused smile. Perhaps he blamed the circumstances that forced me to deceive, lie, and play the hypocrite to meet him, and blamed those same circumstances that allowed him to support me in my deception, lying, and hypocrisy. He then turned his back to me and put a record on, opening the door to our world with songs.

At midnight, Mustafa took me home like I was Cinderella. I was afraid I'd be late and the fairy godmother's spell would be broken!

I continued to go to Mustafa and stay with him until midnight. Each time, I'd find a new plan—a tightly plotted plan that was never exposed and didn't stir up anyone's suspicions. It only stirred up my stepmother's silent, frozen looks, as if she could read my secret on my face.

Despite that, I wasn't happy.

As soon as I got home, I felt anxiety in my heart. I felt ashamed at myself—a sharp shame, like a knife cutting into my chest.

I could hear the voice between my ribs screaming.

"Why?" it would ask.

Why was I doing all that?

Why was my love driving me forward like this?

Why couldn't I control myself?

These questions swarmed around me in a huge empty ring, as if they were coming from a distant world, a world in which everything was old, everything was emptiness, and its residents had huge turbans, long beards, gaunt faces, and wide eyes—very wide. I felt as if those turbans were falling hard on my chest, almost smashing my ribs. I felt as if those beards were wrapping around my neck until they almost choked me, and those eyes were devouring me until I almost disappeared into them. I was surrounded by terrifying darkness.

It was as if I'd been sucked into a nightmare, so I hid my head in my pillow and whispered in a muffled scream, "Mustafa! Mustafa!"—as if I were calling out to him for help, calling out to my love for help.

In these fits, I pitied my father. I pitied him as I betrayed his faith in me. I pitied him as I tore up the pure, innocent image he had of me. I pitied him as I destroyed the future that he was hoping for for me.

I tried to deceive my conscience, tried to reason with it. I'd tell it, "My father is regressive. He doesn't live in the same world we live in. He doesn't understand the mentality with which we think. He can't appreciate the needs that modern society pushes us to." I kept trying to convince myself, thinking about the stories of the girls I knew and whom I heard about. They were all like me. Every one of them had a man she went to and gave herself to. All of them were like me. If

I kept going, it was only because the circumstances in my life allowed me to.

But my conscience refused to be convinced.

It was torturing me.

I felt as if a hand were coming out of my chest, grabbing me by the neck, and trying to choke me.

When this torment got severe, I'd swear to God that I'd resist, that I'd impose my will on myself and cut Mustafa off.

But that was impossible.

It was too late.

I'd become addicted to Mustafa. I'd become addicted to his delicacy, simplicity, and honesty. I'd become addicted to meeting him, to the apartment where I met him, to the world with the golden dome that he was building in my mind. I'd become addicted to his kisses and touches, to my confusion about him and my jealousy for him.

I was like an addict.

The farther an addict goes, the worse it gets.

When they think about their crises, they are consumed by them.

When they resist their addictions, they're driven closer to them.

Mustafa was the drug that made me forget my conscience and my sins, everything that happened to me in my life.

It was no longer enough for me to take the drug. It was no longer enough to meet him every day or stay with him until midnight.

I had to increase the dose.

I had to spend a whole night with him. I was tired of playing the role of Cinderella, going back to her miserable life when the clock struck midnight.

I wanted to be more than Cinderella.

Like someone crazy, like an addict, I began to set my plan in motion.

It was simpler than I'd imagined. I put it off for a few days, and then I convinced my father that my mother was having a party for her son's birthday and I'd promised to spend the night at her house.

My father objected a little, but then gave in.

I was confident that he wouldn't ask my mother about the party or check on me when I was supposed to be at her house, as my father and mother hadn't talked since signing their divorce papers.

Despite that, I was careful. I wanted to check every box, so I called Mustafa before leaving.

"Listen," I whispered to him. "I'm going to block my phone line. Call me back now."

I put the receiver down.

Mustafa called me right back.

"I'm going to hang up again now," I said, still whispering. "But you don't. Leave your receiver off the hook. Put it on the side of the phone and get there before me."

"Where?"

"The apartment."

"Now?" he asked, surprised.

"Right now!"

I hung up.

And Mustafa didn't.

That way I was sure that my father wouldn't call my mother to check on me. And I knew that if someone called him, they wouldn't be able to get through.

Then I went to him.

It was different this time. I spent my whole day thinking about this night that I'd spend with him. I was like a bride getting ready for her wedding night.

I got myself ready like a bride.

I prepared all the details like a bride.

As I was getting ready, all of me was trembling—the tremble of adventure, a delicious tremble mixed with fear, hesitation, and breathlessness. The pleasure of the gambler as he plays with everything he's got, looking at the wheel of luck as it spins before his eyes, waiting to win or lose. Or the pleasure of the addict as he reaches out to take the drug, waiting to be intoxicated or die.

I got a white dress ready, like a wedding dress. It was so tight on my body that it almost stuck to me. It was open at my chest, revealing my shoulders and the tops of my breasts. I took long gloves that went to the tops of my arms, covering my elbows.

I couldn't go out in front of my father and his wife in this dress, since it was too much for a young boy's birthday party. I wanted to dispel any suspicions, to eliminate even simple questions. So I put on this white dress, and then put a long wide skirt and a loose blouse over it. I took a big purse with me, and put in it a white silk nightie, my long gloves, and my diamond ring. I then passed in front of my father and his wife on my way out.

They had no suspicions or doubts.

I was sure of that.

Nonetheless, as I stood in front of my father, I felt my face turn red and the ground shook beneath me. I felt the voice between my ribs almost rise up in my chest again, but I quelled it. I did everything I could to suppress it. I said to myself, "My father is happy with his wife. He wouldn't deny me happiness with my love."

I leaned over and gave him a quick, cold kiss. But as soon as I lifted my lips from his cheek, I kissed it again. The second time was hot, as if I were crying with my lips on his cheek. I rushed to leave, saying goodbye to my father's wife in a loud voice, louder than necessary, I almost shouted: "Bonsoir, Auntie!"

I reached the building where Mustafa was waiting for me, the feeling of adventure overwhelming me with an inexplicable fervor.

I took the elevator, but stopped it between two floors. I took off the skirt and blouse and put them in the bag. I took out the gloves and put them on my arms. I put my big diamond ring on my finger, on top of the gloves. I then turned to the mirror to tidy myself up. I took out my eyebrow pencil and shaded over my eyebrows. I took out my eyeliner and penciled it around my eyes. I then took out my lipstick and pressed it over my lips.

I started the elevator again.

And the door of paradise opened.

Mustafa stood staring at me with his mouth open. I'd never seen him looking at me like that.

"What's all this?" he asked, his voice rattling with surprise.

I gave him a conceited smile. I knew at that moment that I was more beautiful than ever before. I was truly a bride. I only lacked a veil.

I went in without saying a word.

Mustafa looked at the big bag in my hand. He was so surprised that he looked like an imbecile.

"What's going on?"

"Nothing," I said, trying to appear natural. "I'm going to sleep here tonight."

Mustafa's smile disappeared. He gave me a serious look with confusion in his eyes, as if he'd encountered something dangerous.

He didn't say a word.

"Am I mistaken, Mustafa?" I asked.

He stayed silent as if he was still thinking. Then the look in his eyes softened. A sweet smile returned to his lips. He reached out and pulled me to him tenderly.

"Of course not, Nadia," he whispered in my ear. "It's the world that's mistaken about you and me."

He moved me away from his chest and pulled me to the bar. We sat on the stools.

"Tell me," he said laughing, filling a glass of whiskey for me and another for himself. "What exactly happened?"

I started telling him everything that had happened that day. I thought I saw bitterness in his smile. But he laughed. He laughed a lot as I told him how I'd put on the skirt and blouse over my white dress and how I'd taken them off in the elevator.

I finished my drink.

It wasn't the first time I'd drunk a glass of whiskey. I'd had a number of glasses before, and I'd drunk it with Mustafa before. Mustafa didn't give me whiskey to get me drunk. He never encouraged me to drink more than I wanted. I'd never gotten drunk in my life. The whiskey didn't affect me but, with this glass, I felt an intoxication I'd never felt before.

Mustafa pulled me by the hand. We went into the other room that I called the office. It was dimly lit with yellow light from the big table lamp in the corner.

Mustafa began putting some records on the turntable. He then turned to me and enveloped me with his eyes—hot, breathless looks.

"You know what I'm in the mood for now?" he asked as the first record started playing. "I want to take you out, walk with you in front of people, and tell them, 'She's mine. All this beauty is mine.' Your eyes are mine. Your lips are mine. Your hair is mine. Every part of you is mine. You know what the sweetest part of you is?"

"What?" I said, proud of myself and my beauty.

"Me. My love," he said as if trying to make me angry.

"Not at all. Everyone says that their most beautiful part is the color of their eyes."

"If you didn't love me," he said, laughing, "the color of your eyes wouldn't be so pretty. They'd be wilted and your cheeks would be asleep on top of your lips. Your lips would be asleep on top of your chin. Say it, Nadia. Say that the sweetest thing in you is my love."

I didn't say a thing.

I threw myself on his chest.

I let him hear my love from the beats of my heart.

I believed him and I believed myself. I believed everything when I was with him.

We danced to the second record. Our steps started getting heavy, until we stopped dancing, my lips on his, his breath burning my face, his arms squeezing me to him, squeezing me hard.

I didn't feel Mustafa's fingers as I was drifting off in his kiss, as they were searching for the zipper of my dress, pulling it to take my dress off.

This wasn't the first time that I'd taken my dress off in front of Mustafa. In the months I'd known him, nature had given him what he wanted from me, and gave me what I wanted from him. But this time I grabbed his fingers as they were taking off my dress.

"No," I said, with a determined smile.

Mustafa looked at me in surprise, as if I'd disturbed his dreams.

"Look away."

Mustafa didn't understand. He kept looking at me in surprise.

"Turn away," I said spinning him around with my hands. "Don't look until I tell you."

Mustafa smiled. He stepped to the other side of the room, next to the lamp, turned away, and waited.

I walked to the opposite corner. Opening my bag, I took out the white silk nightie. Then I took off my dress.

"Don't look!" I told him a few times.

I put on the nightie.

"You can look now," I said in a shy whisper, as if meeting Mustafa for the first time.

He turned to me, staring as if he couldn't believe his eyes.

I looked away from him as if I couldn't face him or the intoxication blazing in my chest.

He reached out and turned off the lamp. There was only a faint, hesitant light sneaking in from the next room.

I felt him next to me.

I felt him pull me to the wide couch. We fell on it as if we were as light as two leaves blown to the ground from a tree.

I felt myself in his arms.

At that moment, I wished there was a bedroom in the apartment where we could consummate the dream of the wedding.

The night ended without either of us sleeping.

I went back home the next morning. I went back a virgin. I don't deserve credit for that. Mustafa insisted on keeping me a virgin, maybe because he wanted to leave something of me that society recognized.

I didn't see my father. He'd left. And I didn't look at my father's wife. I couldn't.

I took off my clothes and lay in bed with my eyes open, looking up at the ceiling as if I were looking for my fate there.

I felt an urge to cry, but I resisted. I didn't know why I wanted to cry. I took the phone and called Mustafa, as if turning to him for help from my tears.

"I miss you!" I said, trying to laugh.

"Me too," he said, yawning.

I hung up.

Then I cried.

8

I DON'T KNOW WHEN MUSTAFA and I started talking about my father's wife.

She would come up all the time, but was never the subject of conversation. As soon as I mentioned her, I drove her off my tongue as if I was blocking her from sharing the pleasure of talking with Mustafa.

Every time I did mention her, I tried to incite Mustafa against her. I tried to make him hate her as much as I did, to envy her as much as I did. I only told him about what I thought were her shortcomings. Even the good things about her I made shortcomings. But Mustafa didn't rise to it. He didn't hate or envy her. Instead, I felt he tried to defend her for no reason other than that he sensed how much I hated her.

"You know that Auntie Safi is very hard on me," I told him once.

"Why?" he asked indifferently.

"Because Daddy doesn't love her," I said as if pitying her.

"What makes you think that?" he asked, still indifferent.

"I know. I'm sure."

"So why did he marry her?"

"For me," I said, pretending to ignore his tone. "He wanted to bring someone into the house to live with me and take care of me."

"He chose this woman just so she could live with you, not because he loves her?"

"Because she's pathetic," I said as if trying to convince him. "Because she's just a housewife. You know housewives who do nothing but go from the bed to the kitchen and from the kitchen to the bed? She's one of them."

"So she must be ugly and fat, and not know how to read or write," he said with a sarcastic smile.

"She's so-so," I said, angry at his smile. "Not very fat and not very ugly, and she doesn't read or write much."

He withdrew his smile and took my hand.

"Regardless, Nadia," he said seriously and respectfully, as if giving me a lesson, "if your father doesn't love her, you have to make him love her—"

"How do I make him love her? Is love by force?"

"If he married her for you, you can make him love her for you too," he said calmly. "What matters is that she's happy, so that your father's happy and you're happy too. You can't be happy in a house with miserable people, a house with no happiness."

He squeezed my hand, looked into my eyes, and smiled tenderly as if I were his daughter.

"I won't believe that you love me until you love other people, including Auntie Safi," he continued. "When you're in love, your heart gets so big that you accommodate and forgive everyone."

I knew this was Mustafa's philosophy on life and love. I knew that whenever I talked with him, I couldn't avoid his philosophy or make him hate anyone, so I changed the subject.

"Not at all," I said quickly. "I love Auntie Safi very much."

I raised my eyes to him. "You still don't believe that I love you, Mustafa?" He pulled his hand away and put it on my cheek as if he were embracing my face with his palm. Raising his hand, he plunged his fingers into my hair. He pulled me to him and pressed his lips against mine.

"I don't believe that you understand the meaning of love," he said as I was still breathless from his kiss.

"Make me understand."

He let out the smile of the strong self-confident man who knows what he wants. He then started pulling out the clasp holding my hair to let it down on my back, as he usually did when he wanted me.

From then on, I didn't talk to him about my father's wife. Evil and hatred were flowing in my depths and I couldn't tear them out. I couldn't hide them—even from myself.

Everything about my father's wife was inviting me to love her and be friends with her, but I couldn't. The best I could do was to ignore her.

I no longer scrutinized my father's desire for her or his pampering her. I no longer kept tabs on Uncle Aziz's interactions with her. I no longer resisted when I saw her stamp on everything in the house or when I saw her as the center of every party.

My love for Mustafa helped me with all of that. I always said to myself, "I now have a man who is a substitute for my father and my uncle. I now have a house taking the place of this one. Mustafa is that man and the apartment where I meet him is that house."

My love for Mustafa was my remedy against my evil and my hatred. Whenever they tried to spark a fire or come to the surface of my mind, I would set myself on stamping his apartment with my own character so that I became more confident that his apartment was my house. I spent every penny I had on buying things and arranging them there.

I bought a lot of little things and put them everywhere. I bought a set of crystal glasses and put them in the bar. I bought dozens of records and books—books that neither Mustafa nor I read; but I was happy when I saw them on the shelves. I learned how to do needlepoint, and I embroidered two small cloths that I put there. I sometimes moved a picture or a chair from one place to another. I did all that feeling that I was the mistress of the house. I wanted to convince myself that this was my house, which no one shared with me, especially not Auntie Safi.

I was missing one thing: for Mustafa to give me a key. I wanted to go to my house without ringing the bell and without anyone opening the door for me. I wanted to be the one waiting for Mustafa, to welcome him home instead of him waiting to welcome me.

But Mustafa didn't give me a key. He didn't even offer. Maybe because he didn't think I wanted one. Or maybe . . .

The thought of the key tortured me. I always thought that he was avoiding giving me one so he could maintain his freedom to invite over any woman he wanted.

Sometimes my jealousy made me imagine the apartment door opening as some other woman walked in, Mustafa greeting her just as he greeted me, taking her by the hand and sitting with her on the big couch.

I'd go crazy from these fantasies, the craziness of a wife when she imagines her husband's lover in her bed. In the middle of these fantasies, I saw myself lifting up my hands like they were holding an axe and smashing the door separating me from them. I'd then tell myself, "If only I had the key!"

Despite that, I didn't dare ask Mustafa for one. Maybe I was ashamed, or maybe it was enough that when I was with him, I forgot all those fantasies and the torment that gripped me when I was alone.

A year passed like that.

A year in which I ignored my father's wife and ignored the house I was living in. I gave everything to Mustafa. I was happy with him. I was tortured by him. I used his love to fight my evil inclinations and my hatred.

Then one day . . .

My father, his wife, and I were invited to a dance party that a friend of my father's was putting on for his wedding anniversary.

I didn't want to go with my father and his wife. That year, I'd gotten used to turning down invitations. I preferred to stay home alone thinking about Mustafa, talking with him on the phone, or sneaking out to meet him at his apartment, coming home before my father got back.

But my father insisted this time. I knew he was insisting because of his wife. She was always opposed to me keeping to myself and staying home alone. She wanted me to appear in social settings to increase the odds of my finding a husband.

I agreed to the invitation that evening, to please my father. I called Mustafa to tell him I was going out, but I didn't reach him.

We left.

That night, my nerves were calm. There was tranquility in my heart. I stood for a long time in front of the mirror. I dressed up as beautifully as I could. I put on a gray evening dress with a wide rose-colored bow, a Dentelle Jibir design that revealed my back and shoulders. Over it, I put a blue fox fur. My father's wife wore a black duchesse-satin evening dress with gold and silver buttons like stars hiding the shyness of the moon under the curtain of night. It was modest, not revealing her back or shoulders. She put a mink stole on top of it.

I was beautiful, with fair skin. She was beautiful, with dark skin. My father walked between us, the world not big enough for all his happiness, as if he were holding the sun in one hand and the moon in the other.

We arrived at the party.

Eyes did double takes around us.

The hostess walked with us, seating my father and his wife at a small table. I stood a few steps from them as a group of young men and women gathered around me. As usual, I was listening more than I talked. Out of the corner of my eye I saw the stares of the young men devouring me, but I ignored them. There were some attempts to flirt with me, but I blocked them coldly. I was, as usual and as is said about me, cold, silent, and beautiful, my face not revealing anything inside me.

There was nothing inside me except for Mustafa. I couldn't forget him in the middle of that crowd and noise. I was looking at every young man and secretly mocking him because he wasn't Mustafa. I was listening to every conversation, but I found it all to be trifling and pleasureless, unlike with Mustafa.

And then, suddenly, I saw him.

Mustafa!

My eyes widened. I caught my breath. My eyelashes trembled as if I were trying to drive away a beautiful specter that my imagination was picturing.

But he wasn't a ghost. It was Mustafa himself. He was wearing a black tuxedo that made him look like a god of the night, charming, mysterious, exciting, attractive. He was moving among the guests with a beautiful smile, as if he were the prophet of love blessing his followers. Eyes wrapped around him as if they were whispering to each other, repeating his opinions about life and love.

I didn't know what to do or how to get control of myself. I thought I was going to rush over to him and throw myself into his arms, yelling, "This is my love!" I'd let him kiss me and pull out the clip holding up my hair so it tumbled down my back.

The hostess walked with him until they stood next to us.

"Of course, you know everyone here," I heard her say.

He raised his eyes and saw me.

I didn't see a trembling in his eyes, or any other sign of surprise. Instead, his eyes fell on my face for a moment with a firm look, as if he didn't know me.

"Not everyone," he said to the hostess.

She turned to my father.

"You don't know Mr. Lutfi?" she said to Mustafa. She began to introduce us to him. "Mr. Ahmed Lutfi and Madame Lutfi." She turned to me and continued, "And this is our sweet bride to be, Mademoiselle Lutfi."

"Of course, you all know Mr. Mustafa, or at least you've heard of him," she said to us.

My father got up to greet Mustafa warmly. All my father had to know was that someone was rich and from an important family in order to greet him warmly.

Mustafa leaned over to kiss my father's wife's hand. I thought I saw him give her a long look as he was kissing her hand, as if he wanted to verify my descriptions of her.

I was standing far enough from him that he couldn't reach out to greet me. He contented himself with nodding to me from afar with a fine smile on his lips that didn't express anything other than a formal greeting.

I didn't know how to return the greeting. Should I nod my head too? Or smile at him? Or stand frozen? I didn't know. But it took all my strength not to keel over.

My father invited me to sit down and the hostess moved away from us.

The only place for Mustafa to sit was next to my father's wife. He sat with his back to me. I couldn't see him. I thought that if I looked at him, everyone would know about us. I stood up, turning my face to my friends around me but setting my ears toward Mustafa.

I wanted to hear every word he was saying.

But I couldn't hear a thing.

The noise of the party blocked me from hearing anything.

I began to get nervous.

Anxiety started flowing under my skin until I felt all of myself shiver, as if a cold breeze had blown past me. I felt as if Mustafa's hand was touching my bare arm, moving over my breasts, pressing down on my back, and creeping over my torso. Those touches that Mustafa had gotten me used to—I felt them as if they were warming me and protecting me from the cold air. I wanted to be next to him so I could touch him, press my shoulder against his, and put my face near his breath.

Anxiety began to overwhelm me and stir up black thoughts in my head.

What was Mustafa saying now?

What was he saying to her?

Suddenly I heard my father's wife let out a happy, joyful laugh, a laugh higher and happier than I was used to hearing from her.

I turned to her as all my nervous energy tugged me toward her. I saw her face absorbed in laughter as if she were drunk. Her eyes were laughing, her cheeks were laughing, and the locks of her black hair swung back and forth in the air as she laughed boisterously.

I was flabbergasted. I turned to my father as if asking him why she was laughing like that. He gave his dignified smile that makes him look older than he is. I turned to Mustafa as if chastising him. He let out a calm laugh—a conceited, self-congratulatory laugh.

Fire blazed in my blood!

I wanted to attack my father's wife, pull her by the hair, throw her to the ground, and then sit in her place and laugh like her.

I left the group around me and went over to them.

Mustafa half rose to greet me. My father made space for me next to him. I sat down and he put his arm around my shoulder and pulled me to him gently, as he usually did when I sat next to him.

"No!" I heard my father's wife say. "You're very bold in your opinions, Mustafa."

"I'm not bold at all," Mustafa replied. "But I'm not convinced by what people do. Everyone is doing it wrong, so when someone is right, they say he's bold. And that's ridiculous."

I looked from one to the other in confusion mixed with a hint of accusation.

I wondered which of Mustafa's opinions he was telling my father's wife about.

What was he trying to convince her of?

I knew all of Mustafa's opinions. I knew they all flowed like a drug in your veins. Was he trying to drug her?

I woke up from my questions to find the conversation flowing between them. They were talking about memories of Europe, food, books, movies, and clothes—about everything. He only became quiet so she could talk and she only became quiet so he could talk. Only the two of them were talking, as if they were tossing flowers to each other.

Nothing could stop this flood of conversation, not even some of the guests coming by the table. My father was sitting and listening, laughing or smiling, making a passing comment here and there.

I tried to open some space for myself between them, to participate in the conversation, to say something.

But I couldn't.

Words abandoned me and topics melted in my head. When I heard them talk about Europe, I'd say to myself, "I'll tell them the story of my friend who went to have a meal at the restaurant at the Tour d'Argent in Paris." I'd start getting the words ready, but as soon as I was about to say them, after hesitating and not managing to butt in, the opportunity passed. They'd already started talking about something else.

That was what happened every time I tried to talk.

Mustafa sometimes tried to include me. "And what do you think, mademoiselle?" he'd ask, turning to me.

I was confused, not finding anything to say, as if I were far from them in another world, or as if my mind had frozen so it could no longer help me. I'd say any passing comment that came to me. After that, Mustafa had no choice but to keep talking with my father's wife.

"Mademoiselle, do you prefer Christian Dior or Carven?" he asked me, as if insisting that I talk. "Which is more stylish?"

I was thrown into confusion again.

"Carven!" God only granted me a single word. Then I went quiet again.

Mustafa looked at me as if he was waiting for me to finish or take the opportunity to open another topic, but I turned my eyes from him and kept quiet.

At that moment, I felt the weakness of my character like never before. I felt that I'd spent my entire life unable to face people except with this beautiful innocent face and this provocative slim body. I'd spent my entire life only talking with myself, only sharing my thoughts with myself. No one shared my conversation or thoughts except for Mustafa when we were alone. Maybe because Mustafa was my psyche, my soul . . . but we weren't alone now. I couldn't face anyone other than him. I couldn't even face him among people except with this innocent, beautiful face, this coldness and silence.

At that moment I hated my beauty. I wished I were less beautiful, but that I had a stronger character so I could attract people to me and drive Mustafa away from my father's wife.

My stepmother's personality swept over me, driving me away from my love, her strong, delightful personality pulsating with life and controlling everything around it.

I felt as if I wanted to cry for myself. My feelings then turned mutinous as I imagined myself scratching my stepmother's face, tearing it with my nails. I imagined myself taking off my clothes, standing naked in the middle of the crowd so they all gathered around me, turning their backs to my stepmother, while I told them my whole story as loudly as I could so they knew I wasn't as innocent as my face suggested, that I was smart enough to hatch plans and carry them out, that I caused a lot of trouble, that I loved Mustafa, going so far with him that I knew all the secrets of men and women—I knew more than any girl my age!

Uncle Aziz's voice woke me up from my insane fantasy.

He arrived late, as he usually did whenever he went to a party.

My uncle leaned over to kiss my head. He leaned over and kissed my stepmother's hand. My father then introduced Mustafa and my uncle to each other.

The three men turned their attention to my father's wife. I was forgotten. The only part that I had of my father was his arm wrapped around me. My uncle only threw me a kind word here and there, the same things he'd say to me when I was four years old. I only got a glance or two from Mustafa, together with a smile, as if he were apologizing for ignoring me.

I escaped sometimes into my imagination, and sometimes I followed their conversation. When I paid attention, I noticed friction between my uncle and Mustafa, a friction between their personalities. Each of them was trying to talk more than the other, each was trying to control the conversation, each putting down the opinions of the other. My stepmother was trying with her personality and social dexterity to bring them together and please both of them.

I ascribed this conflict to the similarity of the two personalities. Each was a bachelor, each had many experiences, each had romantic adventures. Each even had a special philosophy about life.

But was that enough of a reason for this tension?

At that moment, I wanted my uncle to be victorious over Mustafa. I wanted him to be defeated and mine alone rather than see him victorious with another woman.

"Would you care to dance, Madame Safiya?" I heard Mustafa ask my father's wife.

The words "Madame Safiya" rang in my ears. Where had he learned her first name? If he learned it through their conversation, how was he so bold as to break the formality between them so that he called her by her first name? "Madame Safiya" reached her hand out to him and stood up with his help. They headed over to the dance floor.

I watched them, fire shooting from my eyes.

He wrapped his arm around her waist. They danced in slow steps as he pressed her body against his. After a few steps, he pressed his cheek against hers. Their steps became so heavy it was as if they weren't moving. She moved her cheek away from his and laughed as if he'd whispered something in her ear. Then they went back to pressing their cheeks against each other.

It was exactly like the first time I saw him dance with my friend Nagla a year ago.

I became so upset and my chest became so tight I thought that my ribs would break through my skin.

I turned around as if calling to my father for help but my father was calm, sipping from his glass, and looking around at the other guests.

I looked at my uncle. Like me, he was following them with his eyes, pursing his lips in annoyance. He began tapping on the table with his fingers rhythmically as if they were the beats of war drums.

"You're not going to dance with me, Uncle?" I asked him, almost pleading for help. "You've never danced with me!"

As if I'd opened the way for him, he got up immediately and accompanied me or, rather, pulled me to the dance floor. He danced with me until we were next to them.

The four of us exchanged fake smiles.

When my face was opposite Mustafa's, behind the back of my father's wife, he pursed his lips at me like he was blowing me a kiss.

I hated that.

I wanted to slap him in return.

Then, after a number of steps, I saw them walk off the dance floor. They didn't head to our table, where my father was waiting for us. They went out to the balcony.

My uncle saw them too. He yanked me by the hand and we followed them out.

The balcony wasn't empty. There were a number of guests there. Nonetheless, standing there, I wanted to shoot them both—Mustafa and my father's wife.

"Isn't it cold here?" my uncle asked them with repressed anger.

"The smoke inside is suffocating," Auntie Safi responded in a natural tone. "Regardless, it's two in the morning and I think it's time to go."

No one objected.

Mustafa came with us to our table. He shook my father's hand warmly and shook my uncle's hand coldly. He leaned over to kiss my father's wife's hand and then shook my hand, squeezing it as he looked at me, trying to encircle me with his eyes.

I blocked his look with angry eyes, yanked my hand from his, and turned my back to him.

"I hope we'll see each other again," he said as he moved away.

Only my father responded.

"Hopefully very soon."

My uncle put the mink stole on Auntie Safiya's shoulders and my father put the blue fox fur on mine.

We said goodbye to the host and left. "That guy was very conceited," my uncle said in the car.

"All bachelors are conceited like that," my father's wife said.

"So I'm conceited too?" my uncle asked angrily.

"If you don't want people to say you're conceited, get married!" she said, laughing.

"Oh please, Safiya," he continued, still angry. "We know never to take your advice!"

"They say he's a very smart farmer," my father said. "In this past year, the cotton on his land has exploded while the land next to his, which belongs to Mr. Abdel-Latif's family, has only grown a third as much."

I kept quiet, but I was boiling inside.

We got home.

My uncle went upstairs and the three of us went in.

I don't remember if I said goodnight to my father and his wife. I ran to my room and locked the door behind me. I ripped off my clothes without washing my face as I usually do each night.

But I didn't sleep.

Evil began to rise up from my heart, creeping toward my head to spin its threads into a new crime.

9

The crime whose threads were spinning in my head was horrible. I was afraid of it myself.

An oppressive desire had taken hold of me to destroy—to destroy everything, to destroy my father's wife, my father, Mustafa, and myself. I was thinking like a crazy person. I wanted to smash everything around me with my bare hands, for no good reason other than to relieve my feeling of inferiority and ease my anxiety about my weak character, which had been unable to lure Mustafa away from my father's wife during the party.

I tried hard to drive those terrible thoughts from my head.

I tried to prevent the crime before it happened.

I tried to trick myself into believing that there wasn't any reason to feel like this. I was telling myself Mustafa didn't do anything wrong. He didn't ignore me. He had just found a woman who was good at talking, so he talked with her. Maybe he intentionally didn't talk to me so it wouldn't look like there was anything between us. Yes. He purposely ignored me so his eyes didn't expose him, so his heart didn't reveal him. If I was any other girl, he'd have treated me like he treated my father's wife. But I wasn't any other girl. I was the girl he loved, the girl to whom he had dedicated his heart, his life.

I was also trying to justify my father's wife's position. I told myself she was only interested in him as she would be in any new friend. She didn't talk to him more than she usually talked to anyone else. She had a lively nature, a strong personality. If something attracted her to Mustafa, it was only what attracted everyone to him. His bold opinions, his strange philosophy of life. She didn't want anything from him. She wasn't chasing after him. There wasn't a single piece of evidence that could stir up my jealousy or push me to hate her.

I was telling that to myself, and I felt I'd convinced myself to abandon my crime in the making.

But it wasn't long before I pictured the way he'd looked at her, as if she were the only woman at the party. I imagined her looking at him as if she hadn't seen a man before. I then recalled their long conversation, which went on and on as if they were tossing flowers to each other. Fire broke out in my veins—the fire of jealousy and hatred—as I pictured them dancing, his arm wrapped around her back until his palm reached her shoulder, her chest pressed against his, his cheek against hers, his nose plunged into her hair. The way she lifted her cheek from his and laughed as if he'd whispered something in her ear, and then pressed her cheek to his again.

No. That couldn't be just dancing. If that was how Mustafa acted when he danced, how could I let him dance with her that way? No doubt there was something between them or something that could be between them. Maybe they'd agreed that he'd call her or maybe he gave her his phone number or maybe they'd promised each other to meet at his apartment—the same apartment where I met him, to listen to the same records that I listened to and lie down on the same wide couch that I lay down on.

I imagined her naked, lying in his arms as he looked over her, as if he'd come down on her from the sky. Exactly as I had imagined her between my father's arms in the first months after she married him.

I felt I would choke on these images, that my eyes would come loose from their sockets. I heard Satan pour poison into my chest, repeating, "Watch out! Watch out for her! She could take Mustafa from you just as she stole your father! She's a woman who has everything to entice men. A woman! As for you, poor thing, you're just a virgin . . . just a virgin!"

I let out a scream that no one heard but me. I covered my eyes with my hands so I couldn't see what my imagination was showing me, so I couldn't see myself lighting fires everywhere around me as I stood in the middle of them, laughing maniacally. The craving to destroy took possession of me, so I destroyed. I destroyed until I destroyed myself and I made of myself a woman and not a virgin, so my father's wife wasn't better than me in anything.

I lifted my hands from my eyes and started pulling my hair, as if I were trying to tear it out of my head.

Turning over, I started biting the pillow and kicking the bed, as if I were in a terrifying fight with demons.

Finally I cried.

I cried for a long time, in agony.

My tears cleansed my mind of evil, they cleansed my heart of hatred.

I felt better, but I didn't sleep.

I stayed up with my eyes open, as if I'd woken from a nightmare. I was afraid to sleep since the nightmare would come back to me.

I began to think about my whole life slowly.

As dawn broke, I imagined I heard Mustafa say to me, "When you're in love, your heart gets so big that you accommodate and forgive everyone."

I'm in love.

I'm in love with Mustafa.

My heart has to be big enough for me to love so much. So why didn't I try to bring my father's wife into my heart? Why didn't I try to love her? One last time?

I decided to try.

I decided to do everything I could to befriend her, to reveal my secret to her, to open my heart to her and tell her that I was in love, that I loved Mustafa, the man she had danced with last night, that I'd loved him for a year, that I had become his and he had become mine.

I'd tell her everything.

And after that, I'd make sure that she wouldn't take him from me, that she wouldn't take the man a girl the age of her daughter loved.

After that, we'd become friends.

I'd find solace from my sin, my hatred, and my imagination, which concocted my crimes.

The next morning, I left my room at ten o'clock. After I washed my face, I put on my best day clothes. I was tired and worn out from what I'd endured all night. But I was intent on appearing happy. I put a layer of foundation on my face to hide my faded pallor, to hide the dark rings around my eyes.

My father and his wife were sitting at the table, just about finished with breakfast. I kissed my father's head.

"Bonjour, Daddy!" I cried jubilantly, in a tone happier than the house was used to from me.

I went around the table and kissed my father's wife on her cheeks, pressing my cheek against hers.

"Bonjour, Auntie Safi!"

I didn't usually kiss her in the morning. Maybe I exaggerated a little—or a lot—when I pressed my cheek against hers, because she looked at me in surprise.

"Bonjour, my dear," she said with a smile. "You look like you slept well last night."

"Like a log," I said, laughing.

"I'm not afraid of Nadia getting too little sleep," my father said, laughing with me. "When she was young, she slept enough for an entire lifetime. As soon as she got home, she'd close the door of her room and fall right to sleep."

I laughed again. But there was a bitterness in my laugh that I couldn't hide. No one knew what happened to me when I went to my room and locked the door.

"You know, Ahmed," my father's wife said, as if she was finishing a conversation whose beginning I hadn't heard, "the party was too crowded as well. Those people only do one or two parties a year and invite everyone without any thought."

I knew they were talking about last night's party.

"One could still meet nice people," my father said in his sweet, good-natured way. "You know, I liked Mustafa. You think he was snobbish and conceited, but I found him nice. He knew how to talk."

"He didn't *stop* talking!" my father's wife rushed in.

I felt my heart jump in my chest.

"We should invite him over," my father continued.

My heart started pounding. I feared that my face had turned so pale that I didn't have enough foundation on to hide it.

"Not by himself," I heard my father's wife say. "This kind of person is only invited to big parties. Inviting a bachelor is confusing. Do you seat him on the right or left? Do you walk next to him or next to your husband? And—"

"He'll sit next to my brother, Aziz," my father said, laughing and cutting her off.

I felt I had to change the subject before it ended with him setting a day to invite Mustafa to the house.

"You know," I said to my father's wife with a big smile on my lips, "you were the chicest person there last night, Auntie. There wasn't a dress more beautiful than yours. All of the women were eating you up with their eyes."

"Thanks to your father," she said, looking at him. "He's the one who picked out the dress." She turned to me and continued, "You were the most beautiful one at the whole party. If you'd snapped your fingers, all the young men there would have run to propose to you."

"Thanks to Daddy too!" I said, imitating her.

I laughed. My father and his wife laughed. My father didn't have anything to do with choosing his wife's dress any more than mine. But that was how his wife got close to him, always trying to convince him that everything was thanks to him. And that was why I tried to follow her—to get close to him.

My father finished eating breakfast and smoking his cigarette. He got up and came over to kiss me. He then left for the club, as he usually did every morning. His wife got up with him and said goodbye to him at the door, as she usually did.

I finished my breakfast quickly, then got up and went to my room. I picked up my needlepoint and went to the sitting room to wait for my father's wife.

She came back from saying goodbye to my father and walked by, going through the rooms of the house. I heard her give orders to the household staff. She then came and sat next to me.

"It's no use," she said. "These servants—no matter what you teach them, you have to stand there right next to them." She looked at what I was sewing and said, "Show me how much you've done, Nadia."

I gave her the needlepoint and she turned it over in her hands. I was looking at her face as if collecting my courage.

"I want to tell you something, Auntie," I said in a weak, trembling voice.

"Is everything okay, my dear?" she asked, still examining my needlepoint as if she were looking for my mistakes on it.

I hesitated as if I could no longer move my tongue. She moved her eyes away from the needlepoint and raised them to me. Maybe she saw the seriousness on my face. Maybe at that moment, she realized the kiss I'd given her that morning wasn't just a kiss. She looked carefully into my eyes and then reached out and took my hand, pressing it tenderly.

"Tell me, Nadia," she said in a calm voice, as if she were encouraging me.

I lowered my eyes so I didn't have to meet her gaze.

"I—I'm in love!" I said like a naive child, barely able to speak.

"What?" she said in surprise, seeming not to understand.

"I'm in love with someone," I said, my eyes still lowered.

"Oh!" she said, her voice raised in happiness, as she finally understood. "You mean someone has come to propose? That's wonderful! Why are you being so shy, like this is something to be ashamed of? You can count on me, Nadia. I'll talk to Daddy and I'll take care of everything. As long as you love him and he's nice, that's it. You can consider yourselves married from today. Congratulations!"

I raised my eyes to her, appearing to be struck with disappointment. I looked at her, trying to work out who she really was. Was she really this naive or was she acting like this maliciously, just to embarrass me?

"No one has come to propose to me," I cut her off, in a voice not without sharpness.

Her happiness faded.

"Aren't you saying there's someone who loves you?" she asked in disappointment.

"He loves me and I love him," I said, my voice still sharp. "But he won't propose to me."

"How could he love you and not propose?" she asked, with signs of seriousness on her face.

"He's not the marrying type," I said, hesitating, feeling the weakness of my position. I once again lowered my eyes to hide from her stares.

"What?" she asked, the anxiety creeping into her voice.

"I mean . . . I mean," I stammered. "We still haven't talked about marriage."

She was silent for a moment. Then, turning her head, she called out to the butler. "Abdou! Abdou!" She turned back to me. "These servants are a disaster," she said, as if we hadn't just been having an important conversation. "It's eleven o'clock and the upstairs still hasn't been done. Excuse me, Nadia my dear, while I go see what they're doing."

She marched off, doing everything she could to control her anger.

I felt that she'd slapped me.

I felt that when she said "These servants are a disaster," it meant "These girls are a disaster."

I felt I'd been insulted.

I felt everything in me rise up.

I got up to run to my room, afraid my tears would fall.

I locked the door behind me.

I threw myself on the bed and fixed my eyes on the ceiling.

I wonder today what would have happened to me if Safiya had listened to everything I said, if she'd shared my secret with me and learned about my love for Mustafa. Maybe she could have saved me, my father, and herself.

Maybe our lives would have been different.

But she didn't.

She refused to share my secret.

She was above my emotions.

She preferred to be prim and proper, to maintain a thick curtain between us so that she could keep her position in the house, not subjecting it to anything that could reduce her standing.

That was what God wanted, or Satan. One of them wanted to add fuel to the fire burning in my chest—the fire of evil, jealousy, and hatred. A fire breaking out in my imagination and weaving dark crimes in its wake.

I began to think with a malicious calm, as if a poisonous snake had shot out of my head and started slithering on its stomach, venom dripping from its fangs. The same feeling took hold of me whenever I moved forward to commit some evil act. A feeling that mingled the deliciousness of fear, hatred, hesitation, and intellect. It was the feeling of the gambler who puts everything he's got on the table and holds his breath waiting for the wheel of luck to stop.

At that moment, I was searching for a plan.

The plan with which I'd destroy my father's wife.

I'll put an end to her. I'll make her pay for insulting me. I'll make sure that Mustafa is mine alone.

But a part of me was thinking about something else—the part where what my father's wife said had settled . . .

If he loves you, why doesn't he propose to you?

I asked myself, "Could Mustafa marry me?"

I smiled mockingly at myself, my fate, and the man I'd fallen in love with.

There were times when I hoped I'd marry Mustafa, but it was always a distant hope—very distant. I saw it from behind the clouds of my thoughts like a beautiful, unattainable illusion, one that I had no right to keep hoping for, like I was hoping to be the queen of England or Audrey Hepburn.

Mustafa's life, personality, and philosophy didn't suggest marriage. I was even afraid he'd think that I was trying to marry him, so I was always uneasy whenever this thought occurred to me. I couldn't talk about it or even hint at it.

His personality was too strong to stand in front of a marriage official. That was how he seemed to me.

According to his philosophy of life, love wasn't tied to marriage. Love was a simple virtue, like truthfulness, faithfulness, and gallantry. He didn't need official confirmation, procedures, or the intervention of the state and society. Just as the truthful person doesn't go to the notary public to write a contract to confirm the truth, the person in love doesn't need a marriage official to confirm his love.

That was how he talked.

That was how I'd tried to convince myself.

"You're seventeen and I'm thirty-seven," he once told me. "There's twenty years between us. When you're twenty-seven, I'll be forty-seven. When you're in your prime, I'll be at the end. And when you're at your peak, I'll be finished."

He told me this bitterly.

I thought, as he was talking, that he was thinking about marrying me.

"You'll still be fabulous at forty-seven," I said laughing, trying to lighten his bitterness.

"I'll be old and toothless," he said, his smile still bitter. "My hands will shake and I'll walk bent over a cane."

"May you be protected from evil!" I said, wrapping my arms around his neck. "May you be protected from evil! You'll remain just like this, but your hair will be white. Then you won't like anyone but me."

He often brought up the age difference between us. Each time, I'd catch the anguish in his eyes. I'd hear it on his tongue. Each time, I tried to make him forget it with my kisses. I'd distract him with my kisses until he forgot his age and I forgot mine.

All these memories were mixed with my black thoughts about committing a crime. Once again, I collected my thoughts about my father's wife and my love, Mustafa.

She was older than me. Her age was closer to his. There were only nine years between them, so he wouldn't feel the same bitterness with her that he felt with me. Maybe her mentality was closer to his than mine. Maybe she could make him understand more than I could. Maybe she could give him more than me and take from him more than I'd taken.

I imagined Mustafa coming over to our house at my father's invitation. I imagined him sitting with us in the parlor, having a conversation with Auntie Safiya, a conversation just between the two of them. I imagined his eyes meeting hers with subtly meaningful looks. I imagined her fluttering her eyelids and blushing as if she were shy.

I imagined my father sitting between them, not knowing anything. I imagined myself sitting with my blood boiling, unable to join them in conversation, unable to stop them from exchanging looks. I imagined and I imagined.

I felt that I was in a black vortex that circled around me violently. Questions like tarrying ghosts swirled around me.

Would she be his?

Would she be happy to have him without marriage?

Could she marry him?

Was she so strong that she could conquer Mustafa's philosophy of life, love, and marriage?

I pictured my father's wife as a giant, tall and beautiful, laughing enticingly, and then making all men kneel before her, raising their arms to her in supplication. She moved forward, trampling me under her feet, and meeting Mustafa on my corpse.

It was another nightmare—a nightmare that I saw wide awake.

I felt like I was screaming for help. I got out of bed, terrified of my imagination. Rushing to the phone, I called Mustafa.

I heard his voice, calm and lazy, as if it were coming from a distant world, a world in which there wasn't all this torment that I was suffering.

I told him I wanted to see him immediately.

"Yes," he said, as if half asleep.

I stood in front of the mirror for a few moments and then left.

I met my father's wife in the salon.

"I'm going to visit Munira," I told her on the way out.

My father's wife didn't respond.

I don't know why I told her I was going to visit my friend. I didn't usually answer to her and she didn't usually ask me anything. Maybe the feeling of the crime being spun in my chest made me lie to her.

I went to Mustafa's apartment.

I rang the bell. I waited for a bit, but the door didn't open.

I rang the bell again. The door still didn't open.

Mustafa hadn't arrived yet.

It was the first time he was late, the first time he didn't get to the apartment before me and wait for me to arrive.

Was this because of last night? Was he bored of me? Had he begun to open his door to another woman? To my father's wife?

An incredible stubbornness overwhelmed me.

I'll wait for him as long as necessary.

I felt that my feet were nailed in front of the door. Every minute seemed like a month. Some people went by as I stood there. I pretended to be waiting for the elevator. The elevator came occasionally, carrying one of the residents of the neighboring apartments. I had to get in and go down a floor or two and then come back up. I'd get out to stand in front of the apartment door again like a poor lost dog.

Mustafa finally arrived.

He was ten minutes late. He began offering apologies as he opened the door. His excuse was that he'd just woken up, that I'd called when he was still in bed and he didn't have time to wash and get dressed. I accepted his apology in silence. We went in and closed the door.

He took my cold hands and kissed my palms. I didn't feel any relish at his kiss. It didn't flow in my veins. It didn't rise up to my heart.

We sat in the office silently.

The silence between us lasted awhile.

"Were you happy with the party yesterday?" he asked in his lazy voice, breaking the silence.

"It seems you were the happiest person there yesterday," I said, keeping a hold on my nerves.

"I'm always happy, wherever I am," he said indifferently.

"But it seems there were reasons that made you happier than usual," I said, looking at him as if leveling accusations at him.

"You were there. You were so beautiful."

I felt he was lying.

"So that's why you sat talking with me and dancing with me all night?"

"What do you mean?" he asked, feeling the storm blowing in on him.

"I mean Auntie Safiya."

"Oh," he said, as if remembering. "You'd given me a really bad image of her. It turns out that she's beautiful and nice. Your father must really be in love with her."

"Only Daddy?"

"Is there someone else?" He was surprised.

"You," I said, as if trying to pour a bucket of cold water on him.

"Oh, please," he laughed. "Shame on you!"

"Was it 'shame on me' the way you danced with her?"

"You know I've danced like that my whole life. It's nothing new."

"But she doesn't usually dance like that."

"She was dancing in the most proper way. She's a respectable woman. Everyone who knows her must respect her."

He reached out to put his arm on my shoulder but I moved away as if everything in me hated him and was disgusted by him. I began to observe him with a rebellious look in my eyes, searching in his face for the truth. Words were trapped in my throat and questions piled up until I could no longer talk or even think about what to ask him.

"Don't be crazy," he said, getting up to put on some records. "Don't upset yourself."

I didn't respond.

I watched him as he turned his back to me. He seemed very far from me, far, far from my feelings, far from my emotions, far from my heart. He didn't share with me the emotional turbulence that I was suffering. He didn't even try to share or understand it. He was far from my doubts, far from the black thoughts circling my head. He couldn't discuss them or save me from them.

He was another person, not a part of me, not a part of my soul.

He was calm, cold, and sincere, without any worries or concerns. All he thought about was his own pleasure: his records, books, apartment, the parties that he was going to, and his strange ideas with which he tried to appear unconventional.

Could Mustafa's world—a world without responsibilities—be bigger than him?

That's right. He was a person without responsibilities. Fate had spared him even the responsibility of working for his livelihood. I couldn't be something that he'd bear responsibility for. He wasn't responsible for me. I didn't cost him anything. I was just a pretty girl who had thrown herself on him and whom he had taken to please himself with, to spend a nice time with among his records and books. At that moment, I thought he kept me a virgin not because he was afraid for my future or out of respect for my reputation or because he was a refined man who believed in virtue. No, he kept me a virgin so he didn't have to bear the responsibility of turning me into a woman—something that I might hold him to, that his conscience might hold him accountable for, or that people and society might hold him answerable for. He was a coward fleeing from responsibility. That was my love, Mustafa.

I heard the tune of the first record.

I could bear anything at that moment except for music. I wanted to break something, to destroy something, to smash all the records, furniture, everything. But at the same moment, I was hoping Mustafa would try to destroy me instead of enveloping me with this palpable delicacy and those soft tunes. I was hoping he'd hit me, pull my hair, throw me on the ground, and kick me until I found something in his violence to divert me from my emotions and black thoughts.

All these thoughts passed through my head in a single moment.

"You know, your father is very nice," I heard him say as he turned to me. "It's clear he's a model father."

"He liked you too," I said, as if my voice were rattling through the revolt of my soul. "He plans to invite you to our house for dinner."

I saw happiness on his face.

"Really?" he said, jubilant, like a child.

I stood and went over to him.

"If Daddy invites you to our house," I said sharply, fixing my eyes on his face, "I don't want you to accept."

"Why?" he asked idiotically.

"Because," I said curtly. "For me, Mustafa!"

"But not—" he said.

"For me," I said, cutting him off. "Promise me. Afterward, you'll know why."

"Yes, ma'am," he said indifferently. "For you!"

"Merci," I said. "I'm leaving. I need to go. Daddy's waiting for me at the club."

"Really? Why did you want to see me then?"

"Because I missed you," I said coldly. "Au revoir!"

I headed to the door quickly, almost at a run.

He couldn't save me from myself.

I threw myself in a taxi, my breath ragged, as if I were panting after a long run.

Mustafa's voice rose up along with the sound of the car engine: "She's a respectable woman. Everyone who knows her must respect her!"

And me?

Was I not respectable?

Why was she respectable?

She wasn't respectable. She couldn't be!

I arrived home and Nanny Halima met me.

"Where's Madame Safiya, Nanny?" I asked her.

"Upstairs," she responded.

I smiled a wicked smile.

The crime would begin from upstairs.

10

Every morning after my father left, Auntie Safiya went upstairs, where my uncle lived, to oversee the servants.

My uncle didn't usually leave in the morning. He woke up late and stayed in bed for a long time, drinking tea and reading the newspapers. He then got up lazily and wandered through the house singing and whistling, spreading happiness among us with his jokes and boisterous laughter. He got dressed, went out to the garden, and busied himself talking with the gardener or reading until lunchtime, when he ate with us and then went out into the tumultuous world, not coming back until five o'clock the next morning.

That was his life with us.

My father considered himself responsible for my uncle. My father managed his land for him and dealt with his bills, and generally tried to organize his life.

Before my father got married, I considered myself responsible for my uncle, just as I was responsible for my father. I went upstairs every morning to oversee the servants, just as Auntie Safi did after she married my father.

My father and uncle never fought or had a disagreement, despite the big difference in their personalities: the happy-go-lucky, bohemian man who doesn't have a care in the world and the serious, composed, organized man who bears the responsibility of himself and others.

There was nothing new in the life of the house that could sow discord or cause a catastrophe between them.

There was only the black plan forming in my head, the catastrophe that I was preparing.

I spent the night searching for a way to crush my father's wife, for something I could accuse her of or with which I could break her respect, destroy her pride, and tear up the curtain of dignity she surrounded herself with.

I'd say to myself, "There has to be something in her life, a secret, every woman has . . . a secret. What's hers?"

I started saying to myself, "She has to have a man in her life—a man other than my father. I knew a lot of married women and they all had lovers. Why wasn't she like other women? Who was her lover?"

I began to go through all the men who frequented the house, all the men we knew. I tried to find her lover among them.

But I didn't find anyone.

She interacted with all men the same way. She'd attract them all with her dynamic, lovely personality and they'd all gather around her wherever she went.

When I didn't find a lover, I imagined one.

The man I imagined as my stepmother's lover was my uncle.

Uncle Aziz.

Why not?

He was the closest man to her. His personality made up for what my father lacked. So why wouldn't she seek to bring them both together, so that he completed for her everything women love in men. Seriousness and mirth, order and spontaneity, stability and excitement—the most contradictory characteristics.

That was what I imagined.

I had to convince myself of this fantasy so I could spin from it a truth that filled me with the courage to commit my crime.

When I set myself on this path, I noticed a lot of things I hadn't noticed before, things that hadn't stirred up any doubt in me.

Since my father got married, I noticed my uncle had started having dinner with us, which he never did before.

I noticed he accepted every invitation we received, even if he got there late. Before my father got married, my uncle used to refuse all these invitations and detest our social circles, even those that included our relatives and close friends.

I noticed that I had never seen him dance until when he began to dance with Auntie Safiya. He danced with her at almost every party, especially since my father was always too lazy to dance.

I noticed he gave himself certain rights over her, rights that weren't those of a man over his brother's wife. He always said what he thought about her clothes and he always opposed inviting this friend or that. He always caught her eye if she was late, wanting to know where she had been.

I noticed many things.

I began to be convinced.

When I came back from meeting Mustafa that day, Nanny Halima told me Auntie Safi was upstairs. My new conviction began to show me images I hadn't seen before. I started telling myself, "It's now one o'clock. What's keeping her in my uncle's apartment for so long? Is she still supervising the servants? Or is she taking the opportunity of me being out to stay up there with him? Who knows what they're doing!"

I tiptoed upstairs, sure I'd find her in the compromising position I was imagining.

The outer salon was empty.

There was no sign of the servants.

I tiptoed down the hallway leading to my uncle's bedroom.

The door to his bedroom was open. I heard their voices.

I walked forward, still on tiptoes.

I saw them.

My uncle was sitting on his bed, still in his pajamas, with newspapers and magazines strewn around him and tea on a table next to him. Auntie Safi was sitting on the far edge of the bed.

"Are you getting up or do I have to make you?" I heard her say.

Suddenly she turned and saw me.

She was confused, like she'd just discovered I was spying on her.

"Come here, Nadia," she told me simply, still holding her smile. "Come help me. Let's get this lazy man out of bed."

"My God!" my uncle said, turning to me. "Where did you come from?"

"From downstairs," I replied, trying to smile.

Auntie Safi got up and took hold of my uncle's foot.

"Come on, Nadia, take the other one!" she yelled, laughing.

I went forward, pretending to be happy, and grabbed my uncle's other foot. Working together, we started pulling him from the bed onto the ground.

"Hey! How is this my fault? My brother gets married and it's my fault? It would have been better for me to get married if I'd known you were going to get me out of bed at dawn every day."

"Dawn for you is one o'clock in the afternoon," Auntie Safiya said. "Let's go! Don't be lazy. Lunch is at two o'clock."

Still laughing artificially, I tried to leave them.

"Nadia!" my uncle called out, stopping me. "Come here next to me, my dear."

"What do you mean?" I said, laughing. "No one can go close to you except Auntie Safi!"

"Come kiss me so I can get up from the ground," he said.

He grabbed me by the hand, pulled me into his arms, kissed me on the cheeks, and held me to his chest tenderly.

This affection couldn't divert me from my plan.

I wiggled away from him with the fake smile still on my lips. I then pretended that I was pulling him by the hand to get him up from the ground.

"I'm going to see if Daddy's back," I said, leaving the room.

I went downstairs.

I heard Auntie Safi coming down behind me.

Why was I more convinced that day that there really was an improper relationship between them? Maybe because I wanted to be convinced. Everything I saw could have been happening innocently and could have been a normal part of our family life, but I didn't want peace and calm, and I didn't want our normal family life—this life whose throne my father's wife sat on.

After that, I had to convince my father of what I had convinced myself.

I had to convince him that his wife was cheating on him with his brother!

That was my plan.

That was my horrible crime.

The only result I imagined for this crime was for him to expel Auntie Safiya from the house—for my father to divorce her, to depose her from the throne so I could go back to sitting on it.

But how could I convince my father?

It wouldn't be easy. His good nature would not let doubts rise up in him. His strong morals prevented him from thinking badly about anyone. His firm love for his wife was too strong to simply accuse her of suspicion or caprice.

He was always calm.

He was never jealous, never upset.

How could you convince this kind of man that his wife was cheating on him?

How would I convince him?

I set a long-term plan in motion.

I began by always seeming worried and sad in front of him, as if something terrible was bothering me.

He'd ask me what was wrong.

"Nothing," I'd respond.

My father's wife was watching the shows that I'd put on, but she never said anything. She believed, as I surmised, that I was upset because of the love I had revealed to her and whose details she had refused to hear. Maybe my father had talked to her about me, but I was sure she hadn't told him what I revealed to her. Her policy was not to push her nose into my private life and not to make me a subject of discussion between her and my father. She didn't want to open on herself doors that I could close.

One day, as I sat having breakfast, my father got up as usual to go to the club.

"Don't go today, Daddy," I said suddenly in a loud voice. "For my sake, please don't leave!"

My father looked at me in surprise. It was the first time I'd tried to alter his schedule, the schedule he followed precisely, like the minutes on a clock.

"Why?" he asked, surprise lingering in his eyes. "Is something wrong? Are you sick?"

"No, not at all," I said dejectedly. "I only want to spend time with you."

"I won't be late today," he said with a tender smile. "I'll be back at one o'clock."

I bowed my head silently.

Two days later, I spoke to him again as he was leaving.

"Why are you going to the club? Aren't we more important to you?"

"You know I do all my work at the club," he responded, again with a look of surprise.

"Yes, I know," I said sharply. "But we need you too!"

"Have I neglected something, Nadia?" he asked accusingly. "Are you lacking anything?"

"No," I said, lowering my head. "I just mean that I miss you. I don't spend enough time with you."

He pulled me tenderly to his chest.

"I'll be gone for an hour," he said. "Then I'll be right back."

He did come back in an hour. He came back to find me worried, as I'd gotten him used to seeing me, and he asked me about it, pressing me with questions.

"Nothing," I kept saying to him, giving him the same response. "Nothing, I swear, Daddy. Nothing."

I buried my head in his chest and sighed as if I were holding my breath forever.

Then one evening . . .

I was in my room, spread out on my bed. I left my door open.

It was dinnertime and the servant came to call me. I loafed around until my father came up himself. When I heard the sound of his steps in the hallway leading to my room, I pretended to be sobbing, and made sure he heard it.

As soon as he came into my room, a look of anxiety appeared on his face. I sat up and rubbed my eyes and even started drying my tears.

My father sat down next to me. "Listen, Nadia," he said with a serious, sad, tone, as if his heart were breaking on his lips. "I'm very worried about you these days. You have to tell me everything. What's bothering you? Why are you so upset? You've never hidden anything from me before."

"It's nothing," I said, shaking my head like an innocent child. "I swear, it's nothing, Daddy!"

"For the first time, I feel like you're not telling me the truth, Nadia. Why are you lying to me? Tell me the truth, Nadia. I'm your daddy. You have no one but me and I have no one but you."

"Believe me, it's nothing. I'm just annoyed, fed up. I don't know why."

He put his hand under my chin and lifted my innocent face.

"Maybe you need a change of scenery. Maybe you're worn out. Tomorrow we'll go see Doctor Barrada."

"No, no doctor," I said. "I'm sure I'm fine. I'm just worn out these days."

My father smiled as if he understood the meaning of the words "these days."

He took me by the hand and we went together to the dinner table.

I repeated these little shows for a number of weeks, until my father was certain something serious was bothering me, tearing up my heart, and filling me with worry.

Until one day . . .

As we were having dinner, I intentionally appeared even more anxious than usual, pretending that grief had overcome me until I could no longer bear it. Right after dinner, I got up, went to my father's study, and sat at the desk. I started writing a letter to my mother, who was traveling with her husband and kids to Alexandria.

Dear Mother,

I send you a thousand kisses, even if I'm afraid to wet your face with my tears. I'm crying, Mother. I've been crying all day and night, until my eyes turn red and I can no longer sleep. What's making me cry even more is that I don't know if I have the right to write you this letter or not. Do I have the right to tell you everything, even if it's about my father, his wife, and my uncle—about our life at home? Or do I not have this right?

I have to tell you. I can't be quiet anymore or I'll go crazy. Imagine, Mother, that I'm living in a house that consists of nothing but cheating, that I'm witnessing betrayal with my own eyes but I can't speak.

> Imagine that the traitor is Auntie Safiya and that she's betraying my father! Who's she cheating on him with? My uncle! Yes, Mother, she's cheating on Daddy with Uncle Aziz. It's a betrayal that's been going on for months. I saw them once together in my uncle's room. He was kissing her, and she was . . . no! No, I can't describe to you the scene I saw. Since that day, she's been going up to his room every day after Daddy leaves and staying with him until he gets back.
>
> I've been crying since that day, crying because I can't do anything. I can't tell Daddy and I can't beg my uncle to leave Daddy's wife alone or beg her to protect the honor of my dear father, the good father who trusts her and doesn't know anything about her and . . .

This was the poisoned letter that I wrote in a naive, innocent style, when I was still seventeen.

I didn't finish it. I put it in the center of the desk with the lamp shining on it and the pen sitting next to it. I then left the room with the lights on as if I was about to come back.

My father usually went to his study around ten o'clock to pick a book for himself and read it in the parlor or bedroom.

I was hoping he'd go into the study, find the letter, and read it . . . and after that, I'd let whatever happened happen!

But would he read it?

He might not go into the study.

He might do something different this evening. He might not feel like reading a book. He might go into the study and not see the letter, or he might see the letter and not read it out of respect for my privacy. He didn't usually read any of my letters.

My heart pounded. I felt as if a crazy devil were beating on my chest with both hands in violent rhythmic blows like the pounding of African drums.

I took my troubled heart and snuck like a neophyte criminal through the next room and onto the balcony of the study. The balcony door was closed but I could see what was happening in the room through the glass door. I stood there leaning against the wall so no one could see me, my eyes almost melting the glass as I was looking through it.

I waited for a while as the crazy devil continued to beat on my chest with his fists.

I got tired of waiting. I felt like I waited forever.

I got so tired of the pounding of my heart that I thought I was going to pass out or die of a heart attack.

I started thinking about abandoning it all, about going back to the study, tearing up the letter, and then throwing myself down on my bed. Maybe my heart would calm down. Maybe the crazy devil would stop beating on my chest. Maybe my breath would become regular, and maybe after that I'd sleep.

But right before I gave up, the study door opened.

I saw my father.

He walked around the room, surprised to find the light on. He looked even more surprised when he found the desk lamp on too.

He went over to the desk and reached out to turn off the light, standing with his back to me.

I saw his head lean over the piece of paper on the desk, but he turned away quickly before having enough time to read anything.

He then reached out again to the lamp.

This time he turned it off.

I let out a sigh and put my hand on my chest, as if thanking God that the crime had been averted.

But at that moment, my father came back and turned the lamp on again. I saw him lean over the piece of paper on the desk once more. He stayed there and appeared to be reading it.

He pulled the desk chair over and sat down, his back still to the balcony where I was standing.

I saw him lift the paper up in his hands and read it.

He then tossed it aside nervously, as if it had lit a fire in his hands.

He leaned his elbows on the edge of the desk and lowered his head into his palms.

I saw his fingers rise up to the top of his head and pull his hair violently, as if he wanted to tear something out of his head.

He sat up in the chair, took the letter, and began reading it again. He then hurled it onto the desk. He got up and started pacing around the room.

I saw his face, and almost screamed.

I did scream, but it wasn't audible since I put my hands over my mouth to muffle it.

What had I done?

What had I done to my father?

His face at that moment was strangely terrifying.

His lips were pursed violently and had retreated inside his mouth. His nostrils were flared as if they were breathing fire. His eyes were bulging and confused, circling around feebly. His eyebrows were knotted and one of them seemed to be grabbing the throat of the other. His cheeks were shaking, as if the flesh on his face had come loose from his skull. His hair stood up on end on top of his head and every hair looked like it wanted to take off by itself.

It was as if he'd aged a hundred years in a single moment.

I felt like a knife had plunged into my side.

I felt like a sharp whip was coming down on me, tearing up my face and body.

I wanted to run to him, throw myself at his feet, wash his shoes with my tears, and confess . . . to plead with him not to believe me, not to trust the letter he'd read, and go back as he was, to let his pursed lips loose, to relax his frenzied eyes and his knitted eyebrows, to go back to being calm, good, and handsome.

All those feelings enveloped me as I clung to the wall, my eyes looking down from behind the glass, not moving.

All those feelings couldn't save me from my crime or push me to save my father and his wife, to save the whole house.

It was as if I had two people inside me. One who felt things and was tortured under the whips of her conscience and another who didn't feel anything, who wasn't tortured at all, but was a deformed criminal standing coldly frozen, the blood of her crime dripping between her fingers. The criminal was victorious, the one ruling my being.

I saw my father pace back and forth in the room like a wild animal who found himself trapped, not knowing where to escape.

Then he turned and headed to the door.

I hurriedly left the balcony through the next room. Going into the bathroom, I closed the door behind me and opened the faucet all the way. Even if my father tried to look for me, he'd find me in the bathroom and think that I left the letter before going back to finish it.

But my father didn't look for me.

I waited for a bit, until I was sure my father had left the study. Then I left the bathroom.

I ran into him in the hallway between the two rooms.

I tried to avoid him, but he called out to me in a hoarse voice.

"Nadia! Nadia!"

I lifted my beautiful innocent face, like the face of a child, unpolluted by the crush of life.

"Yes, Father?" I asked in a low voice, unable to look at his sullen face.

My father was silent. It seemed like he was silent for a long time. He then slowly came close to me, wrapped me in his arms, and pulled me to his chest with a roughness I wasn't used to, as if he were asking for help from something inside him, or as if he were apologizing for not taking my worry seriously.

"Nothing, Nadia," he said and he sounded almost tearful. "Good night."

I gave him a quick kiss on his trembling cheeks, as if afraid to pollute his noble face.

"You too," I mumbled.

He left me and went out to the parlor.

I hurried to the study, took the evil letter, and turned off the lights, which my father had left on as they were. I then went back to my room and began ripping up the letter, tearing it into a thousand little pieces, as if I were tearing up myself.

11

I COULDN'T SLEEP.

I was thinking about my father, picturing that strange, terrifying look he had after he read the letter. I was imagining how much he was suffering, thinking that his wife was cheating on him with his brother, the torture of a man stabbed in his honor, stabbed in his pride, stabbed in the heart.

I felt my insides creep up inside my body until they wrapped around my throat and choked me.

I was disgusted at myself.

I needed someone to hit me, to slap me, to make me feel pain, to punish me for my crime.

Why didn't my father hit me?

But instead of imagining my father hitting me, I imagined Mustafa doing it. I imagined him raising his hand up and bringing it down on my cheek. I imagined him pulling me by the hair, throwing me to the ground, taking out a whip and bringing it down on my body until it shredded my clothes.

This thought calmed me. Something about it distracted me from my crime. I unconsciously lifted my hands and covered my face as if protecting myself from Mustafa's blows. I writhed in bed like I really was being whipped.

But this anguish didn't last long.

I knew I had to keep going. I knew the letter was just the beginning. Now I had to prove the affair to my father—prove to him that his wife really was betraying him with his brother.

Otherwise he'd discover my lie and punish me for it. And I'd lose him forever. Anything would be easier than my father discovering that I was a liar or losing him.

Morning came.

I was still in bed when my father came into my room, still wearing his pajamas. I was surprised. Since he'd gotten married, my father never came into my room early. He'd get up from bed, leave his room for the bathroom, and then go back to get dressed. I wouldn't see him until breakfast.

Sitting on the edge of the bed, my father leaned over to kiss me.

"Good morning, my dear," he said with a broken smile. "Did you sleep well?"

"Good morning, Daddy," I said, trying to hide the traces of my insomnia.

I knelt on the bed, threw myself into his arms, and hugged him. I pressed my cheek to his.

"I love you so much, Daddy," I said with childlike naivete, as if apologizing for my crime.

My father wrapped his arms around me and pressed me to his chest. He then moved me away gently and looked at me with a sad smile hanging below his worn-out eyes.

"You know, Nadia," he said, "I feel like we've grown apart. Remember when we used to live alone? We always understood each other, always talked to each other, and . . ." He lowered his head as if he'd never lift it up again. "Those were nice days, Nadia," he continued in a sad voice. "I only had you and you only had me."

I felt a wicked happiness.

I felt that my father had come back to me, to me alone. But he was sad and broken.

"I've never wanted anyone but you, Daddy," I told him, hiding my evil delight.

"Me too, Nadia," he said, raising his head to me. "I only have you. Whatever happens, we'll always have each other. I'll be there for you to make you happy. I'll sacrifice everything to make you happy."

"Your happiness is all I care about, Daddy," I said, kissing him again.

"Good. Go wash your face and let's have breakfast," he said, patting my shoulder. "You need to eat well. You're losing weight these days and I don't like it."

"You go wash your face first," I said, laughing.

"Right. I haven't been to the bathroom yet," he said, smiling, touching his face with his hand. "I think I've become lazier than you!"

My father got up to go to the bathroom.

I went to wash my face and get dressed.

We all met at the breakfast table.

My father's wife was unusually quiet and sad. It looked like she hadn't paid as much attention as usual to her appearance.

My father, sitting next to her, was also silent, his face taut as if he were suppressing a volcano on the verge of erupting. Unlike most mornings, he was paying me more attention than his wife.

I sat silently between them, moving my eyes from one to the other, trying to figure out where the storm would blow in from.

We finished our silent breakfast as if bidding farewell to someone who had died.

My father got up to leave for the club.

Auntie Safiya stood up sluggishly after him, like she was carrying out a burdensome duty by going with him to the door to say goodbye.

I got up too, and sat in the parlor. I waited for her to come back.

"I don't like how Daddy's acting this morning," I said innocently, trying to find out what had happened between them the night before. "What's wrong with him?"

"I really don't know, Nadia," Auntie Safiya said, nervously straightening a cloth on one of the tables. "Yesterday, he changed all of a sudden. He was sitting with me calmly, and then got up and left. I don't know what he was doing, but he came back sulking, really upset. He sat in the parlor by himself until midnight. Afterward, he came into the bedroom but he didn't sleep. He was tossing and turning, sighing and moaning. I kept asking what was wrong, but he didn't respond. I'm afraid he's sick, but he doesn't want to tell me."

"So why don't we call Doctor Mufti?" I asked innocently, pretending to be worried.

"I suggested that. But he doesn't want to. You know your father. When he doesn't want to talk, no one can make him."

She sighed, as if resigned to the situation. Then she went to the kitchen to reprimand the cook.

I took the phone, went into my room, and called Mustafa.

We didn't talk about much. I was trying to get him to distract me from my thoughts, but it didn't work. I had one ear on the receiver while keeping tabs on my father's wife with the other. I was talking with him while my mind was picturing what might happen in the next few days.

Mustafa was trying to get me to talk, but he couldn't get through to me. He made jokes, but I wasn't paying attention. He'd ask me a question, but I wouldn't respond.

"What's wrong?" he asked finally. "What's distracting you?"

"Nothing," I whispered. "Safiya's standing at the door."

"Say hi to her for me," he said, laughing. "And remind her about the invitation. Am I still banned from your house?"

I didn't respond.

"I'm hanging up now," I whispered. "I'll call you later."

"Okay. I'll talk to you in the afternoon. Au revoir."

I hung up. Taking the needlepoint I was working on, I went to the parlor.

Auntie Safiya was supervising the servants.

After about an hour, she walked past me in the parlor and went upstairs as she usually did every morning.

I sat by myself, thinking.

It wasn't long before the door flew open and my father stormed in.

As soon as I saw him, I knew.

I knew he had started monitoring his wife. He never came home at this time of day.

In his anger, my father forgot to say hello to me. He went into the house with quick, nervous steps, and then came back to me.

"Where's Safiya?" he asked, almost yelling.

My eyes widened with fear.

"I swear, I don't know," I stammered as if hiding a big secret. "She's—she's—she's not in her room?"

"No, she's not in her room! Tell me, where did she go?" He came up and grabbed my arm. "Where is she? Tell me!"

"She must have . . . must have left," I said, still stammering.

"Left where?" he said, shaking me.

"I don't know, Daddy! I was in my room. Ask Nanny Halima. Or maybe she went upstairs."

My father let go of my arm. He didn't ask the nanny anything. The storm blew directly upstairs.

I ran after him, as if worried about him.

Upstairs was dark and calm. My father went in as I ran after him. All of a sudden, we saw Auntie Safiya standing in the hallway, organizing the clothes that had come back from the ironer. Abdou the butler was sweeping the opposite room.

My father stood staring at her, trying to get hold of himself.

"Where's Aziz?" he asked, less harshly than before.

Auntie Safiya gave him a cold look. "He's still sleeping."

"And what are you doing here?" my father asked, still fighting to control himself.

She looked at him, surprised.

"You can see what I am doing," she said coldly.

"If you're organizing the ironing, what are the servants doing?" he asked, his voice starting to rise.

"Since when do the servants organize the ironing?" she said, looking back and forth between us. "You know I never leave these things to the servants." She was quiet for a moment. "What's wrong, Ahmed? What's happened? What's bothering you?"

I saw my father press his palms together as if trying to quash his nerves.

"Nothing, nothing," he said with forced calm.

He turned to go downstairs.

"Wait, I'm coming with you," she said.

The three of us went down.

We sat in the parlor without anyone saying anything. Suddenly, my father jumped out of his chair.

"I'm going back to the club." His voice was rattled.

"You're not staying with us?" Auntie Safiya asked with an anxious look. "It's noon and lunch will be ready soon."

"I've got work," my father said, heading to the door. "I came to talk with Aziz about something, but he's still asleep. What kind of man is that?"

And he left.

Auntie Safiya didn't get up to say goodbye. She sat in her spot and leaned her head on her palm as if she was thinking. Then she got up nervously to go to her room, and closed the door behind her. Maybe to cry.

I imagined her tears—the tears I'd never seen. I pitied her at that moment, but my scheme was too big for pity to destroy.

The criminal that lives in my chest was controlling my nerves and my mind. It made me vigilant and alert, watching everything happening around me silently and dryly, without pity.

My father came back after a few hours, later than usual. When I kissed him, I could smell beer on his breath, but he was calm. He seemed as if he'd made a decision and he was following some kind of set plan.

We sat at the table for lunch with Uncle Aziz. Maybe no one else noticed how distastefully my father greeted him.

"Everything okay, Ahmed?" my uncle asked, taking his seat at the table. "Safiya said you wanted to talk to me."

My father looked at his wife sharply, as if accusing her of revealing a secret to his brother.

"She told you already?" he said scornfully.

His wife looked at him in surprise.

"What does she have to do besides pester me to wake up, order me around, and give me lunch?" Uncle Aziz said, laughing. "It's enough. Safiya's turned the house into a barracks: everything's scheduled down to the minute and second!"

My father looked at his brother as if he was trying to discover his secret. He then moved his eyes to his wife and started eating.

"Regardless," he said without responding to my uncle or his laughter, "I don't need you. I was planning on talking with you about the farm, but I decided these things don't interest you."

"Thanks to you, Ahmed," my uncle said.

"Of course, thanks to me," my father said bitterly. "I'm like the donkey that pulls the cart. Everything's on me. I'm the one who looks after the farm for you. I'm the one who takes care of your bills for you. And I'm the one who got married so you could have someone wake you up and—"

Safiya slammed her knife and fork onto her plate. "You married me, Ahmed, to wake up Aziz?"

My father inhaled deeply and angrily, doing his best to calm himself. "I didn't mean—"

"I won't let you call me 'someone' and talk about me like that," she said, cutting him off.

"I'm sorry," my father said, collecting himself. "Forget about it, Safiya. Bear with me for another few days and everything will be fine."

"God willing," he added in a whisper, as if talking to himself.

Auntie Safiya was silent.

"What happened, Ahmed?" my uncle asked calmly. "What is it? What's wrong?"

"Nothing," my father said, not looking at him.

"Maybe there's something I can do."

"You've never known how to do anything other than what you're doing now," my father said, raising his eyes to him.

"That's right," my uncle said, trying to remain calm. "You're the one who wants it like that. You're the one who always wants to do everything yourself. If you were me, you wouldn't do anything, because all I want is to make you happy."

"We're done talking about it now," my father said, going back to his food.

A long period of silence ensued.

It was the first time I'd seen this kind of exchange between my father and uncle. It was the first time these dark clouds had gathered over the dining table. I felt the entire house shake and myself shake with it. I felt that its foundation would collapse and it would collapse on me, but what could I do?

"My uncle invited us for dinner tonight," my father's wife said as we were finishing our food. "Do you want to go?"

I looked at her. She gave a weak smile as if she was trying to defend her happiness with it. There was confusion and hesitation in her eyes, as if she didn't know what to say or do. Her strong, attractive personality was beginning to crumble . . . crumble before me and my wicked plan.

"Let's go," my father said. "Why wouldn't we?"

"No reason," she said weakly. "I'm only asking."

"And you, Aziz?" my father asked after a moment, slicing into an apple like he was butchering it. "You're not coming with us?"

"Are you inviting me or kicking me out?" my uncle asked, trying to regain his cheerfulness.

"Right," my father said, continuing to cut up the apple. "It's just that before, you didn't like these kinds of invitations. But I see you like them these days."

"Thanks to Safiya," my uncle said, looking at my father's wife appreciatively. "She's the one who made me like everything, even these dull invitations."

My father raised his eyes at him briefly as if he admired his courage. He then went back to butchering the apple. And silence reigned again.

That evening, they went to Auntie Safiya's uncle's house.

I excused myself from going, saying there wouldn't be any girls there my age. The truth was that I needed to take a break from myself, from the criminal inside me.

But when I was alone, I couldn't relax. My torture returned. I started wandering through the rooms of the house as if fleeing from terrifying images traced in front of me on the walls.

I had to do something—to embark on a reckless adventure to make me forget myself.

I had no option but Mustafa, the drug I'd gotten addicted to. But this evening, the usual dose wasn't enough. It wasn't enough for me just to go to him, listen to his records and bizarre opinions, and give my body to him. Even spending the night at his place, as I did once, wasn't enough. I wanted a bigger dose, a rougher and more exciting adventure.

I was home alone.

I picked up the phone and called Mustafa, but he wasn't there. I started calling all the places he usually went, until I found him at the Semiramis bar.

"I want to see you now," I said as if giving him an order.

"I'm with people," he said apologetically.

"I don't care. Leave them and come," I insisted.

"But I'm the one who invited them," he said.

"Listen, Mustafa, if I don't see you now, you'll never see me again," I snapped as if I meant it.

"But why?" he asked, confused. "What's going on?"

"None of your business," I said tensely. "I just need to see you."

"But I can't stay," he said, giving in. "Half an hour, and then I need to come back."

"Fine."

"I'll be at the apartment in five minutes."

"No, come here."

"Here where?"

"My house," I said firmly.

"Are you crazy? How could I come to your house?"

"No one's here," I said. "I'm all alone."

"What if someone comes back?"

"No one will. They're all out for dinner and they won't get back before midnight."

"What if one of them gets a stomachache and comes home early? What'll we do then?"

"I'm not worried about that." I was completely calm. "They're all in good health. Are you coming or not?"

"Why don't you go to the apartment since you're alone? Get dressed, take a taxi, and I'll be there waiting for you."

"No, I can't," I said stubbornly.

"Listen, my dear," he said. "Nadia, sweetie, spirit of my heart. Be reasonable. It's been twenty years since I was in high school. I don't jump over walls and I'm not ready to start today. I'm too old for these things."

"Didn't you say you wanted to see my room so you could imagine me everywhere? This way I can show you."

"Not today, please. You can just describe it to me bit by bit or take pictures of it and bring them with you."

"Okay, forget it. Whatever you say. But next time, don't ask to see me."

Mustafa was quiet for a little. I'd hooked him with the seed of adventure. He began imagining it and savoring it.

"If I come, how do I get in?"

"You'll find the garden gate open," I said quickly, delighted at my victory. "You'll find me on the veranda."

"Okay, I'll be there in ten minutes."

"Ten minutes exactly. But listen. Don't park in front of the gate. Park on the next street over."

"Yes, ma'am," he sighed.

It was nine o'clock. All the servants had left except for Nanny Halima, who was asleep in her room, and Idris the doorman, an old man who'd worked for us for more than fifteen years.

I began to arrange everything.

I first wanted to be sure that Idris was asleep, so I went to the balcony and called out to him a few times. All of a sudden, he woke up and responded.

"Listen, Idris," I said, thinking quickly. "Go to the ironer and tell him I have to have my white dress immediately."

The ironer was in Galaa Square. With his slow pace, Idris couldn't get there and back in less than an hour.

"But they're closed now, miss," Idris said in surprise, almost pleading.

"No, we went there once at eleven o'clock and they were open," I said mercilessly, in a commanding tone. "Please, Idris. Abdou went home and I have to have that dress now!"

Idris muttered some words I couldn't hear and then put on his scarf as if he were slapping me with it.

I stood watching him closely until he left the house and went on his way.

I went to my room, took off my clothes, and put on a white silk shirt with a light rose-colored nightgown on top of it. I undid my hair and let it fall down my neck like a cascade of gold. I put on some Femme perfume, which Mustafa loved. I then rushed to Nanny Halima's room and locked the door to make sure she couldn't get out unless I opened it for her.

I went out to the garden and opened the gate, which gave an annoying squeak.

I went back and stood at the top of the stairs leading into the house.

A few minutes later, I spotted Mustafa's car pass by. Mustafa looked at me, and then drove his car to the side street.

After a few moments, he came back. He hesitated, looking around like a thief, and entered through the garden gate.

My heart thundered. I felt like an airplane in the sky plunging down into a bottomless abyss.

I signaled to him with a trembling hand and he started tiptoeing up the stairs. He took my hand with a scared smile. I put my finger to my lips, warning him not to say anything.

We went inside.

I locked the door behind us as a precaution.

Mustafa was raging. His fingers were cold, his face was flushed, and his eyes were darting around. I could almost hear his heartbeats. He was whispering as if he were choking. Despite that, he was trying to appear steady and courageous: he was like an old retired officer who suddenly found himself on the battlefield.

He looked around at the parlor and the furniture, trying to act like he was used to these kinds of adventures. Then he turned to me.

"You know, I had to have two neat whiskeys to be able to come here," he whispered.

"Me too," I said. "My heart's in my stomach!"

"Where's the bedroom you wanted to show me?" he asked as if hoping to end the ordeal.

"No, I won't show it to you," I said, trying to make him mad.

"Why?" he whispered.

"Because."

"What's this 'because'? Why don't you want to show it to me?"

Mustafa was agitated. It was the first time I'd seen him like that, and my room wasn't the reason. It was this whole set up.

I wanted to see how angry he was.

"No," I said, coquettishly. "I won't tell you."

He grabbed my arm so hard it hurt.

"I have to know why you don't want me to go in your room," he whispered loudly. "What are you hiding?"

I was afraid he'd raise his voice and press so hard on my arm that I'd scream.

"Because it's a mess, that's why. I don't want you to see it like that."

Mustafa smiled and loosened his grip. "So, why'd you bring me here?" he asked, whispering again.

"Because I missed you," I said, clinging to him. "And I couldn't go out."

Mustafa looked at me as if he were in heaven. He pulled me to him violently and fell on my lips.

His kiss was different from what I was used to. His lips trembled on mine feverishly. His cheeks were on fire and he was panting. His fingers pressed down on my side so frantically they almost dug into my flesh.

I floated in this roughness.

I then woke up all of a sudden at the sound of bangs on the door.

Mustafa woke up too. "What's that?" he whispered, terrified.

"It's Nanny Halima," I said, trying to calm him.

"What's wrong with her? What does she want? Where is she?" he asked, looking around quickly.

"Don't worry," I said calmly. "She's in her room. She must want to go to the bathroom. I locked her in."

"What should I do?" he asked, trying to get a grip on himself.

"Come, sit here."

I brought him into the dining room and waited for more knocks on the door. I then went and opened it for Nanny Halima.

"Who locked you in?" I asked with a big laugh.

"Bismillah, bismillah!" she exclaimed. "I don't know, Miss Nadia. I thought the jinn locked me in or I'd died and got stuck in my grave."

"There aren't any jinn. Someone must have locked you in by accident."

I let her go to the bathroom, and went to calm Mustafa as he stood in the darkness of the dining room. From a distance, I indicated that he should keep quiet.

Then I left him and stood in the parlor so that Nanny Halima could see me after she left the bathroom.

"You're not asleep yet, Miss Nadia?" she asked as she reached the end of the hallway.

"Not yet, Nanny," I said, standing in the parlor. "After I finish reading my magazine."

She went back into her room and shut the door.

I didn't try to lock it again. Instead, I locked the door separating the bedrooms from the parlor, salon, and dining room. I went back to Mustafa.

As soon as I reached him, he whispered, "What if she'd seen us?"

"Don't worry," I said, unconcerned. "She couldn't say anything."

"And what if someone comes now?"

"I'll sneak you out the kitchen door," I said, pleased with myself for my quick thinking.

Mustafa didn't wait for another word. He pulled me to him roughly and impatiently, as if he wanted to put an end to this, to get himself out of this situation and flee to safety.

His trembling lips returned to mine. He reached out to open the buttons of my nightgown, but I resisted. I wanted to see him angry and aroused again.

He couldn't bear my resistance. He lifted his lips from mine and a terrifying look sparkled in his eyes. With both hands, he ripped off my robe as if he was crazy.

He then grabbed me by my hair and pulled me violently to the ground.

Mustafa left.

He disappeared quickly from the house as if he were running from the devil.

I went after him to lock the garden gate, which let out a squeak.

I then went back to my room, took off my ripped clothes, and hid them in the dresser.

I sat on my bed, thinking about everything that had happened. I was pleased with myself—with this person I'd become.

I heard the front-door bell.

I got up to open it.

"The ironer isn't open, Miss Nadia," Idris said, panting. "I told you before, but you didn't believe me."

"Don't worry, Idris," I said, almost in tears. "You're right. Thanks."

And I locked the door.

12

I DIDN'T KNOW WHAT HAPPENED when my father, his wife, and my uncle went to Auntie Safi's uncle's.

Maybe my father discovered new evidence that his wife was cheating on him with his brother. Maybe he became more convinced of what he read in the poisoned letter that I wrote to my mother. I didn't know.

The next morning, my father was quiet and placid. He wasn't upset or happy, just totally silent, as if his soul had become tired of him and had withdrawn to a far corner of his body, leaving the rest of him empty.

He then surprised me by announcing he was going to the farm. My heart almost jumped when I heard him ask his wife to get ready to go with him.

It was the first time he'd asked her to go to the farm. I'd only been there two or three times in my life, even though it was close to Cairo, not far from the Giza train station.

My father always insisted that none of us visit the farm. His explanation was that the house there wasn't suitable. It wasn't in an appropriate state to receive women or guests. So why did he want his wife to accompany him today?

Why?

Did he want to confront her about her cheating there?

Could she convince him of her innocence so that he would discover I'd lied in the letter?

Did he plan to keep his wife there so she lived far from his brother, far from his suspicions?

Dozens of questions circled my head. I imagined dozens of scenarios.

I knew I needed to defend myself, to conceal the terrible crime I'd committed before my father revealed it, and with it, revealed that his pure, innocent daughter was nothing more than a criminal.

I waited for him to invite me to go with them, but he didn't. Instead, he just gave me an empty look.

"We won't be gone long, Nadia," he said in a weary voice, as if he didn't want to speak. "Two days at the most."

I didn't respond. I opened my mouth as if I was going to say something or smile, but I shut it again.

My father wolfed down his breakfast.

Auntie Safi busied herself, submissively getting her bags ready as if she'd decided to leave the matter to God, to do what He wanted. She then followed my father without having her breakfast, setting out with him as a thick, heavy silence surrounded them like a black fog.

I was so distracted that I didn't feel my father give me a quick, cold kiss or notice his wife as she looked at me in misery, as if appealing to me for help.

"I've instructed the cook on everything," she said.

I was distracted, thinking about what I had to do.

What should I do to make sure this surprise trip wouldn't ruin my plan?

My mind began to spring to life, as I felt something black start to move, like a poisonous snake when it feels warmth.

I realized that my only choice was to hitch my father to his doubts about his wife, to transfer the bitter whispering from the house to the farm, so he could experience it there as he was experiencing it here.

I got dressed, and then went upstairs and woke up my uncle. I pestered him until he opened his eyes and looked at me. Throwing myself into his arms, I started kissing him.

"I'm not Auntie Safi," I said to him. "I'm Nadia. If Auntie Safi can't get you up, I can!"

"What?" my uncle said, rubbing his eyes. "What happened? Where is she?"

"She left," I said with a big smile. "She and Daddy left for the farm."

"What time is it?" he asked, yawning.

"Ten thirty," I said.

My uncle closed his eyes, turned on his side, and pulled the blanket over his face.

"You woke me up at ten thirty? Do you want to kill me?"

"I said that Auntie Safi left," I said, pulling the blanket off his face as if alerting him to something serious.

He sat up in bed.

"Oh, right," he said as if he really had heard something serious. "Why'd she leave? Why'd she go to the farm?"

"How would I know?" I said innocently.

He was quiet for a bit as if he was thinking.

"Your father's never taken anyone to the farm. He runs it like a holy temple. No one enters except for the great priest, its lord."

He was talking about my father with a bitterness I hadn't heard from him until yesterday.

"But he took Auntie Safi with him today," I said with a shrug. "He didn't ask me to go with them."

"There's something on your father's mind. I don't know what it is. God help us! Because your father inherited all the craziness of the Turks from your grandmother, may God rest her soul. He stays quiet and then, all of a sudden, something rises up in him that drives him crazy."

"Only my uncle is better than Daddy," I said, laughing.

He let out a meaningless laugh.

"Please, Uncle," I continued, "I want you to call the farm and tell Auntie Safi to have Umm Atiya make pancakes for me. I'm dying for them. I forgot to tell her before she left."

"You woke me up for that?" he asked with a grave look, as if staring at a problem. "Why don't *you* call her?"

"Because they still haven't gotten to the farm," I said, kissing him again. "And I have to leave now because I have an appointment at the tailor. Please, call her!"

"Yes, ma'am," he said, still with the grave look.

"Don't forget!"

"I won't."

I kissed him one last time and left.

I went to Qasr al-Nil Street and spent an hour wandering around the stores, not seeing anything in the windows except for images from my sick mind. I then spent another hour at Ramère, the hairdresser. As I had my head under the dryer, I thought about asking the hairdresser to turn up the heat until my head melted, dissolving everything in it, burning up my imagination with it.

I went back home.

I waited for my uncle to come down. We sat for breakfast.

"Did you speak to Auntie Safi?" I asked, trying not to look at him.

"Yes, my dear," he said bitterly. "I spoke to her." He was quiet for a bit and then continued, raising his voice. "I'm sure something has happened to your father. He must have gone crazy. I asked for Safiya. He told me, 'Why do you want to talk to her?' I told him, 'Nadia wants to tell her to bring back pancakes.' He told me, 'That's ridiculous, Aziz. You think you're the only one who's clever?'" My uncle went quiet as if he was stunned.

"Did you talk to her?" I asked calmly.

"No, ma'am," he said, shaking his head. "Your father didn't let me. He told me she was busy in the garden . . . as if she understands anything about gardens or has even seen one before. I tell you, he's crazy—absolutely crazy!"

"Shame on you, Uncle," I said as if scolding him. "Don't say that about Daddy. Who knows what's bothering him?"

"Is it not shame on *him* for treating us this way?" he asked sharply.

I was quiet for a bit, pretending to eat. "I'm very afraid for Daddy these days, Uncle."

"May God protect us," he sighed.

I was quiet again. "What do you think if we go to the farm now?"

"What? Have you lost your mind? Do you want him to shoot at us?"

"No matter what, we have to be at his side."

"You can go by yourself."

"You're his brother," I said, imploringly. "He doesn't have anyone but you. Neither Auntie Safi nor I know how to understand him or talk to him. You're the only one . . ."

My uncle calmed down.

"It's true: he's my brother," he said after a moment. "And I've never seen him like this before."

"That's why we need to be at his side. Who knows what's wrong with him or what he's planning to do."

Now my uncle was quiet.

"Please, Uncle," I begged. "Do it for me. I won't be able to sleep or calm down as long as I'm so worried about Daddy. Do it for me. You have to, please. Let's go to the farm."

My uncle didn't respond but gave me a hesitant look. His lips trembled as if he was fighting his emotions.

"Would you really let me take a taxi and go to the farm by myself?" My uncle threw the napkin he had in his hand onto the table.

"Let's go," he said, getting up from the chair. "We'll see what's happened to this man."

I got up immediately. I got a small bag ready with my nightclothes and toiletries. My uncle went upstairs and came back with a small bag. We then got in his car and left for the farm.

Neither of us spoke on the way.

We were each busy with our own thoughts.

My uncle was driving with his face gloomy and eyes confused, and seemed not to be concentrating on the road. Instead, he seemed to sense a darkness creeping up on him.

We arrived at the farm.

The farmers' kids surrounded the car, so my uncle had to honk a number of times to clear the way.

We drove into the garden and stopped in front of the big old house whose exterior paint had fallen off most of the walls. Its façade had become like the face of a giant sieve, sifting through history—the history of our family.

At the sound of the horn, my father rushed out to the big balcony at the front of the house. As soon as he saw the car and who was in it, his eyes widened and he seemed to take a deep inhale of breath. He then stood up straight with his hands on his hips.

We got out of the car.

Wearing forced smiles, my uncle and I walked toward the house and went up the stairs. My father stared at us angrily, until we stopped in front of him.

He didn't kiss me as usual. Instead, he turned his angry glare on my uncle and focused it on him. My father didn't reach out to greet him. He kept standing there stiffly, hands on his hips.

"Why did you come?" he asked in a hoarse voice, as if the words were exploding out of a volcano. "What brought you here?"

My uncle looked at me with a mocking smile, as if he was saying to me, "Didn't I tell you?" He then turned to my father. "I came to check on you!" he said, trying to remain calm.

"Are you sure you came just for that?" my father asked, still standing there like a rock.

My uncle didn't understand what my father was insinuating. "I want to talk with you," he said curtly. "You've been exhausting us all recently. At the very least, I want to know what's bothering you."

"I'm sorry," my father said, smiling in pale bitterness. "I'm very sorry I've exhausted you. I don't have the right. How dare I exhaust you? How could I? A donkey like me doesn't have the right to make anyone tired. Everyone has the right to ride him without him saying a word or braying."

"What are you saying, Ahmed?" my uncle said, looking at my father as if he was examining someone crazy.

"I want to know why you came here now!" my father said, raising his voice. "Why did you choose this moment to come to the farm? It's been twenty years since you set foot here."

I thought my father was about to reach out and choke his brother. I saw his face just as it was when he read my poisoned letter. Terrifying and strange. His lips pursed as if hiding from his face. His nostrils flared as if spitting fire. His eyes bulged as if the hand of hatred and malice were squeezing his neck. His eyebrows knotted as if the flesh of his face had come loose from his skull. At that moment, he seemed like someone dangerous and crazy, someone capable of anything.

"We came, Daddy, because we were afraid for you," I found myself saying as if asking for help. "Auntie Safi said you were sick."

"Be quiet, you!" my father screamed at me, perhaps for the first time in his life. "This has nothing to do with you!"

A moment of silence passed.

"Safiya said I was sick?" my father continued. "Of course, I have to be sick. The sucker, when he opens his eyes, has to be sick!"

"I don't understand anything," my uncle said. "What are you saying?"

"You'll understand soon enough," my father replied scornfully. "You'll understand soon enough that your brother isn't a sucker!"

At that moment, Umm Atiya, the old peasant my grandfather had left to take care of his estate, came out to the balcony. She rushed over and stood staring at me in surprise.

"Miss Nadia!" she said with simple pleasure. "How wonderful! Your presence is an honor to the farm and everyone here." She put her hand over her mouth and let out a weak trill of joy, as much as her lungs would allow. "This brings us happiness and much to celebrate, Miss Nadia," she said. "How wonderful!"

She tried to embrace me, but I stepped back. I let her scaly, dry hand take my hand. I tried to yank it away quickly, but she squeezed it and leaned over to kiss it.

"Get going, woman!" my father yelled at her. "I can't bear your nonsense right now."

"Mr. Ahmed, you won't let us celebrate our bride?" she asked, letting go of my hand and standing up straight. "How beautiful she is! She's the image of my mistress, may God have mercy on her soul. Where have you gone, my mistress?"

"How are you, Umm Atiya?" I asked coldly. "I missed you."

"I missed you more, my dear," she said, kissing me with her eyes in delight and veneration. "Let's celebrate and open a bottle of sherbet!"

"That's enough, woman!" My father cut her off. "Get going."

"Oh," she said as if chastising him. "Why have you changed so much, Mr. Ahmed, sir? Why don't you pray and calm yourself down?"

She turned around to kiss my uncle's hand, and then started to go.

"Where's my wife?" my father asked, following her.

"I saw her in the mistress's bedroom," she said on her way.

"Go call her," my father ordered.

My father went inside the house and we walked silently behind him in a sad procession. As soon as we reached the middle of the big parlor, which was lined with Istanbuli couches with old white covers like shrouds containing the remains of our ancestors, Auntie Safiya appeared.

She looked like she'd lost half her body weight in the few hours since she'd left the house that morning. She looked pale and breathed in a broken rhythm, her eyes confused. I thought she was resisting violently, so she didn't collapse, so she didn't go out of her mind.

She stood opposite us and looked at Uncle Aziz as if his presence were a source of relief. She muttered a quick hello that I couldn't make out, and then nodded her head. I noticed my father move his eyes between her and my uncle as if he was trying to catch every gesture, every hint between them.

Auntie Safi got close to me and took my hands in hers. She looked at me for a moment with sad, cowering looks as if thanking me for coming. She then pulled me to her chest and embraced me.

I felt like my heart was being ripped out.

I felt like I was going to cry.

But the tears clustered in the corners of my eyes were blocked until they became like grains of burning sand.

In that brief moment when I rested in her arms, I thought I could no longer bear it. I thought the good inside me would be victorious over the evil. I thought the angel would be victorious over the devil.

But this fleeting moment passed without me collapsing, without me screaming out a confession of my crime and washing their feet with my tears.

I didn't want that moment to end. I was hoping to spend my entire life pressed against her chest, to feel her tenderness, to feel my importance in her life and her heart, to feel that I was a human being.

But that moment passed.

I felt her kiss my cheeks. Then she moved me gently away from her chest.

"What brought you here?" she asked, turning to my uncle with a weak smile still on her lips. "This is a lovely surprise!"

My uncle didn't respond.

"His excellency came to check on me," my father said. "Because when I go to the farm it means I've gone crazy or I'm sick. My brother had to check on me. Right, Aziz?"

My uncle smacked his palms together in frustration.

"*There is no power and no strength save in God*," he said, throwing himself down on one of the couches. "I was right to come."

"How's that?" my father asked mockingly. "How could you leave me alone? And leave Safiya alone?"

We were all quiet.

"The prophet said, 'Fear the anger of the mild one,'" my father continued, looking at each of us as if delivering a lecture. "But the mild one still isn't angry. Not yet. There's still a little time."

My uncle sat up straight.

"Listen," he said as if trying to be logical. "You know I've never intervened in your affairs. You know I've always liked you, and I trust you and care about you. If today I try to ask what's wrong, it's because you've changed. If you don't believe me, ask Safiya or your daughter."

Auntie Safiya didn't speak.

"It's true, Daddy," I said in a low voice. "You've got to go to the doctor."

My father turned quickly to me, but then looked like he'd decided he should keep me out of it. He stared at my uncle.

"If you're so sure I've changed," he said furiously, "you have to know what it was that changed me."

"That's what's confusing me," my uncle said sincerely. "May God have mercy on our mother and father. I don't know or understand anything. If I knew, I would have helped you long ago or let you do whatever the hell you wanted. You're driving me crazy."

My father gave a nasty smile. "You'll know soon enough," he said and then he walked off.

My father went to his room, which was on the right side of the big parlor. Propelled by an unknown force, I found myself following him inside.

My father sat on a big chair. He lifted his head and saw me come in behind him.

"Come here, Nadia," he said in a tender voice as if seeking refuge in me from his grief.

I closed the door and went over to him. He pulled me by the hand and sat me down on his lap. Wrapping his arm around me, he gave me a hesitant glance, as if he was thinking about revealing his secret to me. Then, as if he'd decided not to, he lowered his head.

"I'm tired, Nadia," he said in a low voice.

I felt as if something was being torn up in my chest.

"You're the one who doesn't want to rest, Daddy," I said, leaning my head on his shoulder. "Get rid of the worry of the farm, the worry of everything. Since the day they took four hundred acres from us in the agricultural reform, you've been anxious and tired."

It was a huge lie.

"I wish it were only the acres," my father said miserably. "They took it all, my dear, but . . . but . . ." He didn't finish.

"Your exhaustion is making me tired too, Daddy."

"I know, Nadia. I know everything. Everything will be straightened out and go back to how it was. May God help me with the rest."

He tried to smile.

"As long as you're mine, nothing else matters," he said. "Everything else can go to hell."

"At least it's taken some of the burden away from you," I said, as if I meant the confiscated land.

I got up from his lap.

"I'm going to wash my face after the trip," I said.

I opened the door and looked out, then slammed it suddenly.

I'd seen Auntie Safiya and Uncle Aziz sitting close to each other on the couch, my uncle holding her hand and talking to her as if he was comforting her.

It was natural for my uncle to hold the hand of his brother's wife in this condition and console her. I don't know what pushed me to slam the door so suddenly that it would stir up his suspicions, as if I'd seen a horrible scene that I wanted to cover up.

The evil spirit was controlling me and ruling all of my actions. My father noticed what I'd done. "What?" he said, jumping up. "What is it?"

I stammered. It was a real stammer because I didn't know what to say. "It's just . . . I—" I said hesitatingly. "It's just I—I forgot to ask when we'll ride horses. . . ."

My father didn't respond. He stormed toward the door.

"Aren't my horses still here?" I asked as if screaming to stop him from committing a crime.

My father didn't respond. He opened the door as if breaking it and went out to the parlor.

My uncle had dropped Auntie Safiya's hand, but they were still sitting close to each other.

My father stood opposite them, looking at him and then at her.

"I think it's better if we go back to Cairo," he said.

We all looked surprised.

"Because the house here isn't big enough for us all," my father continued, staring at his brother. He let out a loud laugh as if he'd gone crazy.

"Isn't it better to wait until morning?" my uncle asked calmly. "It's getting dark and driving at night is dangerous."

"I'm going to Cairo now," my father said, looking at him as if he despised him. "If you would, sir, with your permission I'll take my wife and daughter with me."

"What do you think, Safiya?" he said, turning to her.

She got up without a word and went to her room to get her bag ready.

"Don't bother yourself, Aziz," my father said. "Or are you unable to stay alone, either here or in Cairo?"

"What's important is that I'm somewhere I can talk to you," my uncle said, remaining calm and dignified.

"No!" my father snapped. "It's not necessary to talk. Don't bother."

My father went into the bedroom and came back wearing his coat. After a bit, his wife followed him dressed to leave, holding her small bag.

"Could you take my bag, please?" she said, approaching my father as if deciding neither to submit to him nor to challenge him.

My father looked at her for a moment and then took the bag from her.

Before we left, Umm Atiya came out with a tray of glasses of red sherbet.

"Take one, sir," she said with her sweet smile, presenting it to my father. "Calm yourself. The visit of Miss Nadia is so nice."

"Get lost, old woman!" my father yelled as he shoved her arm away. "Is this the time for that?"

His hand slammed down on the tray and it fell from Umm Atiya's hands. The glasses smashed to the ground and the red liquid ran everywhere.

We went out to the garden without knowing if my uncle would come back with us. We didn't say goodbye. We didn't say a word. Auntie Safiya and I rode in my father's car. His wife sat next to him with an angry look in her eyes, as if she'd shaken off her weakness and submission. I rode in the back, looking at their heads as if watching a movie in which what would happen next was obvious and I knew everything they were thinking.

We drove off.

As soon as we went through the garden gate, we heard the sound of my uncle's car behind us.

We all went back to our house in Dokki.

13

THE ENTIRE HOUSE WAS COVERED by black doubt, pale jealousy, hatred and malice, tension and insomnia. We were living on pins and needles, broken, exhausted, like crazy people, like a group lost in a dark desert. We started to collide with each other as we looked for light and salvation.

My father's wife decided to challenge my father. She no longer submitted or kept quiet. She no longer just bore his anxiety. If she didn't like what he said, she'd scream in his face. If he was quiet, she'd pretend to ignore him. If he issued an order, she didn't obey. The situation overwhelmed her. She was like a pressure cooker full of steam that she'd kept in for too long, and she was bound to explode. She revolted against the suffering inflicted by my father—suffering that she didn't understand and he didn't explain.

My uncle's joyful spirit disappeared. He was silent and miserable, as if he'd lost everything. He no longer tried to find out what was upsetting my father. He didn't even talk to him anymore. If they met, they only exchanged a quick, meaningless hello, neither of them hearing it from the other. Many times, my uncle excused himself from eating lunch with us. Other times, we didn't even see him before he left. It seemed that all that kept him in the same house with us was his affection for Auntie Safiya, his love for me, and a residue of feeling for his brother.

My father was the most miserable of all. He wasted away and dried out like a piece of wood. He always seemed like he wanted to smash something or cry. He sometimes controlled his nerves, appearing cold and frozen like he was made of stone. Other times, his burden oppressed him and he screamed and lashed out with sharp words like a whip. He seemed always to be operating according to a plan he had in his head—a naive plan, like something concocted by a child. It amounted to nothing more than keeping a close watch over his wife and surprising her from time to time. He was trying to catch her in his brother's arms. He'd come home at unusual times and tiptoe into the house. He'd pretend to be on the phone but it would be clear there was no one on the other end and he was just observing her. When she'd leave to visit someone or run errands, he'd follow at a distance.

I remained the same as I was, except that the crime started speeding up my plan, like a horse race approaching the end. And as the finish line got near, my torture became even more severe—the torture of my conscience. I'd listen to the whistling of the storm, waiting for it to uproot the house.

I committed dozens of little crimes to stoke the fires of doubt inside my father. Every day, I'd throw a piece of wood on the fire. I didn't have any mercy on him, not for a single day. Not on his downcast eyes, not on his body wasting away, not on his face becoming pale and thin—none of that could stop me or save me.

I knew that my father, by monitoring his wife, was looking for tangible proof with which to convict her, something that he saw with his eyes or touched with his hand. All I cared about was providing that for him.

Until one day . . .

My father, Auntie Safiya, and I finished lunch silently, as if it were our last supper. Auntie Safiya got up and went into her room. She came back after a bit, dressed to go out, holding her small handbag.

"I'm going to the tailor," she said to my father as if giving him a formal report.

My father didn't respond.

She left without waiting for a reply.

A few minutes later, my father got up and left to follow her, to keep tabs on her, to be sure that she really was going to the tailor.

I got up to say goodbye to him at the door, as Auntie Safiya usually did.

"I'm going to have coffee at the club," he said, placing a cold kiss on my cheek. He said it as if suppressing an accusation that no one had made.

After he left, I wandered among the flowers in the garden, as if looking for a poisonous bloom. I saw my uncle leaving without having lunch with us once again. And suddenly, I had an idea. An idea that, if it succeeded, would bring about the end. It was a small idea but it would be the straw that broke the camel's back, and the camel bearing the load was my father.

I gave a big smile to my uncle and ran over to him. I clung to his neck and started kissing him dozens of times on his face.

My uncle embraced me and kissed me back.

During that time, he went to great lengths to spoil me and show his affection for me, as if he was consoling me for the pain my father was inflicting.

"Where's your father?" he asked, still embracing me.

"He left," I responded. "He went to the club. Auntie Safiya went out too. There's no one here but me."

"That's better!" he said, letting out a laugh, trying to hide his pain.

"I need to go out too," I said, "but I have a friend who's coming to visit."

"What do you need? I'll get it for you or have it delivered."

"That would be great. You'd be doing me a big favor. May God preserve you!"

"What is it?" he asked, smiling. "What do you want?"

"I want you to go to the tailor and tell her to send me my dress by five o'clock."

"No." He cut me off, moving me away from him gently. "Anything but the tailor. I've never gone to a women's tailor before."

"Please, Uncle. Please! I have an invitation for tonight and I've worn all the dresses I have a hundred times. Please, do it for me!"

"Why don't you just call her?"

"Her telephone doesn't work. I've been trying to call since this morning and it's no use. I even called the operator and it's still no use."

"Where did the driver go?"

"He went with Auntie Safiya."

"But it doesn't make sense for me to go into the tailor."

"You don't have to go in at all," I said quickly. "All you have to do is tell her from the door, and when she sees that you've come yourself, she'll take care of it quickly."

"You always have a lot of requests, Nadia," he grumbled. "And they're all ridiculous. Where's this tailor, my dear?"

"You know the Doss Building that's near Café À L'Américaine? That's it."

"Fine," he said, getting ready to leave from the garden gate. "But why didn't you ask Safiya or your father to do this for you when they were leaving?"

"I was still thinking I'd get her on the phone," I said, kissing him affectionately.

"Fine, my dear," he said and left, shaking his head submissively.

"The sixth floor," I said, joining him at the gate. "Her name is Madame Bruna."

He shook his head again to signal that he'd heard me. He then got in his car and left. I watched until his car disappeared, my eyes wide and my heart pounding.

The tailor was in a big building like the one with Mustafa's apartment, a building with doctors, lawyers, tailors and, no doubt, "apartments" like Mustafa's.

At that moment, I knew, my father was standing at the door of the building, keeping tabs on his wife as she was going in, hiding until she left.

I wanted him to see my uncle go into the same building, to make him believe that he was meeting his wife.

Could I provide better proof than that?

Was there a crime simpler than that?

But would my father see him going into the building?

Maybe my uncle would go in from the other side.

Maybe my father was content with checking to see that his wife went into the building with the tailor and left without waiting for her to leave?

Maybe my uncle wouldn't go to the tailor at all and would break his promise to me.

The feeling of the gambler began to overwhelm me, the feeling I'd gotten used to whenever I moved forward in one of my schemes, the horrible feeling in which the pleasure of fear broke out, the pleasure of anticipation, the pleasure of testing my intelligence.

A long time passed—a very long time—as I was in the throes of this wicked, delicious feeling.

I stared into space as if looking at the wheel of fate spinning in heaven, the wheel of this black fate.

I came to at the sound of a car stopping at the gate.

I saw my father come into the house, taking steps so wide and tense that he almost fell on his face.

He didn't notice me as I was sitting in the parlor. Instead, he went straight to his room.

I followed him.

I saw him like a crazy person, opening his wife's dresser and pulling her clothes from it, one after the other, tossing them on the ground.

I knew my plan had succeeded.

But I wasn't happy.

No, I wasn't happy.

The feeling of the gambler left me and terror took its place. I felt a terrifying fear that almost tore out my heart.

"What are you doing, Daddy?" I cried out, reaching up as if I were feeling my way through the darkness of myself.

He turned his head and looked at me with maniacal eyes that seemed not to see me or even know who I was.

"This has nothing to do with you," he said in a rattling voice. "You get out of here!"

"Tell me, Daddy," I pleaded, trying to get close to him. "What happened? Why are you acting like this?"

He pushed me so hard that I almost fell to the ground.

"I'm telling you to get out of here!" he shouted. "Get out of this room!"

I left, stumbling, leaning against the walls. I felt that everything in me was screaming, crying, breaking down. I found myself thinking seriously about aborting my plan before it was completed.

What was I doing?

Oh God, what was I doing?

Forgive me. Forgive me, Lord. Save me from myself. Save my father from me!

What was I doing, Lord?

I started moving my eyes along the walls in terror, as if I were afraid they'd close in on me. I lifted my arms up as if protecting myself from a fire blowing onto me.

I started thinking quickly, with the quickness of an insane person. A voice in my chest was repeating a monotonous refrain, round and round like the wheels of a train: what was I doing? What was I doing? What was I doing?

But I didn't do anything.

I couldn't.

I was suddenly struck with a stupor, as if evil Satan, when he set out from my chest, had taken my mind with him.

Another car stopped in front of the gate.

I saw my father's wife come in slowly and firmly, not knowing anything about what was awaiting her.

"Bonsoir," I heard her say.

I didn't respond. I looked at her with pity, my eyes bathed in tears as if she were a chicken about to be slaughtered in front of me. At that moment, I wanted to bow down to her feet and kiss them, begging for forgiveness, imploring her to pardon me.

"What's wrong?" I heard her say anxiously. "What's wrong, Nadia?"

Before I could respond, my father turned his back stiffly to us like an angry rebel who'd decided to destroy the entire world.

"Go collect your clothes," he said, his voice was a mere echo from a miserable unknown world. "Go back to where you came from."

Auntie Safiya was perplexed. "What are you saying?" she asked in amazement, as if she were addressing someone crazy.

My father took a deep breath as if trying to get control of himself.

"Listen, Safiya," he said in a trembling voice, trying to stay calm, "I don't want a scandal. No scandals. What's happened is enough. Get out of the house! This house isn't yours anymore. Since the days of my grandfather, this has always been an upstanding house and only decent people have lived here."

"What are you saying? What are you saying, Ahmed? Have you gone mad?"

My father couldn't take it anymore.

"I'm saying that I'm divorcing you!" he screamed with everything he had. "You're divorced, divorced, divorced! I'm saying that you're a cheater! A criminal!"

Auntie Safiya backed up as if she'd been stabbed in the heart. She leaned on the small table to stop herself from falling.

"You're crazy," she whispered with a terrifying look. "You're crazy! Crazy!"

"I was crazy the day I married you!" my father screamed again. "I was duped about you and your family. A family whose origin is slime. Only now have I come to know you. Only now do I know. I've given my honor and name to someone who doesn't deserve it. You're divorced—divorced three times. The official is on his way. I sent for him so he can divorce us and you can go to hell, you and the despicable dog who betrayed his blood, my good nature, and the honor of my mother and father!"

Auntie Safiya straightened and raised her head. She looked at my father in disgust. "I won't respond to you," she said as if collecting her entire life in a single moment with which to protect her dignity. "I'm leaving. I'm not picking up my clothes. I'll leave that to you. You can be sure that as soon as I step foot outside this door, I won't be coming back. All I want to say is that you have to see a doctor!"

She grabbed her small bag and walked toward the door.

I found myself unconsciously rushing to her and clinging to her. "No! No!" I screamed. "Impossible. No, Auntie! Don't leave!" I looked at my father with tears in my eyes. "Auntie Safiya isn't a traitor, Daddy!" I yelled, my whole body shaking. "Auntie Safiya is innocent. I—"

"Silence!" my father screamed, cutting me off.

"She's innocent, Daddy!" I said. "Auntie Safiya is innocent and—"

"I know why you're defending her." He cut me off, still screaming. "She's blinded the entire house. She's blinded my brother and my daughter. She's a criminal, and you know she's been cheating on me, betraying me with the closest person in the world to me. You know, and I know you know. Today I saw it with my own eyes. I saw them both!"

I threw myself on my father.

"Don't believe me, Daddy!" I said between sobs, wetting his chest with my tears. "I'm a liar. I'm the criminal. Your daughter is the criminal. I—"

"She's nothing compared to you!" My father cut me off, shouting until he lost his voice. "You're worth ten of her. *She's* the criminal. *She's* the traitor. This is the fate of cheating criminals. Look! Look at her! Look at her face that spites our Lord. She'll be tormented. All her life, she'll be tormented. Our Lord will make sure of it."

He turned to her. "Go. Get out of here! Get out of my house!" Safiya turned her head away in disgust and walked toward the door silently, still preserving her pride. As soon as she opened the door, the divorce official appeared.

She looked at him, at his black beard, pale face, and dark cloak, as if she saw my crime as a snake slithering on two feet.

I felt a gloomy darkness surround me. It got closer and closer until I could no longer see a thing.

I felt myself collapse on the ground.

I don't know how long I was passed out for. But when I opened my eyes, I found myself spread out on my bed. Auntie Safiya was sitting next to me on the side of the bed with a bottle of cologne in her hand.

As soon as my eyes met hers, I tried to smile. I felt as if I had woken up from a heavy, terrifying nightmare. I sat up and wrapped my arms around her neck. I tried to talk, but she put her finger on my lips. I took my arms from around her neck.

"Thank God you're awake," she said with a sad smile.

She eased me back down on the bed and leaned over to kiss me. Her kisses were wet with tears. Then she got up.

"Stay and rest, Nadia," she said, leaving the room.

"Auntie! Auntie! Don't leave me, Auntie!" I screamed.

She didn't respond.

I tried to follow her, but darkness enveloped me again. I saw the walls of the room encircle me as if a vortex were swallowing me up.

*

Things moved quickly after that, faster than I could follow or contemplate, as if all the devils had gathered in our house to take it to another world—to hell.

My fainting was real. There was no fabrication or acting. The ugliness of my crime had overwhelmed me until I could no longer bear myself. The intensity of the crime had become greater than I could handle.

But this didn't prevent my father from moving forward with the divorce proceedings, without any more thought, without more questions and doubt. When I collapsed the first time, as Nanny Halima later told me, my father didn't even notice. He didn't try to help me. He looked at me disinterestedly, as if a cup or a flowerpot had fallen on the ground. He left me there and took the divorce official into the study to sign the repulsive document.

The one who helped me was Auntie Safiya. She carried me in her arms, with love and tenderness, despite everything that was happening to her. She put me in my bed. She sat next to me until I came to. And then she kissed me and left the house.

My father finalized the divorce there and then and had the driver deliver the papers to Auntie Safiya at her family's house.

Then he came to my room. He stood distracted, staring through the window while Nanny Halima was dabbing me with cologne until I opened my eyes. No doubt my face was dreadfully pale. My father looked at me in terror and pity. He came to sit next to me and took my hands in his.

"Shame on you, Nadia," he said as if he was crying. "Don't do that to yourself. There's nothing that should make you so upset. Shame on you. I don't have anyone but you. Nothing matters but you!"

I looked at him.

He looked like he'd grown old, like he wanted to put his head on my chest and cry. Everything about him was limp. His eyelids hung loosely on his eyes, his lips on his jaw, his cheeks on his cheekbones, every part of his face appeared weighed down by the weight of his worry.

I tried to get up, but I couldn't. I felt weaker than I ever had.

"You made a mistake, Daddy," I said in a soft, weak voice, putting my head back on the pillow. "A big mistake. Auntie Safi didn't betray you."

"That's enough, Nadia." He cut me off as if driving away a ghost from in front of him. "It's over. Be sure I wasn't wrong. I didn't believe it at first, but I kept watching her until I was sure. I know you love her. I used to love her too, but I have to sacrifice my love to preserve my honor."

I tried to speak, but he got up, rearranged the blanket around me, and kissed me.

"Relax, my love," he said tenderly. "Try to sleep a little."

He left. I didn't know where he went.

I didn't sleep.

I stayed in bed, broken, weak—extremely weak, as if I'd lost control of my body, as if my blood was abandoning me and spilling out of my pores. My tears flowed in a sad silence as if they were clearing a path on my cheeks for the torture to come.

This weakness came with a horrible pain, a terrifying pain. It started getting more and more severe. It began on my side and then encircled my body until it reached my fingers.

I welcomed the pain.

I found solace in it.

I kept submitting to the weakness and pain until I heard my father come back in the evening. Maybe he was drunk. He walked around the house loudly, without coming in my room to check on me.

Then I heard the doorbell.

Was it my uncle?

Yes, it was him. I heard his voice as he was talking to my father in the parlor. The conversation between them became so tense that they were almost screaming. I could only make out random words, all of them harsh and nasty.

I then heard the sound of the door slamming.

My uncle had left.

Afterward, I heard my father's steps as he came up to his room—slow, tired steps, as he dragged his feet. I then heard the sound of weak, suppressed sobs.

My father was crying.

I felt my entire body freeze. My blood flowed sluggishly through my veins like sand. Despite that, I tried to get out of bed to go to my father.

My father was the one crying.

I suddenly let out a sharp scream. I lay face down, contracting every muscle in my body, gripping the pillow.

I screamed again.

Then I bit the pillow so I couldn't scream.

I felt as if a red-hot skewer had plunged into my side.

It was pain that I couldn't submit to or bear.

My father came at the sound of my scream, tears still in his eyes.

"What's wrong?" he asked anxiously. "What's wrong, Nadia?"

"Nothing," I said through my teeth, my face still pressed against the pillow. "Nothing. This is Auntie Safi's fault!"

I lifted my head and my father saw my contorted face and how much pain I was suffering. He called the doctor.

The doctor diagnosed me with a severe case of renal colic, and gave me an injection of morphine.

I got up in the morning, my head heavy and tired from the morphine.

I still had some hope that I'd find a way to atone for my crime, to bring my father's wife back to the house. But my uncle unintentionally put an end to that hope. The next day, he announced that he'd marry Auntie Safiya, and he actually went to propose to her at her family's house.

Maybe he did that because of his resentment of my father. Maybe he was convinced that Safiya was innocent and had been treated unfairly. Maybe he did it as a sign of gallantry after my father accused him of having a sinful relationship with her.

But my father took this as more evidence of his wife's betrayal.

I believe my uncle went to propose to Safiya to fix his mistake . . . or maybe he was always hoping to marry her.

Of course, Safiya refused to consider it, even after the legally mandated period of waiting after divorce.

She refused completely and categorically.

My uncle left the house. He didn't live with us anymore. He went to live in a hotel. He cut off his relationship with my father and started liquidating the accounts of the farm so that each of them managed his share independently.

The story spread through our social circles—the story of my father's wife cheating on him with my uncle.

Delegations of family, friends, and acquaintances started coming over on the pretext of checking on me and my illness. But they were all hiding their delight at our misery, and suppressing a desire to hear more juicy details.

I was still sick. What made it worse was that everyone thought that I was sick out of love for Auntie Safiya and grieving her divorce from my father. Everyone thought I was an innocent, naive angel who couldn't bear the sight of sin so I fell ill.

"She's going to kill herself because of it!" I'd hear them say.

Or: "It's as if Safiya bewitched her. The girl hasn't been able to get out of bed since the day of the divorce."

I was at the point of screaming at them, telling them that they were all idiots, that they didn't know . . . they didn't know that I was a criminal, that I was the killer.

Part Two

14

I ASK YOU AGAIN.

What pushes the toddler to destroy a doll and then cry about it?

What pushes the boy to climb a tree to tear up a nest and torture the birds inside, and then burst into tears when the birds die?

What is the secret of this unknown strength that controls people their whole lives?

What are people?

And me . . . what am I?

Why was I born to this father? Why did I find myself in that house? Why did I destroy the beautiful doll? And why did I cry after I destroyed it?

Let the psychologists say what they want. Let them search in the human psyche and write dozens of books. But me? What was my crime?

What was my crime from within this complicated psyche that I found inside me?

If I was born a criminal, why is my criminality torturing me?

If I'm tortured by my criminality, why do I commit crimes?

Oh Lord.

Take me.

Take me so I can ask why.

Take me so I can ask about Your great wisdom in torturing me.

Take me, or put an end to the torture so I can rest.

But I'm afraid of You. I fear You. I'm terrified of You. I fear Your power and I fear Your wisdom. I fear Your revenge.

Yes, God must punish me, since this is His way. This is His wisdom.

It's His wisdom to inflict the killer on his victim and then punish the killer. To inflict some of His creation on others and then take the perpetrator and the person harmed to task. Both of them are His slaves, His creation, the work of His hands.

I've become an infidel!

No. No, Lord, I haven't lost faith in You. You're my firm faith, but my mind is oppressed trying to understand You, and it's weakened by the secret of Your wisdom.

I ask God the Great for forgiveness! I ask God the Great for forgiveness! I ask God the Great for forgiveness! I ask for Your forgiveness, and I ask You to be kind to me. I ask You to have pity on me in Your punishment.

I was overwhelmed by a strong feeling that God was punishing me.

Whenever I was hit by a sharp pain during my illness, I began to think it was divine justice. I'd clench my teeth as if chewing on the pain, repeating to myself, "This is for my crime against Auntie Safiya." Even when small things happened, I thought they were God's punishment for "Auntie Safiya's crime." When a bottle of perfume spilled or a glass broke or I lost something or the price of cotton dropped, all those things were God's revenge for what I did to Auntie Safiya.

I spent two months in bed, until I regained my strength and my illness abated.

In the eyes of the people who knew me, I spent those two months as a weak, pure, innocent angel who couldn't take the blow and couldn't bear to live in the same house with sin. It had made me ill.

Auntie Safiya called Nanny Halima from time to time to check on me. She'd ask about what the doctor said, what I ate, and when I took my medicine. She'd asked her questions warmly and precisely, as if she was still living with us and still responsible for me.

She called once when I was on the way to recovery. I heard Nanny Halima talking with her. I thought I could hear her voice too, like an echo in a crystal glass. I felt an urgent desire to talk to her, to embrace her clear voice with my ears, but I hesitated. I felt as if my ears didn't have the right to embrace her voice. Up to that point, I hadn't talked to her because of how unwell I had been. I'd hear her voice only in my imagination, and I'd get what she said from Nanny Halima.

I had an incredible desire to hear her voice.

I was like the criminal who wants to hear the voice of her victim, to be reassured that she has survived.

I rang the bell next to my bed.

"Nanny! Nanny!" I called out in a weak voice. "Bring me the phone."

"Please wait a moment, ma'am," I heard Nanny Halima say. "Miss Nadia will speak with you."

A moment of silence passed.

"Yes, ma'am," I heard Nanny Halima say. "May God preserve you and prescribe peace in every step you take."

She hung up.

"Madame Safiya says hello," she came and told me with a sad smile. "She says, 'Thank God you're feeling better.' She couldn't talk because she was in a rush. She'll call you later."

I knew she didn't want to talk to me.

She didn't want to let me hear her voice or hear mine.

I wasn't angry. I didn't get upset. I didn't feel like I'd been insulted. I didn't even think about the reason she gave to avoid talking to me. Maybe she didn't want to continue a relationship with me after the divorce. Maybe she was afraid I'd construe her talking to me as courting my father, as her trying to get back in the house. Maybe anything. But I didn't dwell on her motives. Instead, I had a deep feeling that it was her right to refuse to talk with me. It was her right to insult me and for me to submit happily and silently to this insult.

After that, Auntie Safiya didn't call, as if she was satisfied that she'd checked on my health and could now disappear far away, very far, to a place where I couldn't find her or set eyes on her.

Weeks passed before I had the courage to call her, before I convinced myself that I had to thank her for her concern.

I heard her tender voice on the phone—the voice I'd lost forever. I felt that I was weaker than this voice—too weak to face it or catch it or respond to it. I felt as if the tender voice was swallowing me up and dissolving me in its folds until I could no longer find myself.

"Auntie, how are you?" I made a big effort to say in a cheery voice.

"How are you, Nadia?" she said calmly. "How's your health now?"

Like a shy child, I responded, "I missed you, Auntie."

It seemed like happiness had abandoned her, or that she was making a big effort to hide it.

"Take care of yourself, Nadia," I heard her say in a cold voice, like it was coming through the cracks in an iceberg. "Do what the doctor says. Renal colic is terrible and needs attention."

"I don't care about my health," I said as if apologizing for something she didn't know about. "All I care about is that you come back home. Without you, the house is worthless. It's empty, with no feeling. Please, Auntie!"

"Merci, my dear," she said, cutting me off, her voice becoming colder and more rigid. "I have to go. Au revoir."

I didn't believe her.

"Au revoir," I said miserably.

I didn't try to talk to her on the phone after that.

I was sure there was no hope to atone for my crime by bringing her back to the house, back to my father.

Auntie Safi was lost.

The ideal wife who shone light on my father's life until I extinguished it with my own hands was lost.

She was lost.

I was the one who ruined her.

I was the one who destroyed the doll.

I sat crying out of grief for her.

During my illness, my uncle also checked on me by phone. If my father picked up, he'd hang up without saying a word. If Nanny Halima answered, he'd question her at length. When I was on the way to recovery, I began talking with him. He always avoided talking about what happened. But I pressed him. I wanted him to tell me the details, about everything that happened between him and my father, everything that happened between him and Auntie Safiya. I wanted him to confirm that he was going to marry her after my father divorced her, as if I wanted to convince myself that what I'd done wasn't a crime and that Safiya would replace my father with my uncle.

I would have been happy if my uncle had married Auntie Safiya, just as he tried. My conscience would have been relieved.

But my uncle avoided talking about any of it. He avoided my questions and his evasion only increased my torture. He slammed in my face all the doors through which I could relieve the burden of what I'd done that weighed on me so heavily.

I begged him to come to the house so I could see him. I pleaded. I insisted. I tried to squeeze my tears down the phone to him, but he refused and kept refusing.

"Soon, when you recover and get out of bed," he'd tell me, trying to seem funny and happy as usual. "I'll make a rendezvous with you and we'll meet like lovers!"

I let out a bitter, miserable laugh.

My mother would come visit me.

She'd come with her husband as if she were on an official courtesy visit. She'd inform us when she was coming so my father could leave the house, so they didn't see each other. She'd sit right next to me, but I felt that she was far away. She'd smile, but it wasn't from the heart. She'd talk, but I felt that she was talking to someone other than me. She didn't understand me. She didn't try to know my true self in order to understand me. For her, I was a sick dear friend, and she had a duty to visit me and check on my health. She'd come to cheer me up, to tell me the news from our social circles and the plots of the latest movies.

That was my mother.

That was her simple nature. She didn't take anything seriously. She was a pampered, dreamy, happy person who looks at the entire world through her own simple, indifferent way of life.

I loved her.

But could I confess to her?

Could I tell her the details of my crime and then throw myself in her arms and cry—cry until I emptied all my tears on her tender chest and then ask her to show me the way to atonement?

Never.

She wouldn't understand.

She wouldn't believe me.

I could imagine the confused, hesitant look that would come into her eyes when she heard my story.

"What you're saying is not possible," I imagined her telling me. "It's not possible. You didn't do that. I don't believe it. Your whole life you've had a wild imagination. Like Ingrid Bergman in *Gaslight*. It's the same idea—that she's a criminal. But she's not a criminal at all. It's her imagination."

That's what my mother would say if I confessed to her.

But I didn't.

We didn't even mention the divorce. My mother didn't ask about the details, unlike the other visitors, who were persistent in their questioning. She ignored the whole thing. It was a disgrace, a subject that should not pass across the lips of a respectable lady, or before a pure, innocent, virginal girl like me.

My mother would come to visit me.

But . . . nothing more.

Mustafa tried to call me too. My father would answer, and he'd hang up. Nanny Halima or the butler would answer, and he'd hang up. Then he'd give our agreed-upon sign when I was far from the telephone, which was to let it ring twice and then hang up before someone picked up, so I'd understand that he was waiting at home to talk to me.

But I didn't talk to him.

Even when I began to recover and I could have talked to him on the phone, I didn't.

I was thinking about him. I was thinking about him a lot. He was a part of my life that I couldn't forget as long as my heart was beating and my mind was functioning. But thinking about him took on a new aspect. It began logically and calmly, like a lawyer researching a complicated legal problem. I no longer devoted my emotions or caprices to him. Mustafa was no longer a drug that I was getting more and more addicted to. Instead, he became a man occupying my life. A man who couldn't move my emotions without moving my mind. It became clear that I used to love Mustafa irrationally, unconsciously, and I now felt that I'd woken up. It was as if the blow I suffered after committing my crime was like the electric shock they give patients to jolt them out of their insanity.

I woke up.

I started asking myself, "Is it true that I took revenge against Auntie out of jealousy over Mustafa?"

I couldn't answer this question.

I knew I'd be lying if I tried to tell myself that I did all of this for Mustafa.

Why couldn't it have been my father?

Yes. Why couldn't the real motive have been my love for my father and my jealousy over him? My father who was everything to me, and was captured by another woman.

I loved my father.

But did I love him to the point of committing this crime?

I couldn't find an answer for that either.

Could it simply have been an evil spirit that took control of me? Simply egotism. Or hatred. Or my feeling that I was weaker than Auntie Safiya. If she hadn't been perfect, if she hadn't crushed me with her personality, I wouldn't have taken revenge against her.

These questions inundated me as I thought about Mustafa. I was left with the firm belief that my love for Mustafa wasn't the motive, rather it was a piece of evidence that I used to convince myself to commit this crime.

But Mustafa had something else.

He was the only man I'd let take possession of my body.

Why did I let him?

Why did I give him my body?

Because I loved him.

Why didn't I resist this love and put limits on it, to protect my body? Why didn't I assert my willpower over myself so that I didn't give him anything prematurely, so that I didn't pluck the flower before it bloomed, before marriage?

I conjured up the exciting, violent days I spent with Mustafa—the days when I was melting in his arms, when I forgot myself in reckless adventures.

Was that love?

Do all girls do what I did?

No. Impossible.

It was something else.

Maybe it was "mischief." Maybe it was simply wanting to take my femininity in hand. Maybe it was me seeking to imitate or challenge my father's wife, or maybe it was me fleeing from something inside me.

Yes, I was fleeing from myself.

Yes, I was fleeing from crime to crime.

I felt ashamed as I pictured those days. Ashamed of myself. I felt humiliation and lowliness. I felt I couldn't bear myself. And I felt I'd remain obedient to Mustafa forever.

I gave him my entire arsenal, so how could I resist him?

He revealed my secret, my body, so how could I refuse him?

This body became his—his right. How could I pull it back from him?

I believed, during those days, that my body was my dignity, my pride. If I'd given my dignity and pride to Mustafa, I had to stay with him, to stay with my dignity and pride as a possession of Mustafa.

Finally I decided to call him.

I heard his voice for the first time in two months. He sounded the way he always did, slow and lazy, his words coming out like sighs.

"Nadia," he said when he heard my voice. "Where are you? Where have you been all this time?"

"I've been sick, Mustafa," I said with a weak smile on my lips as if recalling memories that had passed . . . distant memories that wouldn't return.

"I know you were sick. I heard about it. But you still could have talked to me on the phone."

"I could not, Mustafa," I said, defensively. "I was very sick. The doctor forbade me from talking on the phone. Daddy didn't let me have the phone in my room."

"How are you now?"

"Better, thank God."

"When will I see you?"

"Not yet, Mustafa," I said, in a pleading tone. "The doctor still isn't letting me get out of bed."

He was quiet for a bit.

"What happened to you?" he asked reluctantly.

I hated his question. I felt as if he had left me lying on the bed, as if he were leaving me behind for something else, for another woman. I wanted him to talk about his longing for me, his desire for me, his sleeplessness, his helplessness during the time I was sick. I wanted to seek refuge in his tenderness and love from my suffering, the suffering of my sick body, the suffering of my sick self. But the glass he brought me was empty, dry. There wasn't any tenderness or love in it.

So I ignored his question.

"And how are you, Mustafa?" I asked. "I missed you."

"May you never know any unpleasantness," he said, formulaically. "I've been worried about you—about the whole family. Really, no one could believe what happened."

"What happened?"

"I mean, the story of the divorce," he said. I heard in his voice a desire to hear all the details. "Your father, your uncle, and Madame Safiya. The story everyone is talking about."

"Don't believe people," I said sharply. "They're all liars. No one gets divorced without people making up a thousand and one rumors."

"But the divorce has to have a reason."

"There's no reason," I said, still furious. "There wasn't harmony. They couldn't live together. That's all that happened."

"You mean this story about your uncle isn't true?"

"No, not true," I said, almost screaming. "Lies, lies, lies!"

"Okay. Swear on it."

"I swear to God, lies!" I said forcefully.

"No, swear to me," he said coldly and conceitedly, as if I were a child he knew was very attached to him.

"I swear to you, Mustafa," I said. "Lies!"

"Have you ever lied to me before?"

"Never!" I said, my voice still raised.

He was quiet for a bit.

"I agree," he said at last.

"What did you say?" I asked in surprise.

"Safiya couldn't have done that. She doesn't seem like the kind of person who could do all those things."

I started quickly thinking about what Mustafa had said. He was intent on convincing himself of Safiya's innocence, intent on confirming that she hadn't had a relationship with my uncle. Why? Why was he so interested in her? What was her value to him? Why did he care if she had a relationship with my uncle or not?

I was surprised at myself.

I didn't feel jealous.

I wasn't jealous about Mustafa.

His interest in Safiya didn't stir me up, didn't mobilize the forces of evil inside me.

My pulse didn't race and my heart didn't pound. My blood didn't pump in my veins and my chest didn't tighten.

What had happened to me?

What had become of me?

I was shaken out of these thoughts by the sound of Mustafa's voice as he spoke nonchalantly and coldly, as if he was remembering something trivial he'd forgotten.

"What did the doctor tell you?"

"It's over," I said listlessly. "The crisis is over, thank God. I had colic in my kidneys. It's better now, but I have to stay in bed for three more days."

"You can call me, right?" he said, trying to show me some affection.

"Yes."

"Every day?"

"Every day, Mustafa."

"Every hour?" he asked, letting out a small laugh.

"No," I said, trying to laugh too. "Impossible. Maybe every two hours."

We had a moment of silence. It seemed an unknown hand was trying to separate us, but we feared this abrupt separation, as if we feared that the silence between us would last forever.

"Au revoir," I said hurriedly, before the distance between us grew even greater. "I have to take my medicine now."

"Au revoir," Mustafa said at the same moment, as if he'd been spared from the weight of a duty.

I buried my head in my pillow and plunged into myself once more, looking for the truth . . . my truth.

That was how my illness ended: I found no one who could help me justify my crime. My father, my mother, my uncle, Mustafa, Auntie Safiya—they were all strangers to me. None of them understood me. They all saw me as the weak, pure, innocent girl. They saw my innocent face like the face of a child, unpolluted by the crush of life. They didn't see my sick, oppressed, complicated self—the self in which the howl of wild beasts and the tweeting of sparrows were mixed, in which storms raged before being blown away by fresh air.

I found a doctor to treat my sick kidneys, but I didn't find a doctor to treat my psyche. I felt that I alone would bear the secret of my crime forever. The horrible secret, the secret eating me up, sucking my blood, tearing me up inside, dissolving my youth.

A secret that no one could help me with except God.

If God forgave me.

After a few days, I got out of bed.

I got up to find the house was all mine. I was its mistress, sitting on its throne. My father was all mine. I was the only one who bore his name. I was the only one he came home to.

As soon as I looked around, I saw the truth I'd been trying to ignore.

I saw the house that I'd regained had been demolished.

I saw that my father had come back to me a broken man.

I saw that when I toppled Auntie Safiya, I destroyed everything with her, even myself.

Yes, I'd been destroyed.

I was on the verge of turning nineteen, but I started feeling like I was forty, weighed down with worry, always miserable, always bored, always hopeless, always afraid, always feeling suffocated. I moved with slow steps as if I were afraid that with each step, the earth could split open under my feet and swallow me, afraid that my mind would move to commit another sin.

When I looked in the mirror I did not see the Nadia that I knew. This wasn't my face: the sunken eyes surrounded by dark rings as if the hand of the devil had stroked them; the faded cheeks, as if my blood couldn't reach them; the pursed lips that looked like they were suppressing pain; the knotted brow and the sharp look in my eyes. No, this wasn't my face.

I'd rush to put makeup on, trying to hide the blackness under my eyes, but I'd give up and throw it all down on the ground.

The defect wasn't on my face. It was inside me.

My psyche had become senile and decrepit.

I had become senile and decrepit before I was even nineteen.

Then the punishment began.

God's punishment.

15

My father became a different person.

He was no longer dignified, calm, responsible, or tender. He became miserable—an unbearable drunk who could not get enough to drink.

It didn't happen gradually but all of a sudden, as if, when his wife left the house, she took with her my father's mind, conscience, and will, leaving him an empty box, an empty body. There was nothing in him. You couldn't rely on him for anything.

The day after the divorce, my father left in the morning after checking on me and he came home very late for lunch, drunk, stumbling, slurring his words, his eyes unable to focus on anything.

He came to my room and stood at the door.

"How are you now?" he mumbled.

I looked at him in surprise and disapproval, without responding.

Ashamed at my look, he didn't say anything else. He turned and went to his room.

At that moment, I remembered that I'd become the mistress of the house, so I pressed the bell on the side of my bed to call Nanny Halima.

"Go tell Abdou to take lunch to Father," I said in a tone that had been absent for a long time. A tone that I tried to make commanding, despite my weakness.

"Master says he ate lunch out," Nanny Halima said when she returned.

From that day, throughout the time of my illness, my father would eat his lunch out. He'd insist on seeing me in the morning and waiting for the doctor when he called on the house. But other than that, he didn't insist on anything. I no longer saw him except at random times for just a few minutes. He was always drunk, making a great effort to hide his slurring and stumbling. A great effort that occupied all his thinking and all his will, so I saw none of what he used to give me—none of his tenderness.

He no longer took care of me as he did in my youth.

He no longer worried about my comfort.

He no longer sat beside me to talk to me about his problems.

He became a stranger—a stranger from me and the house.

When I recovered from my illness, I found myself alone. I'd even lost my father. His drinking made him too ashamed to face me, so he kept away, he disappeared. Whatever sense he had left that he was a father responsible for his daughter made him return home each day . . . or maybe it was just out of habit.

I was at a loss as to how to bring him back to me, to bring him back to his caring self.

I'd go into his room in the morning and find his clothes strewn on the ground. I'd find him sleeping, his face puffy, the stench of alcohol on his breath. I'd collect his clothes and set them in their place, open the windows, and go over to him to try to wake him up with my kisses, but it would take a long time. Even getting him to open his eyes was a struggle. As soon as he saw my face, he'd give me a wide smile and a tender kiss. Then, as if remembering his condition and misfortune, he'd withdraw his smile and his kiss would be cold and fleeting on my cheek. He'd turn his eyes away from me.

"I think I was out too late last night," he'd say apologetically.

Every morning, he'd repeat the same words until they no longer had any meaning, either on his tongue or in my ear.

I'd wait until he finished his morning shower—a silent shower, with no singing as before when his wife lived with us.

I'd then help him get dressed and sit with him during breakfast, which he always ate by himself, since he got up around noon. We didn't talk much during his breakfast. Just a few short questions and shorter answers. He'd finish his breakfast quickly and rush out as if he was fleeing something, as if he was fleeing me. I'd go out after him to say goodbye at the door, but he wouldn't turn back, as if he was afraid he'd find his wife following him, as she used to.

I was tortured in my loneliness.

It was tearing me up. I felt I was living in mourning, as if my clothes were black, my chest was black, my head was black . . . I was mourning myself.

I submitted to this torment, to this mourning. I was atoning for my crime, like a monk in the temple of fire, burning herself to be cleansed of her sins.

I sometimes tried to escape from it all.

But I didn't know where to hide.

I tried by supervising the servants. All of a sudden, I noticed that, without realizing it, I was imitating Auntie Safiya. I was imitating her smile and her liveliness, all of her traits. I'd even repeat the same words that she used to direct the cook and the butler.

The servants received my orders unenthusiastically. It seemed like they had mocking smiles on their lips, as if each of them was asking me: "What are you compared to her?"

When I noticed this, my misery and my feeling of mourning increased. I rushed to my room and threw myself down on the bed. I tried to summon my tears but they didn't come. They had run dry. I had already cried enough for an entire lifetime.

I sometimes tried to escape by calling some of the girls in my family, or by inviting them to visit me, but the conversation wouldn't last long and it wouldn't take long for their visits to become boring. It was like I was hearing them talk from a distance and could barely make out what they were saying. It felt like I was looking at their faces from a distance and that I barely knew them. I was so tormented by what I had done I could no longer see or hear clearly.

I talked with Mustafa on the phone, turning to him for comfort, pleading with him to give me some relief. But Mustafa was distant from me too. His words encircled me without entering my heart or head. He didn't know what was wrong with me, so how could he soothe me?

I refused to meet him. I don't know why. But I resisted and refused his repeated invitations. Maybe I was trying to atone for my crime by denying myself Mustafa. Maybe I wanted to confirm for myself that I could be a responsible mistress, responsible for the house and my father's trust. Maybe my suffering was stronger than my love and my desires. Maybe the forces driving me to meet Mustafa had gone.

What were those forces?

I didn't know.

But I no longer felt the need to meet him—that pressing, insane need pushing me to him.

I remained in the loneliness that my father would leave me in. Unable to sleep, I'd spend the night wandering the house like a sad ghost, or like the arms of a clock moving through the minutes and the hours. I'd drift from room to room, feeling like I was fleeing from Auntie Safiya chasing me. I could almost see her image on the walls. I almost felt her breath behind my ears. I almost heard her footsteps following me. She was everywhere in the house. She was sitting here, eating there, standing to supervise the servants, knitting a sweater . . . I felt afraid, to the point of terror. I'd run to Nanny Halima's room and pound on her door with both hands, screaming, "Nanny Halima! Nanny Halima!"

The poor thing would be jerked awake, terrified to see me standing in front of her scared and shaking.

"Come sit with me, please, Nanny!" I'd implore her. "I can't sleep."

She'd walk behind me to my room.

I'd lie down on my bed wide-eyed, afraid to close my eyes because armies of devils would attack me. Nanny Halima would sit on the ground next to the bed talking about anything. And whatever she was saying would always end with Auntie Safiya. She'd let out a sigh for her as if she were lamenting the virtues of someone dear who had passed away. I felt this lamentation like a whip burning my chest and back. My tears and the screaming in my heart would flow.

Nanny Halima would get tired of talking and lamenting, and her eyelids would fall over her eyes as her head drooped to her chest. She'd slouch down to the ground and sleep under my feet like a guard dog. I remained wide-eyed, keeping my eyes open so the devils wouldn't attack me.

That was how I was living after I recovered from my illness.

That was how I was.

I tried to fight it, to change my state and find any other way to live.

I believed that if we moved from this house, my condition would change and I'd be able to begin a new life without this torture. I'd be able to forget my crime and my father would be able to forget his wife.

I began to convince my father to move.

I thought he'd never agree. This big house had always been dear to him. He was born there. I was born there. It had housed our family since my grandfather.

But my father was easily convinced, as if he no longer cared about where or how he lived.

He wasn't interested in the details that I went into, as I tried to convince him how expensive the big house was compared to a small apartment in one of the modern buildings. He simply agreed to move without discussing it, without even paying attention.

I started searching for an apartment in one of the new buildings. One of the women of the family always came with me. In this search, I found something to distract me, at least during the daytime.

We finally found an apartment in a building on Mohamed Mazhar Street in Zamalek.

An apartment with five rooms. In my mind, I divided it up into a room for the salon, one for a dining room, a third for an office, a fourth for my father, and the last for me.

I tried to put my own stamp on the apartment.

But I failed. I had failed to develop my own taste. In everything I bought or planned, it always seemed to me that I was adopting Auntie Safiya's taste. I tried to resist this but, in doing so, I found myself abandoning her standards too.

I took some furniture from the old house, things from the study and my room, and some of the chairs from the parlor. I insisted that my father's bedroom have new furniture. Everything in it needed to be new. I wanted to help him forget, to distance him from everything that made him remember his wife: the bed that brought them together, the dresser that kept their clothes, the mirror that her image was stamped on. Maybe then, he'd forget.

It took me three months to prepare the new apartment and then we moved in.

I stood and looked at the big house one last time before I left it forever and left all my memories there—memories of my childhood and my youth, memories embedded in its walls and inscribed on its floors, memories traced by the tears of a tortured girl who didn't understand what had happened to her, other than that she was created in this world and found herself in this house.

I started feeling like I bore in my chest a heart wrapped in spiderwebs, a decrepit heart.

*

Were we happy in the new apartment?

I certainly felt a great deal of relief from what I had been suffering. I felt I was more active and better able to face the reality around me. I also felt I'd started shaking off some of the dullness that had been creeping into my youth, and that my blood was beginning to rise up to my cheeks again, even if with difficulty at first.

But my father's state got worse.

He persisted in his drunkenness.

When I went into his room in the morning and collected his clothes strewn on the ground, I began finding traces of cheap lipstick on his shirt.

One day, I happened to be coming back from the doctor in a taxi when I saw his car parked in front of one of the buildings near al-Azhar Square. Another time, I saw his car again in front of the same building. I decided to go by the building a third time, and saw it there again.

I was sure that my father must have his own apartment there.

An apartment like Mustafa's.

I didn't say a word. I tried not to think about it. I didn't try to hold my father accountable or put him under surveillance. It seemed to me that he had the right to have his own apartment and to meet whatever women he wanted there.

But that wasn't my father.

It wasn't the father I knew before he got married, who was living for me and sacrificing his youth to care for me and raise me. My father was always a different kind of man than Mustafa.

I began to hate Mustafa because my father had become like him.

Until one day . . .

The doorbell rang around one in the afternoon. Abdou came to tell me that there was a woman at the door who wanted to meet my father. When he informed her that my father wasn't home, she asked to wait for him until he got back.

I went out to meet her.

I stood aghast when I saw her.

I didn't know how to address her, how to pick the first word that I'd direct toward her. I couldn't imagine what this kind of woman could want from my father. My surprise turned to haughtiness and derision. I stood up straight, pursed my lips, and began inspecting her, as if taking her measurements.

She was a cheap woman, who looked like a prostitute. Bright makeup was plastered on her face. Her dyed hair fell on her shoulders. She wore a yellow dress that revealed half her breasts, even though it was the middle of the day. Over her dress was a loose red coat two years out of style.

Had my father sunk so low?

Had he lost everything, even his taste and dignity?

Was this the kind of woman who visited his apartment?

I thought of Mustafa's apartment at that moment and began measuring myself against that woman. Both of us were going to the apartment of a bachelor. I was going to Mustafa's and she was going to my father's. Was I like her? Like this woman?

I felt my insides surging up toward my lips as I heard myself scream out in my chest: "No, I'm not like her! I'm not like her!" I was in love. I had suffered. An unknown force had pushed me to Mustafa's apartment.

All those thoughts passed over me in a moment. Then, as I stood there haughtily, with my back straight, I heard myself say to the woman, "Who do you want?"

"Mr. Ahmed Lutfi," she said, turning and looking at me as if she were undressing me. "Doesn't he live here?"

"Yes," I said coldly. "But he's not here. He's out."

"Can I wait until he comes back?" she asked, taking another step inside the house.

"Why? Is there something you need?"

"A lot of things," she said, giving me a mocking smile, not seeming to notice how coldly I was addressing her. "Do you mind?" She walked into the apartment and sat on the chair in the entryway. "Let's hope Mr. Ahmed isn't too late!"

I stood looking at her from a distance, half admiring her boldness and shamelessness. I gripped my nerves so I didn't explode.

"I'm his daughter," I said in a light voice, as if trying to skirt around a scandal. "Can you tell me what you want? Maybe I can help you."

"I didn't know," she said with a raised eyebrow.

"What didn't you know?"

"I didn't know that he had a grown daughter, a bride like you. You know, you look exactly like him. The first time I saw you, I thought you were his sister."

"Well, now you know. Could you tell me why you want to talk to him?"

"It's better not," she said, moving her eyes over the pictures hanging on the walls. "It's better that you don't know."

"I know everything about my father," I said, challenging her.

"I don't think so," she replied coldly.

"You can't wait here!" I exploded. "My father isn't coming home for lunch and I'm going out now. I can't leave you here alone!"

She stared at me as if she were looking at a child.

"Do you have five hundred pounds?" she asked in a calm voice, ignoring my screaming.

"Five hundred pounds for what?" I asked, taken aback.

"A promissory note that your father wrote me," she said, looking me over while straightening the arms of her coat.

"A promissory note?" I asked, as if talking to myself. "For what? What did he take from you that he wrote you a promissory note?"

She let out a loud, intense laugh.

"He took the dearest thing from me, sweetie!" she said, raising both eyebrows.

I didn't argue with her.

"He must have written you the promissory note when he was drunk," I said, again as if talking to myself.

"He'll have to explain that in court," she responded indifferently.

I dropped into a chair and felt my head spin. I imagined my father in court, standing next to this woman before a judge. I imagined the courtroom packed with wagging tongues—tongues of people, tongues on chairs, tongues hanging from the ceiling, tongues planted in the ground, all of them long, very long, moving around like snakes and cracking like whips, then turning around my father, raising him and lowering him, tossing him around in the midst of maniacal cackling laughs. As I saw all of that—saw my father's honor violated and the tongues crushing his reputation—my eyes opened wide with terror and I cried out, "Daddy! Daddy! My dear father!" And the tongues of the people responded to me with maniacal laughs.

Then the fantasy was gone.

"Can I see the promissory note?"

"When I see the five hundred pounds!"

"When is it due?" I asked, thinking out loud.

"It's two days past due," she said, starting to take me seriously. "I've been looking for Ahmed everywhere and I haven't found him. I had to come here. He owes me."

"Can I ask you a favor?" I asked meekly.

"What?" she looked at me in astonishment.

"Delay the promissory note for a week. If you don't get the money by then, do what you want."

She examined me closely and was silent for a moment.

"Where will you get the money from?" she asked hesitantly. "Your father?"

"I'll get it," I said. "It doesn't matter how. Just don't look for my father. Don't ask anything from him. I'll bring the money to you. Give me your phone number and address and I'll bring it to you myself."

"And if you don't?"

"You won't lose a thing. The promissory note is in your hands and you can file a case at any time."

"Fine," she said, getting up. "But only for you. May God grant me patience. If you bring me what I'm due, there won't be any courts and scandals."

"Merci."

She gave me her phone number and left, without me shaking her hand goodbye.

I slammed the door behind her, as if sweeping her from the house, as if I was getting rid of something odious poisoning the air around me.

I sat thinking, thinking. My mind felt choked, unable to breathe. But, after a while, I thought I'd found a way I could get the five hundred pounds.

I decided to hide the news of this strange visit from my father. It would kill him if he knew that this woman had come to the house and that I'd met her and learned about this dirty promissory note.

I decided to deal with the five hundred pounds myself.

I called Mr. Gerges Shanouda, the manager of the farm, and asked him to come to Cairo to meet me that day. I was careful that he would arrive when my father was out of the house.

Mr. Gerges came, surprised. It was the first time I'd called him and asked him to meet me. He had a look of urgency on his sweaty face, desperate to know what was happening.

"Mr. Gerges," I said as he sat down opposite me, "I want you to get me five hundred pounds, either tomorrow or the day after."

He raised his lips from his coffee as if fire had burned his tongue.

"My God, Miss Nadia. My God!" he stammered in surprise.

"I'll write you a receipt for it," I said, trying to calm him down. "At the end of the year, when the bill is due, my father will know."

He took out his folded handkerchief and wiped his fine lips with it. He lifted it to his face, blew his nose violently, and then raised his silver glasses and wiped them.

"That's not what I mean, miss," he said. "But . . . but . . ."

"But what?" I said sharply, as if the blood of all the Turks since Sultan Suleiman was surging through my veins.

"There's not a penny at the farm," he said as he settled his glasses back over his eyes. "The safe is empty. It's been a long time since the farm workers were paid. Some were paid in advance, but whoever wasn't has nothing. Your father this year has needed money urgently. He's never been like this. We only see him from time to time. He comes, sits for a half an hour, collects the money, and leaves."

I was quiet for a bit. I remembered that my father had spent two nights every week out of the house, on the pretext that he was at the farm. I always chose to believe what he said. I preferred not to let my imagination run wild, picturing him spending the night at his bachelor apartment.

"You mean there isn't even five hundred pounds?" I was unable to look Mr. Gerges in the eye.

"I wish," he said shaking his head, driving away flies with his antique fly whisk. "Really, Miss Nadia." He paused for a moment and seemed to be thinking what he should say next. "Only two months ago," he said, his voice raised, as if he'd been holding his breath, "your father sold forty acres to our neighbor Abdel-Ghaffar Pasha at a dirt-cheap price. He took the money in cash, and since that day we haven't seen him."

My eyes widened in surprise and terror, before I caught myself and quickly tried to hide my horror.

"I know your father, but what does he do with all this money?" Mr. Gerges asked after a bit, becoming bolder. "He's never been like this before!"

I gave him an angry look. I understood he was attacking my father.

"My father has entered into a new company," I said, my eyes fixed on him. "He's building a new factory."

Mr. Gerges shook his head as if he didn't believe it.

"May God grant him success, Miss Nadia. But there's nothing more bountiful than the land. What are these companies and factories?"

"Regardless," I said, shutting him down. "Thank you very much, Mr. Gerges. I'll get the money from somewhere else. Don't forget to pass my greetings to Umm Atiya."

I left him and walked toward my room.

"Thank you, miss," I heard him say behind me. "But Umm Atiya passed away three months ago."

I stopped in my tracks.

Then, without responding or saying, "May God have mercy on her soul," I continued to my room.

I began pacing back and forth as if imprisoned in a black, windowless jail.

What happened?

What happened to us, Lord?

Umm Atiya died—the last person from the days of my grandfather, whom we all loved. She died and my father didn't know. Or maybe he knew and forgot to tell me, as if her death wasn't worth discussing.

And my father was selling his estate!

My father was the one who almost lost his mind when the land reform law took four hundred acres from us, and here he was selling the estate to squander the money on women who resembled prostitutes.

What had happened?

How could I prevent these catastrophes? How could I save what was left of my father and our land?

Why couldn't I think?

Why couldn't I find a solution?

Why was my mind so energetic and alive, sparkling and glittering when I was plotting something devious, and why was it so lazy and confounded when I tried to set out on the path of goodness, tried to atone for my crimes and save my victims?

I needed someone next to me.

Someone to help me.

Someone to take my hand and lead me onto the path to goodness.

Mustafa jumped to my mind.

Why Mustafa?

Why him? I thought I'd grown apart from him. He was no longer in my life, he was just a memory that I could neither forget nor recapture.

I don't know. Maybe because he was an experienced person who could show me how to deal with this kind of woman demanding money. Maybe because he was a philosopher who could show me the path by which I could regain my father.

I didn't know.

But I went to him.

I went with a pounding heart.

16

Six months had passed without me seeing Mustafa—sad, dark, miserable months that I spent in mourning for the victims of my crime.

During those months, my entire body slumbered, broken and grieving. I had no desire, and it felt like my blood was stagnant. No memories of kisses or touches fluttered on my body. I sometimes touched a spot where Mustafa would kiss or caress me, but I didn't find a trace of those kisses or caresses, as if the waves of events crashing over me had erased all traces of life from the shore, from my body.

The body is a strange thing. It sometimes fasts for a long time, until you think it has forsaken life and given itself to the monastery.

It sometimes moves forward greedily, submitting to violent desires until it seems that it will never be sated, that desire will destroy it and make it explode until nothing is left except a collection of bones.

Why?

Maybe because we can't separate the body from the spirit. There's no pure body and no pure spirit. Each is tied to the other. Each is subject to the other. When the spirit is energetic, the body is energetic, and when the spirit slumbers, so does the body.

This precious body isn't simply an instrument. It's not a tram car that goes on orderly tracks, which people board and dismount at particular stations while society plays the role of the inspector, counting the number of passengers and punishing those who break the rules, while parents play the role of the conductor who gives a ticket to everyone wanting to marry. No, the body isn't a tram car. It's more precious than that. It has a spirit. We cannot control our bodies unless we control our spirits. Is that true?

I didn't know.

But I felt as I was going to Mustafa that my body was still in its long fast, its long slumber.

Despite that, my heart was pounding.

I felt like an unknown hand was gripping my clothes and dragging me backward to the deep past, to the days when I went to Mustafa's apartment to fuse my body, heart, and mind on his bare chest. It seemed to me that those days were distant, very distant, as if they were a childhood memory in the imagination of an old woman.

I went into the entrance of the building and looked around, seeing my past on its door and walls. The doorman looked at my face closely, trying to remember me. Then, he jumped to his feet with a big smile on his lips. But I ignored him and walked straight to the elevator. He ran behind me and opened the door for me.

"How are you, miss?" he asked.

I didn't turn to him. I didn't raise my eyes to his face. By way of a response, I murmured something incomprehensible. I stepped into the elevator and he closed the door behind me. I went up, but felt that I was descending.

He was the same doorman to whom I used to give money to keep tabs on Mustafa and tell me what he was doing, and it was the same elevator that I stopped between floors to change into what was almost a wedding dress to surprise Mustafa on the night I spent with him.

The filmstrip of my memories passed through my mind with an incredible quickness, as if I saw my entire life in that single moment. I then woke up to ask myself again, "Why am I here?"

I'm here to present my problems to Mustafa.

I'm sick and Mustafa is the doctor.

Mustafa, with all his experience and all his philosophical ideas, could be my doctor.

This idea calmed me. I felt calm imagining Mustafa as a doctor.

But Mustafa didn't receive me as a doctor. He opened the door for me with the same look that he used to greet me with, the same smile on his lips, wearing, as usual, a shirt with rolled-up sleeves and the top buttons open.

It was incredible.

He hadn't changed or gotten older or younger. He wasn't happier or sadder.

Time passed and I became happy and miserable, I became sick and I recovered, I sinned and I regretted it. Time passed and my father got married and divorced, he won and he was defeated, he had faith and then lost it. Time passed and brought my uncle something new each day. But time passes and leaves Mustafa as he is. Maybe it forgets him: it disregards him and does not hold him to account for his past.

I stood hesitating at the door.

I couldn't go back and I couldn't go in.

I was confused. I didn't know how to smile or what to say. I didn't know if I was happy to see Mustafa or sorry to have come back to him.

My hesitation must have lasted a while, as I saw a troubled look in Mustafa's eyes. I saw his smile tighten in confusion.

"Welcome," he said in a voice that came out broken, as if it was flowing over a rocky stream.

Then he was silent.

I stepped inside. Mustafa turned to me as he reached out and pushed the door to close it. I turned my head to the door as it was closing, as if making sure that I could open it when I wanted.

Mustafa took my hands, turned them in his, and leaned over to kiss my palms as usual.

His kiss didn't enter my blood. I didn't feel it in my heart or my head as I once had. I took it like an experienced woman for whom kissing her palms no longer served a purpose.

We stood opposite each other.

"How are you, Mustafa?" I asked, trying to clear the silence around us.

"How are you?" he asked, running his eyes over my face. "It seems that renal colic makes people more beautiful. You've become very beautiful, Nadia. But enough of your beauty, enough of your sickness . . ."

"Fine," I said trying to smile. "After this, I won't get sick without your permission!"

Mustafa fell silent as if he was thinking about something he had to do. He then reached out, put his arms around my waist, and pulled me to him. He didn't embrace me roughly, but gently. He was careful, as if he was afraid of putting his weight on me all at once.

I submitted. I felt I didn't have the right to resist. I felt I had to close my eyes and float in his embrace, to give him what he was used to taking from my soul and my body. He had earned that right and I couldn't take it from him. But I couldn't give him anything from my spirit and I couldn't lift my body up to be at one with his. My heart did not beat in time with his. Each heart beat with its own rhythm. In his arms, I felt I was embracing my youth, embracing one of my memories, but I couldn't lose myself in these memories. I couldn't lose my head or forget myself. My mind was alert and active, following each of his actions. I was aware of where I was. I saw his arms wrapped around my waist. I saw his chest and the color of his shirt. I saw the chairs and the furniture around me. I saw the pictures hanging on the walls. I was totally aware, and that awareness prevented me from submitting my body and soul to him.

I felt Mustafa's lips touch my cheek. I didn't flee from his kiss. But it didn't stir up the old feelings inside me. It fell on my cheek and remained there. The feeling did not spread through to the rest of my limbs. It was closer to the kiss of a brother or my father or one of the ladies of our family. Simply the touch of his lips on my cheek. They could have been any lips on any cheek.

Mustafa released me from his arms.

I saw sorrow in his eyes, as if he was grieving for something beautiful that he'd lost. Taking my hands, he led me to the office, as I had called it. I stood at the door, recalling the most tempestuous days of my life before me. I concentrated my eyes on the wide couch that had frequently held my naked body. I smiled to myself. I smiled at my naked body that I saw in my mind's eye lying on the couch. Strange. In the midst of those memories, I felt I was old.

Mustafa went ahead of me into the room.

"What records do you want to listen to?" he asked, opening the turntable.

I gave him a big smile.

He was Mustafa. He hadn't changed.

"Whatever you like," I replied.

Mustafa put the same strange clashing group of records on the player: Chopin, Sayyid Darwish, Abdel-Wahab, Ismail Yassine. At the sound of the first record, I woke up to the fact that I'd come to share my problem, to tell him everything so he could lead me to the right path.

But I suddenly felt that I couldn't tell him anything. I couldn't tell him the story of the promissory note my father had written to that cheap woman. I felt that Mustafa was a stranger who didn't have the right to know my father's secrets and the secrets of our life. I'd feel shame and disgrace if he knew about my father's present condition, and the pit he'd fallen into.

Nevertheless, there was a part of the problem that I could tell him.

"There's something I want to ask you about, Mustafa," I said hesitantly.

"Is everything okay?" he asked, still fiddling with the volume on the turntable.

"It's Daddy," I said quickly, afraid not to say something.

He turned to me in surprise. "What's wrong with him?" he asked.

"He's changed completely," I said, sitting on the couch. "Since the day he divorced Auntie Safi, he's become someone different. I don't know what to do. I don't know how to make him happy, to bring him back to what he was."

"Your father made a big mistake," he said in a low voice, looking at his feet.

"I know," I replied pathetically. "But every mistake can be fixed. How do we fix this one?"

"It can't be fixed." He seemed angry at my father. "Impossible!"

"So, I let Daddy do all those things to himself?"

"Leave him," he said coldly. "It's just a phase. In a while, he'll forget. He'll wake up and go back to how he was."

"I was thinking he'd go back to Auntie Safi," I said, as if talking to myself. "But I don't know how to get them back together."

"Impossible," Mustafa said again, this time raising his voice. "It's not possible to get them back together. When the plate is cracked, it can't be put back together again."

"On the contrary. The plate that's been cracked *can* be put back together. There's a saying that goes: the cracked plate lives longer."

"Maybe it lives longer, true," he said, still agitated. "But it remains cracked forever, with a black line running through it. That black line will always run through the life of your father and his wife, even if they got back together. They'll always see it between them. Your father will always be servile to his wife because he won't be able to forget his mistake. He'll always doubt her, but he'll keep apologizing for his mistake. Your father's wife will always be afraid of him, afraid he'll go crazy and divorce her again. She'll keep thinking about his mistake. Their life together won't go back to what it was. Their lives won't be happy as before. The plate, when it's cracked, stays cracked forever."

I didn't say anything. Mustafa had destroyed all my hopes. I could not raise my head from the rubble to say anything.

Mustafa's tone softened a little.

"Religions forbidding divorce know it's a mistake that can't be fixed," he went on. "When the Prophet said, 'The most odious permissible thing is divorce,' he knew that he was treating bitterness with bitterness. If divorce could be fixed, religions wouldn't forbid it and our Lord wouldn't hate it. They'd let people get divorced and go back on their divorce as they wanted. It's like I told you: the plate that's cracked is cracked forever."

"That means you think there's no hope," I said in a low, broken voice.

Mustafa sat next to me and took my hands in his. "Let things take their course. I know your father's changed. I've seen him in the bars for a while now. I've seen him drink a lot, heard a lot of things about him. But everything must run its course and then it will pass. Soon enough, your father will go back to how he was, but you need to be patient."

I lowered my head and didn't respond. I wanted to cry.

Mustafa put his hand under my chin and raised my face. "Where's your smile?" he said, looking into my eyes tenderly.

I smiled, or I tried to.

Mustafa brought his face near mine. He put his cheek on mine. His lips crept to the edge of mine.

I didn't resist. I didn't close my eyes. I didn't feel his kiss move from its spot. I didn't lose my head or my control. I was conscious. I could still see the pictures hanging on the walls and the furniture around me. I heard the tunes of the records coming from the turntable, not from heaven.

"You haven't missed me, Nadia?" he asked.

"I missed you, Mustafa," I said pathetically, as if intent on saying what he wanted to hear.

Maybe the tears imprisoned in my eyes had burned my cheeks and their heat transferred to Mustafa's. I felt his breath get faster and quiver. I felt his arms rise up to my waist and his palms move slowly over my back. He pulled me gently, then forcefully. His lips opened and found mine. No, it wasn't a kiss. Despite all of Mustafa's skill, I didn't feel the intoxication of a kiss. It was simply two lips on mine—a kiss to which I submitted, thinking about when it would end.

Maybe Mustafa felt my coldness. Maybe he felt that I wasn't responding to him, but he continued.

I saw his hand rise to my head and touch my hair. His fingers crept forward to pull out my hair clip, to let my hair fall down my back, as he used to do when he wanted me.

At that moment, I felt for the first time that Mustafa's breath didn't fall in the right rhythm, that his touches fell on the wrong place, that his kisses came at the wrong moment. I slipped away from him before my hair came undone, and I stood up.

I didn't speak. I couldn't find anything to say.

Mustafa lowered his head, looking at my feet. He shrugged as if he was telling me: I tried. Then he raised his head and got up without turning to look at me. He headed to the turntable.

Trying to fill the silence, he said, "Do you want to hear a new record? It just came out yesterday and—"

I cut him off lightly. "I have to go now, Mustafa. I still have a lot of errands."

He turned to me.

He stood opposite me silently, looking at me wide-eyed. "I'm sorry," he said in an embarrassed voice.

I understood what he meant. I smiled, and felt I was turning the page on him.

He walked me to the door and took my hands in his.

"Whatever happens, Nadia," he said in a tone of honesty and sincerity, "all I ask is that you consider me to always be beside you. Your friend, your father, your uncle, your brother . . . anything. But always beside you."

"You'll always be beside me, Mustafa," I said, and I meant it. "I'll always feel you're all I need beside me."

He smiled gently.

He opened the door.

He let go of my hand.

I started walking out, but then I turned to him and gave him a quick kiss on his cheek. I left without looking back at him.

I pulled the door closed behind me.

I didn't regret visiting Mustafa. On the contrary: as the elevator brought me down, I felt like I was going up. I was rising up from the past to the present and to the future. I felt that I'd gotten a heavy weight off my chest, that I'd recovered from the drug I'd been addicted to, and that it had been only a dream between me and Mustafa. Dreams aren't a sin. May God not punish us for dreams, even if they are beautiful.

How strange people are.

How strange I am.

If anyone had come to me a year earlier and told me that everything between me and Mustafa was only a dream—a dream that would end so simply and quietly, wilting gently like a delicate, beautiful flower—I would have accused them of lying. I would have sworn to them that my love was eternal and endless, that it would never wilt and I would never wake up from it.

But people are like this. They live their lives without knowing themselves, without seeing tomorrow or seizing yesterday.

They can't trace for themselves a static, ever-lasting picture that they put inside a frame and hang before them, saying, "This is me." No. This "me" doesn't have a picture. "Me" today isn't "me" tomorrow or "me" yesterday. I'm happy today, I'm miserable tomorrow. I'm in love today, I'm not in love tomorrow. I'm dreaming today, I'm not dreaming tomorrow.

There isn't anything we can hold onto and call "today." All days are yesterday. All days are tomorrow. As soon as you take hold of your today, you find it's yesterday or tomorrow.

How can we settle down in this world?

How can we put a fixed meaning on our emotions and the self that is ablaze with these shifting emotions?

How can we trace love if the self that's in love doesn't have a single image?

How can you know your emotions if you don't know yourself?

No. There's no love, no hate, no resentment, no decency—none of these things. If there were love, we'd discover its image, shape, and components, and we'd be able to inject ourselves with it when we wanted and shake it off when we wanted. But no . . . all a person's will isn't worth a thing, because we're weak creatures. You love despite yourself. You hate despite yourself. You feel resentment despite yourself. You're decent despite yourself. That's how we were created. That's fate, so we must submit. People submit to their lot in life—their selves which they inherit.

All those thoughts spun around inside me while the elevator brought me down, as I smiled in calm submission.

Submission to myself.

I was astonished. I didn't resist it. I wasn't grieving over my lot in life. I left Mustafa and said goodbye to my past with him there. I felt calm. All that was left for me was a shadow of Mustafa traced in my depths—a dear shadow. Mustafa would always remain dear to me. I didn't resent him, he didn't suffer from any of my evil deeds, he wasn't one of my victims.

I went out into the street.

I remembered that the problem hadn't been solved, that I was still looking for a way to pay this cheap woman the amount on the promissory note that my father wrote her when he was drunk.

Where could I get five hundred pounds without a scandal? Without my father finding out?

I hailed a taxi, got in, and told the driver to take me to the Continental Hotel.

My uncle had been staying there since he split from my father. I hadn't seen him since the divorce was signed and I'd gotten sick. He talked to me a lot on the phone, promising he'd meet me one day out of the house, but he never invited me to meet him. I didn't blame him. The nature of his love for me was that he didn't feel responsible for me. He'd pamper me and be sympathetic and give me whatever I wanted, but that was it. I went into the Continental without looking around me. As I went into the lobby, I felt like I was entering a world for men only.

"Room 202, please," I told the elevator operator shyly.

He inspected me.

"Who does mademoiselle want?" he asked with cold politeness.

"Mr. Aziz Lutfi," I said.

"Please wait in the lobby until we inform him."

"I'm his niece," I replied sharply.

"It's forbidden for women to visit guests in their rooms," he said, cutting me off.

He raised his head to the ceiling and impudently started whistling, without moving from his spot. I thought for a moment, and then opened my bag. He lowered his head, and with a single glance seemed to take in the contents of my purse.

I took out a bill, folded it, and pressed it into his hand, which was hanging down at his side. His fingers moved as if they were looking for something to devour.

"Room 202, please," I said again.

"Mademoiselle is Mr. Lutfi's niece?" he said bowing politely, making way for me inside the elevator. "Please, mademoiselle, go ahead. Mr. Lutfi is an old client. Please, go ahead!"

I averted my face from him in ire and disgust.

When we arrived, he opened the elevator door for me.

"Fourth door on your right," he said, his politeness dripping with poison.

I knocked on the door, but there was no response. I turned the knob and went in.

As usual, my uncle was still asleep. The room was dark even though it was almost one o'clock in the afternoon.

I sat on the edge of the bed, leaned over him, and kissed his brow. I kissed one cheek and then the other. I kissed him on both cheeks again, as I usually did when he'd lived upstairs in the big house in Dokki. I'd gotten him used to me waking him up with my kisses.

My uncle reached out and embraced me, his eyes still closed as if he was dreaming.

I leaned on his chest and kissed him again.

He opened his eyes.

He then closed them and opened them again.

"Nadia!" he yelled.

I laughed and gave him my face for him to kiss.

"Nadia," he said, embracing me firmly, as if he wanted to pull me inside his chest. "My dear Nadia!"

"How are you, Uncle?" I asked, trying to move away from him. "I missed you."

"Not yet! At least a thousand kisses!" he said, laughing tenderly and pulling me to him. He kissed me again. "What a wonderful surprise. I thought I was dreaming. You didn't call before you came."

"I wanted to come and wake you up myself."

He moved me away from him, putting more kisses on my face. I jumped up from his bed and went over to the windows to open them.

"How are you? How are Halima and Abdou?" I've missed you, Nadia," he said, more seriously. "You can't imagine how much I missed you."

"So that's why you've been asking after me every day?" I asked, laughing to lighten his mood. "You even promised that you'd take me out, but I'm still waiting."

"Because I've gotten used to playing hard to get with women," he said, laughing. "I prefer them to come to me."

"I'm not 'women,'" I said, pretending to be angry.

"Girls, too. I play hard to get with them too!"

We laughed.

Our laughing stopped suddenly, as if it had been snipped with a sharp pair of scissors.

"How's Ahmed?" he asked hesitantly, trying to make his voice seem light and turning his head away.

"He's good," I said, but my voice was filled with grief.

He turned to me and took me by the shoulders. "What's wrong, Nadia?" he asked, looking into my eyes. "What has my brother done now? Tell me."

"Nothing," I said, avoiding his gaze.

"Impossible," he said. "Impossible that there's nothing. Impossible that you came here to the hotel and nothing's happened."

"Daddy hasn't done anything," I said, broken. "But—"

"But what?" he asked sharply. "What happened to you?"

"Nothing. But a lot has happened to him."

"You're what's important."

"*He's* what's important," I said, defending my father. "I can't be happy or relaxed until I see him happy and relaxed."

"I know he's changed." He sighed. "I know he's acting crazy. No one knows how to keep him in check, or put him in the insane asylum."

"Daddy's not insane. There are things you don't know. No one knows them. But we have to save him before he destroys himself. Do you know that he's started selling his land?"

"Yes," he said, letting out another sigh.

"You know that he wrote a promissory note that he can't pay to a woman?" I asked, hoping that this would move him so he'd agree to help me.

"A promissory note to a woman?" he asked, surprised. "Who is she?"

"I don't know," I said, on the verge of tears. "A woman came to the house and told me she has a promissory note from Daddy for five hundred pounds. If he doesn't pay it, she'll take him to court."

My uncle was silent.

"Imagine, Uncle," I continued, taking a small kerchief from my purse. "Imagine Daddy standing opposite a woman like that in the court. Imagine the scandal that would happen. I'd be so embarrassed. Wouldn't you?"

"So, you came to me because of that?" he asked, as if staring off at a distant world in which he saw his brother behind bars.

"Who else should I go to?"

"What do you want me to do?" he asked in despair, his emotions beginning to surface.

"I don't know," I said. "I don't know what to do myself. I can't ask anyone. I don't have anyone I can ask but you. Even Daddy doesn't know that I know about this."

"So, you want me to pay the five hundred pounds?"

"Do what you want, Uncle."

"This is perfect! My brother divorces his wife and I'm the reason. He goes out with a woman and writes her a promissory note, and that falls on me too. No, my dear. No way! I'm finished with my brother. I have nothing to do with him. He can do whatever he wants, but he has to do it far away from me."

"I can't wash my hands of my father," I said brokenheartedly. "Everything that will happen to him will happen to me too."

My uncle didn't respond. He got up and started pacing back and forth in agitation.

I tried to cry. Maybe my crying would melt what was left of his resistance. But I couldn't. I couldn't find any tears, so I had to be satisfied with lifting my kerchief to dab at my eyes.

He was silent for a while.

"You don't know this woman? You don't know where she is?"

"She gave me her phone number. She told me if she doesn't get the money by Saturday, she'll be in court the next day."

"Fine," he said, looking at me. "Leave the number at the side of the bed."

"Merci, Uncle," I said, taking out the small paper with the number.

"But listen," he said sharply, turning to me. "Next time, be sure that I won't be able to—"

"May God preserve you for us, Uncle!" I said before he finished, bounding over to him and clinging to his neck. "May God preserve you for me and Daddy."

"May God be at your aid, my dear," he said, allowing me to cover his face with kisses.

Then he kissed me.

"Okay, go, and let me get dressed," he said.

"I'll only go when you give me a date for our rendezvous," I said playfully.

"Later," he said, smiling.

"No, now. Enough playing hard to get, Uncle. Shame on you!"

"Fine, my dear. Tomorrow we'll have tea at Groppi's at five o'clock."

"Thank you so much!" I kissed him again. "Au revoir."

I took off for the door, but before I left, he called out to me in a loud voice that sounded like it was coming from a distant place. "Come here."

I went back to him surprised.

"Yes, Uncle?"

"Kiss me again," he said, gently and lovingly, embracing me in his arms.

I kissed him dozens of times.

Then I left.

I was happy. It seemed that God had forgiven me and He had begun to help me solve my problems.

But the greatest problem hadn't been solved yet.

My father.

How could I make him calm, tender, and dignified again?

How could I save him from the abyss into which he'd fallen, save him from the torture on whose fire he was writhing?

I walked down the hotel corridor, not noticing what was happening around me. I got into the elevator to go down. I left thinking, thinking. . . . It seemed that I was walking in a thick black cloud, searching for the light.

When I got to the street, a flash of light sparkled in my mind.

I found the solution to my big problem.

My father had to get married!

Why not? He wasn't yet forty-two—he was still in his prime. If he couldn't return to his previous wife, let him look for another one.

I was the one who'd look for her.

I'd failed to make him happy. I'd failed to be an angel on the throne of his house, to provide him with calm, stability, and happiness. So let me abdicate for another woman. Maybe she could make him happy.

Maybe my conscience would find peace.

And maybe I could compensate my father for my crime.

17

I BEGAN LOOKING AT MY father in his drunkenness like a doctor eyeing a patient when he prepares a tranquilizer or a shot of morphine for him.

The drug I was preparing for him was marriage: to look for a wife to compensate him for the one he'd lost, so as to return his happiness, dignity, and feeling of responsibility and to bring him back to the house.

This idea distracted me from being tortured by the state of my father—his drunkenness and his ignoring me—that had been caused by my lies, and by my fear of the unknown path he was on, pulling me along behind him.

I began spending my days going over the women I knew, looking for a wife for my father. I made connections between different social circles to widen the scope of my choice.

I became like a child in a toy store, picking a doll to play with and hug in bed. Maybe after that, I'd be able to sleep.

I didn't have in my mind any particular characteristics for the wife I was picking for my father, except one: she had to be darker-skinned. All the women I saw in my father's life were dark. My mother, Auntie Safiya, even that cheap woman my father wrote the promissory note to. It seemed the theory that fair-skinned men preferred darker women and darker women preferred fair-skinned men was true.

I went over dozens of women. I inspected each one of them, putting each under scrutiny for a period of weeks, like a mother searching for a bride for her son.

I told my friends that my father was looking for a wife, and the news spread. A lot of the women began showing affection for me and visiting me at home. They'd invite me and my father to their houses. My father would refuse all these invitations, and he refused to sit with any women visitors. He was lost in his drunken life and acted like he'd started to despise all these women from good families, ever since he had begun to hate his ex-wife.

The rumors swirling around my father, the life he was living, even the story of his divorce didn't diminish the desire of respectable families to catch him. At forty-two, he was handsome and in decent shape, even if he'd become a little flabby from drinking too much. Besides, he was rich. The throne he set up for Auntie Safiya made every girl desire one like it.

I saw with astonishment the hypocrisy of these families who now showed their affection for me and my father. But despite that, I didn't like any of the women I saw. This one was fat, this one was short, this one was uptight, this one was arrogant, this one was dumb. I found a fault in every one of them, until I began accusing myself of not wanting my father to get married. Maybe I was imagining these faults only to justify to myself that he remain a bachelor.

Until we went to Alexandria that summer.

I started getting to know the families summering there, and I sat with them in the cabins and under the umbrellas, looking for a woman appropriate for my father.

The idea hounded me to the point that it triumphed over my usual introversion. I became outgoing and talkative, mixing with people until the whole beach knew me as a well-brought up, if snobbish, girl who only socialized with families and only sat with women, and that I was unattached and didn't have a man.

Until I met my friend Kawthar.

I still remember her as I last saw her when she was my classmate at Madame Orly School in Maadi. She was older than me, nice, svelte, and dark-skinned. She walked as if she were floating on air. When she talked, her voice was lovely and tuneful and her smile was like the setting sun. She'd let her long black hair hang down her back as if she were an angel protecting night from day.

She had been in love with Medhat—a pure, delicate love. Their love could have ended in marriage if I hadn't intervened and inflicted my black plans on them to break them up.

I looked at Kawthar as if looking at a life that had been lost.

But she was no longer weak or delicate.

Nothing about her suggested she still floated on air.

Everything about her had changed.

Her bold smile jumped from her cheeks like kernels of hot corn that burst into popcorn. Her eyes darted about quickly and nervously, like she wanted to collect everything around her in a single glance and satisfy herself with it. Her lips were full, and she'd provocatively leave them slightly open so they'd be even more enticing. Her body had matured and become curvy.

Kawthar got married, and divorced a year later. Since that day, she'd lived as a divorcée. I saw her for the first time on the beach, sitting in a cabin with some divorced women and some women on the verge of divorce.

I don't know why divorced women always get together with each other and why a married friend of theirs seems not to happen among them without divorce following soon after!

It seems that divorced women live in another world from married women. A world with its own customs, morals, and topics of conversation, a world in which the cliques of divorcées meet and spend all day and night together, doing nothing but scheming to ensnare a new man or concocting a plan to wreck some other man's home.

I discovered this world when I met Kawthar.

I was passing in front of this cabin when I heard her call out to me.

"Nadia! Nadia!"

I turned and saw her. "Kawthar!" I yelled out happily. "How are you?"

She jumped up out of the cabin and came over to me. "Nadia Lutfi," she said, hugging me. "It's been so long! You're still tall as you were. Four inches taller than me! But you've lost a lot of weight, Nadia. You must have gotten married. Who'd you marry? Medhat?"

She was talking so quickly and happily that I couldn't get a word in edgewise until she fell silent for a moment.

"Not at all. I haven't gotten married."

"You must be in love," she said quickly. "I've known you since we were in school, and you've always been a temptress."

"I'm not in love," I said, smiling.

"That goes for me too. So, why'd you lose weight?"

"I was sick."

I was pleased to see her and she pulled me by the hand.

"Come," she said, bringing me into the cabin. "I'll introduce you to my friends."

She turned to them.

"I present to you Nadia Lutfi," she said in a comically formal tone. "The most beautiful girl with us at school."

"No. You've always been more beautiful than me, Kawthar."

"What are we arguing about?" she laughed. "You were the most beautiful blonde and I was the most beautiful brunette. Together we were ebony and ivory—intoxicating!"

We all laughed.

She started introducing me to her friends. I sat among them and we started talking. They were initially somewhat reserved, but then opened up. The entire conversation was about men.

One of them turned to me.

"I heard your father is looking to get married," she said.

"Not at all. He's had his fill of marriage."

"The truth is that he had bad luck both times he got married," another said.

"Everyone speaks highly of him. He's nice, manly, handsome," a third said.

"You all only talk about men," Kawthar said. "Come on, let's talk about women for a bit!"

They all laughed and actually did start gossiping about different women they knew.

After a while, I stood up, excusing myself. Kawthar got up with me.

"Wait for me. I'll come with you," she said. "I still haven't done the morning inspection."

We strolled together on the beach.

Kawthar walked next to me as if she were a protestor marching for femininity and beauty. Eyes encircled us and looks of admiration covered the path we trod. We were the most beautiful brunette and blonde on the beach. I felt proud as I walked next to her. I felt as if I was wearing a fantastic new dress, turning men's eyes. I felt as if, alone, I was only half a beauty, but with her I was complete.

Kawthar was talking and laughing a lot, only stopping to say hello to a family sitting in a cabin or to greet a passing friend.

"See that one who walked by?" she whispered. "He's going out with Inji Sherif. He's going to leave his wife and marry her. He looks good, but he's uptight."

She knew everyone and everyone's news. She was a burning candle emitting life. I felt alive next to her. I felt happy and active, as if the world had opened up before my eyes.

We arrived at our umbrella and I noticed my father sitting under it. As usual, he was looking around in boredom and annoyance, impatiently waiting for night to fall so he could resume his retreat into its darkness.

I pulled Kawthar by the hand.

"Come, let me introduce you to my father."

My father turned to her. Then he jumped up, and seemed to shake off his boredom and swallow his bitterness.

"This is Kawthar," I said, looking into his eyes, trying to see Kawthar's reflection in them. "My old classmate."

She reached her hand out to him gently and flirtatiously. He reached out to her, hesitating, as if resisting something that was dazzling him.

"Please," he said, flustered. "Sit down, Madame Kawthar."

"This father of yours is very young," Kawthar whispered in my ear as she sat down. "I wasn't imagining him like this."

A long conversation went on between us, during which my father played the role of a father: wise, staid, and mature. But his nice face and innocent eyes clearly revealed his delight at Kawthar, his delight at her dark-haired beauty and her happy-go-lucky presence.

My father swallowed and turned to me. "Madame Kawthar has to be very young if she was your classmate."

"If I was very young," Kawthar said quickly, "you wouldn't have called me 'madame.' It's Miss Kawthar."

"Am I young, Daddy?" I asked as if defending my friend from an accusation. "Don't forget that I'm almost twenty!"

"And," Kawthar interjected. "I must confess that I'm older than Nadia. I'm now twenty-five."

"Impossible!" my father said, smiling.

"Okay, twenty-three," Kawthar said flirtatiously. "Just for you!"

My father looked up to the sky as if doing the math between my age and Kawthar's and his.

One of my friends walked by, and I took the opportunity to get up from under the umbrella and say hello. I intentionally left my father and Kawthar alone. I stayed away from them for a while on purpose. When I went back, I found them talking. My father's face was bursting with happiness—a happiness that lit up his eyes and was sketched on his lips. I heard him laugh as if his heart was fluttering in his chest—laugh as I hadn't heard him laugh since he'd divorced Auntie Safiya.

I invited Kawthar to have tea with me later that day.

My father didn't go out as he usually did. He delayed until Kawthar arrived. With a happy heart, I watched him dawdle, as if I was watching a child whose mother was letting him dupe her.

After that, things went quicker than I'd anticipated. Kawthar was always with me. My father was always with us. The two families got to know each other. They started visiting us and we started visiting them. My father started inviting Kawthar and me to the movies or parties, to lunch and dinner. He began to return to how he was: calm, good-hearted, and stable. Kawthar's smiles wiped the suffering from his heart and made him forget the blow that had crushed him. They compensated him for going to the bars and the bachelor pad that he rented to meet women. My father became as I wanted him. I delighted at this ordered, calm happiness . . . a happiness extending from Kawthar's cheerfulness, liveliness, and her active personality overflowing with life, beauty, and flirtation.

I felt that I'd regained my father. He came back to me affectionate and respectable, as he was before he married Auntie Safiya, when he was living for me and I was living for him. He started spending time with me and talking to me about some of his problems. He confessed that he'd been neglecting the farm for a long time. He even confessed that he'd sold forty acres of his estate, but he promised to work to get it back.

I was happy.

I was so happy I couldn't sleep. I spent my nights anxious about this happiness, afraid it would slip through my fingers again, that I'd lose it, that I'd return to misery. I knew I wouldn't be able to keep my father unless he married Kawthar.

I no longer had any doubt that my father was in love with her or wanted her. It was a wavering, hesitant love, as if he couldn't forget the age difference between them and couldn't forget that she was my friend, and felt he was responsible for her like he was for his daughter. Despite that, he was moving forward with careful, small steps. When he spoke with her, he made distant allusions, as if he was talking in the language of the eighteenth century. When he danced with her, his face would be anxious and his lips would go dry. He kept a distance between them as if he was afraid that if he embraced her, he'd melt in her arms or lose himself.

I got angry at him, wanting him to be strong and courageous, to impose his will on Kawthar and make her submit to him. I wanted him to be like Mustafa so that when he danced with her, he'd press her to his chest and she'd feel the strength of his arms and the heat of his breath. I wanted him to raise her up on the tunes of an imaginary world intended only for the two of them, only for his heart and hers, his body and hers, to whisper in her ear and sear his cheek to hers. When he was talking, I wanted him to delight her with his opinions, to make her focus all her attention on what he was saying, to forget all her opinions and her whole being, to take life from him more than he was taking from her.

But my father wasn't that kind of man.

He was good-hearted, sincere, hesitant, and reserved.

I got tired of having to prepare the road for him and create chances for him to be alone with Kawthar. I even made him understand that I was intentionally leaving the two of them alone whenever she came to visit me and that I was purposely seating her next to him in the car whenever we went out together. I was openly in favor of the idea of him marrying her.

"You know, Daddy, Kawthar really likes you," I'd say sometimes. "Yesterday, we saw a movie with Van Johnson, and as soon as she saw him, she said he looks exactly like you."

"Please! Shame on you," he said shyly. "That Van Johnson is still a young man!"

"Not at all. He's older than you. He's forty-nine. How old do you think Clark Gable is? He's fifty-five and married to someone who's thirty."

"You're comparing me to Clark Gable?"

"You're better than him. And Kawthar says so too."

"You two are still young," he said, laughing.

"Kawthar isn't young," I snapped. "As soon as a woman gets married and divorced, she isn't young anymore, even if she's sixteen. She grows up all at once like she's thirty years old. Her mind grows up with her heart and soul."

My father was smiling, and then became quiet as if he was thinking.

I was infuriated by his hesitation.

It seemed to me that Kawthar was trying to prepare the road for him too, to encourage him to get close to her. Her attention to her clothes and appearance whenever we met couldn't have been by accident. She was always distracting him from what was around him and paying more attention to him than anyone else, until I was sure she was seeking to marry him.

During that time, I didn't look at Kawthar's past or what people said about her. I knew that this overflowing liveliness, this bustling heart and active mind didn't point to a sedate life. Nonetheless, I didn't try to look past her or dig into her background. I needed her. My need for her forgave everything. I needed her not only to preserve my father, but I also needed the life that she gave me. Her free spirit diverted me from my suffering, distracting me from the sickness of my psyche, from my sins, from my crimes.

I decided to keep her at any price.

"What do you think about my father, Kawthar?" I asked her one day when we were alone.

"It's clear this father of yours is an incredible man," she said, laughing. "He runs away like a timid cat, until someone touches his heart."

I laughed. I knew she was teasing me and that my father was incapable of sneaking away like a cat. "No, Kawthar," I said innocently. "My father is a good, sincere man. I wish he'd marry you."

Kawthar was amazed when I surprised her with this, but she didn't reject the idea.

"My dear," she said, feigning a smile, "it's clear that he's not a marrying type."

"On the contrary. My father is the kind of man who's only happy in marriage."

"When I hear you say that, Nadia, it sounds like you're his mother and you're trying to get him engaged."

"Until now, I've been his daughter, mother, and wife. I want you to help by taking one from me. Pick for yourself: be his daughter, mother, or wife."

"I can't be his daughter or his mother."

"Imagine, Kawthar," I said, trying to push her along. "If we both lived together forever, we'd never get tired of each other."

"Why? Won't you get married? Before you know it, you'll get married and no one will see you and you won't ask after anyone anymore."

"I can't get married until my father gets married," I said seriously.

"Then he has to get married immediately," she joked. "Because I want to see your groom and how he looks."

This conversation was repeated between us. It was always cloaked in joking and fun, as if we didn't mean it or we weren't expressing something we were both hoping for.

But she was working to marry him.

She wanted to marry my father.

No doubt about it.

But did she love him?

I tried not to ask myself this question. Maybe she didn't love him. Maybe she wanted to marry him for his money or for the comfortable life he could offer her. Maybe anything. But why did it matter, as long as my father was happy? As long as I, with this marriage, could atone for my crime, to compensate him for what I'd done.

During that time, I met Mahmoud.

Kawthar introduced me to him as we were walking on the shore one day. He was thirty, not tall and not short. Medium build. Not overly handsome. He didn't have the sort of looks that turn heads. You could pass by him as you'd pass by dozens of other young men. His coloring was rather sallow, as if he was sick or on the verge of getting sick. His eyes were anxious, as if he'd just lifted them from a complicated book, still trying to understand what he'd read. His lips were thin, hiding what was inside him. You didn't know if he was angry or happy.

The day I met him, I didn't find myself trying to make a good impression. I didn't try to prolong standing with him and I didn't force my smile. I didn't try to select my words as I usually did when I met someone for the first time. On the contrary, I found myself acting totally naturally, as if he was my brother or father. I found that I didn't need to try to attract him as he wasn't trying to attract me. I felt so relaxed that conversation between us flowed smoothly—a conversation with no airs, no flirting. He seemed serious, as if everything in life was a problem that deserved deep study and scientific research, even the color of my clothes.

The conversations continued between us.

I always met him with Kawthar in the cabins and under our friends' umbrellas. I then started meeting him alone whenever I left Kawthar with my father.

Weeks passed before I realized his place in my heart; weeks during which I met his mother and his sister. We spent those weeks talking about our hopes and dreams, and I learned that he was a teaching assistant in the Faculty of Science at Cairo University and that he was a candidate for a year-long government scholarship to England. He talked to me a lot about the university and about the program he would attend.

There were never any hints of adventures with women or any insinuation of emotions beating in his chest.

Never. But if we conversed about Paris, for example, he'd talk as if he'd read a thousand books about Paris. We'd converse about clothes, and he'd talk as if he'd lived his life in the atelier of Jacques Fath or Christian Dior. All his conversations were filled with information he'd read in books or observations he'd gotten from life with an attentive mind and sharp eyes. I felt as I was listening to him that I'd grown up: my mind and my being. Everything grew up and the world around me expanded. I discovered more beauty—a beauty that delighted me until I forgot myself in it. I forgot the past. I forgot the present. I only saw the future—a calm, happy future with love, goodness, and peace.

Until one day . . .

"The man who could make you happy and fulfill your dreams, what does he look like?" he asked me. "What kind of man is he?"

I reviewed in my mind all the men I'd seen and all the people I knew, even characters in fiction and movies. I found only him, Mahmoud, as if I'd discovered a truth I'd been trying to deny, a light I'd been trying to cover up and close my eyes from, a dream I was keeping deep inside me and resisting, so it wasn't imprinted on my heart and mind.

Mahmoud the calm, good, serious, and understanding man. His mother, who melted with gentleness and tenderness, whose radiant face was free of makeup and around which the hand of God almost drew a halo of light. His sister, who was younger than me—the beautiful, polite girl, like an honorable angel wandering around the shore to guide people to virtue, to the beauty of the soul, to bashfulness and purity.

What man other than Mahmoud could offer me happiness and well-being, to teach me things with his curious mind, bear me with his calmness, and save me from my psyche?

"The man I like," I responded to him, turning my eyes away, afraid that he'd understand me, "has to have a personality. His mind has to be big. A man before whom I feel that I'm still his student and that he'll always be a teacher. I don't care if he's handsome or rich. I only care that he has a personality, that he's a teacher and loyal, and his heart is mine."

He was quiet. He turned his eyes away as if he had understood what I meant.

"You know, girls' taste in men has developed a lot," he said after a bit. "Girls first liked strong men. Men with muscles who could kill their foes with a single blow. Then girls liked handsome men whose strength was the strength of their looks and physique. And now they like men who have a brain—the educated whose beauty is in their thinking, not their physical form. The entire world has developed like this."

"That's true," I said, like a young student getting a lesson from her teacher. "But not all men these days have a personality. Most of them are still interested in their muscles and good looks."

"Because we're now in a period of transition," he said, laughing.

When we parted that day, his hand squeezed mine as he was saying goodbye. I wished I could give him my hand forever.

18

Is life big enough for more than one love?

I loved Mahmoud.

But hadn't I been in love with Mustafa a year earlier?

Was my heart honest in loving Mahmoud? Was it honest in loving Mustafa or had it misled me in love, deceiving me and lying to me?

I didn't know!

But now, I could swear that I loved Mahmoud as I could have sworn that I loved Mustafa a year earlier, despite the big difference between my love for each of them. They were different kinds of love, in how they emerged and the feelings they stirred up.

My love for Mahmoud was calm, pure, and transparent. It flowed in my heart like a sweet stream with no waves or storms appearing on it. This love didn't inflame me, but slumbered in my heart like an innocent angel. It didn't burst through my body like rockets, but filled my chest like the morning breeze. Even when I imagined him kissing me, almost feeling his lips on mine, it didn't release in me a defiant desire or push me to anything like my adventures with Mustafa. Instead, I felt his lips as a touch of love which made my heart happy and which my body smiled at calmly and sedately.

I never imagined Mahmoud in a tempestuous adventure. I always saw him sitting by my side like a husband: he would be reading with me next to him needlepointing or working on a jacket. I imagined him coming back from the university, me greeting him at the door, taking his bag that had his study notes, kissing him on his cheeks, and leading him by the hand to the dining room. I imagined him walking next to me on Qasr al-Nil Street, and us going into shops together. I imagined him as a father for my children.

I thought about him as a husband.

My entire hope was that I'd marry him.

He was the first man I wanted as my husband.

Mahmoud didn't broach the subject of marriage with me. Despite that, marriage was an idea that brought us together, an idea we both aimed for. It also seemed to me that us getting married became the hope of his mother and his sister. I could see in their eyes and their gestures that they had a plan for us.

Was this plan being realized?

Was God happy with me, and was he withholding the punishment I feared?

God is forgiving and merciful. While I was getting close to Mahmoud, I left Kawthar to my father, and was certain she was trying to marry him. Everything was going as I wanted, as I hoped—as if God had set fate in my hands to make what I wanted with it.

Until we got back from summer vacation.

Not even two days after we got back, my father came into my room early in the morning and woke me up with his kisses. He sat on the edge of the bed.

"You've become lazier than me!" he said, hesitation making his smile falter. "Why are you sleeping so much?"

"What time is it?" I asked, opening my eyes.

"Eight thirty!"

"Because I'm still not used to you waking up early."

My father was quiet.

He spread his fingers on the duvet as if he was looking for what he wanted to say underneath it.

"Go wash your face, Nadia," he said, as if he'd decided to delay. "I want to sit and talk a little."

"Why don't we talk now?" I asked, searching his face.

"No," he said, standing up. "After you wash your face. It's important."

"I'm used to hearing important news while I'm in bed. Please, what do you want to tell me, Daddy?"

"Later. After you wash your face."

"No, now," I said, taking his hand so he didn't get up. "Please stop making me worry!"

He became flustered and he blushed. Drops of sweat like the morning dew appeared on his forehead.

"No, it's nothing," he said. "But you know our life alone is missing something. All day and night, I'm afraid for you. I don't know what to do for you. I don't know what—"

"I know," I cut him off jubilantly.

"You know what?" he asked, surprised.

"You're getting married."

"How did you know?" he asked, shocked.

"And should I tell you who you're going to marry?" I asked, laughing. "Kawthar!"

His mouth dropped open.

"Someone must have told you!"

"Not at all," I said, embracing him. "Don't forget that I've grown up and I understand the world. I've been waiting for this day for three months—the day you'd come tell me you're going to marry Kawthar."

Apologetically, he said, "I didn't plan to think about marriage until you got married, but—"

"And I wasn't planning on getting married until you got married!" I said, cutting him off. "But that's it. As long as you get married, I'll start thinking about marriage right away."

I got out of bed happily and went to the phone to call Kawthar.

"Shame on you, traitor!" I yelled at her. "You did the deed without telling me!"

Kawthar swore to me that my father hadn't broached the subject of marriage until the day before, and he hadn't come to propose formally yet.

The formalities were completed quickly after that. Kawthar and her family moved things forward hastily, as if they were afraid my father might change his mind.

I went with my father, and we bought the engagement ring and the engagement present after Kawthar told me what she wanted. I then started going with Kawthar every day to visit clothing and furniture stores.

I felt that half of my hopes had been achieved. I was happy, and my father was happy. He was generous with Kawthar about everything, to the point that I was afraid he might have resorted to selling land again or taken out a big loan to pay for everything.

The agreement to sign the marriage contract was completed quickly. Four weeks after announcing the engagement, they agreed that Kawthar would move into our house, and we wouldn't look for a new house until after the wedding, and they wouldn't change the furniture except in the bedroom, and they'd limit the celebration, just inviting a small number of guests from the two families.

My father wanted to take Kawthar to Europe for their honeymoon, but Kawthar refused on the pretext of saving money. My father pressed her, but Kawthar insisted.

"My good sir, the honey in Europe isn't like the honey here," she informed him teasingly.

"But I want to open you up to the world, Kawthar," my father responded. "We'd get away from Cairo and all its noise for a little while."

"From now on, the only noise in Cairo that you'll hear is mine! You'd be taking my noise with you to Europe. It's better that we spend the money on the new house."

"My dear, you don't have to worry about money," he pressed her. "We can travel and the new house will still be as you want it, more or less."

"If all you want to do is spend money," she said, still being coy, "instead of traveling, you can get me the brooch Nadia and I saw at Yakim's. Instead of us spending money for a month, we'll spend it on something that will stay with us forever."

I didn't know why I found myself standing next to Kawthar and defending her. At the time, I didn't think about what could be pushing her to call off the honeymoon. I didn't ask myself, "Why is a young bride refusing to travel to Europe with her husband whom she loves?"

I didn't think anything of it.

"That's right, Daddy!" I cut in enthusiastically. "And I couldn't let you leave me for a whole month. I agree with Kawthar that she has half of you and I have the other half. And I don't want my half to travel."

The honeymoon was canceled.

My father bought the brooch for Kawthar.

I organized the small party. In her white dress and short veil, Kawthar looked like a beautiful bronzed angel, touched by the sun on her way down to earth.

I insisted on inviting Mahmoud and his family to the party, on the pretext that his sister was one of my dearest friends. Maybe Kawthar knew what there was between me and Mahmoud, and she didn't object to inviting him. He came with his sister, but his mother sent her regrets because she was sick.

I was happy with him.

I was imagining myself in Kawthar's dress—the bride's dress.

I was imagining him in my father's place—the place of the groom.

"I have to see you today," Mahmoud whispered in my ear as we drank our tea, the faint sound of trilling by one of the servants coming from the distance. "I have to see you alone."

I agreed without thinking. I agreed that he'd take his sister home after the party ended and he'd come back to find me waiting for him at the front door.

The party ended at eight o'clock in the evening.

My father and his bride went to the Mena House Hotel to spend three days there. I stayed home alone with Nanny Halima.

At nine o'clock, I was waiting for Mahmoud in front of the building. I didn't feel that I was heading out on an adventure and the night to come didn't stir up anything in me that I was afraid of or that made me excited. My trust in Mahmoud was stronger than the night. All I was expecting was that Mahmoud would propose to me. All I felt was a slight trembling in my heart, as if it were a small bird waking up to the morning light, shaking the dawn dew from its feathers.

Mahmoud came in his car and I jumped in next to him. He turned to me and smiled. Then, without saying a word, we drove off.

The trembling of my heart became more intense, as if the dawn dew was too heavy for the trembling bird to shake off. I felt the situation was more serious than I imagined.

Mahmoud's silence went on.

I tried to break his silence, to talk with him about the party and what people were saying about it, but Mahmoud just listened, he did not talk. Maybe he wasn't listening either.

We got to the end of Haram Street and turned onto al-Naziliya Street. He stopped under a big tree on a calm street—the same street and tree where Mustafa had stopped his car when we met for the first time.

I was suddenly afraid that Mahmoud was like Mustafa.

He turned to me, and then looked straight ahead once more. "I'm leaving, Nadia," he said in a low voice.

"Leaving?" I asked anxiously, as if he'd slapped me.

"The day after tomorrow," he said, still looking straight ahead. "I was thinking that the process would take more time.

I was planning on talking with you about a lot of things, but I got word that I have to leave in two days."

We were both quiet.

"Will you be gone long?" I asked, my voice cascading out like a flood of tears.

"For a year," he said, still looking in front of him. "But I'll be back in six months." He turned to me with a look of pleading and apology in his eyes. "All I can say, Nadia, is that I hope you'll wait for me."

I didn't say anything. My eyes clung to him in a sad silence.

He got close to me. I felt his calm, warm breath on my face as if it were the wings of butterflies dancing in the air.

"Will you wait for me, Nadia?" he asked in a trembling voice.

I didn't answer. I found my head falling on his shoulder, my face hiding in his chest, my hands clinging to the edge of his shirt as if I didn't want him to go.

He raised his arm and it came down gently on my shoulder. He pulled me to him as if he wanted me to hear the beats of his heart.

With his other hand, he raised my head to him. He looked around again, his eyes on my face as if he was seeing me for the first time. I closed my eyes so I didn't see his lips, to resist my desire and ensure that I didn't kiss him before he kissed me.

His lips arrived, delicate and tender, as if they were bearing the message of God and depositing it on my lips.

I couldn't open my eyes. I wanted to sleep in his kiss, in his breath. I'd finally sleep after the long life I'd spent sleepless.

How long did we spend kissing?

I don't know. Maybe he spoke. Maybe he said something. But I didn't respond. My entire mind was on the home that would bring us together, on the bridal dress, on a calm, stable life. I didn't know what was happening around me. I didn't feel that I was in a car parked under a tree on one of the calm streets of al-Naziliya. I felt like I was at home. My home. That

Mahmoud was my husband and this car was our bed. He could have taken everything. I would have given him everything. He was my husband.

His love and tenderness carried me to a beautiful, distant, calm world. I only returned from it as he was lifting his arms from my shoulders, as if he were abandoning me and letting me fall in space, the damp air filling my clothes.

He reached out and turned the car key.

"It's already eleven," he said.

I loved him more at that moment.

I loved him because he was protecting me from myself and himself. I loved him because he was compensating me for my weakness with his strength, completing my will with his, limiting my freed imagination with his incredibly strong truth.

"I'll wait for you, Mahmoud," I told him as I got out of the car at the door of my building, as if taking an oath to him.

He reached out, took my hand, and kissed it.

I went home and felt I was floating. I lay in bed embracing my happiness. I thought I'd sleep but I didn't. Small black clouds began creeping into my mind and spreading across the sky of my happiness. I started asking myself, "Why doesn't Mahmoud come to propose now, before he leaves? Why isn't he marrying me and taking me with him? He'll be gone for six months. Who knows what might happen during these months! Maybe he'll meet another woman there. Maybe he'll change his mind and forget his love for me. Maybe . . ."

My clever mind began to stir—my evil intelligence. It seemed to me that I needed a plan to stop Mahmoud from traveling—Mahmoud, my husband. I felt forces bursting with malice and hatred in my chest. I hated London, where Mahmoud was going. I hated it so much that I hoped the war would return and German bombs would flatten it. I hated the British. I hated the government that sent Mahmoud on this program. Why Mahmoud? Why weren't they choosing someone else? Why were they taking my love from me? My fiancé. My husband.

I felt like getting out of bed, going to Mahmoud, and screaming at him so he wouldn't leave me. I felt like going to the president and begging him to leave my love for me. I thought I could pack my clothes, join Mahmoud in London, and give myself to him there as his wife.

During the turbulent storms of these thoughts, I asked myself, "Why did I promise I'd wait? Why didn't I overwhelm him with my femininity and overcome his resistance, make him lose his mind so he'd marry me before leaving? Why didn't I claim, as all girls do, that there was another man who came to propose and I was afraid my father would accept? Why didn't I use my intelligence?" I know I'd decided I'd be good and was resisting my evil impulses, which were pushing me to crimes that would torture me. But goodness seemed not to be part of my intelligence. Does every good girl have to be stupid? Why couldn't I use my intelligence in order to achieve happiness? To reach my honorable goal of marrying my love? Why did my clever mind abandon me whenever I needed it for good, and help me only when I wished misfortune on people?

I pulled myself back from these thoughts and said to myself, "No, a marriage based on deception will never last. I have to trust Mahmoud. He's stronger than this doubt. He's not just any man, not just any husband. He's my love!"

I was never as afraid of my mind as much as I was that night.

I shook my head on the pillow roughly, trying to dispel every plan my mind concocted. I clutched the duvet, gripped it tightly, as if resisting a great force trying to push me violently on a path I didn't want to go on. I bit my lips until they bled, trying to muffle the scream that almost burst forth from them.

I resisted taking matters into my own hands.

I wanted to leave everything to God to do what He wanted.

I didn't sleep.

I spent the night scared to close my eyes or open them. I was afraid that if I closed them, black thoughts would invade my dreams, and I was afraid that if I opened them, I'd see those same black thoughts.

I wasn't afraid only for Mahmoud.

The phone woke me up the next morning. It was Mahmoud asking to meet me at six o'clock that evening.

"Okay," I said weakly. I was afraid that I'd let myself inflict some kind of harm on him.

I spent the day with Nanny Halima. For the first time, I found I couldn't resist mentioning him to her.

But she didn't understand what I was hinting at. She hadn't noticed Mahmoud at the party, so she couldn't share my interest in him. Mahmoud was the kind of man people didn't notice or pay attention to unless they knew him.

All of Nanny Halima's talk was about the party. She purposely talked around Kawthar, with a tepidness that showed she wasn't comfortable with her and didn't like her.

"The truth is that the master won't find anyone like Madame Safiya," she said, sighing and resting her head on her palm. "No one will ever be able to fill her shoes."

"We're finished with that story," I found myself almost yelling. "Are we going to lament that our whole lives? Your mistress Kawthar is my friend and I know her well. She isn't like Safiya. She's better than her!"

Nanny Halima fell silent reluctantly.

I collected myself.

"Go see what the cook is doing today," I instructed her with artificial calm.

Nanny Halima got up, dragging her feet as if she was walking in a funeral procession.

It took me a while to calm down.

At four o'clock, I started getting ready to meet Mahmoud.

When it was five minutes to six, I took one last look in the mirror. I thought I'd never looked as beautiful as on that day.

I left.

I saw the love in Mahmoud's eyes as he opened the car door for me.

He took me to the Mena House, but we didn't stay there. He took me to Heliopolis again. And we talked. We talked about everything, but he didn't try to talk about marriage.

Until I turned my head and looked out the car window.

"I feel like you're going to war and I'm saying goodbye to you," I said.

"Shame on you," he said calmly. "What war? The only war is the one I'm fighting with myself. I'm fighting myself so I can leave you."

"I've read a lot of stories about war," I said, still looking at the road. "The soldier takes a leave of twenty-four hours to marry the girl he loves and then goes back to fight again."

"These are stories that don't end well," he said, authoritatively. "This kind of marriage is illogical. It's entirely egotistical. Before I die, I come and take something for myself. The soldier goes back to fight and die, leaving behind a woman he could have spared from being a widow and a child who'll grow up an orphan. A poor child born after his father has died. What was his crime? What was his crime other than that his father couldn't wait until his life became stable? His father was selfish, and didn't think about the son who'd be born from the short night he spent with his love."

"But they don't all die. Some of them come back and live happily ever after."

"Whoever doesn't die will change," he continued. "Whoever doesn't change comes back to discover things in his wife that he didn't know about, sides of her that he couldn't see in his rush to marriage where he submitted to his emotions and forgot his mind."

"Sometimes it's the circumstances that change," I said. "The circumstances of the girl whose love didn't marry her before leaving. I think it was in the novel *Waterloo Bridge* where the man went to fight and left his love alone. She was worn down and fell victim to those circumstances. When he came back from the war, it was over. He couldn't marry her. But if he'd married her before leaving, it would have protected her from the terrible conditions she suffered. He would have come back to find her waiting for him."

"I believe this time period," he said, "the time when the man is traveling and leaves his girl, is a test to see how much the two can endure, how much they can wait, if they can hold on to their feelings. That creates the strongest marriage."

"But there are things you can't count on," I said. "For example—"

"Marriage isn't a story, Nadia," he said, cutting me off. "It's not a novel. Marriage is something very big. Marriage is all of life. It means stability. It's not possible for someone to get married until they are settled."

"Why?" I asked. "Is it not possible for a homeless person to marry someone? Is it not better than being homeless alone?"

"What about the children?"

I was quiet for a moment. "You're right," I said finally, trying to be convinced of what he was saying. "Thank God you're not going to war, or I'd be afraid you'd change."

With a big smile, he reached out and pulled me to him. I rested my head on his chest as he drove the car with the other hand.

Mahmoud left at dawn the following day, after he'd signed his name on my heart, my imagination, and my lips. He left me in the checkroom of fate.

We only promised that he'd write me and I'd write him.

"Wait for me, Nadia," was the last thing he said as he pulled his lips from mine.

"I'll wait for you, Mahmoud," was the last thing I said.

After that, I considered myself engaged to him.

I was afraid of this hope. I clung to it with each step I took, with every thought I had, with every word I said.

I was like someone walking on eggshells, afraid I'd break something under my feet.

I was afraid I'd ruin something around me, afraid my hope wouldn't be achieved.

My father had married Kawthar.

And in a matter of months, I'd marry Mahmoud.

My happiness would be complete.

I rejoiced. I felt calm. I slept.

But . . .

Had God forgiven me?

Had He shown me His mercy?

Had He forgotten my crime?

19

There was something small that had happened that I hadn't paid much attention to at the time.

It was during the party for my father's marriage to Kawthar.

The phone rang. I lifted the receiver and said hello a number of times, but no one responded. I heard someone hang up. After a bit, the phone rang again. I picked up, and again, no one responded. It rang a third time, and I saw Kawthar rush to the phone in her bridal dress, beating me to the receiver. She spoke in a low voice for a moment, and then put the receiver down and went back to the guests. She stood next to my father with her wide, sweet smile full of activity and life, without mentioning anything about who was calling.

I didn't pay attention to that incident that day. I was happy. My heart and mind were clear. I was happy with my father's marriage and happy with Mahmoud beside me. I wasn't ready to think badly about anyone, and anyway, I couldn't disturb a bride at her wedding party.

Some weeks passed and I didn't notice anything unusual.

Thinking about Mahmoud occupied my entire being and every second that passed. I sometimes went off alone so I could imagine myself talking to him, scolding him, and confiding in him. Sometimes I imagined him on the streets of London picking out a wedding gift for me. Sometimes I saw him in my imagination with another girl, and then I'd get upset and angry, and I couldn't sleep. I waited for his letters as if waiting for an urgent appointment.

My father seemed almost to float from happiness. He went back to walking with pride and dignity, as if the entire earth were his. He went back to singing in the shower every morning and filling the house with joy. He went back to embracing me roughly, trying to lift me off the ground as if he was trying to prove his strength to me, showing off his masculinity. He went back to being organized and steady, just as he had been. He'd go out on time and come back on time. He was never late for lunch or dinner. He once again accepted family invitations and went to soirees with me and Kawthar.

Kawthar always seemed happy and in a good mood. Her wide smile embraced the whole house and she spread lightness and joy. But she wasn't a housewife. Not at all. She was pampered, a flirt or, as the French say, a coquette. She couldn't stand to keep watch over the house or take the servants to task or go into the kitchen or take over the household expenses. She left all those things to me and Nanny Halima. I accepted the duties of the house excitedly and wholeheartedly. To tell the truth, they were diversions for me while I was waiting for Mahmoud. Kawthar thought that continuing to supervise the house was a way for me to maintain my place and importance. As for Nanny Halima, she was always annoyed and always complaining, since she didn't like that Kawthar ignored the running of the house, even if I was the one who took her place.

A few golden weeks went by.

Then I started noticing things.

As soon as my father left the house, Kawthar would take the phone and disappear with it into her room. She'd disappear for a while and then come back with her hair messed up and her ears red from pressing the receiver against them.

Sometimes, after my father had left, she'd leave the house alone without inviting me to go with her, claiming she was visiting her mother or one of her friends. She'd come back nervous and worn out before my father got back.

"No one called?" she'd ask me breathlessly with a weary smile. "No one asked for your father?"

When I responded no, she seemed to calm down. She went into her room to change her clothes and tidy herself up. She then appeared happy and lively, like she hadn't even left the house.

None of this escaped me.

I wasn't so dumb or gullible that I couldn't make out what was behind it all.

I started wondering . . .

Was she having an affair?

Was she betraying my father?

I didn't need to wonder. The truth was so clear that there was no room for doubt.

Yes. She was betraying my father, robbing him of his honor, bleeding him of his dignity with another man.

I had kicked the faithful wife out of his life and put a cheating one in her place.

I'd sold the innocent one and brought in the criminal.

Oh, Lord!

Has Your punishment begun?

Oh, Lord!

Could You not forget?

Oh, Lord!

Oh, magnificent vengeful One. When will You be forgiving and merciful?

I stopped sleeping. I started feeling like there was a snake slithering over my body, under my clothes, making me writhe. I started feeling as if I was living in a garbage bin. Everything around me was filthy. Everything around me was hypocrisy, lies, deception.

Why was she cheating on him?

What did he lack that other men had?

Maybe she didn't love him.

Then why did she marry him?

Maybe because her lover was the kind of man who didn't get married—someone like Mustafa. Maybe she married my father so he could give her the status society demands, give her the easy life that she was living. She married him as a setup to betray him, in cahoots with her lover. She betrayed him with intent and purpose, with premeditation, as the law says.

All those thoughts were swimming around my head. What should I do?

I could crush her. I could kick her out of the house like a dog. If my mind wasn't incapable of destroying goodness and crushing innocent people, it wouldn't be incapable of destroying evil and crushing criminals.

But my father . . .

My poor father . . .

Could he bear another blow?

Could he bear losing two wives, both accused of cheating?

Could a man's dignity bear the weight of all that pain and suffering?

I remembered my father's state immediately after he divorced Auntie Safiya. I remembered him wandering around drunk, squandering everything, cheap women toying with him. No, my father must not know.

Kawthar had to stay in his life at any price. Whatever it cost. Whatever this charade, this hypocrisy, this deception cost me.

What is adultery anyway?

Adultery is a crime that is only committed once the husband knows. The husband is usually the last to know, and until he finds out, the crime hasn't taken place yet. It's like the crime of swindling. As long as you don't know that there's been a swindle, as long as you don't know that someone has swindled you, there's no crime. As long as you don't know that something has been stolen from you, theft, in your mind, hasn't taken place.

The law on adultery recognizes that it's a crime that takes place only with the knowledge of the husband. If the law gives a husband the right to forgo making an accusation of adultery against his wife, then it no doubt considers the husband who doesn't know to have forgone his right.

Society, too. It doesn't punish the cheating wife unless her husband knows. Society might whisper and it might point from a distance, but it doesn't scream, doesn't accuse, and doesn't punish unless the husband finds out. And the day he finds out is the day the divorce takes place and catastrophe ensues. Society opens its mouth, and thousands of tongues come out to crack like whips.

Was that true?

I didn't know. Nothing mattered to me those days except for looking for a logic to convince myself to cover up for my father's wife, to preserve my father's happiness.

I was determined, to the point that I began accusing myself that I was the reason for what Kawthar was doing.

Why not?

Kawthar, when she was a student, was as innocent and unblemished as a crystal. Then she fell in love with Medhat, my cousin, with a pure love that could have ended in marriage if I hadn't intervened and torn up their love. It drove Kawthar crazy. She shriveled up as if she no longer had any blood left in her. Then they married her to a man far from her heart, personality, and dreams. She divorced him after a year. After the divorce, she let herself go into the world, into corrupt society. She no longer had hope to protect herself with. Fate didn't leave her any virtue to defend herself with. She was sinning now. Maybe she'd sinned a lot. But why? Because she didn't find happiness in virtue. She only found in it torture and degradation and living with a man she didn't love.

If she'd married Medhat, would all of that have happened to her? Would she have cheated on him as she was cheating on my father now? Would she be as frivolous and greedy as she was now?

I didn't think so. A wife either loves her husband or she's an adulteress. There isn't a wife who loves her husband and cheats on him, and there isn't a wife who doesn't love her husband and doesn't cheat on him, even if she cheats on him with herself. That's what Mustafa said. I think he was right.

I was the criminal in both cases.

I committed a crime the day I broke up Kawthar and Medhat, and then again when I covered up for her so she could be a treasonous wife, cheating with another man.

I committed a crime the day I chose her as a wife for my father, so he would be the duped husband.

That was what I'd tell myself to increase my conviction to cover up Kawthar's cheating, to protect my father's happiness.

Meanwhile, Kawthar strived to make my father happy.

I couldn't accuse her of abandoning my father's happiness.

On the contrary. She'd come back from meeting her lover and then bestow on my father double the pampering, tenderness, and submission, as if she were trying to compensate him or ease her conscience.

My good, naive father was happy all that time. I hadn't seen such happiness on his handsome face before.

I, alone, was being tortured.

I, alone, smelled the scent of betrayal, a bitter heavy stench that entered my lungs.

With the passing days, Kawthar knew that I was on to her secret.

She knew that I was covering it up.

It wasn't possible for us both to live in a single house without one of us discovering the secrets of the other. Kawthar wasn't so stupid that she thought she could hide on the phone in her room, leave the house for those supposed appointments, and come back looking suspicious without stirring up my doubts.

Despite that, we didn't talk about it.

Maybe she could see my distaste toward her. But we both ignored it. We both kept control over the disgust between us, so we seemed like close friends whenever my father was with us.

I didn't bring it up, and neither did she.

Until one day . . .

As we sat at the breakfast table, Kawthar said she was going to visit her mother.

I swallowed my pain along with the food that I was chewing.

"Why don't you tell her to come and have dinner with us tonight?" my father asked lovingly and kindly. "We haven't seen her in days. I've never seen a mother-in-law like that."

My father left.

Soon after, Kawthar went out.

I was left alone. Then I started reading Mahmoud's letters for the thousandth time. Those letters were my solace, my hope, everything I was living for. Between their lines, I imagined Mahmoud coming back from London to marry me, to carry me far from this house, far from Kawthar, far from my father whose love had exhausted me, the love that had ruined my life and with which I'd ruined his life.

I only had one hope: Mahmoud.

Mahmoud's letters were always delicate—more delicate than I had expected. They were more delicate than his calm talk, his tender glances, his refined culture, his kisses, which rested on my lips like the touches of angels, more delicate than his breath, which encircled me like the wings of small butterflies in love.

In one of his letters, he wrote:

"It's strange—I didn't know that the women of

London were faceless. I haven't seen a single woman's face here. I see only one face, which I took with me from Cairo in my imagination. The face of a girl with golden hair, green in her eyes, a sweet stream on her lips, and a rose on her cheeks, her skin woven by goodness, her breath innocent, and her smile like a child's."

In another letter, he wrote:

"I wonder sometimes what brings us together. Are we similar or are we contradictory? No, each of us completes the other. You're light and I'm dark. You're a little too tall and I'm a little too short. You're emotional and I'm logical. You're heart and I'm mind. You look at the sky and I look to the depths. You're an angel and I'm human. You and I form a complete person. Each of us is half of the other. Here, far from you, I feel that I'm half of myself. I want to return to my other half!"

I was deeply in love reading these letters, seeing in them a beautiful, sweet, and kind image—the image of me through Mahmoud's eyes.

Suddenly, the phone rang. It was my father.

"Where did Kawthar go?" he asked, his voice going up and down as if driving over potholes. "I called her mother, but I didn't find her there. Do you know where she went?"

I was nervous, but I did everything I could to hide it.

"Daddy, I think she went to the doctor," I said, as if throwing myself into the ocean to save someone drowning.

"Doctor? What doctor?" he asked, surprised. "When I left this morning, she felt fine. I'll go see her right away."

"Don't worry, Daddy," I said quickly. "She should be home any moment. I don't think it's serious. She's been complaining for two days and she didn't want to tell you so you wouldn't worry."

"I'm leaving now," my father said, hanging up.

I walked around the house like a crazy woman. I looked out the windows, searching for Kawthar, hoping she'd get back before my father.

But she didn't.

"Did she tell you she was going to the doctor?" my father asked when he didn't find her at home.

"No," I said. "I was cleaning up my room and I didn't think to ask her."

I started calming my father and consoling him, even though I was the one who needed calming and consoling. I asked my father if I could go to the neighbors' apartment to get a needlepoint pattern from their daughter. I didn't wait for his permission. I left quickly, went out to the street, and stood waiting for Kawthar. I looked all around until I convinced the doorman that I was waiting for a car that I was going to take.

Kawthar came after a bit in a taxi.

Before her feet hit the ground, I went up to her, whispering in her ear what had happened and advising her to tell my father that she'd been at the doctor, not at her mother's.

I then let her go up before me.

When I got to the apartment, I heard my father talking to her anxiously.

"But you're not telling me what's wrong or why you went to the doctor."

"No, I'm not telling you," Kawthar said playfully.

I intruded in the conversation.

"You're back. You made us worried!"

"Please," my father said again, pleading. "Put my mind at rest."

"My dear," Kawthar said, so lightly that I envied her for her nerves of steel, "what do you know about women's things? I'll tell you later, when we're alone!"

She went up to him, kissed him on the cheeks, and looked at him with fake tenderness.

My father's face lit up. His eyes sparkled and his mouth dropped as if he'd suddenly understood something.

My father was aghast, as if what he understood surprised him so much he couldn't speak. He looked at Kawthar with a mixture of shock and admiration.

"Is it really true, Kawthar?" I said, to tighten the great lie.

"The doctor still isn't sure," Kawthar said, putting on a show of being bashful.

From that day, my father pampered his wife and looked after her, paying attention to everything she was eating and every step she took. He bought books about pregnancy, until Kawthar was forced to take him to the doctor. No doubt she gave the doctor another lie, and then left to tell my father that she wasn't pregnant after all.

From that day, the situation between me and Kawthar was out in the open.

She was open about cheating on my father.

And I was open about covering it up.

The caller no longer hung up when I picked up. It seemed that Kawthar had told her friend that I was in on their secret and that I was covering it up for them. He then found the courage to speak to me.

"Hello? Miss Nadia? Can I please speak with Kawthar?"

I knew it was him, her boyfriend, but I pretended to ignore him. Perhaps he'd pretend to ignore the truth too—claiming, for example, that he was the brother of one of her friends.

"Who's this?" I asked him coldly.

"Samir," he said in a polite but impudent voice.

I could do nothing but give her the phone.

That was how I learned his name.

Samir!

Despite that, I didn't give Kawthar the chance to talk to me about him. I wanted to keep myself far from them, to stay as far as I could from this heavy stench that clogged my lungs —the scent of betrayal.

I'd prevent her from talking about herself or her boyfriend. I'd be dry and resolute in blocking her. But she didn't notice. She would smile sarcastically as if she was sneering at me. She knew she had me by the neck and that I wouldn't be able to do anything about her treachery. She knew I was drinking the poison silently and that I was letting her trample my dignity, that she could whip me whenever she wanted and I wouldn't moan or complain.

She knew I'd cover up for her, not out of love for her but to preserve my father's happiness. She knew I'd sacrifice everything—my dignity, my comfort, my entire life—for this love, the love of my father.

She exploited my love for my father. She held me by my most delicate and sensitive part and had started torturing me.

I was tortured horribly.

I was tortured by the wound from having my own dignity trampled. I was tortured by the deception of my father. I was tortured by my hatred for Kawthar, a hatred branding me, burning my heart.

I was quiet about this torture for a long time.

I was afraid it would explode in me and stir up the forces of evil inside me, to bring the house crashing down on my father's head as had happened once before.

I was trying to flee from this torture to Mahmoud. I'd write him at length, telling him everything about Kawthar—about her cheating, and my duped father. I'd complain. I'd seek refuge in him. I'd beg him to come back to save me.

Then I'd tear up what I wrote.

He didn't have to know.

He must always stay out of all these problems that I was immersed in, clean and pure so I could live with him . . . clean and pure.

Fighting this torture exhausted me. My body withered, and everything inside me became broken. My eyes dulled, my lips seemed to deflate, my cheeks become sallow, as if my blood were too ashamed to face my father and people in general. My silence grew, but I was trying to seem happy before my father, so I didn't make him worry. I intentionally went out with him and Kawthar, so I didn't upset him by staying home alone, so I didn't give Kawthar the chance to rejoice at my misfortune.

I once went with them to the Auberge Restaurant, and on the way to our table, I saw Mustafa.

With who?

Auntie Safiya!

Safiya's brother was with them, as well as some friends.

Mustafa and Safiya were so absorbed in each other that they were ignoring everyone around them. Each was immersed in conversation with the other, as if they were continuing the conversation they'd started when they met the first time.

My father saw Safiya and pretended to ignore her.

Kawthar looked at her with cheap haughtiness, and then put her arm on my father's arm, letting out a loud laugh as if she wanted to snatch everyone's eyes away from Safiya.

As for me, I looked at the two of them pathetically and submissively. I looked at them for a long time.

Mustafa looked at me as if suddenly remembering that he'd seen me before.

Safiya smiled broadly at me, appearing happy to see me. She nodded hello from a distance.

In that moment, I didn't care about Mustafa. I didn't feel his presence. Instead, all my emotion was directed at Safiya, all that I'd done. I felt as if I wanted to throw myself on her chest and cry, to tell her what was happening to me. I wanted her to take me with her to her house far from Kawthar, far from her betrayal, far from the deception, hypocrisy, and lies, and the terrible stench of it all.

I spent that evening in a daze.

I wasn't thinking about Safiya and Mustafa or what could have brought them together. I was thinking about myself, my life, my bad deeds, my fate, my torture, my misery.

My dazed state didn't dissipate, and finally my father suggested we go back home, since he thought I was tired. Kawthar refused—she didn't want to leave before Safiya so she didn't seem to be having less of a good time than her.

I kept looking at Mustafa. He was dancing with Safiya as if embracing an angel that he was afraid he might harm. I looked at them like I was looking out through black bars into a beautiful world from which I'd been banished.

When I was back home in bed, every part of me longed for Mahmoud.

He was the only hope that I had left of being saved.

20

ONE DAY . . .

We were invited to the wedding of one of our friends. Kawthar and I went to the hairdresser in the morning. They finished our hair at the same time. It was noon.

After we left the hairdresser, Kawthar suggested that we go to Groppi's to have a glass of orange juice.

I didn't want to.

Kawthar insisted.

"Please, Nadia," she begged. "I feel like I just got out of the oven. The hairdryer melted my brain and I'm dizzy. Let's sit in Groppi's for five minutes. We'll have a glass of juice and go."

"We'll be home in five minutes," I said dryly. "You can have the whole fridge there."

"Shame on you, Nadia!" she said with a pleading look in her eyes. "Do it for me."

"It's not appropriate for two women to sit in Groppi's by themselves."

"You've totally changed, Nadia! You're like my grandmother. Come on, look, Grandma, all the men are at work. Groppi's is empty at this time of day. There are only women there."

She pulled me by the hand and let out a mischievous laugh.

I yielded to her, simply to avoid the scene Kawthar could cause in the middle of the street.

Groppi's was only a stone's throw from the hairdresser.

She was still gripping my hand as we went in, as if she was afraid I'd flee.

There weren't actually a lot of men there—at a table or two, some old men read newspapers. At other tables sat some older foreign women. The entire place was dominated by a silence. The humid air hung heavy, with a gentle light spreading through its darkness.

My chest tightened. I had a feeling deep down that I was being pulled into something.

Kawthar picked an isolated table and we sat down. She asked the waiter for two glasses of orange juice.

I started looking around, annoyed, trying to collect my strength from the dim light.

Before the waiter brought the two glasses of juice, a young man suddenly stood before us as if the earth had split open and spat him out of its belly and then closed itself up after it was relieved of him. I didn't know where he came from or what wind had tossed him to us, but I found him standing up very straight before us, like a plank of wood.

Every line on this young man seemed to have been drawn precisely with a compass and ruler, as if an engineer, not a tailor, had made his suit, as if it were made from stone, not cloth. His tie looked like it had been knotted by someone trying to choke him and his face shone like limestone, as if he had been shaved by a sculptor, not a barber.

His eyes bulged, his life seeming to have collected under his eyelids. His lips were thick and wide, greed and hunger drawn on them. His black hair was long and shiny, each strand clinging to the next with pomade, making it look fake. All his movements were theatrical, as if he was showing off his muscles, elegance, and coolness.

Kawthar reached out to him coquettishly, a drunken smile on her face. He leaned over and kissed her hand with an ugly attempt at gracefulness. He then turned to me and gave me an impudent look, as if he were undressing me with his eyes. I felt his smile like a sticky liquid running down my face.

"Of course, you've spoken on the phone," Kawthar said, introducing me to him, her smile widening. "This, my dear, is Samir. Samir Husam Eddine." Turning to him, she continued, "And, of course, you know who this is. Nadia."

I let out a stifled cough.

He reached out and I extended my hand hesitantly. He leaned over, trying to kiss it, but I pulled it back quickly.

He pulled a chair over and sat down without asking permission, like he had an appointment with us.

I stared at Kawthar sharply, shooting daggers at her. But she ignored my looks and devoted herself to talking with Samir as if it was natural that she met him in a public place, as if it was natural that I was with them. Me, the daughter of the duped husband.

I inspected Samir out of the corner of my eye. His odiousness, his trivialness, the artificiality of his movements, his effeminacy, his empty words. What did Kawthar see in him? Was there anything in him better than my father?

I was furious. He could not be compared to my father. He didn't measure up even to the sole of my father's shoe. He was trifling, despicable, wretched.

I knew this kind of guy. I knew the type well. He was from an old, well-known, but dissolved family that had lost its moral standing and material wealth. He grew up with a well-known name and false sense of belonging to the aristocracy, but what he lived on was tricking women, duping them, snatching their honor and everything they had. He was the kind of guy who specialized in pursuing a woman and ruining her.

Yes, I knew this type.

I was enraged. I felt that I couldn't bear any more or I'd explode. Everything in me was wounded—my dignity, my honor, my love for my father.

I hit the table with my hand.

"I think we'll get going, Kawthar," I said in a hoarse voice, choked by the fire bursting through my veins.

"We haven't had our juice yet," Kawthar replied indifferently.

"It seems that Miss Nadia is in a big rush," Samir said.

I didn't respond.

"Not at all," Kawthar said, attaching no importance to what I'd said. "She's just a bit agitated these days."

I wanted to slap her.

My hand almost moved on its own.

Samir gave me a bold look from beneath his thick eyebrows.

"Kawthar is always telling me about you, saying that you're beautiful. But I didn't think you'd be this beautiful."

"Samir," Kawthar said. "Is your eye roving?"

"We're very late," I said again, getting ready to go.

As soon as I stood up, the waiter came with the glasses of juice.

"Can't you just let us drink our juice?" Kawthar said, looking at me angry and irritated.

I sat back down in my chair, resigned to my fate.

I looked at the juice like it was poison. I didn't reach for it. I turned my head to the door, searching for a way to save myself. Then I let out a muffled scream.

I saw my father.

I saw him come in through the door, heading over to buy sweets.

My eyes clung to him as if I were trying to push him away with my eyelashes.

In a fleeting moment, I imagined him standing in front of us and then pulling a revolver out of his pocket and shooting two bullets to kill Kawthar, two bullets to kill her boyfriend, two more to kill me, and the final bullet to kill himself.

I turned to Kawthar in terror.

"Daddy . . . Daddy!" I whispered.

Kawthar raised her head and saw him. Her face went pale, as if all her blood had drained out of her. Her lips trembled. Her eyes filled with confusion and terror. She turned her head to Samir as if to protect him from the shots of the gun. She then turned to me as if she was pleading, begging for help.

Samir turned to look at my father and started fiddling nervously with his tie. He tugged his neck from the shirt collar and bit his lip. Pushing down on his nose with his finger, he mumbled words that I couldn't hear or understand and that sounded more like the hissing of a snake.

Before any of us could move, my father was right next to us.

The eyes of the three of us met in a fleeting glance, as if we were weaving a net to trap my poor father.

"What a surprise! What brought you all here?" I heard my father say in confusion, as if calculating something. "Didn't you tell me you were going to the hairdresser?"

I don't know how much time passed before I heard Kawthar speak. Maybe an hour or two, maybe a minute or a second.

"We came to have orange juice," I heard her say. "Because . . . because . . . because you feel dizzy when you leave the hairdresser, and—"

Samir stood up next to my father, still fiddling with his tie and tugging his neck from his shirt collar.

My father turned to him. I saw an unreadable look in his eyes, as if he was waiting for one of us to introduce them before defining the meaning of his look.

I don't know what happened to me at that moment.

I don't know what happened to my mind.

At that moment, I thought Kawthar wouldn't ever speak, that her tongue was paralyzed from the terror of the situation. I thought that if she spoke, she'd confess and say that this was her boyfriend, that she'd been betraying my father with him since they got married, that she was in love with him and she was his. I imagined my father hearing this confession, letting out the word *divorce*, then collapsing on the ground dead . . . dead from a heart attack. I pictured myself screaming, clutching him, drenching him with my tears.

All of this passed through my mind in that split second. I had to do something. I had to say something to save this situation, to save my father from death as Joan of Arc saved her nation, and then was burned alive.

"This is Mr. Samir," I heard myself say to my father. "Mr. Samir Husam Eddine."

My father extended his hand to him and they greeted each other.

My father looked at me wanting more details.

"I'll tell you everything later, Daddy," I said, lowering my eyes in faked shyness like I was a bride on her wedding night.

Samir turned to me in surprise.

Kawthar's eyes clung to me as if she were searching for what was in my head.

"I'll know what?" my father asked, forcing himself to remain calm.

"Later, Daddy," I said, still acting shy and bashful. "Kawthar will tell you everything."

Out of the corner of my eye, I noticed a wide smile spread across Kawthar's lips. I thought I saw the blood starting to flow back to her cheeks.

She understood what I was hinting at.

Samir understood too. "Sir, I've been wanting to have the honor of meeting you for a long time," he told my father boldly, as only a real crook could. "I'll let Nadia pick the time that's appropriate."

"Appropriate?" he asked. Then, as if he finally understood, a small smile came to his lips. "Oh, okay, but—"

Kawthar cut him off, jumping up and calling up all her powers of persuasion and deception. "Now's not the time," she said, putting her arm on my father's arm. "We'll talk later. Let's go, Ahmed."

She reached her hand out formally to Samir. "It was very nice to meet you, Mr. Samir," she said. "Rest assured that everything will go well, God willing!"

She then turned to me.

"Let's go, Nadia, my dear!" Her tone was tender like a mother who was happy with her daughter.

If she'd reached out to me, I would have strangled her.

Samir took my hand. He gave me a theatrical look and then leaned over and kissed my hand, pressing his greedy, hungry lips to it.

We left after my father bought some sweets and pancakes.

We three sat in the front seat of the car, my father at the steering wheel next to Kawthar. I slammed the door behind me.

"I don't understand what's going on," my father said, looking in front of him. "What's the story exactly?"

"Later, Ahmed," Kawthar said, tugging her dress around her thighs. "Just be patient until we get home."

"Yes, but," my father persisted, "whatever it is, why were you sitting at Groppi's with someone I've never seen before?"

"Trust me," said Kawthar without missing a beat, "it has to do with Nadia."

"Where do you know him from, Nadia?" my father asked, still looking in front of him. "Have you met him many times before this?"

"Not at all, Daddy," I said, about to cry from anger and rage because of the position I'd put myself in. "I saw him in Alexandria last summer. Then he called me on the phone once a day. Of course I ignored him. Until he asked to meet you. I thought I'd introduce him to Kawthar first so she'd be the one to talk with you."

"Is he related to Fathi Pasha Husam Eddine?" my father asked, clearing his throat.

"He's his nephew," Kawthar said quickly.

"It's an important family," my father said. "But penniless."

"He's not rich," Kawthar said, as if defending him. "But he has a good job in an insurance company."

We reached the house.

Kawthar and I got out at the door of the building while my father headed to the garage. My nerves had frayed and rage burned in my heart. I was ready to explode.

I leaned toward Kawthar.

"Get me out of this," I whispered sharply. "I swear on Daddy, Mother, and God that this is the last time I have anything to do with you or this whole thing. After this, let what happens happen. I've had enough humiliation."

Kawthar smiled wickedly. She was sure she had me by the throat and could do whatever she wanted.

"Don't upset yourself, Nadia," she said. "Everything will be fine. It'll all work out."

My father came back.

We both smiled at him as if we'd just been chitchatting about something.

My father put his arm on my shoulder as we went toward the elevator.

"I didn't think that you were hiding something from me, Nadia," he said tenderly and good-naturedly.

I didn't say a word.

I thought that if I opened my mouth, my tears would come pouring out.

We had lunch quickly and quietly, each lost in our own thoughts.

I was distraught.

I was thinking about this dilemma I'd put myself in.

Why had I volunteered this great lie?

Why didn't I wait? Maybe Kawthar would have found another way out for herself.

I was deluding myself if I believed I could find a solution to every dilemma, a way out of every crisis.

Or maybe it wasn't delusion. My longing to protect my father's happiness and my determination to cover for his cheating wife were what had pushed me to this charade.

I didn't think for long about the results of this deception and the trouble it could bring me. I found myself thinking about Mahmoud instead.

I felt I'd betrayed him with this lie.

His pride would be wounded when I claimed I belonged to another man.

I was pulling Mahmoud with me through the mud to a despicable world in which only cheats live.

I jumped to my feet and ran to my room without saying a word to my father. I took out Mahmoud's letters and his picture, and started kissing them as if apologizing to him, as if begging him to forgive me, as if promising to rise up to the world of decency he lived in and not drag him down into the black realm I inhabited.

I only left my room in the evening when it was time for us to go to the wedding party, not knowing what my father and Kawthar had talked about.

That night I tried to appear beautiful and chic, but I failed. I was dejected. Something inside me whispered terrifying things. I felt weak and pathetic, as if my wings had been clipped. Mahmoud was the only means I had to fly into a happy world.

I sat with the guests at the wedding party, silent and depressed. I didn't respond to people saying hello or partake in any pleasantries.

I was thinking about Mahmoud the whole time, feeling sad and miserable, as if I'd lost him, as if he'd never come back to me.

During the bridal procession, I stared at the bride and groom, trying to put Mahmoud in the groom's place and myself in the bride's place, to feel happy with this fantasy. But I couldn't. This sweet image kept disappearing. Whenever I tried to bring it back, it moved farther away as if I couldn't convince myself that one day I'd be Mahmoud's wife.

I was on the verge of tears.

The sound of the tambourines rose up around me, violently like the screams of devils circling. The body of the dancer twisted before my eyes like a huge snake coming to swallow me up.

My eyes filled with tears. It took everything I had to keep them in, to keep from crying or screaming.

Why, oh Lord, couldn't I have a wedding like this?

Why wasn't Mahmoud next to me now?

Why was I surrounded by this depression and misery?

We left right after the procession. I was staggering, as if about to collapse.

"May it be the same for your wedding, Nadia," my father told me as we were at the door, giving me a smile full of insinuation.

"Merci," I mumbled.

As soon as I found myself alone in my room, I cried.

I cried so much I thought I'd drown in my tears.

I didn't leave my room until late the next morning.

My father had left.

Kawthar was in the sitting room. Before we'd even said good morning, the phone rang. Kawthar rushed over to answer.

"Good morning," I heard her say. "How are you, Samir?"

She started talking with the phone in her hand, heading to her room and closing the door behind her.

I didn't care.

I was exhausted, so tired that I didn't have the strength to care about anything. I called Nanny Halima and asked her to make me a cup of hot milk. Maybe it would calm my nerves.

After I drank the milk, I went back to my room and started writing Mahmoud. As usual, I wrote him two letters. The first in which I told him everything, everything happening to me, as if recording my memories and confessions, and another in which I told him about my love and longing for him, repeating my promise that I'd wait for him.

I'd tear up the first letter.

And send the second.

I found solace in confessing to Mahmoud. I was happier writing the first letter than the second. But could I send it to him? Those confessions? Would he be happy with me as a wife after he read them?

I didn't think so.

While I was writing, Kawthar came in.

"Samir says hello," she said teasingly.

I didn't respond and kept writing.

"You know, he likes you very much," she said, coming to me.

I didn't respond.

"He talks about you all the time," she said, putting her hand on my shoulder.

"Please!" I cried, turning to her. "Don't talk to me about him. I don't want to hear his name, ever. You have no shame. Isn't what you're doing enough?"

Kawthar moved away from me with a look of disgust and hatred. But she quickly regained her composure and wiped the harsh look from her face.

"Please," she said with a mocking laugh, "don't get so mad. I know what's making you so anxious. It's these letters that you're writing. Be reasonable, my girl. Far from the eye, far from the heart!"

"You have nothing to do with him!" I shouted, wanting to protect my love, my only hope. "Don't say anything. Don't come in my room. Please leave. Leave me alone!"

She shrugged disdainfully.

She left the room and I got up and slammed the door behind her.

Like a woman possessed, I tore up the letters I'd written and threw the pillows on the ground. I smashed a vase and pulled my hair.

When I had calmed myself down I went to have lunch with my father, quiet, sad, depressed, not looking at Kawthar, not wanting to lay my eyes on her face.

"Mr. Samir hasn't called today?" I heard my father ask.

I raised my head in surprise.

I was thinking that Kawthar had put an end to the subject of Samir with my father, that she'd told him any old thing, given him any old lie. I never expected that my father would ask me about him.

I collected my nerves. "No," I said.

"Really?" my father said with a big smile. "So that's why you're grumpy."

I looked at Kawthar in confusion.

Kawthar turned away from me with a wicked smile.

I looked at my father again. He still had a broad smile on his face.

I tossed my napkin onto the table, got up nervously, and headed for my room. My father laughed loudly and the sound followed me until I threw myself on my bed.

What did my father mean?

Was he making fun of me?

Why didn't Kawthar say anything?

What was the meaning of that wicked smile?

How long could I keep quiet about this situation?

Oh, Lord!

I couldn't stand staying in the house. I left at four in the afternoon and went to visit one of my friends. I couldn't bear staying with her either, so I left and went to visit my mother.

As I sat with her, I asked myself again whether I could share my problems with her. Could I tell her what Kawthar was doing to me, the story of her cheating on my father? Could I tell her about my love for Mahmoud, my waiting for him and longing for him? Could I open my whole heart to her so that all of my emotions and thoughts could rush out, and then ask her for advice?

I came to the same sad conclusion: Of course not. She wouldn't understand me. She's distant from me, very distant, in a world other than mine, an innocent, naive world in which neither my problems nor my complicated life could enter.

I drifted off as she talked about clothes and movies. The whole time, I felt there was a catastrophe awaiting me, a hole into which I'd fall, a wind that would blow over me, but I didn't know when and where it would come from. I was afraid—afraid to go back home, afraid to think, afraid of a huge black specter closing in on me.

I had to go home, so I got up to extract myself. I hugged my mother as if seeking protection from her, as if I was leaving her forever.

I got back at seven o'clock. As soon as I went in the house, I found the parlor lit. I heard my father's voice, Kawthar's voice, and the voice of a man I didn't recognize.

I went to the parlor and stood at the door, flabbergasted. I felt nailed to the floor.

I looked from Kawthar to my father and back again, in surprise and confusion. Then I felt something repressed inside me would erupt.

It was Samir.

Samir Husam Eddine.

Kawthar's lover.

What had brought him here? What was he doing in my house?

I didn't wait for the answer. I turned around without greeting anyone, even my father, and went to my room.

That shameless woman. That criminal! All that was left was for her to bring her lover to the house, to get him and my father together in the same room.

But why?

What was her pretext for inviting him to the house?

I heard the sound of the front door open and voices saying goodbye, and then the door closed.

My father came into my room with a big smile on his face.

"Why did you run off like that—like a little girl?" he asked happily and tenderly. "Come, come, let's talk together in the office."

I got up and went with him, stunned.

He called Kawthar to join us.

Then he closed the door on us as if he was preparing an important meeting. He turned to me and put his hands on my shoulders, looking at me as if he was seeing me for the first time. Pulling me to his chest, he squeezed me gently and tenderly, and kissed me on the forehead.

"Congratulations, Nadia," he said as if his heart was trembling. "Congratulations, my dear!"

"Congratulations, Nadia!" I heard Kawthar say at the same time with false happiness.

She got up to kiss me as I was still in my father's arms.

I moved away from both of them.

"For what?" I said, not understanding anything.

"That's it," my father said. "I've agreed."

"To what?" I said, beginning to feel the wind blowing and the catastrophe looming.

"To Samir," my father said patiently.

"What about him?" I said, frustrated.

"Come on," Kawthar said coldly. "You're taking this too far, Nadia."

"What do you mean?" I said, beginning to lose my patience.

"Quiet, Kawthar," my father said.

"My dear," he said, turning to me, "Samir came to propose to you today and I've agreed. The young man was very shy, but between you and me, I was even more so. I thought he was coming to propose to me. I agreed that he'll come tomorrow to have dinner with us and we'll all sit together."

My eyes widened in terror. I saw the dark, bottomless abyss open wide under my feet.

"Who said I want to marry him?" I said, my nerves like snapping violin strings. "Who?"

"Who said?" my father said, surprised. "Kawthar told me everything!"

The threads of the plot became clear.

"But I don't want to get married," I said calmly, collecting myself and shooting daggers at Kawthar.

"You don't want to get married?" my father said, raising his voice as if he could no longer bear me. "What? You want to get to know him without getting married? You were going to meet him, taking Kawthar with you, without intending to marry him? So why were you meeting him? Help me understand!"

I looked at my father silently. I felt my blood boiling and rising up inside me.

At that moment, I thought about confessing—telling him that this man was his wife's lover and that he and I were becoming victims of a despicable, vile plot being spun around us.

But could I confess to him? Could I put an end to his happiness with a single blow? No. I loved my father too much. I'd already seen what happened when he divorced his wife for adultery.

I'd experienced it and I'd learned my lesson.

"Kawthar was with me so she could go and have you ask around about his morals and his situation and—" I said, trying to stay calm.

"I asked, my dear." He cut me off as if hurrying to put an end to the conversation. "You think I'd meet him without asking around about him? Today, all my friends at the club spoke highly about him and his family. I asked the director of the insurance company about him and he praised him highly, said he's a smart young man with a future and—"

"Let's still wait a little until we're sure," I said, cutting him off, trying to keep calm. "Right, Kawthar?"

"I don't see any reason at all why we should wait," she said with astonishing coldness. "Your whole life you've been hesitant, especially about marriage."

"Listen, Nadia," my father said, as if completing what she was saying. "You've been proposed to since you were sixteen, but you've rejected everyone who's come along. You're now twenty and you have to get married. I can't leave you like this until you wind up losing your future."

"Are you tired of me living with you, Daddy?" I asked, trying to make him feel bad.

"I don't know how I'll be able to live without you, my dear," my father said in a low voice, coming close to me and wrapping his arm around me. "Your whole life you've been a part of me—a part of my morning and my night. I was thinking when Samir proposed that I'd stipulate that you stay with us."

"I'd love that, Ahmed!" Kawthar cut in.

My father paid no attention to her.

"It's clear he's a good guy, Nadia," he continued, running his hand through my hair. "From a good family, educated, not a bad financial situation, and you love him . . . so what's missing? He's not rich, but you don't need him to be, thank God. You have enough for the two of you and then some."

I put my head on my father's chest but I couldn't get hold of myself and I cried.

It was the first time I'd cried in front of Kawthar.

I thought my tears falling at her feet would cause her to have mercy on me.

But it didn't.

"No," I heard her say, as if her heart were made of stone. "Honestly, enough crying. You're acting like a twelve-year-old girl whose groom just showed up."

My father embraced me and patted my back.

"Why, Nadia?" he asked. "Why are you crying?"

"I don't love him, Daddy!" I said through my tears. "I don't love him!"

"How's that?" my father said. "Am I the one who chose him or you? You're the one who took Kawthar to meet him." He laughed as if he'd told a joke.

His laugh reverberated in my chest as sobbing.

"Please, Daddy," I said, my weeping cutting through my words. "Don't rush. Don't force me. Let me think a little."

"I've never forced you to do anything, Nadia," my father said, still patting my back. "It's always your choice. We'll do whatever you want. But don't forget that you're almost twenty and you have to get married. If not today, then soon. I want to tell you too that this Samir seems like a good guy."

"Okay, let me think, Daddy. Let me think!"

I pulled free of his arms and stumbled out of the room.

My father started to come after me.

"Leave her, Ahmed," I heard Kawthar tell him without moving from her seat. "She'll calm down. We're all like that the first time we get married."

I slammed the door behind me.

Throwing myself on my bed, I let out all the tears I had left in me.

Then I felt strangely calm. I lay on my bed with my eyes open. Staring at the ceiling I saw the threads of the plot that was being spun around me.

The threads were now clear.

Samir and Kawthar wanted to exploit me, covering up their adultery and deception once I'd convinced my father that Samir was my friend, not Kawthar's, to save her when he surprised us at Groppi's.

They wanted to exploit the situation. Samir agreed with Kawthar to marry me. I'd be a filthy rich bride. My father had six hundred acres, in addition to houses and a share in a big endowment that hadn't been liquidated yet. My uncle was rich too and didn't have an heir. My mother was rich. And, more important than that, my father had set up a huge trust fund that was mine the day I got married.

All of that would go to Kawthar and Samir!

Samir would swindle my trust fund while guaranteeing himself both an easy life beside me, and that he'd always be near Kawthar. He could move their betrayal inside the house instead of having to trek out to his bachelor pad. The husband leaves, and the lover comes in without anyone suspecting or saying a word about it.

How happy Samir must be about my poor father. He was going to take his daughter, his wife, and his money!

But how could Kawthar be happy about surrendering her lover to me?

Who said she'd give him up? He'd stay hers after the marriage, as she stayed his after her marriage. Didn't she marry a rich man and stay in her relationship with him? So why wouldn't he marry a rich girl too and stay in his relationship with her?

I smiled bitterly as I saw the black threads of this scheme drawn before my eyes on the ceiling.

But were they going to succeed in executing this plot? Would their despicable hopes be fulfilled?

I had believed once that I was evil.

Then God delivered me someone even more evil than me.

That night I tried to talk to Kawthar alone. I went out of my room, my eyes puffy from crying.

"I want to talk to you," I whispered in her ear.

"Not now, Nadia," she replied. "I can't leave your father alone. If I did, what would the man say?"

I understood that she was avoiding me.

I understood that she was preparing something—another thread of the plot she was trying to hide from me.

I went back to my room, broken and abject, as if she'd slapped my face with one of her shoes.

And I didn't sleep.

I was thinking. I channeled all my mental power to try to come up with a plan, to protect myself from this marriage, to take revenge, to subdue Kawthar as she'd subdued me, to torture her as she'd tortured me, but my mind let me down. I didn't come up with a plan. I didn't think of a way to take revenge. I was like a cat trapped in a cage, pacing back and forth, its tail on fire.

I will not marry this monster Samir.

I will resist to the end.

I couldn't sacrifice myself to that degree—sacrifice all my hopes, sacrifice Mahmoud, my love, and give in to those crooks. No. Never. Impossible.

I began to confide in Mahmoud.

If he was beside me, none of this would have happened. I would have sought protection in him and his love, and he would have come forward to marry me and save me.

My fear turned into violent revolt building up inside me. I dreamed I had a knife in my hand and I was ready to stab Kawthar. I stabbed her until she fell to the ground and I washed my feet with her blood. Then I cut her body into pieces and tossed them to the dogs.

In the morning, my father came to my room and sat next to me on the edge of the bed. He looked at my sallow face.

"You look like you haven't slept," he said, kissing me.

"I slept," I said with a weak smile. "I'm just a little anxious."

"Listen, Nadia," he said, looking at me tenderly. "I didn't know what to say to you yesterday. You were so upset. I wanted to tell you that, as happy as I am, my happiness can't be complete without your happiness. My happiness only increases whenever I think about yours. I love Kawthar. You can't imagine how much I love her. I never thought I could love someone this much. But as much as I love her, I think about you more. I think about you loving your husband as much as I love Kawthar. You'll be happy, like I am with her. That's why I want you to marry Samir—not just because I want you to get married, but because I want you to be happy. I trust that you'll be happy with him."

I looked at him in pity.

He seemed like an overgrown child who didn't know anything about what was going on around him. He was a child I loved: my child.

Should I open his eyes to see the world as it was, to see his wife betraying him, to see that the lover of his wife was coming forward to marry his daughter?

Should I put a stop to the beautiful dream he was living?

No.

I pitied him at that moment as I'd never pitied him before. He'll stay happy.

He'll live in his beautiful dream. He won't ever wake up from it as he had before to find his happiness was a fantasy.

At any price, no matter what happens.

"I know, Daddy," I said. "I know we belong to each other. I'll be happy, God willing, to complete your happiness. Tonight you'll know everything."

He left.

I got up after a while, and found Kawthar in the sitting room, flipping through a magazine. I stood up straight and took a deep breath, preparing for battle.

"Listen, Kawthar," I said firmly, without saying good morning. "A word. This wedding won't happen. Understand what that means? It won't happen."

She raised her head from the magazine and gave me a cold stare.

"Why?" she asked listlessly. "That Samir is a good guy!"

"Strange. What do you mean? Make me understand."

"I don't mean anything," she said, enjoying torturing me. "He's a man who likes you and is coming to propose to you. Is there something wrong with that?"

"He doesn't like you?"

"That's just an innocent interest. Believe me."

"Innocent or not," I said, starting to lose control, "I won't marry him. Please tell him I won't marry him even if they slaughter me. He should do the right thing and not come for dinner tonight."

She gave me a harsh look, and shrugged. "Then I'll marry him," she said calmly.

"What?" I cried. "What are you saying?"

"Because I feel sorry for him. Poor guy, living alone, not meeting anyone to marry. *I'll* marry him."

"You're a criminal!" I screamed. "A scoundrel! I've never come across a woman like you!"

"Save the insults for yourself," she said without flinching. "It's better for you to marry him."

"If I don't marry him," I said, exploding with rage, "what will happen?"

"Your father will know that I love him," she said, still flipping through the magazine. "That I'm going out with him and that I'm betraying him with Samir . . . and after that, he'll know everything else."

I collapsed into a chair as if I'd been shot.

"What did my father do to deserve this?"

"Nothing," she said without looking at me. "But that's what will happen."

"You know I'm in love with someone else," I said, pleading with her. "He's coming back from Europe to marry me. Shame on you. Shame on you, Kawthar!"

"You're in love?" she said, tossing the magazine aside. "So what? I was in love with Medhat when I was a student, but I didn't marry him. I married someone else I didn't love or even know. I was in love with Samir, but I didn't marry him. I married your father instead of the person I love. Love is one thing and marriage is something else."

"You've never been in love," I said weakly. "If you loved Samir, you wouldn't let him marry me."

"I already told you," she said with a nasty smile. "Love is one thing and marriage is something else."

"Very good," I said, clutching my chair so I didn't jump up to slap her. "He'll marry me, but he loves you. I'll marry him, but I love Mahmoud."

"My dear, that's just the way things go."

"No!" I screamed. "That's disgusting! Despicable! Criminal! You're both crooks, greedy for my money and my father's money. I won't marry him. Let what happens happen!"

She jumped up.

"That's it!" she said sharply. "You've gone too far. I'm going out so I don't lose my temper with your stupid words. When Ahmed comes, tell him I'm having lunch with Samir—with my love, Samir. He'll like that. He'll be happy with that. Won't divorcing me make him happy?"

She went out and slammed the door behind her.

She left me in a black hole.

I was looking for a thread to grasp at, to pull my way out.

21

I HAD TO CHOOSE

Me or my father.

My happiness or his.

My love or his.

My life or his.

There wasn't any other way. I couldn't find a solution that would reconcile his happiness and mine. Kawthar and Samir had laid their ingenious plan without leaving me a way out.

Maybe the blame lay with me, since I'd covered up Kawthar's betrayal. Kawthar knew I wasn't covering up for her out of love for her or support for her cheating, but out of love for my father and my desire to keep him happy. She turned that love and determination back on me, as a weapon to swindle me out of my money and my life.

But what could I do?

Could I expose her? Bring the house down on her head, on my father and myself?

And why was God punishing me?

Was covering up her sin a crime that deserved this retribution?

Was that my only crime?

My life flashed through my mind like a movie. I watched my victims. The young man I'd lured to the house for the doorman to beat up. Kawthar herself, whose love for Medhat I'd destroyed—her first love. Then my friend Mervat, when

I made up a story about her and told it to her mother. Then Auntie Safiya and my uncle, whose relationship with my father I cut off with a vile plot. And the nights I freed myself from all of society's chains and spent in Mustafa's arms. I even saw my doll that I destroyed when I was a child, as if it was one of my victims. And the servants I got fired. And Nanny Halima, whose love I blocked and who I treated harshly. Whenever an image of one of my victims passed through my mind, I felt like something inside me was screaming out in terror.

But I tried to atone.

I tried so hard, Lord.

So why do You not forgive me?

Maybe I was too clever for my own good and possessed an intelligence without principles. I didn't have principles that I protected and that protected me.

That was it. I didn't have any principles.

No one had tried to teach me principles. As a result, my intelligence was not guided by a moral compass. It set out alone, my impulses leading the way, my feelings of hatred, egotism, conceit, and jealousy. It meant I made mistakes and would go too far, and then I would fall and not be able to get up.

I had made a mistake when I picked Kawthar as a wife for my father.

This was a terrible error.

Regret wouldn't do me any good. But should I give in to this mistake? Should I bear all its consequences without resistance?

Still sitting in my spot, I asked myself again: was Kawthar serious about her threat? Would she divorce my father if I didn't marry Samir? Would she sacrifice all that my father provided her? And why? To marry Samir if I didn't? But if she wanted to marry him, why was she letting him marry me?

I almost believed that Kawthar couldn't be serious in her threat, but feared that if I didn't marry Samir, he wouldn't leave Kawthar alone. He'd push her until she divorced my father. What did he care if she divorced him? He could then marry her or not—it would make no difference to him. Even if my father didn't divorce her, she'd ruin his life. She'd turn his life into hell. I knew her. She was capable of anything.

I felt my heart pounding as this terrifying nightmare crouched on my chest. I hid my eyes in my hands as if I was cowering before the knife she was brandishing. I didn't want to see myself as a victim trampled under the feet of Kawthar and Samir, as they relished tearing me apart.

There was a severe pain in my head. Through this pain, I tried to think. I was trying to figure out what to do.

Why didn't I leave my father? What would I do if this was his lot in the world? Why didn't I reveal the truth and be done with it? Then I could rest. After that, let what would happen happen. But he was my father. More than that, he was my father and my mother. My father, who deprived himself of his youth until I was sixteen. He had lived for me—for me alone.

I remembered him carrying me to bed when I was a child. I remembered him reading books to me. I remembered him standing next to Nanny Halima as she changed my clothes. I remembered him worried when I was sick. I remembered the nights he spent by my bed until I fell asleep. I remembered him surrounding me with love and tenderness when I was a young girl and then a teenager. Every one of my days was a part of him.

I imagined him looking over me with his kind, handsome face, smiling at me with his sweet, innocent smile, looking at me with kind eyes. I heard the words he had told me that morning: "I love Kawthar. I love her more than you can imagine. I never thought I could love someone so much."

Could I abandon him?

Could I open his eyes to the fantasy that he was living?

No. No, I couldn't. Impossible. My love for him was stronger than for myself.

So . . .

I'll abandon Mahmoud.

My love, Mahmoud.

I'll abandon my love, my happiness. I'll destroy all my dreams with my own two hands. I'll leave the garden and throw myself into hell.

I felt as if my heart was being torn apart. I could almost hear the sound of my ribs being broken like pieces of kindling.

Mahmoud, the decent honorable man. The fortress I'd prepared to seek refuge from myself and the world. Could I sacrifice him now that I'd found him—this man I wanted as a husband?

Why, Lord?

Lord, are You there?

Where are You to show mercy on me, to save me?

I don't know how long I spent in this state, but I woke up at the sound of the door opening and my father coming into my room.

He looked at me in surprise.

"What's wrong?" he asked. "What are you doing? You still haven't washed your face?"

"No, not yet," I said. "I woke up tired. I got out of bed and came to sit down on this chair. I've been here ever since."

"Okay. Go wash your face and come back," he said, passing his hand over my hair as if trying to straighten my scattered locks. "I brought a surprise for you."

He turned around.

"Kawthar!" he called. "Where are you, Kawthar? Kawthar!"

He left my room. I got up and I ran after him.

"Kawthar is having lunch today at her aunt's," I said, trying to keep my voice natural and calm. "Her mother called and said her aunt is sick. She went to her mother's and they went together to go see her."

I knew there wasn't a phone at Kawthar's aunt's house.

"Very sick?" my father said, his eyes troubled, as if it was hard for him to be deprived of Kawthar for even one lunch.

"I don't think so," I said, avoiding his eyes.

"Why don't we go check?"

"Why? There's no need. You know Kawthar's family. When one of them is a little sick, they all rush to see them."

"She didn't say when she'll be back?"

"Right after lunch, I think."

"Why don't we go and get her now?" he said. "We need to plan what we'll do for dinner. Samir is coming tonight."

When he said Samir's name, it felt like a slap in the face, but I collected myself.

"If we go now, they'll keep us for lunch. It's not worth it."

My father sighed, as if letting out all of his breath.

"Fine," he said submissively.

He headed to his room, and I followed.

"What's the surprise?" I asked, managing to put a smile on my face.

"When Kawthar comes," he said listlessly.

"Tell me, Daddy," I said playfully.

"It's only a surprise if Kawthar's here."

He went into his room and stayed there for a few minutes. Then he came back out and sat in the sitting room.

I went to my room, washed my face and put foundation on, and then went back to him.

We sat down for lunch.

We didn't talk much. I didn't raise my eyes to him. I had a grave expression on my face, putting the food in my mouth without noticing how it tasted. I didn't think about Mahmoud or Samir or my father. I was only thinking about Kawthar. I was collecting all my energy and trying to turn it into evil.

I wanted to become evil again.

More evil and cunning than before.

I no longer had a crime that I was regretting and trying to atone for. Instead, there was one facing me and I simply could not submit to it. I had to fight evil with evil, to take revenge against the criminals, to grip the reins myself. I needed all my strength, all my cunning, and all my intelligence.

"So, what have you decided about today, Nadia?" my father asked as we were finishing lunch.

"We agreed you'll know tonight," I said in a low voice, as if I was shy.

My father smiled trustingly as if he knew everything in advance.

I got up and went to the sitting room to wait for Kawthar.

I had to see her before my father.

As soon as I glimpsed her behind the glass door at about four o'clock, I got up and opened the door for her.

She gave me a defiant look, a mocking smile on her face.

"I said you had lunch at your aunt's," I told her in a low voice before she said anything.

"When will Samir come?" I continued. "Did he tell you?"

Kawthar smiled.

She thought that I'd given in to her.

She went in and gave her cheeks to my father for him to kiss longingly, as if she'd been gone for years.

"I'm sorry, Ahmed," she said. "I had to go to my aunt's."

"How is she now?" my father asked as if gathering his spirits.

"Thank God, she's not sick. You know my aunt. As soon as she coughs, she thinks she's going to die."

"May God keep evil away," her good husband said.

Kawthar went in to take off her tailored jacket and came back to us after she'd tidied herself up. She sat down, looking at me questioningly as if she didn't believe that I'd actually given in to her, and so easily.

"I was preparing a surprise for Nadia," my father said. "I didn't want to show it to her until you came."

He put his hand in his pocket and took out a small box covered in blue velvet.

"This is the surprise, my dear."

He opened the box and an eighteen-karat solitaire diamond ring flashed from it. He presented it to me, the flash of his smile almost overshadowing the flash of the diamond.

Before I reached out to take the box, Kawthar snatched it from his hand.

"Wow!" she said, staring at the diamond with eyes so wide they seemed to swallow half her face. "What's that? Look, Nadia, look! How lucky you are! I've never seen a stone so beautiful!"

She handed me the box reluctantly. I looked at the diamond coldly. I tried to be happy about it, but I couldn't. I felt choked.

"Merci," I said, lowering my head as if I was a fortune teller looking at a dark future in the crystal ball. "What's the occasion for this surprise?"

My father leaned back in the chair, stretching his feet out before him.

"This stone belonged to my mother, may God rest her soul. She gave it to you the day you were born. I took it, set it in this ring, and then put it in the bank. I decided no one would see it until I gave it to you the day you got married," my father said proudly.

"But I'm still not married," I said.

"I feel like you've gotten married." He was silent for a moment. "I'd love to see you wear it tonight at dinner."

"Yes," Kawthar said quickly. "That's a great idea. It will be a surprise for Samir."

"We'll see," I said, getting up.

I went to my father and leaned over to kiss him. He pulled me and embraced me.

"May you be happy, my dear," he said.

"Merci, Daddy. Merci beaucoup."

I left the two of them and went to my room gripping the small blue box as if clutching a burning ember.

I opened the box before I put it in my dresser and looked at the big diamond again. I tried again to be happy about it, to feel its beauty, but I couldn't.

I wasn't happy and I wasn't sad.

It seemed to me that I'd never be happy and I'd never be sad.

I'd lost my heart.

I'd lost my feeling.

I tried to think about Mahmoud, to confide in him as usual, to conjure up his image, which was suspended in my mind, to summon his opinions and principles, but I couldn't. Mahmoud seemed very far from me, his image blurry in my imagination as if he was fleeing from me.

I found myself cold.

Cold as ice.

I felt like I'd remain as cold as ice my entire life: heartless, emotionless, not loving or hating, not happy or angry, not calm or upset, not delighted at beauty or upset by ugliness. Cold, dry, hard, like a beautiful stone statue.

Kawthar came to my room. She stood at the door, resting her arm on the doorframe and sticking out her hips.

"You know, that ring is very valuable," she said, looking at it with a wicked smile on her lips. "There aren't any others like it."

"I know."

"I couldn't believe you agreed to Samir so quickly," she said, getting close to me.

"Why? He's a good guy and I like him."

"But you didn't like him this morning."

"You want the truth? I was afraid you'd be upset."

"Me? On the contrary!"

"The truth is that I do like him. But I can't say I'm in love with him."

"Aren't you in love with someone else?" she asked.

"Yes," I said, raising my eyes to her and then lowering them as if I was being shy.

"That's it?"

"As the saying goes," I said, echoing her, "marriage is one thing and love is something else."

She came up and embraced me. She started swaying with me as if she were a child playing with another.

"We're going to do some things, my dear," she said in a loud, happy voice. "We'll have a blast."

We both laughed.

Her laugh was loose and pure, as if she'd achieved all of her dreams.

My laugh was loud and hollow, like a bell.

"I'll go see what the cook is making for dinner," she said. "I know what Samir likes."

And she left.

I threw myself on my bed. I felt the fumes of hatred collect in my chest and then rise up to my head. Something in my head began moving, crawling and writhing. I began feeling as if I were in darkness and could see the devils of revenge dance in front of me. Their leader came forward, picked me up in his arms, cackling, and threw me to his followers. They tossed me back and forth between them. I felt intoxicated as I flew up and down into the arms of the devils: the intoxication of fear, darkness, cunning, the intoxication of the gambler as he plunges into the unknown, gambling with all his money, greedy for the win.

I was setting my plan. I was weaving its threads precisely and skillfully, like an experienced old spider. It seemed to me that the fly had fallen into its web and I would soon be sucking its blood.

It was seven o'clock in the evening when this darkness began creeping around me. I got up and sat in front of the mirror to get myself ready for dinner.

I looked at my face.

It was just as it had been.

The innocent face of a child, untouched by age and crowds of people, her purity unpolluted by the crush of life.

My eyes the color of green fields wet with dew. None of what was inside me ever flashed in them. Even when I cried, they didn't express my grief. Instead, tears flowed over them like a strange hand coming forward to cleanse them. My small mouth traced by two firm lips. I never needed to put on lipstick—my lips were always the color of cherries, so you imagined blood would burst out of them the instant you touched them.

I smiled at myself. I opened a drawer next to me to take out a jar of cream. My eyes lit on a picture of Mahmoud in the drawer, so I closed it again quickly. The drawer closed on my finger. But I wasn't in pain.

There was nothing left in me that could feel pain.

22

A WEEK LATER, MY ENGAGEMENT to Samir was announced in a small, sedate party, as if we were celebrating the anniversary of the passing of someone dear.

We all played our roles perfectly.

Samir was happy, as if he'd closed the deal of a lifetime.

Kawthar was happy, as if she was marrying Samir. Was he not going to live with her in the same house?

My father was happy, believing he'd achieved my happiness.

My family and his family and all the guests were happy. Everyone was happy except for me. Rage and fury were tearing up my insides. The craving for revenge hung a pitch-black veil before my eyes. But none of that was visible on me. I was in total control of my feelings. I kept a close eye on everything around me, as if watching a play in which my only role was of someone watching.

The effort I was exerting to control my nerves pushed me to seem snooty, arrogant, and cold. Inside, I felt a kind of disgust. The sharp, odious scent—the scent of the crime— filled my lungs. I gave Samir quick, furtive glances, and I envied his brazenness. No trace of the crime appeared on him, as if his tight, shining skin had been made especially for this occasion. Everything about him looked like it had been drawn with a ruler and compass, even his smile, which seemed like it had been neatly pressed before being hung on his lips.

Looking at him made me feel a kind of lament and hatred—a lament for the black future I was preparing for him, and hatred for him, his ambitions, and his depravity.

Samir put the engagement ring on my finger and leaned over to kiss my hand. As soon as he touched me and pressed his lips down on a part of me, I felt his kiss like drops of cold oil running across my hand. Every part of my body shuddered and revolted, and I almost wiped his kiss off the top of my hand.

I looked at him without smiling or appearing happy.

I couldn't.

I looked at him, asking myself: could I be this man's wife? Could I bear to have him next to me? Could I bear his lips on mine? His hands on my body? No. Impossible. No matter what I did, no matter how hard I was on myself, I couldn't bear him. I couldn't.

I raised my eyes to my father, as if blaming him, as if holding him responsible for my torture, as if I were a saint they were crucifying on the door of his happiness.

I saw my father's wide smile and the happiness in his eyes. I smiled at him bitterly. I smiled at my big child who didn't know the extent of the suffering that he was bringing down on me.

I then turned to my mother. It was the first time she'd come to our house with my father present since the divorce eighteen years ago. She sat next to her husband as if he were protecting her from distant memories. She was like a stranger, a guest at the engagement party of a neighbor's daughter. She didn't share in my feelings—neither my happiness nor my sadness. Maybe she and her husband were counting the minutes until the end of the party, to end the discomfort of having to be in my father's house.

I looked at Kawthar. She was happy because her plan had succeeded, because she'd achieved what she wanted. Despite that, when I looked in her eyes, it seemed like her happiness had been shaken—a happiness in which there was fear and doubt, as if she were afraid she'd lose her way on the road. She was looking at me with quick glances that I caught by chance, finding within them hatred and jealousy. Sometimes she'd examine me as if she were probing my depths, as if she wasn't certain about my naivete, as if she wasn't totally sure that the victim had submitted to slaughter. She then looked at Samir as if there was something confusing her, as if she'd left something with him before she got on the train.

I looked around for someone missing.

For my uncle.

Uncle Aziz.

If he was here, would he save me? Would he lead me to the light? To virtue? To the way out? To clean air?

But could I confess to him, tell him that Kawthar was betraying my father, betraying him with the person I was being forced to marry?

He wouldn't believe me.

He'd think the story was just another fantasy, like the fantasy that erupted in my father's head when he accused him of cheating with his wife.

Despite that, my uncle's absence left an emptiness. I felt I'd lost my support.

When the last guest left at ten o'clock in the evening, there were only the four of us: my father, Kawthar, Samir, and me.

"You know who was missing today?" I asked my father.

"Who, Nadia?" he asked tenderly.

"Uncle Aziz," I said.

His face became gloomy as if a black cloud had swept over it. He didn't say a word.

"I called him today to invite him," I said. "I wanted to give him a surprise."

"What did he say?"

"I didn't get him," I said, grieved. "I called him yesterday too, but I didn't get him then either. I think he's traveling."

My father was silent, disappointed.

"It's true, Ahmed," Kawthar said, butting into the conversation. "You should have invited him no matter what happened between you two. On a day like this, your brother should have been invited."

I looked at her as if to say, "What's wrong with you?"

"He'll be invited to the wedding, God willing," my father sighed.

My heart smiled. I felt like a heavy weight had been lifted from me, like I'd been forgiven for part of my crime.

I hugged my father and kissed him.

"May our Lord keep you for me, Daddy!" I said.

My father understood why I was so happy. He hid his own happiness at the feeling that he may have forgiven his brother.

"Let's all go have dinner at the Semiramis!" he then said.

I jumped in fright.

That would mean that I'd have to spend more time with Samir, dance with him, ride next to him in his car alone.

"Not tonight, Daddy," I said quickly. "I'm tired. I've been on my feet since yesterday."

"Really, sir," Samir said in a respectful, formal tone, "I say we go somewhere quiet because—"

"I'm tired." I cut him off. "Next time."

Samir fell silent as if he'd gotten an order to be quiet.

"We'll all have lots of time together," Kawthar said, looking at my father.

"Really?" my father said. "Okay, let's get going, Kawthar."

He took his wife's hand and led her to their room. Kawthar hesitated a little, but my father gave her a wink as if reminding her that the rules of etiquette required them to leave me alone with Samir.

As soon as they left, even before they got to their room, I reached my hand out to Samir to say goodbye.

"Bonsoir, Samir," I said. "Very sorry. I'm tired."

Samir looked at me, surprised. He then smiled, with the expression of someone experienced in the ways of women, and leaned over to kiss my hand. He left another drop of cold oil on it.

"Bonsoir, madame," he said.

Then, he left, moving with an attempt at elegance that made him appear as if he were walking on springs.

I wanted Kawthar to see me before she went to her room.

I saw relief on her face that I was no longer alone with Samir.

I went into my room and looked at myself in the mirror, at the expensive dress that Madame Safeds had made just for my engagement party. It was a dress of Brighton toile in a light rose color. It was my most expensive dress, and perhaps my most beautiful. But I didn't feel its elegance. I felt it was made from tin pressed against my chest, that its rose color was like blood poured over me.

I took off the dress and left it strewn on the ground under my feet as if it were the remains of my corpse.

I began circling the room in my slip, trying to find something to entertain myself with, to quiet the noise that started rising up in my head. I then sat trying again—maybe for the tenth time—to write a letter to Mahmoud.

Since Samir had invaded my life and I had agreed to announce my engagement to him, I'd been trying to write Mahmoud. I wrote him many letters in which I confessed the whole truth with all the details, but I then tore them up, as well as other letters in which I tried to lie to him about it, to beat around the bush and justify my engagement to another man, but I tore those letters up too.

I grabbed a pen and started writing.

"My dear Mahmoud,
Don't ask, but trust that I love you and will always love you."

I tried to finish the letter, but couldn't think of anything else to write. I folded it quickly before I could tear it up or sign it. I put it in an envelope on which I wrote Mahmoud's name and address with a trembling hand, as if I were writing from my death bed.

I left the letter on my small table. Then I got up and threw myself on the bed.

I began reviewing in my mind the plan I'd set.

The night passed, and I did not sleep.

My plan was simple and easy—the height of simplicity.

I had to make Samir fall in love with me, to fall in love with me for real, so that I controlled him and completely distanced him from Kawthar. When Kawthar saw that she'd lost Samir and that he'd abandoned her, jealousy would blind her and make her abandon her plan. She'd revolt against him and work to annul his marriage to me.

In order to execute my plan, I had to play two roles: one role for Samir, to convince him that I loved him, that he was mine, that he could be satisfied with me instead of Kawthar, that he could control me with my love for him instead of by threating me—threatening to reveal that Kawthar was cheating on my father.

And another role that I'd play for Kawthar, so she didn't see what I was up to, so she was reassured about me, stood with me, and directed all her anger toward Samir.

That was my plan.

I couldn't think of anything else.

It had to be executed before I signed my marriage contract.

Could I do it?

I asked myself thousands of times: was Samir so naive that he'd believe me and surrender the weapon he and Kawthar had been threatening me with?

I asked myself thousands of times: was Kawthar so stupid that she wouldn't catch on to my plan? And when she agreed to marry me to Samir, had she really tamed her own emotions so she wouldn't be jealous, so she could bear me living with him as his wife? Could I inflame her jealousy so that she revolted against Samir and deserted him?

I didn't know.

I had doubts about whether my plan would succeed, but I moved forward with it, gambling with my life.

For days after the announcement of the engagement, I avoided being alone with Samir. I wouldn't sit with him or go out with him unless Kawthar and my father were with us. Kawthar was reassured. She knew that I accepted to be Samir's wife, but within narrow limits that I didn't want to overstep or encourage him to overstep.

"The truth is that he's good husband material," I told her one day. "But it doesn't make sense for me to love him. He's not my type at all."

Kawthar smiled.

"Don't you have someone you love?" she asked.

"Pray that he comes back safe and sound," I said, sighing.

I was trying to win Kawthar's trust. I was trying to convince her that I was persuaded by her way of thinking: marriage was one thing and love was something else and I would leave Samir to her, to her alone.

We went to the movies, all four of us. Whenever we went to the movies, I always let Samir sit between me and Kawthar, to reassure her that I was leaving him to her.

On one occasion, when we left the movies and headed to the car, my father said: "I think you should ride with Samir, Nadia,"

I didn't say anything.

I looked at Kawthar as if asking for help.

Kawthar smiled dismissively as if she didn't care about these trivialities and got in my father's car. I then got in Samir's car.

"Do you want to drive around a little?" he asked.

I didn't respond.

He drove toward Heliopolis.

"I feel, Nadia, that we're very distant from each other," I heard him say as I was purposely turning away from him. "We don't sit together. We don't go out together—it's like we're not engaged."

"You're the one who wants it like that," I said in a sad voice, turning halfway toward him.

"Me? How?" he asked.

"You know," I said, as if angry.

"Know what?" he asked, with a feigned ignorance.

"You know you don't love me," I said. "You love someone else."

"I don't love you?" he said as if reciting a line in a play. "All this and I don't love you? From the moment I saw you at Groppi's, everything in me changed. My principles changed. My morals changed. I never thought about marriage until I saw you."

"I was thinking that too," I said, exaggerating my anger. "But unfortunately . . ."

"Don't believe anything, Nadia," he said. "Believe me, I—"

"You mean don't believe my eyes, don't believe my ears?" I asked sharply. "But believe *you*?"

"I know who you mean," he said. "Kawthar, right? I swear to you, it's all over. It was just a fling, I was young and stupid."

I turned fully to him, holding my breath as if I believed him.

"Really? Really, Samir?"

He stopped the car on a dark side of Baron Street. Sidling over to me, he put his arm on the seat rest.

"What am I swearing on?" he asked.

I let him bring his arm down on my shoulder. He brought his face close to mine, and I felt his breath, like an unpleasant hot dusty wind. I turned my face to him with my eyes closed, as if waiting for him to kiss me.

Before his lips touched mine, I opened my eyes and turned away. I pushed him gently from me.

"No," I said. "Impossible. You don't love me."

"I love you," he said, leaning his face in toward mine, overcome by desire. "I love you, Nadia!"

"Prove it," I said, moving away from him. "Prove that you love me."

"How?" he asked. His breath hissed from his chest, sounding like air being released from a torn tire pump.

"I don't know," I said. "Just convince me. You should take me home now or Kawthar will be mad."

"Fine. To prove to you that I don't care about Kawthar, I'll stay with you all night."

"All I care about is that Kawthar doesn't get mad," I said, coldly and decisively. "Don't forget she's living with me in my house. She's my father's wife!"

He sat up straight.

"So we're going back?" he asked.

"Yes," I said firmly.

On the way back, I began speaking, as if talking to myself: "I had thought that you tricked Kawthar to marry me. It turns out that you tricked me, that you still love Kawthar."

"You'll know everything soon enough," he replied. "You'll know how much I love you."

We arrived home.

I didn't let him say goodbye so he couldn't put another drop of cold oil from his lips onto my hand.

I went into the house to find Kawthar waiting for me in the sitting room with a magazine in her hands.

"Welcome back," she said as soon as she saw me, feigning a big smile, trouble in her eyes. "Imagine: I couldn't sleep, so I've been sitting and reading, hoping you'd come back soon so we can sit and chat."

"Listen, Kawthar," I said sharply, tossing my purse on the table and pulling my gloves off. "I can't bear these tricks of

Samir's. Why did he insist on showing me Heliopolis when I didn't want to go there? We're engaged, but we have a clear understanding. So why does he have to do these things?"

"What did he do?" Kawthar asked with great interest.

"Do?" I responded sharply. "That was all that was missing. Of course he didn't *do* anything! He sat talking about himself, giving me his life story."

"Samir loves talking about himself," she said, smiling happily, trying to calm me.

"Please, Kawthar," I said, grabbing my purse and heading to my room. "First thing tomorrow morning, call him and tell him to stop. We have a lot of days before us for him to tell me his life story."

"Okay. You're not going to sit with me for a little?" she asked.

"No," I said. "I'm in a bad mood."

I went to my room with the wicked feeling filling my chest, the feeling of a gambler watching the wheel of luck spinning in front of his bulging eyes while his heart clamors and pounds. The feeling that always came over me whenever I hatched a plan and waited for its results.

The next day, Kawthar relayed my message to Samir. She told him I was angry because he took me to Heliopolis against my will.

Of course, Samir denied it.

He called me afterward.

"You said that to Kawthar?" he asked me, angry.

"What do you want me to say to her?" I yelled at him. "You want me to tell her that I love you so she lights the house on fire to drive you away from me and kills me in the process?"

"I didn't think about that," he said, surprised.

"You don't know a lot of things, Samir." I cut him off, lowering my voice as if crying. "You don't know the torture I've been suffering. You don't know that I can't mention you in the house. I'm afraid of Kawthar. You don't know that I have to go on saying that I don't love you and that I can't stand you. I have to say those things to comfort her, so she doesn't bring the house down on my head or on my father's head. Even worse than that, Samir—much worse—is that I can't tell you anything. I feel like anything I tell you, you'll go and tell it to Kawthar. I'm now living alone. I can't confide in you or my father or her."

"You think I'd tell Kawthar?" Samir said forcefully. "You don't know me, Nadia. I swear, I've never told her anything we've said."

"Listen, Samir. I agreed to marry you because I thought you loved me, but I've discovered that you don't. I started living in the hope that you'll love me after marriage, but if there's no hope tell me now. Tell me and have mercy on me!"

"How can I make you believe me?"

"I wish I could believe you, Samir."

That was how I began to execute my plan.

I lived those months with my mind alert and my eyes wide open, day and night. I observed everything around me so that no movement or whisper escaped me. I kept track of everything so I didn't make a mistake, so Kawthar didn't get ahead of me in anything.

Samir was easier than I thought. His conceit and confidence in his good looks and intelligence blinded him to everything. He believed that I was in love with him. He believed that I was innocent and naive. He then began to be convinced that Kawthar was an obstacle in his path: in the path to controlling me and my wealth. He started purposely showing interest in me and hinting at his love to me whenever Kawthar was with us.

He made sure not to sit between me and her whenever we went to the movies. Instead, he sat next to me, far from her. He began talking less with her on the phone after he learned from me that she was telling me everything he said to her.

During this time, I used all my tricks on him, laying down an emotional rollercoaster. I fought with him and then made up with him, got close to him and then moved away, raised his hopes that he had me and then deprived him of me. And I made sure to stir up his greed for my wealth.

"I don't know what to do with my trust fund," I told him one day. "Should I buy land or a villa with it? Or, say, don't you know about stocks and bonds? You could take it and buy some stocks with it. That's the best way these days. Land isn't as valuable anymore."

"True," he said, as if the money was already burning a hole in his pocket. "There's nothing I understand better than stocks and bonds. Yesterday, the stock of the Bank of Cairo went up and—"

"Don't bother," I said, cutting him off, laughing. "I don't understand any of that. I bet you can make a million from twenty thousand." I was quiet for a bit, then went on sadly, "But is money everything? Would a million pounds buy me love?"

"You're going to have both a million pounds and love!" he said, squeezing my hand.

"We'll travel to Europe every year for six months," I said, squeezing his hand in return.

"I want to go to America too." He let out his disgusting laugh. "And we'll never come back! We'll go live in Hollywood forever."

As soon as I left him, I ran to Kawthar.

"Did you hear Samir's new plan?" I told her, playing the role of someone oppressed. "He wants to go to America right after getting married!"

"America?" she said anxiously. "What's he going to do in America?"

"Emigrate. He'll take me and we'll live there forever. I don't know what the man is talking about."

"Samir has changed," Kawthar said, as if talking to herself. "He's changed a lot." She turned to me. "And you agreed to this story about America?"

"Absolutely not! It's madness!"

Of course, after that, I told Samir that Kawthar was angry when she heard the plan about us going to America, so he believed she was standing in the way of his dreams.

Kawthar, meanwhile, began to believe that Samir's love for her had begun to change. I noticed her angry looks as she observed him whenever he flirted with me and ignored her, directing all his attention to me. I saw the confusion, trouble, and suppressed rage on her face. Her desire to cling to Samir had begun to get the better of her greed, and of the evil plan that she had set in place to marry me to him.

I noticed all this, but I kept going with my plan. I continued to turn the screws on her, but I was careful and bided my time—I couldn't lose her trust. The most important thing I relied on in keeping her trust was her knowing that I was in love with another man—with Mahmoud. I was always talking about him, and about my love for him. I even wrote imaginary letters to him and showed them to her, then tore them up.

Little by little, Kawthar began expressing her fears to me: her doubts about Samir's intentions, her doubts about his love for her. The things she said at first were like bubbles floating up to the surface. Then she burst open, revealing everything to me.

"These men, you can't trust any of them," she'd tell me.

"You don't know men?"

"It's clear Samir isn't a good guy. I think I was duped by him."

"You know him better than me. You're responsible for all this. The truth is that I'm not comfortable with this marriage."

Until one day . . .

Three months had passed since the announcement of my engagement to Samir.

I knew Kawthar was going to meet Samir from the way she got herself ready to go out, from her apprehension, the look in her eyes, the distracted way she talked to me on her way out.

As soon as she left, I called Samir.

"I wanted you to go with me to Baroukh the jeweler," I told him coldly. "But of course you can't. It's Kawthar's time with you."

"Kawthar?" Samir said, agitated, as if he didn't know where to flee. "Who told you that?"

"Don't try to lie," I said sharply. "She's the one who told me. All I ask is that you tell me so I'm not embarrassed in front of her, so I don't feel humiliated. What did I do to you, Samir? My only mistake was that I fell in love with you. Everything I had hoped for in our life together is being destroyed."

"The truth, Nadia," Samir said, as if confessing to a priest, "is that Kawthar has been begging to see me for a month. I was willing to meet her, to end it between us. But since she's told you about our meeting it's clear she has bad intentions, she now wants to ruin us. I'll toss her out. I'll—"

"No," I said, cutting him off and sounding terrified. "If she knows I talked to you and told you anything, she'll come back and take revenge against me and make me miserable. Please don't!"

"She won't know that you talked to me. But I'll get rid of her. She'll be right back at your house."

"Do what you want, Samir," I said in sad submission.

And I hung up.

Less than an hour later, Kawthar came back. Her whole body was shaking. Her eyes were shaking, her lips, her cheeks, her fingers, every strand of hair on her head. She came into my room immediately, and began pacing nervously back and forth in front of me, grinding her teeth as if she were tearing up her entire past with them. She then started pressing down on her arms with her hands. "The scoundrel! The dog! The criminal!" she yelled.

"What's wrong, Kawthar?" I asked in fake surprise.

She didn't respond, but kept pacing back and forth in front of me.

"Are you bent on this wedding?"

"What's making you ask this now?"

"Answer me. Are you determined to marry Samir?"

"Oh, the wedding," I said with a shrug. "Aren't you the one who brought him? Aren't you the one who wants me to marry him?"

"Not anymore." She was almost screaming. "I don't want you to marry him anymore. He doesn't deserve you. He's a criminal, a scoundrel, a deviant!"

She suddenly threw herself on my bed, turned her face away, and broke down in tears. Her entire body began convulsing.

I wasn't moved.

My heart didn't soften.

I didn't feel any sympathy for her.

I stood staring at her, taking pleasure in her misery, feeling satisfaction. I observed her as if watching a chicken being slaughtered in front of me, and hoped she'd choke on her tears. I felt I could use those tears to wash away Samir's vile touches, to ease the grief that engulfed my heart, and erase the days and nights that I had spent unable to sleep.

I had to continue with my plan until the end.

I went and sat next to her on my bed, and began patting her back.

"What happened, Kawthar?" I said hoarsely, as if crying along with her. "Tell me, my dear. What happened?"

Her crying calmed down a little.

"I tricked you, Nadia," she said through her tears, not raising her face to me. "I deceived you. After all you did for me, why did I deceive and ridicule you? Samir is the one who made me do it. He was greedy for your money. He made me greedy with him. I went along with him because I was in love with him, but now I know that he wanted to trick you, and me too. Forgive me, Nadia. Forgive me. I'll kill myself. I'll commit suicide!"

I leaned over to give her head a cold kiss, my heart completely unmoved.

"May evil stay away from you," I said with feigned emotion. "We all make mistakes, Kawthar. When we're in love, we don't know what we're doing, but thank God you've turned back from that."

Kawthar's sobs got louder. Her tears started to flow again.

"You know that I agreed to him for you," I said after a bit, sounding sad and sorry. "I never loved him."

Her sobbing got louder.

"I was wrong," she said. "Wrong! Wrong!"

"So, what do we do now?" I asked after a little.

She raised her head to me. "We'll break off the engagement," she said with a wicked glint in her eye, as if she were imagining the dagger she'd plunge into Samir's chest to take her revenge. "You'll leave him. He has to understand that even if he could trick one of us, he can't trick both of us!"

"And Daddy?" I asked, playing the role of the innocent little girl.

"I'll convince him," she said, the glint still in her eye.

We sat waiting for my father, preparing what we'd say to him.

23

It wasn't easy for Kawthar and me to convince my father to break off the engagement, despite the masterful performance that we put on for him.

As soon as we heard the front door open and my father walk toward us, I turned my face to the bed and pretended to cry. Kawthar leaned over me, patting my back as if she were consoling me. My father stood at the door of my room, aghast.

"What—what happened?" he asked as if he'd lost his voice. "Why is Nadia crying?"

Kawthar stood up, in complete control of her nerves.

"Come, Ahmed," she said. "I want to talk with you."

She pulled him by the hand and took him to the study. She told him that I was determined to break off the engagement with Samir and that I couldn't stand him anymore. She told him that during the three months that we were engaged, I hadn't let him kiss me even once because I didn't love him, that she and I discovered he had an Italian girlfriend and he hadn't ended his relationship with her, and that he'd proposed to a girl in Alexandria before, but the engagement was called off after he stole diamond bracelets from her. The girl's family decided not to notify the police to avoid a scandal. And so on. She told him Samir's history and all the rumors about him, which she knew better than me.

Despite that, my father still didn't want to break off the engagement.

Breaking it off was more serious in his mind than going forward with it.

My father was afraid of what people would say, afraid that it would damage my reputation.

He came into my room with Kawthar behind him. I had moved over to the mirror and sat down, pretending to dry my tears.

"I can't believe all this, Nadia," he said, standing behind me, his distraught expression reflected in the mirror.

I decided to follow a new tactic. Instead of crying again and trying to stir up his love and sympathy, I turned to him, trembling, and screamed in his face.

"You're the reason, Daddy! You're the one who threw me into this. You're the one who sold me to a scoundrel criminal! I didn't think you wanted to get rid of me that badly! It would have been better if you'd just killed me instead of this torture!"

"Me?" my father said aghast. "Me, Nadia?"

"Yes, you!" I cut him off, still screaming. "You should have asked around about him before ensnaring me in this!"

"I *did* ask around," he said, worried.

"But did you really? You went and disappeared for two hours at the club and then came to tell me he's a good guy."

"Aren't you the one who agreed to it, Nadia?" he said, trying to calm me down, trying to deny responsibility.

"I agreed to it for you," I said, hitting the commode with my hand. "You kept pressing me until I agreed. I'm ready to die for you, Daddy, but not like this. Shame on you! Shame on you!"

"But, Nadia," Kawthar said, rubbing my shoulders. "Everything has a solution and this can go away."

She turned to my father.

"The truth is, we're the ones who were wrong, Ahmed," she said.

"But how were we wrong?" my father asked, as if he were about to go crazy. "I saw her with my own eyes sitting with him at Groppi's. I understood she was in love with him."

"So, if I talk to someone on the phone or say two words to him on the beach, that means I'm in love with him?" My voice was so loud it was going through the walls. "Someone asks me to marry him. What else do you want me to do than take Kawthar to hear what he has to say and come tell you? What more do good girls do? More than let their fathers deal with their marriage and future?"

My father was silent. He seemed to be persuaded that he really was wrong and that he really had hurried to announce my engagement to Samir.

I calmed down.

"Do what you want with me, Daddy," I sighed. "It's in your hands."

"I'll only do what you want, Nadia," he said, not looking at me, as if he was embarrassed. "But I say we wait a bit until we confirm what we've heard about him."

"It's not what we've heard. It's the facts. For two months, I've been trying to lie to myself. But I can't. I curse everything I see and hear. I didn't tell you anything until I knew it was no use and they were true."

"Fine. Let me think about it. It's not so easy . . ."

"I've thought a lot," I said in the same sad voice. "Kawthar thought a lot with me. You think about it on your own."

My father looked at me silently. He moved his lips as if he wanted to say something, but he didn't. He turned and left with slow, sad steps. Kawthar walked out behind him, giving me a look to reassure me about the success of the plan.

I smiled.

A smile of victory.

I stayed in my room. I refused to leave for lunch. I refused to leave for dinner. I left my father to Kawthar, so she could convince him and instill our revolt against Samir in him.

At seven o'clock, the phone rang. Samir was calling, as he usually did every evening. I didn't tell him anything. I even spoke to him gently and sweetly, and as usual I apologized for not meeting him, since I was sick and had a headache, but I promised to meet him the next evening.

He couldn't know anything before the plan was finished. He needed to be surprised so he wouldn't try to ruin it.

The next morning, my father left early. Kawthar told me she was able to convince him to break off the engagement, but he insisted on asking around about Samir so he was sure he wasn't making a mistake. Kawthar's tone was harsh and bitter. She was wide-eyed. Her lips were trembling. Her hair was a mess and she didn't change out of her nightclothes, as if she'd given up making herself look nice for anyone. In this state, I saw in the hateful way she looked at me a clear accusation—I was the cause. I was the one who had broken her heart and taken her away from her love. Maybe at that moment, she remembered this wasn't the first time I'd broken her heart: I'd done it before when we were students and she was in love with my cousin Medhat.

I could feel it.

I was afraid of this feeling.

I had to be sure she was on my side until the engagement was called off. I had to blow on the fire of her hatred for Samir and her desire for revenge against him, so she didn't backtrack on the plan we'd hatched together.

"I really don't know if what we're doing is right or not, Kawthar," I said, sighing. "Maybe Samir is being treated unfairly."

Her eyes glinted. It was that terrifying glint that I wanted to keep lit until my engagement was broken off.

"Treated *unfairly*?" she exploded. "He deserves the noose! He's been driving me up the wall for three months. He'll do the same to you, more and more. Let me tell you, he's a criminal!"

Until my father got back, I pretended to hesitate and act confused as she encouraged me to continue the plan, insisted on it.

He returned with the worry of the entire world on his head.

He'd gone to ask a lot of the people he knew about Samir, his morals and his past. Maybe he asked some people he'd asked before the engagement was announced. But when people saw signs of worry and anxiety on his face, they guessed he'd learned what they already knew about Samir and they began revealing the truth to him—the horrible truth about Samir's past. Maybe they made up things to make it even worse.

That's how people are.

They don't tell you their opinion. They tell you what they think you want to hear. If they think you want to hear praise about someone or support for an idea, they'll praise or support. If they think you want criticism or opposition, they'll criticize and oppose.

I wonder how many girls were made miserable after marriage because people lied when they were asked before the engagement.

My father sat next to me, destroyed and embarrassed, as if he were a sinner coming to beg for forgiveness.

"I really made a mistake," he said in a weak voice that pierced my heart. "Forgive me."

I threw myself on his chest. Each of us felt like a sinner asking the other for forgiveness. I wanted to tell him with my kisses that he was an angel, that he was cleaner than the world, that I was the sinner, the criminal, and he was the innocent victim.

Kawthar couldn't control herself as she watched us kiss each other, and she cried. My father thought she was crying out of love for him and me, but I guessed she was crying out of grief for herself.

My father looked between me and Kawthar. A small smile came to his lips as if he were praising God for our love for him. He then drew from this love strength to puff up his chest. He went over to the phone, called Samir at the insurance company, and made an appointment to meet him at four o'clock at the club for an important matter.

I pulled Samir's ring off my finger as if extracting a thorn dug into my hand, and I gave it to my father.

"Don't forget this," I said happily.

Samir went crazy when he heard my father announce the end of the engagement.

My father told us what Samir said to him, how he started pleading and asking for sympathy, claiming that what was said about him were lies and swearing on his love for me. "I know who's behind this," Samir said. "I know the one who did this. It's Madame Kawthar, sir, because she didn't accept me. She's angry with me, and—"

"I won't let you talk like that about my wife!" my father cut him off. "Please go."

He tossed the engagement ring at him and left.

Samir didn't say anything to him about his relationship with Kawthar, since he was still hoping he'd find a way to get back to me, but we had closed all the doors in his face. He sent all of our common friends around to us, but we refused even to talk about it. He tried to contact me, but I refused to speak to him, hanging up as soon as I heard his voice. He tried to contact Kawthar, and maybe he spoke with her once or twice, but Kawthar could no longer do anything after all that, even if she forgave him and wanted him back.

When Samir lost all hope, he started talking openly in our social circles about his relationship with Kawthar. Maybe he meant for whispers about this to reach my father, but my father interpreted it all as slander from a filthy man who thought he'd been cheated, so he didn't pay any attention to him.

I saved myself.

I saved myself.

But did the world settle down? Did my sky clear up? Did I sleep?

No.

I was still sleepless!

24

During all this, Mahmoud's letters had stopped coming. He no longer wrote me. I no longer heard his sweet words like gentle knocks on the door of hope. I no longer found him next to me to rely on him, to draw goodness from his goodness, strength from his strength. I was alone. I plunged alone into the flames surrounding me to get to him—to Mahmoud. Maybe if I hadn't been so determined to reach him, I would have stayed in the flames, in the fire.

I guessed that his sister or mother had written to him with news of my engagement and then he stopped writing to me. I didn't write to him either, after the short letter I sent him asking him to trust my love. I didn't want to write him until after my engagement to Samir was called off. I didn't have anything to tell him before that. It was enough for me to hold his picture all evening and fill my eyes with it, a sad smile on my lips, looking at him and confiding in him with my neck under the guillotine. I'd then say good night and put the picture in my drawer. During those days, whenever I was upset at myself and my situation, and almost despaired and gave in to the schemes hatched around me, I took out his letters. I didn't read them. I had memorized everything in them. I opened them before me as if they were white sheets whose lines my eyes had drunk up to soothe my heart. I drew from them the strength I needed to plunge into the fire, to be able to return to him.

After the engagement was called off, I sat down to write him.

I didn't tell him the whole truth. I told him I had been forced to be engaged to Samir and that I couldn't break it off. But I was still keeping my promise. I was living every day waiting for him. I was living only for him, and I loved him.

Two days after I sent this letter to him, his sister came to visit me unannounced. Maybe she didn't want to see me, since she was coming to drop something off for me. But, by chance, I opened the door myself. I was happy to see her, as if Mahmoud had reached out to me from London. I embraced her as if embracing a part of him. I kissed her as if kissing his cheeks.

But she was reserved.

She seemed anguished.

She hesitated before agreeing to come in and sit with me.

"Congratulations, Nadia," she said nervously and timidly.

"For what?" I asked, surprised.

"For your wedding," she said, as if performing a formal duty.

"Don't you know that my engagement was called off? I thought everyone knew."

She got up from her seat as if she hadn't heard what I said. She then gave me a box wrapped in fine paper.

"My mother is sending this to you," she said shyly. "Au revoir. I have to go. My mother is waiting for me in the car outside."

The traces of my laughter disappeared as if a dark hand had choked them. I felt the beats of my heart lighten and grow weak.

"You won't have her come in?" I asked, confused, not looking at the box in my hand.

"No, merci," she said, heading quickly to the door. "We have a lot of visits today. Au revoir!"

Before I had the chance to see her out, she had stood up, got to the door, and then closed it behind her.

I sat down. I looked at the box uneasily. Then I unwrapped it. I found an elegant silver box, which I opened. As soon as I took one look inside, I knew what was there.

My letters.

The letters that I had sent Mahmoud since he left for London.

He was unbelievable.

He never bent the rules. Everything in life had principles and rules. Even morality was a science like arithmetic, with set numbers and inescapable rules of addition, subtraction, and multiplication. The news of my engagement to Samir subtracted my love for him, and the result was that he sent my letters back to me.

How unjust this was.

His inflexible mind had no mercy and didn't make excuses for anyone. The mind controlled the heart, forcing it to submit to these mathematical equations as if people were numbers, as if life and love were numbers.

No.

Impossible.

Life could not be all about numbers, and love and morality could not be fixed into rules and principles like a set of numbers. If someone is starving, you can't blame his character if he steals. If someone is oppressed, you can't blame his character if he kills. You can't take away my love for Mahmoud if I accepted my engagement to Samir. All the people in the world have motives, inclinations, and reasons that make them unique and make their world singular, unlike the ones others live in. It's not possible to issue a single verdict on all of humanity and it's not possible that the relationships between individuals can be reduced to a single calculation. Mohamed + murder = criminal, but Ali + murder = hero; and Khadija + love = marriage, but Saniya and Sami + love = suicide!

Isn't that right?

But Mahmoud didn't believe that. He was a man who lived by his mind, not his heart, and his mind didn't have any mercy and didn't accept excuses. It drew the world in orderly straight lines, and anyone who crossed those lines departed from his world.

But I loved this inflexible man, an oppressor in his harshness.

I loved him.

I desired him.

I wanted him as my husband.

I carried the box of my letters around with me as if carrying my own corpse. I talked to myself, depressed and dejected. I heard an annoying echo of my words, as if they were coming back between a series of towering wild mountains in a dark desolate valley. Among this noise, a single hope waved at me. Maybe, after hearing the news that my engagement was called off, Mahmoud would repent and respond to the last letter that I sent him.

Days passed.

Difficult days. They got more difficult, since I could no longer stand Kawthar and Kawthar could no longer stand me. I saw her as the reason for Mahmoud abandoning me, and she saw me as the reason for her breakup with Samir. We didn't exchange this accusation honestly and openly, but it manifested as a repugnant feeling boiling within each of us, our hearts in turmoil. Nothing brought us together but our individual decisions to remain in this house, since neither had another one to go to.

Mahmoud didn't respond.

I wrote him another letter in which I chastised him for returning my letters. I told him I'd keep my promise even if I'd been married to another man, but I wasn't married and I was still waiting because I loved him and I lived for him.

More days passed.

The harshest of days. My hope began to fade away so that I no longer saw it as anything but a fantasy, a distant illusion.

Kawthar started escalating the way she mistreated my father. She was the kind of wife who couldn't bring happiness to her home except during her adultery, who could only make her husband happy out of guilt for an ongoing sin of—betraying him with another man. I witnessed this mistreatment. I felt every part of me torn apart in rage and anger, but I couldn't intervene. My father was happy. His love for her was deeper than ever. I was on the verge of committing another crime, but I resisted. In my resistance, I hoped to flee this house, to flee my father's love that had brought me all these catastrophes. I wanted to flee to another house, to Mahmoud's house.

But Mahmoud didn't respond. I didn't get any response from him.

I realized that God was punishing me.

It felt that God had only created me so He would have something to punish. He ended my suffering when He broke off my engagement to Samir, only to return it by depriving me of Mahmoud.

Forgive me, Lord! But I want to know. I want to understand.

What did I do to deserve everything that has happened to me? What sin has given me this complicated soul of mine? Who complicated it?

It wasn't me.

I'm a product of my circumstances. I have committed no sin in that.

So why did You punish me?

Why, Lord?

Life passed slowly, boring and empty. I found myself lost, not knowing how to move the days forward or push the boredom away or fill my emptiness. I went out every day in the morning and evening. I wandered around stores, wasting money buying things. I surrounded myself with a huge group of friends and offered myself up to being flirted with by guys. I let them toss their words in my ears and dance with me while rubbing their chins on my cheek. Nonetheless, not a single word landed in my heart. No chin could light my cheek on fire. Emptiness grew around me. Boredom weighed heavily on my soul, until the more I saw my face in the mirror, the more I hated it. It seemed like my hatred had been stamped on it. My cold, narrow bed became like a prison custom-built for me. I hated the house. I hated it. I hated it.

One day, when I went into René's boutique, I ran into Safiya and Mustafa. They were together alone. Safiya was full of joy when she saw me. She hugged me and kissed me, and then introduced me to Mustafa.

"I think you remember Mustafa."

"Yes," I said, reaching out to him. "How are you?"

Mustafa gave me a long look—a look of tenderness. There was no flirting, nothing of the past. He was just someone who asked about me and wanted to be reassured about my happiness.

He squeezed my hand.

"How are you, Miss Nadia?" he said in his lazy tone, a voice coming out of my past.

"I heard your engagement was called off," Safiya said. "Thank God. He didn't deserve you."

A quick thought passed through my mind. If Safiya were still my father's wife, I wondered, would someone like Samir have come into my life?

I didn't think so.

I didn't know what brought my eyes to Safiya's hand and then to Mustafa's, but I did notice something.

Two rings.

Safiya didn't tell me she was engaged to Mustafa, as if it was enough for people to see them alone to know. I didn't feel jealous when I learned about their engagement. Instead, I felt a kind of envy—a white envy. If I'd had Safiya's personality and strength of will, maybe I would have been the one engaged to Mustafa. Maybe I would have been the one to conquer his bohemian principles and his flight from responsibility.

What makes someone's personality?

No doubt it's the circumstances surrounding them since birth.

That's what Mustafa told me once.

What had I done to live in circumstances that gave me this complicated personality?

What was it about Safiya that allowed her the circumstances to create an open, pleasant, strong personality?

None of us had committed a crime or deserved anything.

Each of us was a product of our circumstances.

I smiled as I thought about the advice Mustafa used to give me.

"Congratulations!" I said, with a smile meant for both of them.

"Thank you," Safiya said with her calm smile. "May you be as fortunate, Nadia."

I went home.

At lunch, I hinted to my father about seeing Safiya and her engagement to Mustafa. I did so to try to erase any remnant of anger in his chest that my uncle betrayed him with her.

But my father didn't pay much attention to the news. His love for Kawthar had swallowed up everything, even his past.

During those long months, I called Uncle Aziz often. I'd lie to him and tell him that my father mentioned him. I then invited him over to have tea, but he refused the invitation until my father was the one to invite him.

"You remember when you promised that you'd invite Uncle Aziz to my wedding?" I asked my father one day. "I'm not getting married, but I still want to invite my uncle over."

"Shouldn't we wait for an occasion, so it's natural?" he asked, smiling good-naturedly as if he'd forgotten everything that had happened. "Although, I do want to talk to him about the man who's leasing his land. The man's a crook, and is brazenly ripping him off."

"Talk to him soon. I invited him for tea, but he'll only come if you invite him."

"Okay, give me the phone, my dear. I'll talk to him."

I asked for my uncle on the phone, and my father spoke to him. As soon as I heard him say, "How are you, brother?" the gates of the sky seemed to open for me and the hand of God reached down to pat me on the head in forgiveness.

But God didn't forgive me.

I learned one day that Mahmoud had come back from London without calling me. I hesitated before calling him. But I loved him. I loved him so much that my pride grew weak before my love, so I called him. As soon as he spoke, I heard his natural, dry tone.

"How are you, Miss Nadia?"

"Have you really come back without telling me or calling me, Mahmoud?" I asked, my heart troubled.

"I swear, I was busy," he said in a polite, distant tone. "I came to extend the scholarship and go back again."

"You're extending it?" I asked, receiving this news as if I'd been stabbed.

"Yes," he said. "I'll do another research project. It will take me two years."

"Mahmoud," I said, begging, "I need to see you. I need to talk to you. There are a lot of things you need to know. You're not being fair, Mahmoud."

He was quiet for a bit, as if his heart had jumped from his chest and he was trying to return it and lock it back up.

"Really, it's not possible," he said hesitantly. "I'm leaving tonight, going back to London."

"Tonight?"

"Yes."

We were both quiet for a long time.

"I have something that I wanted to send you," he said hesitantly.

"Don't tell me. The rest of my letters."

He was quiet.

I was quiet.

I clung to the receiver as if clinging to life itself.

"It was very nice to chat with you, Miss Nadia," I heard him say.

"Au revoir, Mahmoud. Good luck."

I hung up before I heard his response.

He didn't ask for forgiveness. He didn't apologize.

There are men of this type. They don't forgive, and they don't marry people whom they don't forgive.

I'm now twenty-one.

I live in boredom and emptiness. I hate my mirror, my bed, and my house. I don't know what's good and what's evil. I don't try to know. I don't try to know anymore. There's nothing in my life that deserves to be good or evil. It's a life like water, with no color or shape. You can't seize it with your hands.

I'm a person of nonexistence, of emptiness, nothingness, nothing. I do things, but my actions have no goals and I don't try to judge their motives. Some of these actions might be good and some might be bad. Goodness might lead me to evil, but I no longer know or try to know. I am just a collection of actions and whims.

I don't think about marriage because getting married requires a motive and a goal. I don't have motives or goals.

My father doesn't try to force me to marry because he's afraid he'll make a mistake, as he did when he engaged me to Samir. He's a man and men who are fathers don't understand their daughters.

My mother is still far from me, happy and spoiled. She doesn't care about anything in her life or mine.

My uncle pampers me, but he doesn't take responsibility for me. He lives far from us, and his relationship with my father is not what it was. It's now characterized by pleasantries and formalities.

I hate Kawthar.

And Kawthar hates me.

This hatred is the only truth in my life—a truth I insist on, since it convinces me that I'm still among the living.

The only happy person in our house is my father.

The duped husband!

I do not sleep.

Sleep no longer tortures me, and thinking about evil deeds no longer makes me anxious. Despite that, I don't sleep.

Maybe because to sleep, I'd have to be awake. And I'm not awake. Today, there's no waking up or sleeping in my life. I'm dead. I move like the dead and I sleep in my bed like the dead, a dead person with open eyes.

I want to close my eyes so I can sleep.

When will I sleep?

Selected Hoopoe Titles

The Lady of Zamalek
by Ashraf El-Ashmawi, translated by Peter Daniel

The Girl with Braided Hair
by Rasha Adly, translated by Sarah Enany

The Magnificent Conman of Cairo
by Adel Kamel, translated by Waleed Almusharaf

*

hoopoe is an imprint for engaged, open-minded readers hungry for outstanding fiction that challenges headlines, re-imagines histories, and celebrates original storytelling. Through elegant paperback and digital editions, **hoopoe** champions bold, contemporary writers from across the Middle East alongside some of the finest, groundbreaking authors of earlier generations.

At hoopoefiction.com, curious and adventurous readers from around the world will find new writing, interviews, and criticism from our authors, translators, and editors.